The Mask Carver's Son

"This reverent, formal, and ambitious first novel boasts a glossy surface and convincing period detail." —*Publishers Weekly*

"Richman has successfully drawn upon her historical research and her own experience . . . filled with historical detail and strong characterization." —*Library Journal*

"A meticulous profile of a man struggling against his native culture, his family, and his own sense of responsibility."
—*The New York Times Book Review*

PRAISE FOR THE WORKS OF ALYSON RICHMAN

The Lost Wife

"Staggeringly evocative, romantic, heartrending, sensual, and beautifully written, Alyson Richman's *The Lost Wife* may well be the *Sophie's Choice* of this generation."
—John Lescroart, *New York Times* bestselling author

"A truly beautiful, heartfelt story . . . I couldn't put it down once I started it. Ms. Richman is a very special talent."
—Kristin Hannah, *New York Times* bestselling author

continued . . .

"Daringly constructed, this moving novel begins at the end and then, in a fully realized circle through the most traumatic events of the twentieth century, returns you there in a way that makes your heart leap. Richman writes with the clarity and softness of freshly fallen snow."

—Loring Mandel, two-time Emmy Award–winning screenwriter of *Conspiracy*

"Richman once again finds inspiration in art, adding evocative details to a swiftly moving plot. Her descent into the horrors of the Holocaust lends enormous power to Lenka's experience and makes her reunion with Josef all the more poignant."

—*Publishers Weekly*

"Tragedy and hope, love and loss, and the strength to endure are examined through Richman's graceful writing and powerful characters."

—*Booklist*

"Begins with a chilling revelation and had me hooked throughout. A love story wrapped in tragedy and survival, I read *The Lost Wife* in one sitting. Tense, emotional, and fulfilling: a great achievement by Alyson Richman."

—Martin Fletcher, special correspondent, NBC News, winner of the Jewish National Book Award

"*The Lost Wife* is a luminous, heartbreaking novel. I was barely able to put it down and can't stop thinking about it. Not only is the writing exquisite but I have seldom seen such skill in sweeping a reader back and forth over sixty years until the journey of Josef and Lenka, both such brave and beautiful people, becomes one glorious circle of the triumph of love over evil."

—Stephanie Cowell, author of *Claude & Camille* and *Marrying Mozart*

The Last Van Gogh

"*The Last Van Gogh* is a balanced symphony . . . Richman's style is gentle and sober. With clear, undulating prose . . . it is as evocative as one of Van Gogh's paintings. Richman proves she can travel through time to re-create the past." —*En Route Magazine*

"*The Last Van Gogh* paints an intricate portrait of a woman's life at the end of the nineteenth century . . . It is a powerful and poignant love story." —*Tulip Magazine*

"[A] beautiful book." —*Vriendin Magazine*

The Rhythm of Memory
(previously published as *Swedish Tango*)

"An engrossing examination of the prisons people create for themselves and the way they accustom themselves to suffering until liberation seems as painful as captivity. This is an ambitious exploration of political and personal struggles." —*Publishers Weekly*

"A heart-wrenching story of loss and love in the lives of people affected by war and political upheaval . . . [marked by] sharp resonance." —*Library Journal*

"Places an Ayn Rand lens on societal ethics against personal loyalty and safety . . . Deep, thought-provoking philosophical questions on the needs of an individual and a family against the demands of deadly leadership and a nation." —*Midwest Book Review*

The Mask Carver's Son

Alyson Richman

BERKLEY BOOKS, NEW YORK

THE BERKLEY PUBLISHING GROUP
Published by the Penguin Group
Penguin Group (USA)
375 Hudson Street, New York, New York 10014, USA

USA I Canada I UK I Ireland I Australia I New Zealand I India I South Africa I China

Penguin Books Ltd., Registered Offices: 80 Strand, London WC2R 0RL, England
For more information about the Penguin Group, visit penguin.com.

THE MASK CARVER'S SON

The author wishes to thank Hiroaki Soto for permission to quote from "Cathedral in the
Thrashing Rain" from *A Brief History of Imbecility: Poetry and Prose of Takamura Kotaro*
(University of Hawaii Press, 1992), translated, with an introduction by Hiroaki Soto from
Twenty Plays of the Nō Theatre, edited by Donald Keene. Copyright © 1970 by
Columbia University Press. Reprinted with the permission of the publisher.

BERKLEY® is a registered trademark of Penguin Group (USA)
The "B" design is a trademark of Penguin Group (USA)

ISBN: 978-0-425-26726-4

PUBLISHING HISTORY
Bloomsbury Publishing trade paperback edition / February 2001
Berkley trade paperback edition / September 2013

PRINTED IN THE UNITED STATES OF AMERICA

10 9 8 7 6 5 4 3 2 1

Cover design by Sarah Oberrender
Cover photos: Seine River © W. Robert Moore, National Geographic Image Collection/Alamy; cherry
blossoms © prasit chansareekorn/Shutterstock
Book design by Laura K. Corless

For Stephen,
whose love, support, and gentle kindness
enabled me to write this book.
For my parents,
with love and gratitude.

O Notre-Dame, Notre-Dame,
rock-like, mountain-like, eagle-like, crouching-lion-like
  cathedral
reef sunk in vast air,
square pillar of Paris,
sealed by the blinding splatters of rain,
taking the slapping wind head-on.
O soaring in front, Notre-Dame de Paris,
it's me, looking up at you.
It's that Japanese.
My heart trembles now that I see you.
Looking at your form like a tragedy,
a young man from a distant country is moved.
Not knowing for what reason, my heart pounds
in unison with the screams in the air, resounds
  as if terrified.

Takamura Kōtarō

*Part
One*

ONE

My memories of Paris are never too distant, the colors never too far removed. My palette runs with the blue of violets, the burnt red of sienna, and the saffron yellow of cadmium, yet I remain chalked in a gray-walled studio on the outskirts of Tokyo. Here, every surface is tacked with newsprint sketches and unfinished canvases, and every floorboard blackened by the dust of crushed charcoal. My mind is captured by a fingernail memory, caged by the fractured glass of a prism that refracts time and reflects only the past.

Burdened by my vision and displaced by my experience, I am bound. My journey prevented me from being Japanese; my face prevented me from being French. I am an artist who cannot belong to the tapestry of either country. But my misery becomes me. I exist with few friends and even fewer followers. I suppose I must be proud of this: like my father's craft, my world remains appreciated by few.

My father was a mask carver. As a young boy I saw his craft overtake his face. While other boys see their fathers' faces become a feathered maze of wrinkles, my father's became a smooth sheet of stone. My father had a broad, flat face and skin stretched so thin that he appeared blue. He, a man who carried with him the faint green smell of cypress and the cool sting of steel, could stammer only a few words to me, yet could stare for hours from behind a pair of bottomless black eyes.

Father was a lonely and famous man, and I his lonely and confused son. He widowed, I motherless, we lived quietly near the Daigo mountain, within the walls of Kyoto. This mountain, the ancient tomb for the emperor Daigo's spirit, served as the shrine of my childhood. As I crossed its earthen path each day, with the sand and rock dust beneath my sandals and the flaming orange gateway above my head, I knew that something was here in this burial ground of my ancestors and their rulers that breathed a rhythm into my own minor existence. It was also here that, as a young schoolboy dressed in my coarsely woven *hakama*, I first noticed the extraordinary beauty of the seasons.

I marked the seasons by the change in the mountain; perhaps this was the first palette I ever owned. From below the belly of the mountain, the fabric of autumn stretched high into the horizon. The colors, loomed by the threads of interwoven leaves, beamed yellow to screaming scarlet, then humbled to a fading brown. Winter ushered the dying leaves to the sepulchre of the earth's frozen floor and blanketed the city and empty branches with a soft cotton rain. It was in those cold, dark months, with the color drained from the landscape, that I was most miserable. The brightest things I saw between late December and early February were my frostbitten ankles, which shot nakedly from underneath the cloth of my uniform, their skin always splashed crimson from suffering the bite of the bitter snow.

Every night my father and I raised a sliver of my mother's dowry to our lips as we sipped fish broth from her dark lacquer bowls. Her ghost most often visited me on icy winter nights. She always came in silence, careful not to disturb my father's solitude, arriving and then dissolving in the cloudlike formations of my soup.

She appeared and she was beautiful. She, my fleeting companion who encouraged me, who I sensed always understood.

Her death had prevented me from knowing her voice, yet her image was revealed to me when I was alone at night. She would come to me as I lay sleeping and lead me through what appeared to be just a dream, but in reality was the story that preceded my life.

Father's arrival into the Yamamoto family was as strange and mysterious as our family itself. His arrival was unannounced. He carried with him no letter of introduction, no ceremonial gift reserved for first meetings. He simply arrived at the Kanze theater carrying with him nothing more than a *furoshiki* filled with masks.

Grandfather's reputation, however, preceded him. Yamamoto Yuji. He was the most famous and most revered Noh actor in the Kansai region, the patriarch of the Kanze Noh family. People came to see him whether he performed by torchlight or within the walls of the Kanze theater. Having played the distinguished roles of both God and Spirit for nearly a half a century, his position had gone unrivaled. To many in that community, he was the closest thing to a living God.

His entrance on the stage was marked by the beating of the *otsuzumi*, the high-pitched cries of the chorus, and the *nokan* whistling its shrill staccato. I can still envision the richly embroidered *karaori* hanging from his broad shoulders and the tresses of the massive wig tumbling down his back.

Most vivid in my memory is the mask, the haunting mask: its hollowed-out eyes and a face that changed with every turn. The mask with a life of its own.

That day in the theater, the first time my grandfather laid eyes on one of my father's masks, he felt his face drain white. Holding the mask between his thick, pulpy hands, he shivered, and his eyes widened with wonder. There was something different about my father's masks. And after Grandfather held each one in the cup of his hands, he swore he could feel each unique spirit seeping into the creases of his palms.

He felt his eyes being drawn into the masks. Their eyes penetrated his own gaze. To my grandfather, my father's masks were just like those carved by the masters over a hundred years before. In particular, the young man's masks reminded him of those of the great Mitsuzane; they were subtle, refined, and possessed a haunting intensity that stirred his soul.

My grandfather looked into the eyes of this quiet young carver and saw nothing. He then looked to Father's hands; he saw genius.

He asked my father about his family. Where had he been born? Who was his father? To whom had he served his apprenticeship?

My father's voice was soft. His response to Grandfather's inquiry was barely a whisper: "I no longer have a family."

If it had not been for the silence of the room, Grandfather would have been unable to hear. He could see that my father's lips were still moving, and because he felt a strange interest in the man, he craned his thickly veined neck toward the young carver.

Father's words were barely audible, but Grandfather found himself entranced. He had, for perhaps the first time in his life, relinquished his role as performer and become the sole member of an awestruck audience.

Within the sanctuary of Grandfather's dressing room, my father relayed his story. A strange and sad story, one of ghosts and plum trees, of an old man and a young boy. A story so unique it could have been a play of Noh.

When Father had finished telling his story, his body echoed his exhaustion. His shoulders sloped under the folds of his kimono and his eyelids weighed heavily, veiled pupils gazing at the ground.

Grandfather was rendered speechless. He had never heard such an outrageous story. Nor had he seen such a young and talented carver in his lifetime. His mind raced. If what my father said was true, he possessed a skill that could rival that of Mitsuzane, one of Noh's most revered carvers.

Truly, the masks before him were unlike any he had seen before. The edges were whittled down to paper-thin proportions, and the features were perfectly formed. But even more impressive was their incredible sense of unearthliness. These masks were not bound to a single expression. Rather, the strokes of the carver had freed their spirit instead of binding them to a single earthbound existence. They refused to be captured; they evaded his eyes like coquettish young girls masked in an innate world of mystery. They existed like blank white ghosts until he manipulated his hands under their backsides.

Grandfather held the Komachi Rojo mask in his palms. His eyes traced the thin curl of her ruby-painted lips, the razor-sharp incisions of her eyes; in her blankness she seemed almost haughty, defiant, all-knowing. But when he tilted his palms forward, he saw her face cast in an entirely different shadow. Suddenly she appeared sadder, older, and lonelier. He jerked forward. Startled by his abrupt movement, he focused his gaze once more. He could not believe his eyes; it was as if the spirit of the aged poet Komachi was transforming there before him.

Grandfather knew this carver was empowered with a gift far greater than even his own acting ability. He pondered the young man before him and then found his concentration shifting to his daughter. With no heir to carry on the Yamamoto name, he marveled at the idea of a possible family union.

Grandfather surmised that because the young carver had no family of his own, he would be proud to be brought into the Yamamoto family and to inherit the prestigious name. He poured sake for the young man and, with great elegance, thanked him for his visit. He commissioned three masks from him and then, before my father bade him farewell, Grandfather slyly inquired if he was married.

"No?" My grandfather repeated my father's answer. "Well, I am not sure of your schedule, but next Thursday my wife Chieko is planning to teach our daughter to prepare *chawanmushi*. Should you have the time, we would be delighted to have you join us."

My father, understanding that this was the old man's way of initiating an introduction to his unmarried daughter, offered a deep and reverent bow to my grandfather. He bade the great patriarch farewell with the promise to visit his home the following Thursday.

TWO

When I think of Father, I think of his hands. Lined with rivers that charted through coarse and tired palms. Rough and callused; yellow skin and white nails. Hands carefully veiled by the sleeves of a kimono.

Hands that had earlier destroyed his family. Hands that later brought him fame.

When Grandfather asked how he came to be a mask carver, Father at first could only extend his hands while Grandfather simply stared. But later it would be revealed that Father had taught himself to carve, as he had no words to express his sadness. He dug deep into the wood, as if to drive a sword deep into his own heart. He wished to feel pain. He wished to know tears. He wished he could fall to his knees like a wounded animal and howl to the moon.

But the gods had stolen his voice. He could not yell in anger. He could not weep in grief. He was driven by a force that grew inside him, one that could not be controlled. It choked his larynx, and it dried the ducts of his eyes.

His hands, however, moved freely and could not be restrained. They belonged to no one. They had a life of their own.

* * *

He first discovers his hands in the forest. He goes there to be alone. To hear no voices other than those trapped inside his head. He feels the soft soil beneath his sandals, inhales the deep, damp smell of humus penetrating his nostrils, and sees the leafy green canopy of branches over his head. Only here does he know he is safe.

He is a young boy and is humbled by the nature that surrounds him. He recognizes its glory as well as its power to kill. Nature has killed his parents and left him an orphan.

He cannot prevent his mind from transporting him to his life before their death. He remembers his old house. He pictures the thatched roof that his father replaced each spring. He remembers the hearth, with its eternal flame. There he was warm. There he spent his evenings sleeping next to his mother, her gentle sighing coaxing him to sleep.

He feels the wind riding through his hair, and he remembers his mother's caresses. He sees her slender throat rising from the neckline of her blue linen kimono, her long black hair flowing over her shoulders. She is his mother and she is beautiful.

He recalls how she would greet him and his brother when they returned from school. "Tadaima," he would holler as he slid his sandals off in the *genkan*, "I'm home."

His brother is older than he. He does not crave their mother's affection and instead purposefully tries to avoid it. The older brother grumbles the greeting under his breath and brazenly drops his satchel. He prefers to play with his friend on the nearby farm. He turns his back and is walking out the door as his mother cries from the kitchen.

"Okaerinasai," she sings to my father. "Welcome home."

She walks toward the entranceway and kneels. She does not

cover her exposed knees. She is not refined. She is not elegant.
But she is smiling. She extends her arms and he playfully presses
her hands to his face.

"*Okāsan, okāsan,*" he says in between giggles. He can smell
their dinner deep in the skin of her palms. Dried seaweed. Bean
paste. Eggplant.

"Yes, Ryusei?"

"May I go into the garden and pick some plums for you?"

"Yes, but you must be careful climbing the branches. The tree
can be dangerous."

"Of course, Mama," he assures her. "I am a big boy now. I
can take care of myself."

She is smiling again. He is her baby.

He changes from his school *hakama* and into his simple navy
yukata. He ties the sash himself and walks to the garden. He sees
his small, plump legs peeking from the cloth. He stops for a
moment. The plum tree stands before him. It is a thousand times
bigger than he.

His eyes are parallel to its ancient trunk. The bark is gray and
gnarled, rough to the touch.

He pulls up his robe and reaches for the lowest bough. He
grabs it and pulls his leg up to the *V* of the trunk. He climbs until
he has reached the highest branches. He can no longer see his
house. He is trapped within a sanctuary of leaves and yellow fruit.

He shakes the branches with his tiny hands. The leaves rustle
and the boughs quiver. The fruit tumbles to the ground. He
shields his head with his forearms. It is raining a yolk-yellow rain.
With a shake of his hand, plums fall from the sky.

He returns to the ground and giggles to himself. A field of
glistening golden fruit surrounds him. He has three baskets to

fill. Each plum fills his hand like a perfect glowing orb. He eats one. He eats two. The juice swooshes through his mouth, then runs down his chin. Its stickiness dries on his hands and cheeks.

"Ryusei . . ." his mother calls from inside. "Don't spoil your supper."

She sees him without seeing him. She is his mother.

He drags his sticky hands across the front of his *yukata*. He wipes his mouth with his sleeve. A storm is coming. Dark clouds are moving across the sky.

He must swiftly gather all the plums. He pulls up the hem of his robe and uses the cloth as a basin and then dumps the fruit into the baskets. He does not examine the fruit to see which specimens are bruised or underripe.

His father has been in the fields all day. He is tired and dirty. The saltiness of his perspiration penetrates the room. He goes to the garden and pours a bucket of cold water over his body. He scrubs his back until it is red and raw. He runs his palms over his wet hair until it is smooth and changes into his *yukata*, later joining his family by the hearth. He sees his two boys sitting at the low wooden table, the steaming bowls of *nabe* beneath their small faces. He meets their gaze with pride and begs them to eat before him.

His wife serves him a large portion of vegetables and tofu from the kettle and lovingly ladles the broth on top. Their evening is illuminated by rapeseed lanterns. They stay with each other until the wick burns low and the night casts shadows across their tired faces.

She clears the table and removes the futons from the shelves. They roll out the mattresses and the buckwheat pillows. They will sleep deeply. Tomorrow the father will stay at home. He must collect wood for the long winter.

His young son touches his cheeks before he slides into his futon. "Tomorrow we will play in the soybean fields together, after you return from school," he gently says. "Off to bed until tomorrow."

The boys return home the next day. Ryusei calls out to his mother as his brother drops his satchel and heads out the door.

"Tadaima," he hollers. *"Okaa . . . san! Okaa . . . san!"* he cries out with childlike glee.

There is no answer. He cannot understand where she could be. He removes his sandals and walks over the house's earthen floor until he reaches the kitchen.

What he sees there is too terrible for words. Words cannot do justice to the horror. His face is red now. His knees give out, and he crumples to the floor.

He shrieks.

Brother arrives. He stands beside him. Both their faces are locked in grief.

One of the baskets of plums rests proudly on the table. They are the golden plums he picked himself. There is a plate with a small knife. One of the plums has been cut and shared. The pit rests alone on the ceramic plate while his parents lie on the floor as white as frost, their fingers stiff, their bodies heavy, and their eyes staring up at him wide open.

"They are dead," his brother says firmly. "It must have been the plum they shared." An underripe plum. What we now know to be as lethal as poison.

He follows his brother to the garden as he turns on his heel and heads straight for the tree. His brother's eyes are fierce and angry; he has the face of a warrior. He is swollen and orange in the face. He has become his rage.

He seizes the trunk with his outstretched arms and tries to lift it with no success.

"We must destroy it!"

The elder brother thrusts his foot into its center and makes his ascent to its sparsely fruited boughs. He tears at the branches and rips apart its leaves. With clawlike sweeps he grabs what fruit remains and smashes the plums to the ground.

The smaller one joins him. He creeps up the trunk, swallowed by his brother's tremendous shadow. He does not shield himself when the fruit falls on his head and splatters its juice over his young skin.

He joins his brother in the breaking of the boughs and the slicing through the leaves. They tear off its few remaining blossoms and smash its yellow fruit. The juice stains their hands as they smear it over their stinging faces and break its branches over their bleeding knees.

In the end, they chop at its trunk until it falls over like a crippled old man. Its roots have been unearthed from the ground, resembling huge fingers clawing at the earth.

Blood mingles with the broken wood. Tears run rivers with juice. Pain rips the golden tree to shreds as dark clouds once again appear in the sky.

The young boy's grief consumes him. He picked the fruit that killed his parents. He handed the poison to his mother in a basket made of ruby straw. He is lonely for his mother's touch. He aches. In his heart he believes he has killed her.

In his *furoshiki* he keeps a little sliver of the murderous plum tree. At first it serves only as a reminder, then slowly it is transformed into a symbol of his pain.

For a long time, perhaps many, many months, he just holds it between his small hands. The wood shines from his oils. It is molded to the shape of his palms, curving from the pressure of his grip.

He holds it to his nose and smells its light floral fragrance. He sees colors: the pink blossoms and the yellow fruit. He sees his mother kneeling in her blue linen kimono; he sees the whiteness of her knees. His nails dig deep into the smooth shard of wood. He feels his nails penetrate the wood's soft skin. For a split second he is at one with the wood and all the memories it contains. His knees are still scarred from where the tree branches splintered into his legs. The wood is now inside me, he thinks to himself. He attributes the thought to his madness. This madness that has forced him into a world of silence.

The home of their aunt, where he and his brother now live, is not at all like the home where they were raised, where they were loved. Thatched roof snapping from the sound of gnawing vermin. Mud walls. Threadbare tatami. Hunger sweeps through the house's dusty hollow like wind through the rib cage of a fleshless carcass.

Their aunt glares at them with hard, stony eyes. Pupilless eyes, eyes that rest in deeply welled sockets. Irises bleeding black. Hunger had devoured her compassion years before. Now all that that remains of her is a bony skeleton swaddled in stinking cotton.

At mealtime she serves him and his brother last, ensuring that her husband and two children receive what nourishment there is to offer. He and his brother eat what remains in the empty iron pot. The ladle banging around its bare inside, that ringing a sign that now they can skim their fingers around the hollow cavity, to sweep up the scum with their fingers, to suck them until they are raw.

At night, when he is exiled to the drafty side room, the younger boy watches his cousins through half-closed eyes as they sleep like silkworms, their futons scattered around the four sides of the hearth. His brother holds him tightly to his chest, not out of brotherly love but rather out of a savage yearning to keep himself warm. It is there that he whispers, with his breath hot in the younger boy's ear, of his plans to leave the next day for the city, to find work and be free of this misery.

"I will come back for you, brother," he says.

But he never did.

It is a month or two later that he finds himself alone in the woods. He has learned to fashion a chisel by hand. He binds a piece of flint to a stick with rope and practices carving on scraps of wood.

He carves nothing but faces. He has no image in his head, and he has no schooling in the craft. The faces simply reveal themselves in the wood. He strips the layers of bark away like a surgeon. He unearths the faces from their slumber with the swiftness of his hand.

One might think that he carves only sad faces, but he does not. He has no control over what he carves. He does not dictate to his chisel. He only follows.

No one knows of his talent. He hides it. It is something that is precious to him, and he fears that it will be taken away. His fingers blister. Callused palms and bleeding skin. But he feels no pain. He feels nothing at all. Nothing except the sensation of wood between his hands.

The faces carved from the wood become his family. They are eternal and will never die. He wraps them in rags and buries them in the soil. "I won't abandon you," he whispers to them as he smooths the earth over their shallow grave. "I promise that I will always return."

He carves faces of young women and wizened old men. He carves warriors and demons with horns. Yet he uses no pattern. The lines of the wood are his only map, his guide to what he believes is his salvation.

He believes that he is alone in the world. The image of his mother and father becomes less clear. He can no longer remember the exact curve of his mother's smile, the precise length of her hair. He tries to recall the pitch of her laughter, the smoothness of her voice.

She is fading from his memory. He carries only stones in the cavity of his mind. His head is heavy but empty. There are no more colors. The young boy has been consumed. His hands are all that remains. The hands with a rhythm of their own.

One day a priest appears, draped in white linen, his shaved head covered by a hat made of straw. He sees the boy in the distance, his back round as a boulder, his head bowed to his knees.

He holds his breath and raises his sandals carefully with each step. Peering over the tiny shoulder and craning his neck to get a better view, he discovers a boy carving. The boy is whittling a face out of a block of wood.

It is not an ordinary face. It is not one that is recognizable to his trained eye. Yet it is extraordinary all the same. It is haunting. It is in the process of being born.

The planes of the face are smooth and supple. The cheeks gently sloping, the forehead high and round. But it is the eyes, staring wide and wild, that are the most disturbing, bulging pupils and raised lids. It is a face whose spirit cannot be contained.

The priest is speechless. He has not seen a mask like this in more than thirty years. He feels himself tremble. He feels his fingers tingle and his wrists begin to cramp.

He too was a carver, a long, long time ago.

He befriends the young boy. At first the boy is frightened and tries to flee. He is like a wild animal feeling threatened by an unfamiliar predator. The priest does not try to follow him. He remains where he first glimpsed the boy carving. He stands there and waits. He waits until the young boy returns.

"I call myself Tamashii," the priest says in a solemn voice, "and the forest is my temple. If you will listen, I shall share my story with you. And you might learn something from me."

It is a long and complicated story. There are elements that the young boy will not comprehend until years later. The words the priest uses are unfamiliar to him. "Without knowing it," he tells the boy, "you have entered the world of Noh."

"Close your eyes," the priest whispers to the boy, "and I will offer you all that I know."

He begins with a story. It is a legend that has been handed down from master to disciple, from actor to actor, from father to son.

The story begins in the ancient capital of Nara, where the wooden shrines are black with age, where torches illuminate the vestige of the great Bronze Buddha, where deer run wild and eat from the palm of your hand. It is here, in a city that stands as a testament to the past, that the ghosts of emperors roam, that the voices of fallen warriors boast their glory, and that love-struck maidens bemoan their broken hearts. And it is here that the great Pine of Noh still grows.

They say that over five hundred years ago, an old man performed a dance under the crooked boughs of the Yogo Pine, a tree that grows at the base of the Kasuga shrine. They say that this man danced in such a way that he awed the people into silence. His limbs floated like wings, his feet slid like sleighs, and his hands extended before him like small paper fans. They say that through his dance he ceased being a man, a divine spirit possessed him, and the gods directed his movements. They say that through his dance he was briefly transformed.

And centuries later the great pine still stands. Its trunk still twists, and its branches still blossom from Nara's ancient soil. And on every Noh stage it has since been painted. For it was beneath the great Yogo Pine that Noh was channeled from the gods in heaven to the humble world of men.

"Noh is a dance," the priest declares. "Noh is a recital of poetry. It is a performance incorporating sound and stage." But the boy continues to look blank; he continues to be unmoved.

It is only when he hears the priest whisper, "Noh was created to pacify the troubled dead," that he hears the message and is forever transformed.

Before the boy ever began to carve, he had heard voices in his head. He saw the whitened corpses of his parents; he heard their piercing shrieks and their wails.

But the carving has made this all stop. He no longer hears the wails of his parents' ghosts; he no longer feels the anguish of his guilt.

Has he placated their tortured spirits through his carving? Has he entered the world of Noh, this esoteric world of transition, where mortals channel the voices of the dead?

"There are spirits trapped in your masks," Tamashii tells him. "You are a son of Noh."

The priest speaks of Noh as a rare and selective family, saying that it was a privilege to be allowed within its walls.

"The carver holds the fate of Noh in his hands. Noh begins with a mask, and the mask gives birth to Noh."

"The gods have channeled the spirits through your hands, and you in turn infuse the wood with their presence. Only the actor can release them into the world."

Tamashii breaks a branch from the pine tree that grows behind him. "Consider the forest our stage," he says as he circles the soil around him. "I will teach you the plays of Zeami. I will describe to you the faces of the stage!"

The boy becomes his disciple. The priest shaves the boy's head and dresses him in the robes of an ascetic. He teaches him to fear the dead more than the living. He teaches him to love nothing but the wood.

Within the grounds of the monastery, the two live in a make-shift hut built from bamboo and straw. Every morning after their ablutions, they carve. They do not stop for meals; they barely speak between themselves. They simply carve until their hands cease to move, till their chisels cease to meet the wood.

The boy consumes the wood; the craft consumes the boy.

"We are driven by our ghosts," Tamashii tells him.

"I feel nothing when I carve," the boy confides in the priest.

"To be in a state of unawareness is the highest goal for a carver," whispers the master, his voice already lost in the wind.

The boy's addiction to the wood can be easily explained. When he carves, he feels no pain, he hears no voices, he sees no ghosts. He is no longer shackled to the mortal world. His mission is to appease the troubled dead.

He need not study models to learn the traditional attributes of Noh masks, as almost all other carvers do. He simply closes his eyes and listens to Tamashii describe each play and its characters. He simply has to glance at him as he carves the Ko Omote mask, the Okina mask, and the countless other faces of the theater. He was born with a gift. He is a son of Noh.

They do not speak of the past. They do not share the weight of their guilt. They share only their meals and their wood. They are outcasts, bound to their only family, the family of Noh.

Tamashii does not reveal his own troubled past until the boy is much older. He does not speak of his exile until he lies on his deathbed, his hoary face white with death. "Come closer," he says, his voice dry with pain. "You must know it is through you that I have finally appeased my master."

He tells the boy of his life before the priesthood. He tells him of how as a young boy he was the prized apprentice of the carver Mitsuzane. He tells of his betrayal.

"As a young apprentice, my talent for carving was spotted early on by Mitsuzane and eventually he had me carving many of the masks which were commissioned to him. I was ordered never to reveal that I had carved these masks. I was instructed to carve my master's seal into their underside and pass these masks on to the theater as if they were his.

"I carved many such masks, but I grew weary of receiving no recognition of my own. One day I stopped imitating his seal exactly. I devised a way in which only I could tell who had carved the mask."

Tamashii's voice is now barely a whisper.

"Should you ever find a Mitsuzane mask. Look at the seal that reads 'Deme Mitsuzane' If the *mē* character extends further on the right, it is mine!"

Tamashii smiles up at his pupil. Death is now consuming him from inside. "My master discovered my betrayal, and I have never known greater shame. From that day on, I was banished and sent away with a curse."

And so the master tells his student what had been his master's last words to him. He tells the boy he should never become tangled in the world of emotions. "It will only ruin you," the priest warns. "Learn from me. Have no ego and avoid emotion. Such worldly burdens have the power to destroy your craft!"

But he is not finished. Death has not devoured him yet. He lifts his frail head from the straw pillow and with great desperation insists, "It is essential, Ryusei, that you be formally adopted into one of the great Kanze families. You belong to the Kanze school, as that was the school of my master." He pauses in an attempt to regain his voice. "A carver needs the official backing of a school. It is imperative that you receive their support. Go forth, Ryusei. Go forth and show them your masks!"

The boy, now a man, does not cry at his master's death. "Life is fleeting, Noh is eternal," echoes the voice of his master. "Spare yourself pain and never become attached to anything but the wood."

These words are difficult to abide by, but his master spoke the truth. His masks will never die. He is their creator. They are a family that will never leave.

He builds a coffin of pine. He does not carve the exterior with flourishes, he does not adorn the coffin with symbols. He simply incises his master's seal on the lid's center. Without tears, without a eulogy, he returns Tamashii to the earth, to sleep with the roots of the trees, to rest his days of eternity at the base of a bending pine.

He brings his masks to the Kanze theater, where the actors are awed. "Go to our patriarch, Kanze Yamamoto Yuji," they all agree. "Go and show him your masks."

He travels the next day to the theater, his masks tied in *furoshiki*, his wooden children tucked warmly underneath his arms. He unwraps them under Grandfather's watchful eyes, he reveals that which has come from him.

Words do not come easy to him. But he need not speak in support of his masks. The masks speak for themselves. He offers them to the great patriarch with the extension of his marble hands, and presses his forehead to the tatami floor.

He sees their magic revealed in the cupping of the famous actor's hands. He feels the ghost of Tamashii smiling at the mention of my mother's name. He bows reverently to my grandfather's request that he visit his home. The priest has spoken the truth. He is a son of Noh.

THREE

W ait until you see his hands!" Grandfather called out excitedly to Grandmother from behind his dressing screen.

Grandmother was busy in the kitchen and could not discern the exact words of her husband. She put down her long chopsticks, took her pot off the flame, and went to see what he was saying.

He stood there basking in the light of his discovery, his legs slightly apart, his stomach puffing through his *yukata*, his palms resting on his forearms.

"I have found a man that I believe is suitable for Etsuko to marry," he told her, his red face beaming.

Grandmother looked at him, wild with excitement and brimming with plans. She fell silent, her eyes locked to the floor.

He stood staring at his wife for a moment, as she had the capacity to move him deeply. He would never tell her this, however, for that would make him appear ridiculously sentimental. Seeing her stand before him, quiet as a squirrel, brought him comfort. She supported his every wish. She had been his wife for almost thirty-three years and, in his days of joy, had borne him a lovely daughter and, in his days of sadness, borne him a stillborn son.

He disliked thinking about his son. It only revealed wounds that could never heal. While his wife's despair manifested itself in weeping, his had revealed itself in anger. He lashed out at the gods with an angry fist and challenged them with the volume of his voice. It was unfair that his son not be allowed a single breath on this earth. It was unjust that the Yamamoto family be denied an heir.

He had watched as his wife, wrapped in blankets and her hair matted to her face, cried until her eyes swelled shut. Their son's face in death appeared identical to hers wrought in grief, both pairs of eyes pink, sealed, and raw, both pairs of cheeks whiter than mountain snow.

He preferred to remember how beautiful she had been when they first met. The vision of her kneeling at the base of the stage, her slender arms extended before her, searching the ground for her missing comb. If he closed his eyes, he had the ability to be transported back in time.

"What are you looking for?" he had asked her as he descended the stairs of the main platform more than thirty years before. He had just finished one of his first rehearsals at the Daigo theater.

"I have lost one of my combs," she said shyly, lifting one arm to contain the section of fallen hair.

"Let me help you," he replied. He watched her as she smiled up at him, her pale cheeks blushing with embarrassment.

After searching for a few minutes, he turned to her and asked why she did not simply redo her bun using the remaining combs in her hair.

"It is so long that it requires nine combs to secure it above my head. Anything less will cause it to tumble." She giggled and her laugh was soft, nervous, and feminine.

He thought her charming. He thought her innocent. And in his heart he knew that one day this woman would be his wife.

He courted her for months. He gazed for hours at her perfectly round face. Her skin as translucent as gossamer silk, her eyes like two shining stones. When he lay in his futon, the night separating their bodies, he could imagine each peak and plateau of her cheekbone, each thread of her eyelash.

Theirs was a love marriage. Their union, rare and precious, defied custom because their parents had not introduced them or arranged for them to marry. Instead, the sacred walls of the theater had cloistered them, led them to each other.

In his sleepless nights, her sweet melodic voice would come to him, whispering into his heart the words of the ancient Heian poem: "If not for you, then for whom shall I undo my hair?"

He ached. He yearned. He envisioned himself swept into the blue-black sea of her hair. When he performed on the stage, with the mask veiling his eyes, he searched for her in the audience. She was there, as promised, with her mother sitting beside her fragile frame. The kimono bound her straight, her head cocked toward the stage. She allowed her body and soul to separate for those three hours. Her ears opened to the sounds of her father's drum, and her heart to the magic of my young grandfather.

The afternoon his family and he traveled to Grandmother's home to ask her parents for her hand in marriage, he was so nervous that perspiration seeped into his undergarments. He tried to comfort himself that he had nothing to worry about; it was a family alliance that benefited both parties.

Both he and his wife, Chieko, had been born into established Noh families. Although they specialized in different areas of that segmented world, they were forever tied by the same traditions. His father was an actor, as his father's father had been, as had those before him. The Yamamoto line could be traced back nearly seven hundred years, a time when his ancestors performed *Gagaku* for the imperial court.

Her family, by contrast, contained a long line of musicians. For three hundred years her ancestors had played the *otsuzumi*, the hip drum that accented the Noh actors' chants on stage. Each child born to that family, his wife included, contended that the beating of the drum was the first sound they ever heard. They believed they heard it through their mother's womb, that the walls reverberated with each beat, and that the rhythm was born into their veins.

During the brief and fleeting moments of their courtship, when they found the time and privacy to meet, he would produce a small *otsuzumi* from the folds of his robe and playfully tease her by pounding the skin of the drum. She in return would pull up the hem of her kimono, only an inch or two above the ankle, circle round him, and slide her sandals over the earth as if to imitate the movements of a Noh actor. In her mirth, she would feel compelled to cover her mouth, as the force of her laughter would pry her budding lips open and expose her flash of white teeth. Grandfather, however, was always relieved that she chose to continue dancing for him, rather than surrendering to a silly rule of hiding her smile.

As her combs loosened and the tresses of liquid black hair fell down her back, he beat the drum harder and faster. He pounded the drum until they both fell to the earth, their bodies exhausted from releasing such an uncontainable amount of joy.

Her family accepted his proposal of marriage. "It is with great pleasure that we give our daughter to your family in marriage," her father said, his head lowered in a courteous bow. "It is a strong union that will fortify our families as well as the theater."

The two families exchanged gifts in the traditional Yuino ceremony to show their support of the marriage. They sat across from each other, each family offering their gifts on exquisite black lacquered trays. Grandfather's family gave envelopes of money. Grandmother's family gave a beautiful spice set comprising five porcelain jars covered in a deep purple lacquer with the Yamamoto crest painted in red and gold. In addition, her family made a promise to provide the new couple with furniture: two *tansu* chests, a *zushi-dana*, a writing cabinet made from the finest paulownia wood, and an entire set of lacquerware.

It was May and the house had been opened up to the garden. Outside, the cherry blossoms danced for the young couple's happiness. Behind the shoji, Grandmother clasped her kimono in an attempt to contain her excitement. Her face glowed like a paper lantern.

The woman who now stood before Grandfather was but a distant memory of that young girl. Her beauty had faded, but she was still handsome. She had long since cut her hair. Now she only required two combs. The color was no longer the blackest black, but streaked with rivers of gray. In her middle age she began to use powder, as her skin had begun to bruise in patches below her eyes and at her temples. Her body seemed to shrink, and her eyes became less clear.

After the death of their son, nearly fifteen years before, she had ceased to laugh. And now, as his wife approached her forty-third year, he detected that her shoulders had begun to slope and her back was beginning to bend forward. Like the great pine always painted on the Noh stage, her body twisted and her outside had begun to show the lines of age. Yet even though she had never given him a male heir, he still loved her. She remained a sacred and eternal part of his life.

* * *

The warm winter sunlight penetrated the rice-paper skin of the window. Grandfather stood there, his lungs inflating his size, the golden light illuminating his face. A tremendous amount of satisfaction flowed through his magnificent frame. He had found for his daughter a suitable marriage prospect as well as a distinguished candidate for an adopted son. He relished his sense of accomplishment. Now his only concern was how his wife and daughter would receive the news.

"Yesterday a young mask carver by the name of Enchi Ryusei came to my studio," he confided to his wife.

"Enchi?" she asked, her gaze rising from the floorboards and settling on her husband's carefully knotted sash.

"Yes," Grandfather confirmed the name once more.

"I am not familiar with that family name. Is he a carver for the Kongo school?" she questioned softly.

"He has studied under a monk whose name and school are unimportant. What is important is that he possesses the greatest talent I have seen in a carver."

"Really?" She appeared intrigued, because her husband rarely showered compliments on anyone. "But if he studied under a monk, he comes not from a family of carvers. Were they at all involved with Noh?"

"His parents died when he was a child, and I did not inquire of their background. He is thirty-three. He is not homely and he is not ill-bred. Above all, he possesses great talent, and I believe he will be the most famous mask carver this century will ever see. He is the next Mitsuzane. And with no family of his own, he will surely be proud to adopt our prestigious Yamamoto name."

With those words she fell quiet. The son I could never give you, she thought, her heart shrinking like oak leaves under a flame.

"It is Etsuko's feelings of which I am unsure. Has she ever mentioned anyone to you? Do you know if she has feelings for another, or what her marital aspirations are? We do have a few eligible men in the theater who could also suit her, although their potential for success is not as great as I believe Ryusei's to be."

She looked at her husband, proud and radiant, his mind swimming with the thoughts of having discovered this young man.

"I know of no other," she said.

But she told me later that she had lied.

My grandmother was capable of great love and enormous guilt. She carried both of these like a woven iron rope around her heart. Without either, she would probably have been carried away by the wind, as she was as ethereal as the heavens and carried no other allegiances than those of her family and those concerning the ways of Noh. She loved her daughter, but despised herself for wishing my mother were a son.

She was not envious of her daughter's beauty, as some mothers are. On the contrary, she lavished attention on the child. They would both enter the bathhouse together. Grandmother would carry in her wooden caddy three scrubbing brushes made from fastidiously polished pine and bristles of wild boar, a pot of ground azuki beans, and a balm made of soybean and almond blossom. She would scrub Mother's back with the azuki paste, circling the grains over her skin with the pine brushes, and rinse her down with a bucket of cool water and the sweeping of her hand. As her daughter became a young woman, she would chide her affectionately, "Concentrate on the elbows, the knees," she would say. "And don't forget the balls of your feet." After their bath, they would rub camellia oil on their hair and smooth the soybean and almond blossom balm over their glistening limbs.

She taught her daughter the art of the tea ceremony, and Mother learned how to sit with her legs tucked underneath her with the cloth of her kimono neatly folded over her knees, and her hands positioned before her. She memorized how to withdraw the powdered green tea from its canister and how to whisk it into a frothy foam. With the utmost elegance and feminine perfection, she learned how to slide the ceramic *chawan* around her cupped palms and imbibe the steaming liquid with one silent swallow.

She had her mother's sense of place and her father's sense of artistry. Her talents were revealed in her preparation of the family meals, in her intricate tying of her obi, and in the ink drawings she made by the mountainside.

When Grandmother had a stillborn son, Mother had the capacity to grieve deeply, even at the innocent age of three. She had seen Grandmother hold the lifeless baby, pale as ivory, to her breast and cry to the gods to give him back his life. Although she could not grasp the full meaning of her brother's death, she understood that he was something the family desired from the deepest channels of their hearts. And so, when she wandered into my grandfather's studio and discovered this great man with his head cupped in his palms, she knew enough not to disturb him but rather to make herself vanish until the darkness had lifted from their home. This personified my mother's innate sense of duty.

Mother's powers of awareness were perhaps her greatest curse. She saw the demon of grief rise from the floorboards of their house. She saw the pain choking the light from her mother's eyes, and the anger puncturing her father's veins. At night she dreamed of her little brother, whose tiny form had since vanished to the confines of a small bronze vessel, whose spirit, her father informed her, was now entrusted to the gods.

In her nocturnal journeys she would travel to his gravesite, bringing with her small fruits and sweet bean paste. She would beg him to eat, she would dig her fingers deep into the earth and beg him to return.

She saw herself in sacrifice, prostrate in front of the altar, the eyes of the great bronze Buddha beating down into her back. She imagined inhaling the incense, throwing all of her coins at his rounded knees. But it was of no use. The gods would not listen to her. They had ignored the pleas of her mother, the angry cries of her father, and her own childlike but pious supplications.

As Mother grew into her womanhood, it became apparent that she had inherited Grandmother's appearance. She had Grandmother's translucent skin, her wasp-thin waist, and her slight bones. She grew her hair long like an empress, and chose to secure it high above her head with nine combs, for that was how her mother had done at her age, and so she would follow.

She learned the correct way to walk, she memorized the correct way to bow her head, lower her gaze, and maintain her posture. She fell asleep to the sounds of family legends and believed it when her mother told her, in hushed whispers, that their family name would protect her from evil.

Grandmother wore the family crest on her kimono at the nape of her neck, like a samurai wears his sword. In her eyes, the Yamamoto name gave her protection and she would never leave the house without it emblazoning some part of her robe.

Proud and stately, she walked the streets of Kyoto with her head high and sandals moving softly beneath her. She had a natural sense of color and her elegance was reflected in the palette of her robes. She chose pastels for summer and vibrant jewel tones for winter. She wore cherry blossom patterns in spring and maple leaves in fall. But regardless of the kimono, whether it was a solid robe in which she had the crest prominently sewn between her shoulder blades, or whether it was a heavily patterned silk in which she had it discreetly sewn behind her neck, Grandmother always had the family's symbol embroidered somewhere in the fabric.

She sewed it herself, choosing the thread from her many spools of colored silk. Her careful and steady hand took delicate pains to re-create the ancient family insignia: the mountain inscribed within the circle. For generations, Mount Daigo had been at the center of our lives. It had, in fact, given a deeper meaning to our name. We were the family of the mountain, protected by its enormity, enshrined by its grandeur; Grandmother wore it like a shield.

Grandmother knew it was her husband's expectation that she inform their daughter of the mask carver's arrival. She dreaded this. She had lied to her husband, something she swore she would never do. But how could she explain to him that their daughter had affections for another. She shuddered to think of what his reaction would be if he learned of the young man who had captured Etsuko's attention.

His name was Kitano Yoshiro and his family owned a tea shop close to Kiyomizu temple. The shop had been there for nearly two hundred years. Grandmother had bought her tea there since she was a young girl. Instructed by her own mother, Grandmother knew the tea at Kitano-ya was the best in the city. As she had learned the ways of running a household from following her mother, she thought it best to bring Mother along whenever she went out on her domestic excursions.

Aside from the theater, the teashop was my mother's favorite place. There the scent of the dried tea leaves mingled with the smoky fragrance of the burning wood and the steaminess of the whistling kettle. She enjoyed being enveloped by the smells and loved the fact that her mother and she had such a wide selection of teas to choose from.

The elder Kitano would appear from behind the navy hemp curtain like a wizened alchemist. He would point to the earthen jars that contained the perfumes of the floral jasmine, the musky *ban-cha*, the nutty *mugi-cha*, and the roasted *soba-cha*. He would often successfully cajole my grandmother into buying more than just her usual green tea.

While Grandmother searched within her sash for her small purse of coins, Kitano's young son Yoshiro would appear from the back room. In his youth, young Kitano Yoshiro was round and pudgy, with a thick mop of black hair and long black eyes. He would always appear with a game or a toy in hand, much to my mother's delight, and the two children would immediately begin to amuse themselves with each other's company. Occasionally, Grandmother would accept Kitano's offer of a cup of green tea and allow the children to play for a few moments. Other times, however, she would hold her daughter tightly to her side and inform her that there was no time for childish nonsense. "We must hurry along," she would say, as they had to meet Grandfather at the theater.

As Yoshiro grew to be a man and my mother into a woman, the magic shared in their childhood still connected them. He stopped bringing toys, but he still had the capacity to hold her attention with the winking of his eye and the lengthening of his smile. Mother would insist to Grandmother that she could attend to the errands on her own, but Grandmother refused to allow her to make the trip alone. The two women would dress in their Nishijin kimonos, their feet bound in white and slippered in geta, and would elegantly make their journey by way of chair men into town.

Over the years, old Kitano-san ceased to wait on customers, and his son eventually replaced him at the counter. Grandmother took notice of the extra attention and generosity he lavished on them, and found it strange and uncomfortable. She would watch with a suspicious eye as Kitano Yoshiro scooped the dried tea leaves with his hollow-bamboo shovel onto the scale and consistently undercharged them.

"You have undercharged me, Kitano-san," Grandmother told him.

"For the pleasure of serving you," he would reply to her in his most polite speech, his eyes traveling down from those of my grandmother and, finally, to the eyes he yearned for, those of my mother.

She would notice how her daughter reciprocated his gaze, how her lips would turn delicately into a smile, and her cheeks would suddenly flush.

"He is the son of a merchant!" Grandmother would sternly tell my mother as they left the shop, their packages neatly packed in *furoshiki* tapping against their sides. "There is no future for you with him!" she would reiterate time and time again.

Later my grandmother would learn to regret her harsh words. She would confide to me how they tortured her, burned her heart, and tore at her insides. But that day, with her young daughter at her side, she thought the girl immortal and forever seventeen.

Indeed, Grandmother was surprised at her daughter's lack of propriety. There could be no future for her daughter and Kitano Yoshiro. Imagine the disgrace of a Yamamoto marrying a merchant! The bloodline of the great families had to be maintained. Ideally, actors married daughters of actors, and musicians married daughters of musicians. But, as with Grandmother and Grandfather, there were occasionally marriages between the related professions.

Her engagement with her husband had been an easy one. Both families could not have been happier. Their marriage festivities lasted for three days, and she wore a heavy wedding kimono as fine as any courtier's. She had always hoped that one day her daughter would wear the same robe. She had pictured her high in the wedding palanquin, her hair piled above her head, her face powdered to perfection.

Her husband seemed so ecstatic about finding a match for his beloved daughter: a man of Noh and an orphan who could adopt the Yamamoto name. He had done well to invite the young man to their home. Should her daughter consent to marry this mask carver, her daughter might succeed where she had failed, giving the family the son they always wanted.

She did not know how her daughter would feel about this young man. Arranged marriages were still the norm rather than the exception. But the child was a precocious girl and had always been aware that her parents had defied tradition and married out of love, not obligation.

Grandmother worried unnecessarily about what my mother's reaction would be. She should have realized that my mother would have always chosen duty over love.

"Your father has found a man he believes to be a suitable husband for you," she whispered to her daughter as she awakened her. "You must get up! He will be arriving at three."

It was early December and, because of the season, Grandmother chose for her daughter a silk kimono with snow-covered plum blossoms over a pale blue background. After Mother had bathed, Grandmother plaited her black hair for her, coiled it on top of her head, and fastened each gleaming sheet of hair with one of the nine exquisite lacquer combs. In order to reinforce the elaborate coiffure, Grandmother secured the combs with a few thin tortoiseshell pins. Mother's long neck was exposed, white even before being powdered, as slender as a reed.

Outside, the wind howled and the first snow of the season arrived. Snowflakes fell cold, pale, and ghostly, dusting the nearby mountain and the carved pigeons perched on the peaks of our house's gables in a flurry of white. The braziers in the house swelled orange, and the shoji, if only for a moment, caught the beautiful flicker of the two women's shadows stretched across parchment.

"Etsuko," Grandmother whispered, as she raised her hands over mother's head and smoothed out the stray tendrils of hair, "Father has found a great man for you. He tells me that his carving is as fine as that of the great masters, that he has the promise to be the finest carver of this generation."

My mother sat squarely on a silk pillow, allowing her mother to prepare her as though she were a doll.

"Do not be afraid of marriage. Learn now, and learn this early," Grandmother continued, "you must not fight marriage or try to escape from it. Because in this life it is our destiny to be the wives of great men. Comfort yourself, as I did, that your future husband is in a position that commands respect. But Etsuko, never forget that a bond is shared among all women, regardless of class or fortune: our duty to our husbands is to give them a son. In this regard, I have failed your father. I have heard that once a woman gives birth to a son, she is finally free. The roles of the marriage reverse and she becomes the one with the power. Of this sort of emancipation, sadly I am ignorant. All I know is that for you, my beloved daughter, I pray you will deliver a healthy son and come to know the freedom I have been denied."

Then, with a long razor, Grandmother deftly defined the hair at the base of mother's scalp, which, when completed, resembled a perfectly formed black triangle.

Later that day, at the *o-miai*, the ceremony of introduction, my mother sat across from my father with her legs tucked tightly underneath her. Her hands were folded neatly on her lap and her gaze directed at the floor. She sat, flanked by her parents: Grandmother silent and beautiful like mother; Grandfather enormous, mighty, and proud. His face red and his neck strong, he resembled the ferocious, bulldog-like thunder guard positioned at the entrances to our temples.

Mother did not dare permit her eyes to meet those of the man who sat across from her. Rather, she allowed herself occasionally to glance at the low lacquer table that separated them. There, in the shine of the silky black tabletop, his face revealed itself. He appeared older than she had expected. His eyes, lowered like hers, already had creases at the corners; his face appeared windburned and cracked. She had pictured him stronger and hoped him to be handsomer. She had imagined that he would be tall, that he would have a full, round face and mischievous black eyes. She had wished, when her own eyes were shut tight and her mother was applying her makeup, that her husband-to-be would have the laughter of Yoshiro and the strength of her father.

She saw the reflection of my grandfather, this mighty man, floating beside that of her intended. How odd they seemed in comparison. She could see behind my grandfather's eyes that he was already planning the festivities of their marriage and orchestrating the mask carver's adoption into their family. And believing there was no way she could have refused this man before her, Mother allowed her heart to soften for him. She wanted to warm to him, to love something about him, but she struggled to find it. She strained to catch a glimpse of his hands, which he tucked underneath the table, so that she might see the tools that bore him such fame.

But to her, he exuded no magic. His pallor appeared dusty and devoid of light. When he spoke, it was in a serious tone, devoid of any humor, punctuated by no points of laughter, and nothing of his soul was exposed in his eyes.

She thought of Kitano Yoshiro and his laughter. She thought of the sparkle of his eyes, the sweet melody of his voice, and shuddered at the contrast between the two men. She had often allowed her mind to wander, to dream of what it would be like to be alone with Yoshiro. But her sense of duty always overpowered her girlish fantasies. Her mother's harsh words still echoed in her head: "You have no future with the son of a merchant!"

Dragging her back from her dreams, she heard the mask carver's faint voice: "I come with humility and great respect for the Yamamoto family. I only hope that Etsuko will allow me the privilege of being her husband."

No longer could she hear her own voice in her head. It seemed so crowded in her mind. And as she lowered her head and agreed to accept my father's proposal of marriage, she could not help but think of the dream that had recurred throughout her childhood. As she uttered her words of compliance, she saw herself once more at the Buddhist altar, offering herself up in sacrifice, so that, in return for her meager life, her family might be bequeathed a son.

To my grandfather, the *o-miai* went as planned. My parents were presented to each other, and on the same day, their engagement was announced. He chose the day of their marriage and then welcomed his future son-in-law as his own.

Grandmother, however, did not respond to the news as she had expected. That evening she lay awake, stray pieces of tatami pricking her like thorns. Her mind and her heart raced. She wanted to wake her husband and tell him to reconsider. It was all wrong. But even in his sleep his noises were loud and furious, and she feared telling him her truest thoughts. So she spent the remainder of that evening sleepless. She would spend every evening thereafter in the same manner: silenced by fear and tormented by her guilt. During the preparation of her daughter's hair before the *o-miai*, she had accidentally inserted *four* tortoiseshell hairpins underneath the beautiful lacquer combs that had been placed in my mother's bun. The word *shi*—four—never to be spoken, the number four always to be avoided in groupings; the word whose double meaning was death.

FOUR

The preparation of a Japanese bride is much like the wrapping of a splendid present, and Mother was no exception.

Her dressing would take several hours to complete. First there was the arrangement of five layers of colored cloth around her neck. Grandmother had carefully selected each color. She chose the *ukon* yellow, derived from the turmeric plant, for its vibrant color; the *suou* red and safflower pink for their sign of wealth; and a malachite green because it personified eternity. But the last layer that she placed on her daughter's shoulders was the prized *konjyou* blue. This dark blue-purple, made from a rare mineral imported from China, was said to evoke dignity and spiritual composure; it was said to symbolize the resolution of the bride stepping into her new life.

Layer upon layer, Mother was prepared for her waiting bridegroom. The temperature of her body soared with each additional garment. Red underclothes peeked from underneath a white silk robe girdled by a small red obi, and then a thicker white robe was placed on top and girdled with a slightly broader white obi. Grandmother's colorfully patterned wedding kimono was placed over Mother and allowed to remain open, revealing the multiple layers of robes underneath, and trailing behind her nearly four feet. Last, a fan was placed in the outermost sash. Gold on one side, silver on the other. The sun and the moon. Closed and compact. Neatly tucked at her waist.

Grandmother went to the corner of the room where the *tsuno-kakushi*, the bride's ceremonial horn hider, and the large black wig remained. She had hesitated the night before, when she went to place the decorative combs throughout the wig. She remembered how she had placed four pins underneath the combs during the *o'miai*. She would be more careful this time, she thought to herself. With all her heart, she hoped the gods had not taken notice of her mistake.

This time she chose five combs. She selected two adorned with auspicious animals, the tortoise and the crane, and one made of red lacquer, one made of silver, and one made of gold.

She stood behind my mother and slowly placed the wig on her head. She smoothed down the strands of hair with her palms and then delicately placed the *tsuno-kakushi* on top.

Mother felt a dull pain in her neck from the increasing weight being placed on her tiny form.

"You look beautiful, Etsuko," Grandmother whispered, as they both stared into the same mirror.

Mother looked at herself in the small glass frame. She believed she looked identical to Grandmother on her wedding day, as she was dressed in the wedding kimono Grandmother herself had worn. She concentrated on her heavily powdered face, the carefully painted red mouth and finely lined eyes. For the first time she noticed that she had her mother's cheekbones and softly rounded chin.

But the weight of the kimono, the tightness of her obi, and the layers of cloth around her neck were suffocating her.

"I can hardly breathe, Mother," she said.

"You will become accustomed to it, Etsuko." Grandmother smiled as she rested her palm on her daughter's shoulder. "I felt the same way on my wedding day."

But Mother knew that those words were half-truths. Her

parents' story was different from hers. And her life would undoubtedly be different from theirs. She knew in her heart that she did not love her husband-to-be and that he could not possibly love her. Her sense of responsibility and devotion was to her family; her husband's was to his craft. But if the gods smiled upon their union and gave them a son, both parties would be content. So when she visited the Zuishin shrine before her wedding day, that was what she prayed for. She did not pray for love or for health. She prayed for me.

Sadly, that was all she ultimately received.

The banquet was the most splendid display the guests had ever seen. Under Grandmother's careful guidance, each course was fastidiously arranged and artistically decorated. Adhering to tradition, the cucumbers were cut into the shape of pine trees, as the evergreen was a symbol of a long and lasting marriage, and the carrots were cut into the shape of bamboo roots, the symbol of a sturdy union. The dried *matsutake* mushrooms had been reconstituted in a mixture of sake and rice wine and folded into heaping mounds of rice. *Shiso* leaves and chrysanthemum petals floated in clear broth like flowers in a palace pond, red caviar roe rolled in seaweed glimmered, and raw jellied quail eggs jiggled their bright yellow yolks in half-open pale blue shells speckled in white. Crisp tempura slices of lotus root and sweet yams were placed on flat basket trays decorated by a spray of winter grasses. The festive *o-seki-han*—rice pinkened with mashed azuki beans—was served cool on the top shelf of a three-tiered lacquer box also containing a small grilled fish on the second shelf, and a selection of *tsuke-mono* pickles on the third. Lastly, and most elegantly, sugar-dusted plums were served for dessert.

Mother had always been particularly fond of plums. She loved their perfectly round shape, their thin translucent skin, and the sweet succulence of their flesh. As she sat displayed next to her new and unfamiliar husband on the wedding dais, she found herself anxious to try the plum that rested on the tray before her.

She looked to her husband, who sat squarely at her side dressed handsomely in his black crested kimono and *haori* coat. With a quick glance she surveyed what he had eaten, as she herself was becoming quite hungry. She noticed that her husband had nearly finished the elaborate meal that had been placed before him in its entirety. He had eaten everything except the sugar-dusted plum.

Mother, however, had been fearful to eat anything all day. Aside from the normal premarital apprehension, her tightly bound obi had severely constricted her eating so much that her intricately arranged meal remained untouched.

I will only have a nibble, she thought to herself. I will only eat the plum.

Then, with great subtlety and refinement, Mother revealed two slender fingers from the sleeve of her heavy silken robe and placed the plum discreetly in her mouth.

The plum tasted wonderful. Sweet and fragrant. Mother let the juice slide down her throat and into her empty stomach. She closed her eyes, savoring its exquisite taste.

When she opened her eyes, she saw Grandmother surrounded by several of the wives of actors in the theater laughing and speaking among themselves. She smiled at Grandmother and watched as she elegantly bowed her head and bent her knees, in a polite departure from her guests. Within a few moments she was at her daughter's side.

"The plums are delicious, Mother," she said.

"Plum blossoms are the first flower to appear in winter. They are hearty and they persevere. Even after the cruelest frost, the plum blossom remains. That is why the image of the plum is ever present at a wedding. Especially a winter wedding like yours, Etsuko."

Father had seen the sugar-dusted plums being neatly arranged earlier that morning. He had frowned behind Grandmother's back as she frantically rushed to place each one on its tray. In his mind, the plum did not bode well for the future.

He was silent as the four of them rode in carriages to the shrine for the Shinto ceremony, he riding with Grandfather, she with Grandmother.

My mother stepped out of the palanquin like an empress. Grandmother steadying her exit with the extension of her hand. Mother held the front placket of her robe with candle-thin fingers, the tips finely rounded and lightly powdered, and stepped to the ground with grace. Grandmother straightened the robe's heavy train and met the eyes of her husband. He was beaming, seeing his daughter dressed in the same magnificent finery in which he earlier had wed her mother.

Father gazed nervously at his young bride. He noticed the beautiful shadow that her headdress cast over her porcelain-white face. He felt the coldness he had harbored in his heart so long grow warm. She was indeed more beautiful than he imagined a woman ever could be.

Their eyes finally met during the exchange of the *san-san-kudo*, the three sips, followed by another three sips of sake, the essential binding part of the Shinto ceremony. And for the first time in his memory, he discovered two eyes blinking back at him.

That afternoon, the Yamamoto household was brimming with food and conversation. Grandfather believed he was uniting the finest blood and talent in the theater. When he lifted his cup of rice wine to toast the new couple he remarked, "This day signified the merging of acting and art. Their son, my future grandson," he declared, "will be the future of Noh for us all!" The other actors cheered Grandfather and the young couple and within minutes they broke into song. With great gusto they began chanting "Takasago" the Noh song that describes the twin pines of Takasago Suminoe, a symbol of everlasting marital happiness. But the actors never finished the chorus. The rice wine had made them giddy and they gave up halfway through, buckling over in their kimonos, their faces as red as pickled plums.

None of the daughters in the other families envied my mother. They all believed that my father was too consumed by his craft ever to be bothered with love. Within the circle of hushed whispers, it was said that a man whose fingers are indistinguishable from the blades with which he slices can never truly caress and love the flesh. His fingers become scythes, and his skin solidifies, hardened by the wood he embraces day after day.

On her wedding night, my mother waited anxiously for my father to join her in their connubial futon. She lay stiff, the virgin bride tucked neatly under the red silk blanket. Grandmother had embroidered the futon's overlay with large white cranes, and mother, her eyes shut tightly and her fists clenched at her sides, wished more than anything that the silken cranes would take flight and carry her far away.

Father, however, had spent nearly an hour soaking in the *o-furo* in what proved to be a futile attempt to calm his nerves. Exhausted from the wedding, and overwhelmed by the crowds of guests, he sought the peace and tranquillity of the bathhouse. To be sure, he knew that his wife waited for him. Her elaborate wedding robe was already folded and she was now elegantly dressed in a delicate *yukata*. Her skin smelled sweet from the almond blossom balm, her lips painted into a demure expression. She waited. Like a lovely bundled-up *furoshiki* waiting to be untied.

He had never been with a woman before. His only memory of a naked woman was that of his aunt. He had seen her shriveled body when she disrobed before bathing with the wooden pail in the outer yard of the old house. Her spindly backbone protruded from her flesh like the snaking spine of a scaled fish. Her breasts, deflated with age, hung like the weak teats of an animal. When she poured the water over her head, letting it cascade in a huge torrent over her whole form, her hair adhered to the blades of her shoulders like a black wig threaded with long strips of seaweed.

He knew his wife would be different. He had studied her face, much as he studied the planes of a mask. Her porcelain-smooth complexion, the slight elevation of her cheekbones, he already knew her features by heart. With ease he could imagine her narrow eyes rimmed in black kohl, the brow bone white and high. Had he a block of wood in front of him, he could carve her from memory. He would begin with the nose. Long and distinctively arched. Not flat like most. He would carve away both the right and left sides of the wood until it rose from the center like a small triangle. Then he would move on to her mouth. He pictured her lips blossoming into a full pout. Red like a poppy. Smooth like a single petal. In his momentary wandering of the mind, he transcended time. It was only when he discovered himself in steaming water up to his neck, the steam rising over his face, that he awakened.

He gathered himself slowly. The heat had made him lethargic, yet he knew he must go to his bride. She would be waiting for him. He wrapped himself in an indigo-dyed *yukata* and pushed his red feet into his rope-coiled sandals. The stars in the evening sky were white and dangled above him like *shimenawa*, the strips of rice paper one knots to mark the most sacred places.

When he walked to the tatami room where his bride lay, he discovered her not exactly as he had imagined. Fearing in her loneliness that her new husband had rejected her, Mother had begun crying. Her once impeccably powdered face was now streaked with red blotches. The rice powder had clumped like glue around the basins of her eye sockets, and her lips were swollen beyond the line of her lip rouge. Seeing his face looking down at her sent her seeking refuge in the sleeve of her *yukata*.

Father knew that what his master had forbidden him was now rising in his chest. Emotion swam inside him, choking him like a salty wave. Indeed, the face he now saw before him was definitely not a mask. Yet the faint noise of weeping and the sweep of milky leg protruding from the slit of her robe reminded him of his mother. He knelt beside her and stroked her arm as if it were the rarest column of wood. He traced the blue of her veins running like the current of a river underneath the skin, branching into thin spiders at the delta of her wrist.

She turned to him, half her face imprinted with the texture of buckwheat grains from the pillow, and smiled faintly. It was easy for him to see beyond the smeared makeup, the faint redness, that blemished her otherwise beautiful countenance. For Father was a carver and could easily disregard the often misleading appearance of a block of wood. He knew that, underneath, she was more beautiful than any mask he had ever carved.

His hands moved over her cheek, and she found herself surprised by their warmth. He fingered the stray hairs that had fallen onto her cheeks and stroked them behind the curve of her ear.

When he caressed her neck, he found himself surprised by the sheer smoothness of skin perhaps more supple than even oiled cypress. When he fumbled over the cloth and moved to untie her sash, he could not help but hear her soft, nervous giggles.

Somewhere deep inside him he wished that she would not make a sound. Sounds increased his nervousness. Brought him out from the recesses of the workings of his inner mind, where he felt uneasy, where he felt unsure.

But he proceeded. He felt the smoothness of her breasts, the contrast of her nipples. He inhaled the sweetness of her perfume.

Underneath his body, he felt her initial tension rise and then release. And he heard the clenching of her teeth fade into soft moans. He wished to see her face, wondered if it too would be transformed like a mask on stage, and searched to find it, to uncover it from the shadows. Once he had discovered it, he held her head in between his palms like a boy who has finally grasped the moon.

His lips fell over hers and he inhaled, hoping to breathe her soul into his, so that perhaps he would release it again in the form of a mask. But the taste was not as he expected. Not the sweet floral scent of almond blossom, not the nutty smell of toasted ginkgo. Something unexpected, something terrible. The taste of plums.

He fell away from her like a slain man. The taste of plum was his forewarning. He had danced with the seductive sensation of emotion, and now he would be punished. The gods would take her too.

Mother turned to him, bewildered, not knowing what she could have done, humiliated by how she had failed. But he no longer saw her. There was no one but him in the room with his darkness and his ghosts. He did not feel her trembling hand on his back. He did not hear the repetition of her sobs.

She was the last thing that he would allow himself to love. And he knew in his heart he would never be able to kiss her again—for he knew now the destiny that awaited them.

And it was on this fated night, when the taste of plums slipped like poison between my parents' lips, that I, their only son, was conceived.

FIVE

I firmly believe that my father began carving only because he knew that whatever he created with the chisel could never die.

Marriage, however, confused him. As he was a husband now, he would be responsible for his wife's protection. This weighed heavily on him. On the night of their wedding, death had lurked in the shadows of their room. He had smelled it. Ripe as a plum. And now he had to either resign himself to fate or try to overcome it.

All of these sensations and feelings scared him. He had not known such fear since he was a child. This must be that which Tamashii had warned him of. That which threatened to weaken his craft. Emotion. Yet Etsuko was not what he imagined a woman to be. She was far lovelier. How could his heart not weaken to her? How could he not thaw when he was in her presence?

She reminded him so of his mother.

Now that they were married, she wore her hair long for him. Shiny as lacquer. Fragrant as camellia oil. He would graze her shoulder just so that he could inhale her intoxicating perfume.

Just as he believed it was his duty to protect her, she believed it was her duty to care for him. To love him. As no one had done in years.

In the morning she would rise before the house awakened,

while her parents still slept and the night braziers still burned. She would slide from underneath their coverlet, careful not to disturb him, and gather herself and her robes. Then, with steps as light as a spirit, she would walk into the garden to scoop the miso paste from one of the earthen jars and pull two or three fish from their salty box. She would steep his rice in citron and rice wine. She would lay a branch of blossoms, to wait beside him and his bowl.

On the days when her early departure left a coldness and an aching emptiness in their bed, he would rise minutes after her. He would walk toward their small paper window and slide it ever so slightly to one side. Just to watch her, if only for a moment, as she glided through the garden as ethereal as a ghost.

He could hear the sound of the latch closing, the gentle whipping of her hair. To him nothing was more beautiful—not even a mask, dare he say it?—than his wife wrapped in her morning robe.

The black of her hair falling like the smooth feathers of a raven bird, the shine of her alabaster brow. He could anticipate the sound of her footsteps, he could watch her for hours and never tire of the sweet melody of her voice. With great voracity, he consumed his breakfast as if it were manna delivered to him by the gods. He saw her image in the cloudy broth of miso, and her tenderness in the wilted greens.

As much as his superstitious mind hated to admit it, the first month of their marriage was nothing short of blissful. Every morning she prepared his meal for him, and his afternoons were free so that he could carve. His father-in-law converted the small room on the second floor into a studio so that he could work uninterrupted on his masks. When he had imagined himself adopted into a household, he never dreamed that one as prestigious as the Yamamoto family would be as kind and as warm as he discovered them to be.

Since their first meeting at the *o-miai*, Father had known that Etsuko felt no love for him. He knew that he was not beautiful and that the years spent in isolation had prevented him from cultivating any charm. He only hoped that she would learn to love him, as his father-in-law promised she would.

"I believe it is far easier for a woman to learn to love her husband than it is for a man to learn to love his wife," Grandfather had told him before his wedding day. "I know my daughter, Ryusei, and I know that she will learn to love you." Father remained skeptical, convincing himself that their marriage was acceptable because it fulfilled desires within both parties outside the world of love. But as much as he knew he should avoid all feeling for the material world—one of his master's strictest rules—he could not help being captivated by its enticing powers.

He knew his wife was particularly fond of the love poems of Ono no Komachi. Those words of a woman who cannot sleep, whose love burns inside her like an inextinguishable flame, how they captivated him too! Only in his most fanciful dreams could he imagine his wife ever feeling that way toward him.

He recognized in himself that he appeared staid, almost passionless. Yet he had been told that his masks had the capacity to move audiences to tears and the finest actors to cries of awe. His spirit was in each and every one of those masks, infused with what he could never convey with words. He worried that his wife could not recognize that. Would she always think of him as just a man of the wood?

* * *

Despite her initial resignation, Mother did learn to love the man who was chosen for her. And perhaps that made the remainder of Father's life all the more painful. For eventually she grew to love him deeply.

As no one else ever did.

Her love for him grew slowly, beginning almost as an abstraction. Undoubtedly, Mother loved that which gave joy to her family. In the beginning, her feelings toward her husband were defined by a sense of duty. For now she had given her parents a sense of completion in their old age. Her father seemed to breathe a new zest for life now that he had a male companion in the house. The family dinners were now convivial, unlike the quiet meals of her childhood, which had become the norm after the death of her brother. Grandfather's eyes sparkled, as they hadn't in years, enjoying the entirely new set of ears to which he could tell his colorful stories. Grandmother's body began to relax slightly as her daughter assumed the chores of head female of the household. With great anticipation and happiness they began the next stages of their life.

When Mother announced that she had forgone two consecutive monthly defilements, the response to the news was overwhelming. She had never seen her parents more filled with joy.

Grandmother walked over to her daughter's side and gently kissed her blushing cheek. "Your father and I are so happy for you," she whispered. In her heart she prayed that the child would be healthy and male—the two things that had evaded her own family.

Grandfather raised his cup of sake and toasted my health, the heir to the Yamamoto name.

"Soon I will have a grandson," he declared, upon rising from the low table. He seemed to believe that since the gods had denied him a son, they would smile on his good deed of having adopted the lonely mask carver, and now bestow on him the grandson he so passionately craved. He knew it would be selfish for him to insist that the boy be raised to be an actor, and so, to appease the gods with one more selfless act, he added to his toast: "And as it is with so much pride and joy that I look upon this day, I hope that my grandson will live to become as great a mask carver as his father!" He lowered his gaze to Father and raised his cup. "With great anticipation do I look forward to the day that Mother and I can bestow on him his first set of chisels."

Father, slightly overwhelmed by all of the emotion that was flowing through the room, managed to awkwardly raise his cup and acknowledge Grandfather's toast. His wife had told him the night before that she suspected she was with child and he had received the news with mixed emotions. Certainly he was thrilled with the thought of creating his own family, perhaps he truly was no longer bound to the wood. It had never occurred to him that he might have the power to create a human life. For the past thirty years of his life he had felt almost nonhuman. Neither a man nor a ghost. Perhaps something in between, a man made of wood.

Now there was a life growing inside the womb of his wife that he was partly responsible for. Another person to protect. Another person who must be sheltered from the clawing vines of death.

He allowed his wife to place his hands on her stomach. So that he might feel the heartbeat, my heartbeat. So that he might feel the difference between flesh and wood.

Her stomach was still as flat as a tablet. He closed his eyes and tried to imagine their child being formed from each of the fibers in my mother's womb, a process so different from his craft. Within that warm, carefully cushioned shrine that contained the cells of generations of tradition and talent, I would be created.

He remembered the eyes of his father and how his life had seemed to begin at the hour when he arrived home. When his eyes fell upon those of his wife and those of his sons. His family.

With each passing day Father found it easier to imagine himself in his newfound role. His masks became less interesting to him compared to his family. Perhaps Tamashii had never known such joy, I believe Father thought to himself as he searched for reasons why his master so strongly advised against an emotional life. Perhaps his life was filled only with sadness. But perhaps Father believed, for the first time, that he could triumph where his master had failed. Over sadness. Over death.

The first thing he did after Mother announced her pregnancy was forbid her to eat plums. "They are no good for you or the baby," he told her, gently sweeping one from her hand as she sat in the garden one day, her hair loosely tied in a bun.

"But why, Ryusei?" she asked, puzzled.

"Hasn't your father told you?" he asked, equally perplexed that his father-in-law had never divulged the story of his past. "No good can come from them. You must trust me. Promise me your lips will never touch one," he pleaded. Not wishing to scare his wife with his former misery, he pretended his superstition was grounded in an old wives' tale he had heard long ago.

"I promise," she whispered, looking down at his kneeling form. "I would do anything to ensure our son's arrival into this world. *Anything.*"

As she watched him return to the house, it occurred to her that she had eaten a plum on their wedding day. The night of the child's conception. She considered whether she should divulge this to her husband. "No need to worry him," she decided. "It is only a silly old wives' tale."

* * *

Father's interest in carving waned over the months of my mother's pregnancy. It seems she was the only one in the world who had the power to distract him from the wood. The orders for his masks continued to pile up even though the number of performances the theater was producing began to decrease. His masks became almost rarities, limited editions that demanded far higher prices than the theaters could afford.

"Don't forget your carving," Grandfather began reminding him after the family dinners. "The actors in the theater are beginning to wonder if you have given up on your craft."

"Don't worry," Grandmother comforted him. "It is just the baby's impending arrival. Once he is born, all will return to normal."

"I hope you are right, Chieko," he sighed with the day's exhaustion. "It would be a shame to let a talent like his go to waste."

Mother, however, enjoyed the attention that her husband lavished upon her. Never in her most colorful dreams had she imagined that he would be so attentive to her. Although he seemed uninterested in lovemaking, his hands would find themselves on her expanding belly. Like a blind man, he would trace the gentle rounding, the sloping that began beneath her breasts and then gently merged with her thighs. At night he would thread his fingers through her hair, gently caress her cheekbones, her eyelids, the soft line of her lips. As if to memorize her.

Indeed, she began to believe he truly loved her, and subsequently her love for him blossomed. No longer did she feel that she was preparing his meals or attending to his needs only out of a wifely duty. Now she truly desired to make him happy.

His sweetness grew. He spent less time carving and more time at her side. When he did carve, he often called for her to come and see something he had just completed.

On one day in particular, he asked her to come to his studio. When she arrived, an exquisite female mask rested on a piece of silk cloth.

"It is you, Etsuko," he whispered to her as she knelt beside him, the strips of cypress curling under her knees.

She recognized the mask as the beautiful Ko Omote mask. White as rice powder. Lips as demure as a doll's.

He placed the mask in her outstretched palms.

"I have made her for you, my wife," he said, almost shyly.

Mother remained silent. She knew that if anyone could interpret her lack of words, it would be her husband.

"She is *you* and you are *she*," he said, pointing to the mask.

Deeply moved, tears beginning, she turned the mask over to examine the lines of the carver. Her husband.

The strokes were deep. Lines like furrows. Channels that wound in a pattern almost too complex to convey. It was now she truly saw him for the first time, not as she had seen him when they first met, when she was limited to the masklike quality of his face. Now she saw beyond it.

"You have shown me your soul, my darling," she said, her words almost lost in her sobs.

He placed his hand on her shoulder and he knew that he probably appeared clumsy. But, for the first time in their marriage, that did not bother him. He knew she now saw him for what he was. A man far deeper than the wood.

According to Grandmother, by her seventh month, Mother's stomach was as large as a small bear. She carried all of her weight in the front, which grew so large that, when she walked, her back seemed lost in its perpetual arching and her shoulders pushed even farther behind.

Every morning, however, she continued to rise to prepare her husband's breakfast. She never tired of heating the pails of water for his bath, no matter how great the strain. It seemed as though each of them had finally discovered what the other needed.

In the last month of my mother's pregnancy, she announced that she would like to make a trip to Kiyomizu-dera in order to pray for my entrance into the world and buy a blessed *anzan o-mamori* charm from one of the priests. Grandmother insisted that the three-hour journey from Daigo to the temple would be too exhausting.

"I must go," she said obstinately. "Ryusei will accompany me. We will visit the inner shrine, Jishu Jinya, the shrine of the love rocks. We will pray together and ask Ubugami to look over our child. It is the only way."

Her parents lowered their eyes, knowing they could not argue.

"Are you sure you feel up to such an arduous journey, Etsuko?" Father asked with concern.

"I am sure. Please do not worry. Seeing the temple and praying to the birth deity will calm my nerves."

The three of them looked at her, swollen with my unborn form, and nodded in weak consent.

The next day Mother, too fragile to be carried by chair men, was placed in the palanquin that had carried her as a bride. Her parents, still concerned that she might damage the child, made one last attempt to dissuade her from making the trip.

"Thank you, Mother and Father, for your concern, but I will be fine," she insisted. "My husband and I want to pray for our child together."

Grandfather shook his head, and Grandmother clutched her wooden prayer beads. The two of them watched as the carriage took them away.

When they arrived home late that evening, Mother was as pale as the inside of a Chinese guava. Her lips, no longer the pink of lotus blossoms, suddenly white as ash.

The rains had begun late that afternoon, after they had departed, and they could find no shelter along the way. The roof of the palanquin had collapsed, and Mother lay drenched and covered in thatched straw.

Wiping her brow with his soaking wet sleeve, Father helped Mother from the carriage. When she proved too weak to stand, he hoisted her weary body in his arms. He cradled her like a child, the *anzan o-mamori* charm dangling from her hand.

Grandmother and Grandfather stood in the rain transfixed. They did not flinch even as their silver hair fell like wet grass over their scalps, as their kimonos became so drenched one could see the outlines of their forms. How could it be, they thought, in only eighteen hours' time, their beautiful child had paled to nothing more than a ghost?

"Bring her into the center room," Grandmother ordered. "The braziers are warmest in there."

Suddenly, from where she stood, Grandmother noticed a bloodstain expanding from underneath her daughter's loosened sash. That stain, as bright as fire, spread within seconds over the entire front placket of her kimono. Streaking like bolts of red lightning.

"I will run for a doctor," cried Grandfather. "Ryusei, bring her inside!"

He laid her down on the tatami and brought the brazier closer to her side. He lowered the flame of the lantern, untying the sash of his own kimono, covering her belly so she would not see her clothes saturated with blood.

In the few moments that transpired before the quilts were brought to him, he held her face in the gentle basin of his palms. He pushed back the damp locks of her hair. He whispered into her ear all the ancient love poems she had held so dear.

My face white as Fujiyama betrays my red, red heart.

On my way to Edo, I found your face in the weave of my sleeve.

When the blankets arrived, he removed her wet robes, like a mother changing the soiled clothes of her baby. He dabbed her sweating brow with a cloth soaked in fragrant tea. He wound his fingers tightly into hers and looked deep into her frightened eyes, never flinching all the while as Grandmother pressed strips of boiled cotton between Mother's bleeding thighs.

When his mother-in-law appeared finished, he stood up to retrieve the stack of blankets. Hoping to appear helpful, he placed each warm layer over his ailing bride.

"Take the *fourth* off, Ryusei," Grandmother told him before the blanket had even reached my mother's chin. "You, if anyone, should know better."

He grew pale, realizing his near mistake. "You are right, Mother," he said wearily. "Indeed, I should."

When the doctor arrived, my mother had already lost consciousness.

She had spent her last hours of memory pleading with my father to save their child's life before her own.

"Please," she had begged him. "Save our son."

He had not wanted to hear her. She was the one he most wanted in this world. He did not need an heir. He did not need a disciple. All he truly needed was her.

He held her hand even when she no longer had the strength to grasp his fingers. He pressed her smooth wrist to his cheek, inhaled the sweetness of her lips, even when the breaths no longer seemed to come.

When the doctor arrived, he tried to pry the mask carver's fingers free. My father would not budge.

"Yamamoto Ryusei-sama," the doctor insisted. "You must let me attend to your wife."

My father lay next to her, his forehead lowered to her brow.

He heard the doctor's words, but no more would come from his lips. He only stared.

It was finally Grandmother who pried his fingers from hers. She never forgot the sight of those two interlocked hands. Laced like two tendrils. Clutching until icy white.

SIX

My father's greatest betrayal was caused by neither his wife nor his former patrons but by me, his son.

Had my father not believed in magic, perhaps the reality of my birth would not have been as painful. But he was no ordinary man; he created faces that lived on the stage, and he did this all with the sheer sorcery of his hands. He believed that happiness was owed him for his suffering. But he should have known that the gods do not reward those who believe themselves owed.

Journeying to Kiyomizu, they had each prayed separately for a son. They rang the temple bell, clapped their hands, bowed their heads, and prayed for my health. But unfortunately they forgot to pray for my mother's.

Yes, I was born from the waters of my mother's blood and in the blue-black darkness of her death.

"I am not sure we can save her," the doctor had informed them as he walked to the adjacent room lit with coal. "Her placenta has disengaged."

"And the child too?" Grandmother asked.

"The only chance for survival is if I cut," he said with resignation.

All eyes fell onto Father, already collapsed in anguish.

"Do what you can, Doctor," said Grandfather.

And so the doctor did. Carved me out from my mother's belly, with a small knife, not with a chisel.

My mother, nothing but an empty gourd, resting on a blood-soaked tatami, her eyes as vacant as two black stones. Her greatest duty fulfilled, she departed without a sound.

The three of them stood in silence. Grandmother whispered to herself: "I have killed her." Father thought to himself, Death follows me wherever I go. Neither could speak the thoughts aloud. It was only I, screeching my newborn cries, and Grandfather, who thrust his fist into the bamboo pole of the *tokonoma*, and cursed the Gods for taking his children, who refused to be muzzled.

Grandmother looked at me and then at the room where mother lay, her womb ripped to shreds. She remembered the four tortoiseshell hairpins with a shiver. She recalled her last words to her daughter on the day of her *o-miai*: "When you give your husband a son, you will be free . . . I hope you know a freedom that I have been denied." And the pain inside her was overwhelming.

Her daughter lay in the same room where Grandmother had given birth to her stillborn son years before. The room was dark and rank with death, "a cursed room," as she would later describe it to me. It was there within the claws of the timber that she had first lost her son and now her daughter. She crumpled to the floor.

But now, crying in the arms of the man my mother was forced to marry, was I, the grandson. The much anticipated heir who had arrived under the greatest sacrifice.

Father held me in his arms, but no warmth could be detected in his embrace. He looked at my newborn head: my features shriveled, my skin a mottled mixture of pink and blue, my eyes and mouth oozing with newborn wetness, and at that moment, all his fears and anxieties were confirmed. He believed that all he touched and hoped to love was cursed, for even my image in infancy echoed his haunting memories; I was another poison plum.

He should have given me up. I am sure he thought that often

during the earlier years of my childhood. He should have left me to my grandparents. They had wanted a son so desperately that they had taken my father as their own. He slept in their house, ate at their table, and adopted their name. But, later, it was I who they considered their own. To my grandfather I was a true Yamamoto; the blood that flowed through my veins was his, red and strong.

But, to everyone's surprise, Father insisted on raising me.

"Let us take him," Grandfather implored. "You are still young enough to remarry."

"I will never remarry," he replied, almost taking offense at Grandfather's suggestion.

Father had taught himself to carve on the *ume-ki*, the very plum wood whose fruit had killed his parents. The fruit had brought him misery; the wood had brought him fame. He did not know what his son would bring him. But he believed that I was his burden to bear.

Perhaps my father's actions were admirable; perhaps they were plainly selfish. Of this, I am still unsure. I am, however, certain of this: it was *I* who fought for eighteen hours not to be born, not to be given to a father whose expectations I could never fulfill. For my birth coincided with the birth of a new era, and as I would later discover, my artistic calling was in sharp contrast to those of my ancestors.

I have heard that my mother's death nearly destroyed my father. Grandmother once told me: "Had your father not had the support of the wood, he surely would have died. It was the only thing that could heal his wounds. The only thing that could absorb his silent, bleeding heart."

But much like a tourniquet, it stopped all feeling.

After Mother's burial, he walked up to his studio and shut the door. No longer did he sleep in the room he had shared with her; now he slept on the sawdust floor, beside the masks he carved by blade. He refused to eat his meals with his in-laws, requesting that they leave only a bowl of rice and a jug of water outside his door.

They did not know what faces he carved. They did not know how many masks cluttered his shelves. They only knew that he carved from dawn to dusk. I, the newborn babe, was put to sleep in the room where my grandparents slept, and according to Grandmother the hum of my father's saw was the only sound that lulled me to sleep.

Nearly fourteen days after my mother's death, my father walked down the stairs.

"Forgive me," he muttered. "I am in need of a cup of tea."

Grandmother stood in shock for what seemed like minutes, she told me. The man who stood before her now was as gray as a ghost, his skin ashen.

Clutched tight to his side he held in his right hand a shard of wood. Had he been thirty years younger, he would have appeared identical to the image of himself as a young boy after the death of his parents.

She told me he grasped the wood so firmly that the skin around his knuckles betrayed his bones. The flesh under his eyes had slackened, his cheeks sunken like two valleys. He stood there, a man deflated. That which had existed underneath his skin had been consumed.

When Grandmother asked him if he would like to hold his child, his first instinct was to decline. His son, his heir, lay in a long basket lined with white cloth, crying for an embrace.

"He is your son," she told him, her voice suddenly firm, "and,

Ryusei, you have told us that you wish to raise him. How, may I ask, do you intend to rear a child you are incapable of holding?" For the first time in her life she seemed to reveal her anger.

"I do not wish to betray my son with an embrace," he replied vacantly.

"What ever do you mean?"

"Should I raise him to depend on me, to love me, as I let myself love his mother, when I die he will only feel betrayed. Should I raise him to love nothing but the wood, that which he will know will never leave him."

He paused. His body felt heavy and dead around him. He would now live his life and rear me as his master Tamashii had urged him.

"Your son needs to know that he has a family that cares for him!" she cried.

He looked at her, his eyes suddenly aflame. "My child needs only to know that he is a son of Noh!"

With those words, Grandmother fell silent. There were certain boundaries that she knew were forbidden to trespass. This was one.

"But, Ryusei," she said, her frustration curling inside her like a snake, "your son has no name."

"I'm so tired, I can hardly think of such things." He brought his long white hand over his brow and sought the support of the banister.

"I am afraid that you have little time. By law, we must name him by the fourteenth day after his birth."

He stood there for several moments.

"Call him Kiyoki," he told her finally. "Use the Chinese characters *kiyo* meaning 'pure' and *ki* meaning 'wood.'"

"Yamamoto Kiyoki?" she asked, trying to disguise her disapproval. In her mind she had always hoped that he would let her choose my name. She would have chosen something stronger and more lyrical like Shotaro, with the characters meaning "shining first," or Zenkichi, meaning "the very luckiest of names."

"Kiyoki is a fine name!" he said. "He should have a name that evokes the strength of wood and the purity of his mother! Those are the two forces from which he was born."

Grandmother fell silent again. The son-in-law who had become her adopted son by law was a difficult man to comprehend. There were so many opposing forces enshrined within him. She had seen him fall in love with her daughter right before her very eyes. He had arrived at their house as stiff as a wooden doll, but over the months spanning her daughter's pregnancy, he appeared to have been transformed. His gaze softened, his touch no longer sounded like the dropping of lumber. She believed he had changed. That love had penetrated a heart that had petrified long ago.

She had not anticipated that death would propel him back to his original state. She would have never guessed that a young man could grow ancient in a day. But here he was, standing before her. Had she never met him before, she would have mistaken him for a mountain pilgrim, hoary as the snow.

Undoubtedly, her daughter's passing had a severe impact on her, too. She held herself personally responsible for her death. Had the gods been so vengeful that they would not overlook her mistake with the hairpins? Had her own criteria for a husband been so strict that she could not have divulged to her husband that she suspected Etsuko had burgeoning affections for another?

Guilt consumed her. Now that my mother was gone, Grandmother could no longer escape the realization of how selfish she had been.

She could not deny her self-loathing. She knew on the surface that she appeared the dutiful wife. She spoke to her husband only when he addressed her, she maintained a large and beautiful home and ensured that she, her husband, and Etsuko were always dressed appropriately. The death of her son, however, had affected her deeply, and perhaps that had been the turning point in her life, when she realized that there were some obligations for which she was responsible and others that she could never control. Etsuko had become her extension. Perhaps, even before her daughter's death, Grandmother knew in her heart that it wasn't fair to expect her daughter to sacrifice herself, her dreams, her love.

But her husband so desperately wanted a son. This mask carver was the perfect solution. That which they believed would fill in the missing pieces of their family. And when they heard that Etsuko was with child, oh, how they had rejoiced! Once again her husband and she had thought only of themselves. The child was to be a boy. They felt it in their veins. They believed that the gods would reward them for the losses they had endured.

How gravely they were wrong.

She could not help but consider herself responsible. The omens were there but she refused to see their fate. She feared upsetting her husband and, even worse, feared upsetting the fulfillment he gleaned from having another male in the household. Foolishly, she believed that if she supported the union of the mask carver and her daughter, her husband would no longer look at her as the wife who had failed to give him a son.

Now, however, as she stared at my father, she came to realize the impact of her mistakes. She found her shoulders beginning to slope even lower and what black was left in her hair succumbing to gray. Yet from the distance of the corner six-mat room where she now slept, she was awakened by my cries.

SEVEN

I was my grandmother's child for a time. Hers completely. The two males of the family coexisted under the blackened rafters of the old house, each in his own mind anxious for the day when I would be old enough to be initiated into the world of Noh. Grandfather imagined the day when I would be old enough to appreciate the theater and the craft of both him and his peers. Father, the day when I would pick up my first chisel and come to love the wood.

But Grandmother loved me as if I were her own. Her own children lost to her, I became the only living connection she had with her daughter.

So she raised me as if she were starting anew. In a world where she tried to shield me from the burden of my birth. To love me as she wished she had loved Mother. Without imposing the contagious notion of sacrifice.

In my infant years I was treated like a young prince. I was weaned on ox milk and washed in water steeped in Manchurian violets and Chinese bell flower. My swaddling clothes were made from the threads of silkworms, harvested after weeks of feeding from a diet limited solely to mulberry leaves and yellow rape blossoms. Grandmother constructed my crib from thatched dried *suzudama* stalks and cushioned its interior with soft gauze pillows. And as if to ensure my safety, she pinned a tiny ornament of *jizo*, the god of protection, to my underclothes and embroidered a tiny version of the family crest to drape over the canopy of my cradle.

She swore she would never offend the gods again.

Thirty-one days after my birth, as dictated by tradition, I was placed in the center of my grandmother's obi, tied in silk, and taken to the local temple. This ceremony, the Hatsumairi was my first journey outside the home. And as the custom specifies, the males of the family followed Grandmother as she carried me, the child, in front, secured ever so safely by the tightness of her sash.

Both Grandfather and Father wore black and slid their sandals silently as they walked behind us. Neither wished to pay his respects to the Gods, as both were angered by their loss.

Father had lost love, and Grandfather had lost his link with his last surviving child. And of these two great losses I dare not judge whose loss was greater.

Grandmother dropped a few drops of water from a bamboo ladle onto my infant fists and then carried me up to the great altar where incense clouded the air. She stared at the flicker of candles; she bent her knees and bowed her head.

And it was there she thought she saw a vision of Mother nestled under the swollen calves of Buddha. Cloaked in the white of a pilgrim, hooded like a bride, she slept.

She turned to her husband, her face as pale as the robe of the priest who passed behind the altar, "Do you see anything at the base of the Buddha?" she asked.

He looked at her strangely and shook his head to show he did not know what she saw. But as his gaze fell on that of his new grandson, he noticed how the small child extended his hands toward the bronze statue, how the child's eyes widened, transfixed.

"I do not see what you see, Chieko," he told her, "but perhaps the child does."

Looking down at me, she saw the top of my forehead grow pale, cast by the light of the tall temple tapers, my small, plump hands reaching toward the sagging belly of the statue.

He sees her too, she thought to herself as a warmth flowed through her body. It never occurred to her, however, that another person besides her husband might have seen her as well.

For she did not see Father, or perhaps even think of him, as he stood there motionless behind her. But he saw more than either of us. Mother. The image of his lost love. Transparent as wet cotton. Floating toward him and then evaporating in midair.

EIGHT

One of the first things I learned from Grandmother was that when spirits of the dead wished to visit the mortal world, they often used the bodies of small children to reveal their lost souls. "Before the age of seven the spirits can enter and leave you at any time," she said to me one night as she placed the coverlet beneath my chin. "So we must take care of you." She looked down at me with her sad black eyes. "You are your mother's shrine."

I grew up believing those words. That my mother lived inside me. That I was a vessel for her soul.

My dreams, I believe, were unlike those of most young children. Colorful and rare. Mother would appear like poured liquid, suspended by air, her robes a blurred lavender. I would see her, and she would lean down and touch me with the sweep of her hand, create a cradle from the weaving of her thick black hair.

When I awakened, I would tell Grandmother, "I have seen her! She has come," and she would kneel by my futon and hold me so close that I could feel her ribs. Her small nose pressed into the sprout of my hair, her arms tightening with each of her breaths.

I often wondered, as I grew older, if in his dreams Father saw her too. I never believed he dreamed wooden dreams cast forever in brown. But had he seen her, reached out in a half-awakened state to touch her, his fingers would merely have grasped the air. And he would certainly have have had no one there to hold him when he realized, as he collapsed in the shadows of those dark nights, how truly deep was his despair.

NINE

There were certain things that my grandmother knew she could not protect me from. Things that were chosen for me before I was born. For she had witnessed her husband's declaration and my father's reaffirmation: I was to be a son of Noh.

Originally she did not think anything of the decision. She had expected such. That was how the Yamamoto family had lived for centuries. Emperors had strained their ears to hear my ancestors' melodies, Shogunates had fought to be patrons of our troupes. She herself would have preferred that I grow to be an actor like Grandfather. Proud and stately. A man who commanded respect. The great patriarch to whom she was wed.

But her husband had deferred, promising even before I had my first breath, that I be a mask carver like my father. It hadn't pleased the gods as much as he had hoped. But at last he was given an heir.

She confessed that she wondered in private what kind of child I would develop into. Which part of me was stronger, my mother's "purity" or my father's "wood." She had vowed to make sure I would not become encased by the wood, as her son-in-law had sworn. She felt it was her duty to her daughter to ensure that, despite my future vocation, I would always know love.

When she called me by name, she often dropped the last character of my name and just called me "Kiyo." The character for *ki* would vanish at the tip of her tongue, and she would concentrate on the character that symbolized the image of my mother. For she secretly hoped that I'd be pure, like her. But when the time came, she would not expect me to sacrifice myself, as her daughter had done.

For, in a Buddhist world, she believed, there were certain wrongs that must be righted. And that the wishes of the dead must always precede those of the living. Even if those who were living were male.

TEN

I have always believed that it was my destiny to become a painter, as I have a tremendous talent for memorizing images, and less strength for remembering words. I can tell you with ease the first time I saw crimson, yet struggle to recall your name. I do know, however, that some of my first memories—the ones that come with ease and great vibrancy—are not the ones of my father and his masks but rather those of my grandfather and his stage.

Although I was no more than a mere child at the time—perhaps I was five, as it was the year I began wearing a *hakama*—I can still recall walking through the forest, treading the carefully groomed pathway to the formidable Kanze theater. Its wooden hood loomed. The pine baseboards gleamed. I can remember with great clarity pointing to the twisting pine tree painted on the backboard of the stage and questioning my grandmother: "Who was responsible for putting it there?"

"It has always been there," Grandmother replied, indirectly trying to explain to me one of the cardinal principles of Noh philosophy.

"Yes, Grandma," I insisted, "but someone must have painted it."

"You are right, Kiyoki, but the name of the artist is not as important as the image that he has painted. In this case, the pine is a symbol of Noh's eternity."

I remember being disappointed by her explanation. I remember wanting to know who was responsible for painting the enormous tree with its twisting boughs and flourishes of green. I thought to myself, If I know it is my Grandfather who is responsible for making the mask come alive, and it is my Father who is responsible for carving the mask, why should I not know whose hand was responsible for creating the great pine?

The question haunted me, and had Grandmother's explanation been more intriguing, perhaps my attitude toward Noh would have been different. Aside from the splendor of the costumes and the beating of the drums, Noh was incomprehensible to me.

For as I sat there watching my grandfather perform the role of the *shite*, the haggard mountain woman, Yamamba, in the play of the same name, I was visually stirred by the richness of the costumes and the intensity of the masks, yet I remained completely unmoved by the poetry of the words. The loud and slow chanting booming from underneath Grandfather's mask was difficult to understand and unpleasant to my ears. I detested the shrieking of the *nokan* flute, the incessant beating of the *otsuzumi* and *taiko* drums.

In contrast, the painting of the great pine stirred me. I strained to discern each brushstroke, marveled at the enormous patches of green. Perhaps it was the first painting I saw in person. An image in the second dimension reaching out toward me, pulling me inside its sprays of leaves, clutching me in its thorny spindles. I can still see my restless hands reaching toward its luminous branches, eager to capture the sensation of paint underneath my infant nails.

At a very early age, it seems, I recognized that I was moved by color and by paint. Sometimes, as was the case with me, we are incapable of changing these passions. They grow inside us like vines. Wrapping around veins and our heart. How much easier my life would have been had my destiny not been written before

I was born. That I should love the wood. Had I not been born the mask carver's son.

Three months prior to my sixth birthday, my grandfather gave to me my first set of chisels. Grandfather and Father sat at either end of the table, their legs carefully crossed, the fabric of their kimonos carefully veiling their knees. I can see my grandmother across from me, her hair lined with gray, her eyelids soft and draping. With great clarity I can see the lacquer plates from our night's dinner stacked in a slender column and our empty rice bowls pushed to the side. The taste of our Kyoto miso, the sweet saltiness of the broth, tingles at the tip of my tongue. The deep fragrance of the roasted pumpkin and *shiso* leaves floats through the air. It is as though I can close my eyes and be there once again.

"This is a special evening," Grandfather announced proudly. His voice resonated with the confidence of a man accustomed to speaking and remaining unchallenged. The room swelled with each of his breaths. The soft lantern illuminated his whitened brow. Briefly he fastened his eyes on Grandmother, who acknowledged his gaze with a gentle nodding of her head, and then Father, who met the intense gaze of Grandfather, if only for a moment, before lowering his eyes. There was a hush in the room, a pending sense of ceremony.

Grandfather reached underneath the cloth of his kimono and placed what appeared to be a rolled pouch of leather on the table. With his thick fingers, the knuckles cracked with age, he unfurled the long white cord that bound the supple ox-hide pouch and revealed five gleaming blades.

"This is your first set of chisels, Kiyoki. They are a gift from your grandmother and me." He placed his hands on the leather edges and bowed his head slightly. From the side of the table I caught sight of the blue-gray sparkle of the steel. I believe that this was my first memory of seeing the color silver, and I marveled at each of those edges as they sparkled in the moonlight like five radiant swords.

"Would you like to see them, Kiyoki?" he questioned.

I nodded my head bashfully and reached for the edge of the leather casing as Grandfather pushed the chisels toward me. I saw Father look at me, and I believe he smiled as I picked up the *tsukinomi* chisel and caught my reflection in the shining blade.

Although Father was the carver of the family, he knew the honor of bestowing on me my first set of chisels was not his to give. Such ceremony was reserved for the patriarch, the man who gave him his name and his only semblance of family. Grandfather. As he had promised even before I was born.

Sitting quietly at the table, I remember thinking that, in comparison to Grandfather, Father seemed small.

Certainly he could not compare in girth. Father's concavity was foiled by Grandfather's convexity. The hollow of Father's cheeks hung whereas Grandfather's swelled. His stomach retreated whereas Grandfather's expanded. And then there was Father's voice. Almost a whisper. A faint, gravelly murmur of words strung out over the smallest breath, forever channeled into the wood. A silent dialogue with his ghosts.

He smiles and his lips are slightly cracked. With fixed eyes and sloping shoulders, he watches as my small hands grip the smooth wooden handles, blonde with youth. I am surprised at how warm they feel to the touch and how icy cold the steel tips are in comparison. I can barely lift the tools more than a few centimeters from the table. That is how heavy they are to me. Like slender weights, loaded with responsibility. With only one in my tiny palm, I feel as though I can hardly move.

"Use them well, Grandson," echoed the voice of Grandfather. Father and he exchange contented glances once more. The two of them need not speak. They have been looking forward to this day since my conception. To them, my destiny was sealed seven years before.

I wore my destiny like a too-tight robe in which I could not breathe. Each thread of fabric was woven by an ancestor, the color chosen by fingers not my own.

Within weeks of receiving my chisels, I found myself in the forest. Father's slender form in front of me, his delicately veined eyelids are closed, and he walks with his hands stretched outward, his palms facing the sky. Paper-thin butterflies flutter at his hem.

He has awaited this time, *his time*, since the very day of my birth. He will teach me to love nothing but the wood.

"Kiyoki," he says, "someday you will be a mask carver like me, and you will be able to see all the world in a single block of wood."

His words fall like slices of cypress. Fragments that I learned to interpret since birth. He has taken me into the forest, an earthen stage for my initiation, a place where he too once learned the ways of Noh. I wonder if here he sees the ghost of Tamashii, the father figure who brought him into the world of Noh. Sees his face hovering over him like a mask swaddled in a wig of leaves.

"Father," I say, "what am I to do here?"

He holds the single-sided saw, shimmering in the forest.

"You will choose your first *hinoki* tree. From this tree I will teach you to carve."

Carve. The Japanese word is *horu*. And every time Father

articulated the word his eyes closed, his lips slightly trembled. It was as though his world suddenly came to a standstill.

"But, Father, how will I learn to carve? I will never be as fine a carver as you."

There is a flurry of leaves falling to the ground. Green. Brown. Yellow. Their edges have curled, and their veins have reddened. Leaves fall over our heads, crowning us. Shadows stretch over soil, like silk on felt. Father and I stand side by side, our reflection emblazoned in a saw.

"You are my son, Kiyoki. Your hands will lead you, as mine have led me."

He extends his hands before him, white fingers as slender as icicles.

"Choose your tree, Kiyoki," he utters once more.

All around me the forest looms vast as an ocean. I cannot distinguish a cypress from a cedar, a juniper from a spruce. I cannot differentiate between a fir tree and a cryptomeria. I am too young.

Help me, Father, I am pleading. *Help me to learn what you already see.*

For the first time in my memory we are the near-perfect image of father and son.

"The leaves of a cypress tree are pale green in spring, dark brown by midsummer, and on the forest floor by the first week of the ninth month," he tells me. "The bark, a cinnamon red."

My eyes survey the forest before me, and I still cannot find the tree that he describes. Yet I stand there listening, so unaccustomed to the sound of his voice.

"You can trace its roots to the closest source of water," he says as his fingers graze the earth. "Its smell is high and green."

We walk the forest floor until we arrive at a soft, marshy expanse. The cool water ripples in the afternoon light.

With a light in his eyes, he points to a single tree. More imposing than a pine. More statuesque than a red maple. "That is the *hinoki*," he says, "the cypress tree from which you will carve your first mask."

"The *hinoki* was the first wood in which you carved, Father?" I ask, my face turning up to him like a sunflower.

The light in his eyes is fading, clouding over his pupils. A distance forms between us.

"No, Kiyoki," he says with a pause. "I learned to carve on a shard of plum wood."

The Japanese word for plum, *ume*, falls from his lips.

"I have always hoped you would learn to carve the proper way," he says gravely. "A way without sadness. The way that generations before you have always learned. The way that begins with the cutting of your first cypress tree."

We walk toward the tree. We kneel on the cold and damp soil. The silver saw rests between us. Father extends his hands and grasps the sides of the trunk like a husband grasping the waist of his bride. Tenderly. Passionately. Possessively.

"She is yours, Kiyoki," he says as he turns to me, his hands still firmly planted on the trunk. "Pick up the saw."

I bring him the saw, its very image heavy and dangerous, its glimmering teeth cutting the air. He takes the handle from me and places it to the right of the trunk's lowest part.

"Place your hands on mine," he says quietly, as if he wishes not to awaken the spirits of the forest, "and follow me."

The Japanese saw is not like the Western saw. In the West you pull the instrument toward you and then push it away from you. You cut two ways. In Japan, however, our traditional saws cut only in one direction: toward the cutter.

The saw becomes much like the sword.

And so Father and I, with my childlike hands placed on top

of his aged ones, my stomach placed on his back, begin to cut through the thick middle of the cypress tree with long, careful strokes. Strokes that, with every repeated movement, come closer and closer to us.

The tree becomes weakened by our incision. We have severed it from its roots. Three quarters through, Father orders me to retreat.

"The tree will soon fall, Kiyoki. You must step back!"

I take two steps back.

"Farther," he says as he turns quickly to see how far I have gone.

I take three steps back.

"Farther," he says once more.

I take five steps back.

"Farther, Kiyoki." His voice this time is more impatient. I see him turn his head upward toward the highest peak of the tree.

"Run!" he yells. He is running toward me. I see the back of his hair rising to the front like a small tsunami. The sleeves of his kimono billow like sails.

Behind him, the tall, slender tree begins to creak, teetering to one side before it begins its fall.

Father rushes toward me. He picks me up like a basket. Cradling me for the first time. Holding me in his arms.

There is the sound of a crash. Splintering wood and tearing leaves. And then there is the sound of us. Echoing the sound of the tree. The two of us falling to the ground.

Father rests for only a second on top of me, his rib cage sealed to my back. I taste the feral bitterness of soil on my lips. Smell the dampness of the earth.

He rolls me out from underneath him and rises to his feet, dusting himself free from the blanket of soil and wet leaves.

"It is always the most difficult the first time, Kiyoki," he says with a faint smile. "One day you will be cutting trees for your masks all by yourself."

I stare at him blankly, wishing that his words were easier to believe. Craving for him always to be this warm.

The cypress tree lies on the forest floor like a slain warrior laid out in ceremony. Its proud, long expanses of branches jut from its exposed side; the others lie broken and smashed beneath its fallen form.

I watch as Father begins sawing the trunk into small round wheels, the inner core radiating a paler shade.

He removes a *furoshiki* from his sash and unfolds the cloth on the ground. Then, after several moments of pondering each wheel of wood, he picks up one from the tree's middle and places it in the center of the cloth.

He wraps it without thinking and secures it with a short, tight knot.

"This is yours, Kiyoki," he says while walking over to me. He places the heavy package of wood at my feet.

"Thank you, Father," I say blindly.

He acknowledges me with a nod, then returns to the tree. He places the remaining wheels of cypress in a small pyramid, stacking each piece with care. He leaves three blocks of wood for himself and then lifts them simultaneously onto one bent knee.

"We must return to the house; it's beginning to get dark!" he says suddenly. "We should go now, for tomorrow is a big day, my son. It will be your first day learning to carve!"

At that moment the forest seemed to echo my silence. Obediently I picked up my *furoshiki*. And yet the burden seemed almost too difficult to bear.

ELEVEN

The earlier one learns to carve, the better carver he is, my father believed. So I came upon my apprenticeship at the early age of six.

Through his teachings, I learned that the block of cypress should be no thicker than seven thumbs prior to carving and that the wood should not be so dry that it begins to crack with the insertion of one's chisel. As for the chisels, I learned that a beginner carver uses five, and an expert can manage with three. The blades are made from a special alloy of soft iron and steel. The handles are always made from pine.

Although the chisels that Grandfather gave me rested by my side, I would not be allowed to use them until I turned seven the following year. And so, for twelve full months, all I did was sit and watch Father carve.

I watched as he sawed off each corner until the rectangle of wood became an octagon. I watched as he carved with his chisel until two eyes, a nose, and a mouth rose from the wood in high relief. The features, rough and coarse, become finer, more refined as the thicker blades are exchanged for thinner ones. I learned the difference in chisels, those with a straight tip from those with an arched. I learned how with each tool one could round a corner and hollow out an underside. It was with my eyes that I first learned to carve.

But it was with my heart that I first noticed that, without the connection of Noh or wood between us, I existed estranged from my father. He seemed to acknowledge me only as an extension of the wood. That which planked his heart and freed his creativity. That with which he hoped to link himself with me. So that we would both feel the sensation of wood beneath our fingers, the pulse of Noh in our barely beating hearts.

You see, within the walls of his studio, I was not Yamamoto Kiyoki, the son of Ryusei and Etsuko. I was Yamamoto Kiyoki, the son of Noh. As he had been to Tamashii. The wood connecting them. Where wood absorbed pain.

For me, however, wood caused only confusion. I did not understand why, outside the arena of Noh, Father ceased to reach out toward me. Why he limited our connection to the wood.

Even as a child I made attempts to bridge our two worlds. As my schooling outside the home began, like my peers, I became excited by the information our teacher imparted to us. The new Meiji empire, which coincided with our birth, Omori sensei informed us, "was a time of great change." The emperor was challenging all the youths of our generation to learn as much of Western technology as possible. My generation, I was told, was being cultivated to bring our nation into the new age.

For years, Japan had grown within its own self-containing walls. But with the Meiji Restoration of 1868 this had begun to change. Now, over a decade later, we were free to travel abroad and learn of things that we had never even dreamed existed. We were opened to the West, and the West, with all its newness and foreignness, was open to us. Where we had previously been taught that Japan was the center of the world and that our cultural and technological achievements were unsurpassed, we were now encouraged to learn everything that was Western. The emperor, in a program to Westernize the entire country as quickly and efficiently as possible, sent scholars of every kind to England, France, Germany, and the United States to study modern technology, political science, and languages. Even art, now considered a discipline of its own, found a place in Japan's new agenda.

The curriculum in our schools changed. No longer did our history classes teach exclusively Japanese history; we were also introduced to classical Western civilization. We saw prints of the Parthenon and drawings of the Pyramids. We saw the magnificent government buildings that housed the parliaments of England and France. Our own architects, upon returning from their studies abroad, would later create similar structures for our governmental buildings. The emperor's wish incarnated in stone; our city and our people were transported into the new age.

Whereas Father ignored the futile attempts of a six-year-old to inform his family of the changes that were sweeping across our nation, Grandfather became angered by it.

"No more of this chatter, Kiyoki!" he would boom, stopping me in midsentence. Grandmother would look up from her bowl of miso soup and try to soften the ire of her husband's voice with the gentle shaking of her head.

It did not take me long to realize that Grandfather, Father, and the rest of the Noh community regarded the Meiji reforms as a bad thing. To him, a man firmly rooted in tradition, the Meiji Restoration of 1868, carried out seven years before my birth, was only now beginning to penetrate his world.

The artists and actors involved in the traditional Japanese art circles were clearly suffering as the Japanese government and people rejected the ancient parts of their nation's culture in favor of the new Western elements. Noh theater became unfashionable. The audiences dwindled. The eyes that had watched Grandfather perform the dance of the demon queller looked no longer, and the ears that had once been moved by the age-old melody of the *shamisen* became deaf.

All that had once been considered sacred by the community, by my family, was threatened by the influence of West. And to think that I, seized by those great images of European art and technology, was the greatest betrayer of all.

As my grandfather's audience diminished, his anger grew. He felt he had been betrayed. His patrons had abandoned him and the government turned its back on its cultural support. His title no longer echoed with prestige, but rather seemed ridiculous and archaic.

On December 4, 1881, when I was six years old, he performed for the last time. He left his home, sliding the latch of the gate into its lock, and walked by himself to his dressing room in the old wooden theater. He powdered his face and smoothed out his hair. He dressed himself in his robes and fastened his wig.

Then, as ritual dictates, he sat alone with his mask. He meditated over it, breathed over it, and pondered his role over it. He rightfully acknowledged the power it would bring to him as an actor and the spirit it would bring to his performance. He believed, as all great Noh actors do, that his job as an actor was to free the spirit trapped within the mask.

He raised the mask to his face and greeted it with a reverent nod. He tied the silk cords behind his head, rose to his feet, and tucked his fan into his sash.

He had successfully become one with his character. There was nothing between him and his mask. He was now the red demon Shikami.

He appeared on stage in his splendid robes, the insidious monster in the play *Momijigari*. He slid his *tabi*-bound feet across the stage; he pressed his soles hard against each of the floor beams and flexed his toes at the end of each step.

He moved straight-backed, his head slightly forward. He was moving even when he was standing perfectly still.

"*Iya! Iya! a-ha! Ha!*"

The *otsuzumi* player extended his long, slender arm, anticipating the smacking of his hand against the drum skin.

"*Iya! Iya! Yoi! Yya! a-ha!*" he cried.

From behind the mask, Grandfather chanted his lines slowly, each word articulated in the song of a master. The drums played on as he danced, his body swaying and thumping, the pace quickening with every turn.

He revealed his arm from beneath the *karaginu*, richly embroidered with red, yellow, and pale green maple leaves against a silver-threaded background. He pierced the air before him with the dagger of his fan, then pulled it back to the hollow of his sleeve; he performed the *hataraki* dance.

"*Namu-ya hachiman dai-bosatsu!*" cried the *waki*.

Grandfather stepped backward, then forward, then back again. He stomped one foot, then the other. He raised both arms, his elbows extending from his heavy robes like huge silver wings.

His arms encircled the air in long, calligraphic sweeps. He punctuated the poetry of each movement with his gilded fan.

Suddenly and unexpectedly, just seconds prior to his character's impending slaying, my grandfather stepped to the edge of the stage. He posed, his hands stretched wide.

And then he let out an enormous cry.

The people in the audience covered their ears, and behind the mask, his wrinkled face turned bloodred.

When his cry finally ended, he stiffened for a moment, his arms still stretched wide. The coronary took him quickly. He collapsed, falling dead into the awestruck audience.

The theater, with a capacity of two hundred, contained an audience of five.

TWELVE

Grandfather's death weighed heavily on all of us. But no one felt it more deeply than Grandmother. After the funeral had passed and the actors stopped coming to pay their respects, she decided she could no longer sleep in the house that for so many years she had called her own. She offered no explanation. She simply packed what few belongings she had and converted the old *chashitsu*, the tea shack on the border of our property, into her new quarters.

Constructed shortly before her marriage to Grandfather, the tea hut had complied with the traditional architectural specifications of the tea master Sen-no Rikyu. Built using the lightest materials—bamboo, rice paper, and wood—the rustic structure existed between the ungroomed forest and our meticulously maintained garden.

Inside, the room was Spartan, offering nothing more to its occupants than a straw floor, a charcoal brazier, a place for storing utensils, and a *tokonoma*, a small, narrow alcove for a hanging screen and a vase of flowers.

It was a tranquil place that, since the death of my mother, had gone unused. The thatched roof was in fine condition, the brazier still had its coals. The plaster was peeling in places, "like an old skin," she would say, "like me." The round windows were in need of a new covering of rice paper, but other than that, the place remained intact. All that Grandmother had to do was sweep the straw floor of the years of dust that had accumulated since she and Mother had practiced the ancient tea ceremony within its walls.

I missed Grandmother's presence in the house deeply. The pressures of my apprenticeship weighed heavily on me. During my sessions of carving with Father after school, I could not help but feel as though I had been captured. I sat across from Father in the small three-mat room, our knees barely touching, our heads bowed in concentration.

I took to carving easily, though I disliked the sensation of wood between my hands. Where Father carved to forget love, I carved to obtain it. And as a result, my relationship with the wood was undeniably strained. It became the symbol for that which encased my father and prevented him from displaying emotion. Yet it was the only world in which he allowed his passion to truly be unleashed.

Sometimes as I sat there, the heavy handles of the chisels clasped in my hands, I would recall that day in the forest, when Father's form had rushed foward to protect me.

Now we carved side by side. I listened as he explained the attributes of each character in the plays, the process of a face being born.

My masks were silent in comparison to his. How ironic, I thought to myself, that a man who avoids speech could create such emotive masks. And I, the child who craved conversation, created such two-dimensional blocks of wood.

I would find myself compensating for the dearth of warmth in my life with my daily visits with Grandmother. After I returned from school and completed three hours of carving with Father, I would always end the day by going to the tea shack to pay her a visit. There she would be, hunched over a small lantern, on this day embroidering the family crest into the waistband of my extra *hakama*.

"Hello, *obāsan*," I would say, as I slid open the shoji and entered the humble structure.

"Hello, Kiyoki-chan," she would respond while removing the *hakama* from her lap. "How kind of you to come and visit your old Grandmother."

"It was not a far journey, Grandma," I would reply, and she would laugh with me, if only for a moment.

She would look up at me, her neck stiff with age, her back curving under her kimono. "You have your mother's laugh," she would say.

As she said the words "your mother," her eyes would cloud over, as if she had suddenly entered a world now gone, a world where death had not made her prematurely gray and where ghosts did not wrestle her from her sleep.

In this world the images are timeless. She is not a widow, and she is not guilty of my mother's death. She is the beautiful wife and mother of the Yamamoto family once more.

Here the kitchen fire crackles cinnabar flames, the rice steams through the iron pot and perfumes her hair. She sings songs from her childhood while she works. *"Kaki-tsu-bata, kaki-tsu-bata,"* she hums, as her own mother once sang.

She hears the gate unlocking. Her husband has returned safely from the theater. She hears him holler that he is home and she sees herself greeting him at the *genkan*, the first moonbeams of the evening radiating off his arriving form.

He is red, the winter having breathed its icy gusts over his puffing face. He stands in the entranceway, appearing larger than a god, dropping his satchel to the floor and lifting his eyes to his wife.

"Where is Etsuko?" he asks.

"She is still at the mountain."

He shakes his head with mild disapproval. "She should be concentrating more on her tea ceremony than on those ink drawings," he sighs.

"Sometimes I do not think that I control her," she tells him. "The mountain seems to possess all the power."

"That is ridiculous, Chieko," he says while slipping into his straw slippers. "We are her parents."

"It is not we whom she draws day after day. It is the mountain."

She hesitates for a moment before she continues. She lowers her eyes and then says in a voice so hushed that it is barely a whisper, "Her drawings are actually quite good. It is a shame that she was born a girl."

Grandfather has the capacity to hear everything. He hears Grandmother's words before she finishes speaking them.

"How dare you, Chieko!" he booms. "If Etsuko had been born a boy, she would not be an artist, she would be an actor!"

His eyes dart at her like those of an animal that has been threatened with its life. Again he chastises her. "I do not understand why you bemoan her silly sketches as wasted talent. It would be more of a waste if she had talent as an actor but could not perform because she is a girl." He pauses and looks down at his wife. "Now that would be a shame, Chieko, would it not?"

"Yes, yes," she replies, again almost in a whisper. "I am sorry for my foolishness. You are absolutely right."

She decides to go and fetch her daughter, as darkness has already blackened the sky. Dinner has been ready for almost an hour, and she fears her daughter has lost track of the time.

The path leading to the base of Mount Daigo is rough and winding. Like a thin black serpent, it slithers around the channels of the forest. Pointed branches whose leaves have long since fallen blanket the earth beneath her sandals and thrust their daggerlike boughs into her kimono. They mildly pierce the flesh of her shoulders, bend at the force of her movement, and snap to their death as she pushes onward with her rapeseed lantern dangling from her slender arm.

She finds her daughter at the base of the Daigo, a piece of mulberry paper nailed to a wooden board propped on her knees. She has brought her own lantern, the flicker competing with the shining moon.

"Etsuko," Grandmother calls out. "Etsuko!"

Mother turns her head, revealing her long neck and bewildered eyes. Had she been cloaked in a red blanket, she could have been mistaken for a fawn.

Grandmother finally reaches her. The cold mountain air has weakened her voice and quickened her breath.

"Your father and I have been worried. Do you not see that it is dark and that dinner is waiting?" she scolds.

It has been several hours since Mother has spoken. Words feel strange and unfamiliar to her lips.

"I am sorry, Mother," she manages to say, her voice strained and tired.

"At least show me your drawing, child," Grandmother sighs.

She pushes her lantern over her young daughter's shoulder. The flame's reflection splinters blue and yellow shadows across the page.

Grandmother has known Daigo all her life. She has slept at its base; she has journeyed to its peak. She has walked its winding paths in the season of cherry blossoms and turning leaves. She has watched it from her window as it slept under a coverlet of white snow, and anticipated its thawing from the thick blankets of her bed.

Her nose could discern its particular scent—smoky and green—on her daughter's kimono, the dry earth her husband carries in on his sandals, and the flowers that she gathers for her urns.

Still, until now, she has never seen all of these images captured in a drawing.

She sees nothing but the drawing. She does not see her daughter's hands quivering in the mountain air, shrunken from the cold, and clutching the thin twig that has been sharpened to a thin point and saturated in dark black ink.

The drawing has rendered her speechless. It is as if the mountain has penetrated the paper and the sky has fallen onto the page.

She places her lantern at her daughter's side and kneels on the earth, her kimono getting soiled under her knees. She extends her hands to grasp the drawing, to seize it from her daughter's lap and bring it closer to her eyes.

She traces each tree with the side of her finger. She notices how each bough arches in the right direction, how the texture of the peeling bark has been masterfully executed, and how the edges of each leaf curl.

The mountain seems to be breathing, coming to life off the very page, its soft roundness undulating, its hump curved and bowed to the sky.

"Why do you not speak, Mother?" her daughter inquires.

"Your drawing has brought a hush to my heart," she whispers as she rises and lays her hand on her daughter's shoulder and hurries her to her feet.

There is quiet between them.

"We must get back to Father," her daughter reminds her.

And so with the base of the mountain fading behind them, its charcoal image tightly rolled underneath a tiny arm sleeved in silk, mother and daughter hurry to return, their wooden sandals sinking into the soft, damp earth.

The mask carver's son, that is who I am. But do not be mistaken. I may have been born by a shining silver blade, but I do not intend to live my life by it.

I am filled with images that I cannot shake. They reveal themselves in color, they are born from the strokes of my inner mind. Shape and shadow. Form and line.

In my heart I know that someday I will be a painter. My hands are not like those of my father. They are my mother's. They cannot be restrained.

Throughout my early childhood, I tried to cultivate my talent in secret. Never allowing my father to know that my mind was elsewhere. That to me there was nothing less interesting than a block of wood.

In my heart, I felt like a thief. I stole small pieces of charcoal from the hibachi and wore the face of a diligent son. I drew on old, discarded pieces of paper; I sketched from memory and from what I saw before me. All the while, I visited Father and carved hollow faces, my dedication to this ancient craft as empty as the underside of a mask.

My grandmother's confession of my mother's talent was a revelation to me. The feeling of betraying my father was replaced with the notion that I was fulfilling the unaccomplished dreams of my mother. Suddenly I found myself impassioned as I had never been before. I drew my inspiration from Mount Daigo, just as my mother had. I made studies of each leaf, tracing the spidery vein with my finger and then re-creating it with my hand. I learned to make my own pigments using the juice found in smashed berries and the natural green stain of damp moss.

I sketched the squirrels and colored in their fur with the brown of the earth. I formed the sky by rubbing the petals of irises across my page, the sun by the circling of mandarin rind.

There was nothing that I did not challenge myself to draw. I drew the head of my teacher while listening to the lecture in class. I drew my sandals dangling beneath my desk.

I could not control myself. I looked at the world not in emotional terms, but rather as a place filled with images, a menagerie of objects and subjects that I was to reproduce on paper.

I saw the beauty of nature's simplest things and studied them with such intensity and reverence that they became almost anatomical studies. The cracked skull of a pomegranate, smashed on the earth with its ruby pebbled seeds oozing from its broken seams, could consume me for hours. I remember drawing each kernel, each section of its inner casing. I colored the sketch of the pomegranate with the fruit's own juice, piercing a handful of the red ovules with my fingernail. It was with this self-invented method of creating art that I believed I was bringing nature to my page.

I cannot explain what drove me to seek such creative sources of supplies. It was as though I was born an animal, who hungered for color as though it were prey. I know only that, for me, fresh paper was a far more valuable treasure than a coffer brimming with gold, that the mountain was the god who offered me his bounty, and that the ghost of my mother had manifested itself deep within my soul.

* * *

I shared my modest creations with no one except Grandmother.

"It was your grandfather's hope that you would maintain the family line in the theater. He understood you would most likely follow in the footsteps of your father. That is why he bought you a set of chisels before he died."

"And what is your hope, Grandmother?"

"It is also my hope that you maintain the Yamamoto line in the theater," she said before pausing. "It is more important to me, however, that you be happy." Looking down at me, she added, "I have learned with age that the sibling to sacrifice is pain."

"I want to be a painter, Grandma."

There was silence between us. But it was a comfortable silence. It was not the same silence that distanced me from my father. On the contrary, such silence bound me closer to her. Her eyes were soft and understanding as she listened to me. The words I spoke were difficult for her to hear, but she acknowledged them even before speaking.

Her neck arched slightly forward, her head elegantly bowed, she absorbed my words and acknowledged my presence within her humble walls.

Grandmother looked at me for a long time before she responded. Then, after several pensive minutes, she raised her head and opened her eyes. "Kiyoki," she began, her voice reflecting the seriousness of her impending words, "always remember that it was your mother's blood in which you were born."

"Yes, Grandmother. I know."

"Your mother was a truly selfless child. Her only indulgence was the mountain. How she loved to draw it! Neither the harshest winter nor the most humid summer could keep her away."

Grandmother stared at me with great intensity, and the haze

over her pupils grew thick and cloudy. It was almost as if I, sitting square before her, was being transformed.

As if in a trance, Grandmother rose from the tatami. With careful and delicate steps, she walked to the low *tansu* chest that rested on the other side of the room. Her knees bent slowly and with great reverence she wrapped her ancient fingers around two iron handles and quietly withdrew one of the drawers.

I could hear the brittle sound of paper. Its rolled edges scraping over the wood. The paper was old and yellow, as cracked as the hands that now unrolled it before my eyes.

"I believe that you were born with her talent," she said as she revealed the drawing that had come from my mother's hands, the ink sketch of Mount Daigo.

I looked at the sketch. This was something my mother had created around the same age as I was now. I could discern her skill, her exacting eye, from the preciseness of each of her lines. She had rendered Mount Daigo as if she had buried herself in the back of my mind and viewed its mighty peak from the irises of my own eyes.

I sat in awe, staring at the worn paper with its fading images as if they were my mother's fingerprints. Was this her legacy to me? An inheritance of images bequeathed to me, a reminder that in me she was forever born.

Grandmother clutched my hands with the force of her wrinkled palms and shook them. "Kiyoki, I betrayed your mother in many ways. Her death will haunt me to my grave. I transferred my burden onto her, and she sacrificed her life in order to fulfill your grandfather's and my wishes. She did as we told her and denied herself who and what she loved in order to please us and the world in which we lived. She died as a result. I will not allow you to do the same."

I looked at Grandmother and then at the aged drawing before

me and felt that there were not two but three of us in the small room. I felt Mother's ghost eyeing us from the bamboo rafters, her spirit breathing cool mountain air into the tatami chamber. And I saw how Grandmother sat there, almost relieved. Having waited years to unburden herself of that which she kept contained. Weighing her down like an iron anchor on a ship of fragile sails.

The following Thursday I found her with her eyes wide open and her skin milky white. In life, pain had cracked her countenance, but death had been kinder, leaving her with the face of a sleeping doll. The lines of age that had run rivers into her porcelain skin had vanished, and the cataracts that clouded her eyes had cleared.

For the first time in my life, she appeared beautiful to me. I had always reserved the word "beautiful" for the image I harbored of my mother, but as I scooped Grandmother's tiny head into my lap, and stroked her long strips of charcoal-colored hair, I could not help but think her the same.

I did not call out to my father, as another child might have. I wanted to have Grandmother alone to myself before the priests arrived, before her body was reduced to ashes in an urn.

I had been denied this privilege at my mother's death. I never had the chance to study her face, to hold her fingers to my cheek, to cry over the departure of her soul.

With Grandmother, I mourned her death as if she were my own mother. She was the only one I had made myself vulnerable to, the only one who knew of my dreams, and the only one who seemed to care. My father would not see my tears. I made sure that they had dried before I left the tea hut.

I whispered good-bye into Grandmother's delicate ear and closed her eyes with my two fingers. I covered her with the blanket that she had embroidered as a young bride, knelt beside her, and prayed for her safe journey into the next world.

I walked from the tea hut to the main house. I passed by the main room with the *tokonoma*. The flowers in the vase had wilted, and the hanging scroll tilted slightly to the left.

"Father," I called up through the ladder leading to his studio. "Father!"

He did not reply. After I received no answer from my calls, I decided to go up to the second floor. I had never interrupted him before, but I knew I had to inform him of Grandmother's death.

Exercising great caution, I proceeded up the ladder.

"Father," I uttered again, as I slid open the shoji and craned my neck inside. He still did not answer me. He sat with his back turned to me, as if in a trance, his small body resting on a tiny pillow, a long wooden board extending from beneath his legs.

He held the mask between his slippered feet, his bent legs extending like the small wings of a Japanese beetle and his back curling to shield the face of the birthing form. Within the studio's wooden walls and tatami-mat floors, the smell of cypress, freshly stripped by the blade of my father's chisel, floated through the air.

I felt as though I were trespassing. I was used to seeing him carve, but during those times he was cognizant that I was watching him. Now I felt like a voyeur. All I wanted to do was close the screen and vanish.

"Father, I apologize for disturbing you."

His back stiffened, and I saw him remove the mask braced between his knees. He placed it at his side and covered it with a piece of cloth.

"Yes, Kiyoki," he said, his back still facing me.

"It is Grandmother," I stuttered. "She is gone."

"Gone where?" His voice rose slightly and his head spun to my direction.

"She has died, Father."

He closed his eyes and the blue spider veins of his lids bulged ever so slightly. I stood there, in the small entranceway just outside his studio. He did not invite me in, and I dared not enter.

As he rose from the tatami, he brushed the thin curls of wood from his limbs and placed his mask carefully on the shelf. He walked past me and closed the shoji silently behind him. I allowed him to walk down the ladder before me, and watched as he descended without the assistance of the slender rail.

When we reached the *genkan* he turned to me. "I'll go to the temple and inform the priest," he said to me flatly. He put on his sandals and slid open the door. He walked past the front garden, undid the latch of the gate, and vanished before my eyes.

When he returned, he did not bring the priest inside. He took him around the outer walls of the house, past the formal garden, to where the weeping sycamore trees veiled the tea shack.

As I lay in my futon that evening, unable to sleep, I heard the priest chanting the Buddhist rite in his deep, hollow voice and the striking of a bell. The rice-paper windows glowed from the interior candles and the structure creaked and cracked from the two men moving inside its tiny walls.

I wanted to join the vigil. I wanted to burn the incense and pray for Grandmother, but I had been ordered to remain in the main house, alone with my thoughts and my ghosts.

The two men did not exit the tea hut until the next morning when the funeral palanquin arrived. After it had been carefully shrouded and laid inside a wooden coffin, five silent monks removed Grandmother's body from the *chashitsu*. Father entered the house, and his face betrayed his fatigue.

"It is time to leave for the temple, Kiyoki," he said with a sigh.

I turned to fetch my sandals and watched as he removed

several strings of silver from the *tansu* chest in order to pay for the funeral pyre and the burial.

"Will they burn her in front of us?" I asked with a twelve-year-old's innocence.

"No, Kiyoki," he said, his voice sounding for the first time tender. "You will stay outside while I go to the crematorium and pray for her safe passage." He never told me that he would be there with long chopsticks in hand, picking through her bones.

I remember I stood up and tried to grasp his hand. But I was too late, he had slipped outside the gate and had already clasped his hands tightly behind him. At that moment, I wanted so desperately to be proper, to honor the customs of my family, to make my father and the spirits of my mother, grandfather, and grandmother proud.

And so, with the sunshine of that autumn morning, I walked behind the funeral carriage, imitating my father: my hands carefully interlocked behind me and my head solemnly bowed.

THIRTEEN

After the deaths of my mother, my grandfather, and my grandmother, I was forced to acknowledge that my childhood was to be forever laced with death. The smell of burning incense became familiar to me, as did the sound of the priest's sandals, his small bell, and the drumming of his voice.

Our house became a shrine for the dead, as the dead seemed more alive in our house than the living. In my twelve short years I had watched the family altar, the *butsudan*, become more and more crowded. There were days when I would spend hours watching Grandmother as she knelt, her wooden Buddhist prayer beads wrapped around her withered knuckles, praying to the spirits of my mother and grandfather. She would burn a long stick of *senko*, clap her hands, and chant the sutras over the candles' flicker and around the incense's clouds of smoke.

Almost daily she replenished the vase with flowers, and after every meal she left small offerings of food. She dusted the small tokens of my mother's memory: one of her hair combs, the silver and gold fan she had used on her wedding day, and a canister of her favorite tea. For my grandfather, she placed a program from his last performance and a piece of fabric from his favorite robe.

When Grandmother believed she was alone, she would finger these tangible memories with her weary, wrinkled hands and recall the days when her house was her own and those she loved the most in the world lived within its walls.

Now I was left with the responsibility for maintaining the family *butsudan*. Like my grandmother before me, I replaced the flowers daily and offered small samplings of food. I learned to kneel and recite the Scriptures in front of the small bronze image of Amidah; I burned sticks of incense and kept the small, white candles alight. In honor of my grandmother's memory, I brought red maple leaves in autumn and branches of cherry blossoms in spring.

The tea canister inside the altar intrigued me. The seal and name of the store—Kitano-ya—was strange and unfamiliar to me. Why had Grandmother ceased to frequent this shop, I thought to myself, knowing that she had always bought from Kuniyoshire-ya, a store several miles farther away and whose tea bore no fame that could justify the extra distance?

Now that she was gone, it was my responsibility to pick up the household necessities on my way back from school. Kitano's tea store was not far from the road I took every day, and I decided that I would pay a visit, realizing that it had been a supplier of a tea that my mother obviously cherished. It would not have been placed on the family altar had it been otherwise.

The following Wednesday I took a five-yen note from the household purse and went to school planning to visit the tea purveyor at the day's end. That afternoon I expected to find nothing but a small country shop with an old man behind the counter and bushels of tea leaves lining the shelves. How wrong I would soon discover myself to be.

The blue and red curtain outside the shop marked the store's name and boasted about what goods lay inside. I walked through, imagining that my mother had once touched the curtain, her hands once cupped the bowl of offered tea.

I walked up to Kitano-san, who stared at me as though he had suddenly awakened from a dream.

"Hello," I said cheerfully. "I am looking to buy some Mugi-cha." Hoping to gain nothing more than better service, I added, "My mother used to be particularly fond of your blend."

His nervousness betrayed him even before the words came. His eyes went to a corner of the wall.

Confused by the man's behavior, I found myself following his gaze until I saw the painting of Daigo. Sketched in thin black line, smoothed in loose fading washes. That which could not have come from anyone's hand but Mother's. Like the painting given to me by Grandmother. Here on Kitano's wall, among the barrels of tea.

I pointed, my finger shaking with disbelief.

"Yes," he said, his eyes brimming with tears. "I knew it was you when you walked through the door. Even though you are male, you have inherited her beautiful face."

He walked to the corner and unpinned the drawing from the wooden boards.

"She gave it to me shortly before she was wed," he said as he spread it on the counter's flat surface. "She came in the night, when her parents were asleep."

I looked at the lines that had come straight from her hand. Traced each gesture that had been preserved in ink.

"It was the last time I saw her. She never came again, nor did your Grandmother."

All this information was so much more than I could have expected. I had only hoped to buy some tea, not to discover that, had things been different, my mother could have been the wife of this man.

"She loved to sketch. She used to have bits of charcoal stored between her toes sometimes when she was a young girl and would come to visit. We used to play a game when we were small children, and I would try and dislodge them with my thumb."

"She died when I was born," I said, finding myself jealous of his memories.

"I heard. Your grandmother passed on recently as well . . . The city is very small and a tea man like me hears everything." He paused. "You know, I never stopped listening for news about her, hoping that someday she'd come again."

I looked at him, a man who looked far younger than Father, and who talked with ease.

"What is your name?" he asked staring deep into my eyes.

"Kiyoki."

"Kiyoki? A strange name, eh?" He rolled up the painting and after a minute of silent hesitation, handed it to me.

"As much as I want it, it would be selfish of me to keep it. She was, after all, your mother."

He extended his arms slowly, the rolled-up painting resting on his palms. "Please," he uttered once more, before I finally accepted his offering. With my head bowed in gratitude, I saw how the edges of the parchment were curling, the color yellow like the one Grandmother had showed me.

"Thank you," I mumbled sheepishly, as I was deeply embarrassed by what had transpired.

"Please come again, Kiyoki," he said earnestly. "I would enjoy seeing you . . . " He seemed to catch himself in midsentence. Seeing how uncomfortable I looked, he too turned pale.

"I must apologize for having told you so much. Perhaps I should have kept my memories to myself."

I nodded politely to him and tucked the painting underneath my arm. "Perhaps I'll come again," I said softly. "Thank you for your kindness."

I walked out slowly, turning my head back to see the tea man's face once more. To try to see beyond the lines of age. To see what my mother had loved once long ago.

Then I was beyond the interior's curtain out in the fading sunlight of the afternoon. I found myself walking blindly, trying to comprehend all that I had just learned.

The sun's glare prevented me from seeing more than a few steps ahead of me, so I walked without seeing. Walked while inhaling the faint smell of tea still clinging to my sleeves. Walked while wondering how different my life would have been had I been born the tea man's son rather than the mask carver's.

I returned home that evening to find my father waiting patiently for me to come and eat our dinner. It was the only meal we shared, and it usually began a few hours after I had completed some carving.

We did not join each other for breakfast. He awoke every morning before me. And although we had slept side by side since the death of Grandmother, our bodies never touched and the cushions of our futons never overlapped. We existed like two separate pods, sleeping within the same cocoon but never binding ourselves to each other.

Each morning at dawn, before the birds began to chirp, before the fog lifted its dewy haze from the tall grass, he rose from his futon. He moved stealthily, as if his body was not his own. His movements were performed like rituals: slow and methodical, reverent yet strangely unconscious. Half asleep, I would watch his thin legs protrude from his cotton *yukata*, slim as candles with bony ankles that quivered at his first steps on the floor.

Father looked his most vulnerable in the morning: before he dressed himself in his robe, and before he combed his hair and washed his deeply lined face. Before he left his nocturnal world of dreams and entered the world of Noh.

After having tied the sash of his *yukata* a little tighter and after having rolled up his futon in one of the room's sliding closets, Father would kneel at the base of the dresser, his sleepy, half-molded face floating within the spotted glass.

He stared at himself for what seemed like several minutes. He never lifted his hands, which remained flat on his thighs, his slender calves carefully folded beneath him. He only stared. He stared until his sleep-swollen eyelids began to retract and his face began to resemble the serious and staid man I saw each and every day.

I too would stare, through carefully cloaked eyelids, at his daily transformation. I would wonder whether, if he did not rise from his knees, he would be different. Would his features remain soft, and would his feelings be revealed in a face made of flesh rather than wood?

Each morning as he sat before the glass, my body tucked into the right-hand corner of his reflection, he squeezed the pain from his mind. With tightly shut eyes, he purged my mother from his memories. No longer seeing her laid out on the futon and me cupped in his palms. That guilt so heavy that its weight stifled words.

And with those thoughts pushed from his mind, he shifted his concentration from that of the world of pain and the world of love to the world of Noh.

He rises. He lifts his pale and slender arms, the skin puckered from middle age, to the graying peak of his hairline and smooths the river of silver and black hair with the oil of his palms. His back stiffens for a moment, his shoulders arch so that the blades almost touch, his neck rises from the high stiff collar of his robe, then retreats like a turtle to its starched folds. After a few more moments he heads to the door.

Only once do I recall him hesitating. It was on the thirteenth anniversary of my mother's death. He rested his hand on the outer post of the shoji and turned his head to stare at me sleeping. He paused for what seemed like several minutes, his gaze focused on my heavily blanketed form. He did not smile or speak. He simply nodded to himself and then turned to exit through the door.

FOURTEEN

In the performance of *Saigyo-Zakura*, the Ishi-O-Jo mask is almost always used. It is said that this mask best incarnates the spirit of a wizened old cherry tree. For in the play the tree magically comes to life.

It was my father's favorite mask to carve, and what emerged mirrored his own image. The eyes are forever downcast. Half-moons slit into a wooden face. Eyes that are frozen to the floor.

It is a weary face whose skin is pulled tight to the temples yet hangs heavily beneath the eyes and hollows of the cheek. Brows arched and forehead furrowed, whiskered chin—a mask that can exude both sadness and anger, deep thought and despair. It is a face that captures the range of the spirit.

I could not control my urge to draw him, to capture his strained visage on paper, to trace the lines of his forehead onto my page. It was as if my hands and heart had united. My palms were eager to accept the challenge of his complex countenance, my heart hopeful that if I grappled with the task of reproducing his image, I might also secure the secrets of his ways, reveal the truth of his emotions, demystify the strangeness and severity of his ways.

I climb the stairs on tiptoe, leaving my slippers on the first beam. Sketch pad in hand and wedge of charcoal secured in the well of my first, I stealthily ascend to the top floor, which leads to his studio. As I anticipated, the shoji is not completely closed. A crack of light. Despite this limited view, no wider than a stick of bamboo, I am able to see my subject.

I see my father in profile. His chin resting on his chest. His graying hair combed away from his forehead. He will not see me. I am not the child of wood that nestles between his knees.

It is I who now give birth to a face.

I trace him in outline, a thin river of black snaking across the page. I render the flatness of his nose and the slope of his chin. I draw the peak of his ear and the roundness of the lobe. With the thick side of the charcoal I contour the planes of his cheek, the shadow cast by his lowered eyelids. With the sharpest edge of the lump of black, I delicately outline each hair on his scalp, the few whiskers on his chin.

I draw the profile of his spine, protruding from under the cloth of his kimono, the bending of his neck. I capture the contorted position of his body as it hovers like an overprotective mother over a molting block of wood.

I had been drawing him through the crack, my own body pushed against the wall, my knees cramped to my chest and the paper resting on top. I was forced to crane my neck to get a close look and then retreat quickly back against the wall to reproduce what my eyes have just absorbed. At all costs I wanted to remain unseen.

After nearly two hours, when I had nearly completed his face and body, and I am just about to begin working on the rendering of his hands, my charcoal slipped through my fingers and fell behind me. As I attempted to find the shard of coal, the floorboards creaked underneath me, and from the corner of my eye I caught the image of my father shooting up from his carving like a bolt of lightning.

With three quick steps, he was already at the shoji, thrusting it aside to reveal me.

But Father did not yell. His face did not reveal the rage that I had expected. Rather, the lines of his face ebbed downward. Like a painted mask bathed in a river of soft water, he melted.

For the first time outside our bedchamber, I saw him transform. His eyes shut, blocking out the vision of me crouched in the corner, paper and charcoal in hand.

It was dark where I sat, yet I swear that I saw moisture seeping from the corners of his closed eyes. I believe for that split moment I succeeded in breaking Father from the wood.

In the end, however, he retreated. He gathered himself and stuffed all sentiment back into the trunk of his body.

He did not ask to see my drawing. And I do not know to this day if he realized whom I was straining to sketch. I do not know that if he had known, it would have made a difference.

That evening as we sat down for dinner, I remember that, for the first time in my life, the miso soup that he had prepared was cold and the small grilled fish that we ate along with our bowls of rice was burned.

I consumed the meal without complaint and watched Father as he bent his head into the basin of the soup bowl, his mouth curling into the rim. He slurped unusually quietly that evening. And I could tell, by the way he approached each grain of rice with the tips of his chopsticks, that he remained greatly disturbed by today's episode.

After I finished eating, and our bowls remained empty and neatly stacked before us, he raised his head and spoke to me in a voice that was monotone, as usual, yet seemed surprisingly sincere.

"Kiyoki, I have completed several masks, and I will be going to the theater tomorrow to meet with some of the actors. Perhaps you will join me after you return from school."

"Yes, Father," I stammered quietly, my voice betraying my confusion. "I will be home by three o'clock."

"We will leave then," he said while standing up with the empty dishes in hand. "Go now and attend to your studies."

The next afternoon I arrived home to find him waiting for me at the gate. He was dressed somberly in a gray kimono girdled by a thin navy sash. Clutched in his arms were his treasured masks, neatly wrapped in a black *furoshiki*.

"Place your satchel inside and we can go," he said calmly.

I did as I was told and went inside and dropped my bag in the *genkan*. I returned to the garden and approached him cautiously by the gate.

"I am ready, Father. I am sorry to have kept you waiting." He nodded with his usual serious manner and opened the latch, and I followed him into the dirt road which led toward the path to the Kanze theater.

We walked in silence. The silence was not the same as that I had shared with Grandmother. It was the first time that I recalled walking with him to the theater, for this was the journey that I had made when I was a toddler and Grandfather lived and performed.

Father carried his tightly wrapped package of masks in the basket of his arms, much like the way I imagined Grandmother carried me when I was an infant. I pictured myself, round and plump, squirming in her embrace, extending my short arms so that I might pluck a leaf from one of the boughs.

The masks, however, did not squirm. They did not move from

underneath their wrapping. Father held them tightly to his chest. Children of his, cocooned in cloth, cautiously and carefully handled with love.

I glanced at Father, jealous of the masks' hollow faces rubbing his side.

The path that curled before us seemed unending. The smells of the forest were familiar to me; the colors glowed like precious stones.

The light of the forest is a special light. Pale green. Yellow shadows. The forest floor, damp with last night's rain, shimmers flecks of quartz, cushions your feet like green virgin moss. Mushrooms blossom like brown gardenias under heavy trunks.

The smell of the forest is intoxicating. Like an empress's perfume, rich and floral, it rises from the earth in thick, steamy clouds.

Swallow it with a large gaping mouth. Slide it down with a glass of mountain rain. It is yours for the taking. The forest is but an offering. A gift created in the very images of the gods.

Yes, I am a Yamamoto, born from the base of the mountain. No stranger to the forest floor.

Cypress and ginkgo. Silk oak and red maple. I have hovered by your trunks and gathered your leaves. I have been tangled in the roots of burdock and itched from the sting of nettles. I have eaten the petals of chrysanthemum and slept in the tall grass of pampas. Yet why is it that my legs now quake and, with every step, my ankles tremble?

Is it that structure in the distance? The hooded roof, thatched from cypress bark, whose peak pierces the sky. The Kanze theater. A place, in my father's eyes, more sacred than a temple. An interior that, perhaps even more so than our family home, he considers his own.

We enter under the large canopy of the roof. The audience boxes stretch before us. The hibachis are empty; there are no charcoals in the braziers. The silk cushions on the seats are a faded purple. As we walk along the middle aisle, I allow my fingers to dangle into the wooden boxes so that I might graze one of the cushions, to feel the silk on my finger pads.

I barely remembered sitting on one of them. Although I remembered how vibrant the purple color had once been. The deep color of an iris. Grandmother had a spring kimono she wore to the theater that was the same shade.

Father walked a few steps before me, and I watched as he trod on the side of the gravel that separated the audience from the stage. To the far right, hidden by a curtain, was a small stairway. He removed his sandals and ascended to the stage like a frail gray dove cloaked in cloth.

The stage, constructed from thin planks of cypress wood, gleamed like polished gold, and the large jars underneath the stage resonated with each of our steps. I followed my father without uttering a word as we passed the great twisting pine painted on the backboard and walked over the *hashigakari*, the passageway that bridged the backstage to the main stage: the entranceway for all Noh actors.

I heard the voices of the actors complaining among themselves even before I saw their faces.

"We had only three men at Saturday's performance!" one man grumbled.

"I am not sure we even have enough money to buy coal for the hibachis," said another.

Father hesitated before interrupting the men. *"Shitsurei-shimasu-ga,"* he said quietly. Excuse me for my rudeness.

The faces of the three men reddened with embarrassment. "Yamamoto Ryusei, greetings! Please accept our apologies for *our* rudeness. We are sorry to have kept you waiting."

"I have brought my son, Kiyoki. I hope it is not an inconvenience to you."

I emerged from behind my father's slender back and bowed reverently to the three senior actors.

"I am Iwasaki Hidemi," said one of the actors. "I am Fukuharu Kyoun," said another man, shorter and plumper than the others. "I call myself Hattori Keizo," said the last man. I noticed he had a rather unsightly mole growing below his eyebrow.

"How privileged you must be, Kiyoki, to have the greatest mask carver of our time as your father!" Iwasaki, the eldest of the actors, exclaimed.

I nodded back at him nervously, my eyes darting quickly to the floor.

"Won't you have some tea, Yamamoto-san?" Hattori asked Father while motioning to the iron kettle steaming on a brazier.

"Yes, thank you."

Hattori poured hot tea into five ceramic cups. We walked into one of the small side rooms and sat down on the tatami. My father sat down first and the three actors formed a circle from the point at which he sat. I sat slightly behind everyone, excluded by age and title, there only to observe.

Father unveiled the masks from their silken shroud. He smoothed the dark cloth that radiated like a dark mandorla, a black halo around three pale masks. He tipped each mask to show the actors their range of expressions.

The three men gasped with delight, sighed with appreciation, and rolled their eyes to the heavens to express their awe.

"I have brought with me only the Yase-Onna, Kasshiki, and

Ishi-O-Jo masks, as I am not sure what you are lacking for this year's performances," Father said reverently.

"Perhaps the Yase-Onna could be used for your upcoming performance of Zeami's *Kinuta*, if you think my humble mask merits such a honor," Father said modestly, while holding the mask of the female spirit between his two palms. He had painted her with several layers of white aleurone and tinted her complexion with a mixture of pale yellow and antique brown. She appeared as translucent, eerie in her ghostliness, starving in her apparent ravished state.

Father did not need to explain his carving. The mask's pointed cheekbones, triangular nose, and open mouth were executed with a master's perfection. The distinctive hairline was delicately painted around the top half of the mask's perimeter, with the three sections of overlapping hair, three strands of which were finely articulated in order to help identify the mask.

"Please," Father began, his voice sounding friendlier and more open by the minute. "I offer my masks for your inspection." He handed one mask to each of the three actors.

Hattori held the Kasshiki mask in between his large, creased hands and could immediately imagine himself as the *waki* in *Togan Koji*. Even a god could not have carved the mask of the young boy any better. The shape of the mask was perfectly oval. The size, only a few inches longer than his outstretched palm, was meant to fit snugly around one's face. Hattori had a special appreciation for masks, perhaps even more than the other actors. For in a mask he no longer felt ugly and self-conscious. The mask not only disguised his visage but also covered his mole.

The features of the Kasshiki mask were soft and youthful. The cheeks were round and smooth, almost like one of the female masks. But the eyebrows were painted thinner and arched more.

The hairline was thicker and punctuated in the middle by a large black fan of hair.

"Iwasaki-san," Father said, almost playfully, "won't you try on the Ishi-O-Jo mask so that the others might see how it looks when moving."

As Iwasaki gladly untied the silk cord knotted in the back of the mask, I remained startled by how at ease my father seemed with the actors. I had never seen him socialize with anyone, and yet while he sat there with his glorious masks floating through the room, I had never seen him seem so natural. He was actually almost charming.

Iwasaki-san placed the mask over his face and tied the silk cord behind his head. The two other actors gasped in awe, but none of them louder than I. It was my father's face now floating on another.

"It's perfect for *Saigyo-Zakura*!" Fukuhara exclaimed.

"Yes, absolutely," agreed Hattori. "We were planning to do a performance of *Saigyo-Zakura* in the spring."

Iwasaki untied the cords and carefully returned the mask to my father. He was the oldest and most revered actor of the Kanze troupe. He had ascended to patriarch earlier that year.

"As you know, Yamamoto-san," he began, his voice suddenly sounding grave and dispelling the former ease that had floated through the air, "for several years now the attendance at our performances has dwindled. It is no longer the glorious days of the Tokugawa when almost every seat was filled. At present we consider ourselves lucky if the first box has more than three people.

"Our treasury is almost empty, and we are not even sure we can afford coal for the braziers. You know that we have bought countless masks from you in the past, often during times when we should have saved the money that our forefathers had left for the survival of the theater. But we cannot help ourselves. Your masks have the power to seduce us. They dangle before our eyes, more precious than the rarest jewels.

"And so, Yamamoto-san, although I wish we could afford all three of your masks, I am afraid we can afford none of them. But as I see how my peers have reacted so strongly to the Ishi-O-Jo mask, I am willing to offer you three gold kobans for it. I understand, as you typically charge fifteen kobans, that this might be insulting to you. But, alas, it is all we can offer."

The heads of the other two actors bowed humbly to their chests.

Father acknowledged their humility with the nodding of his head.

"Save your money, patriarch," he said quietly. "I offer you these three masks for the sake and renewed prosperity of Noh."

He wrapped the three masks back in the *furoshiki* and pushed them over the tatami till they rested in front of Iwasaki.

The patriarch pressed the tip of his forehead to the floor, his arms outstretched, his palms flat on the tatami. The other two actors followed, mimicking their patriarch's motions of reverence.

"We will be indebted to you for several generations," said Iwasaki. "I hope I will live to see the day when our sons purchase masks carved by your son, Kiyoki."

The three actors turned and bowed their heads in my direction.

Father did not acknowledge Iwasaki's last statement. "Kiyoki," he said, "we must return home before it gets dark."

We excused ourselves and returned the way we had entered, passing over the *hashigakari*. We slid into our sandals without speaking, and returned home through the forest without uttering a word.

Father would seem forever different to me after that afternoon. I had seen him offer his masks, his priceless treasures, for not even a single piece of gold. He offered them with outstretched hands, like a priest offering sacrifice to an ailing god.

That night I dreamed of my mother. I dreamed that she prayed to the great Buddha to give her brother back his life. I dreamed that, as she raised her eyes to the face of the great bronze deity, she could no longer see his face. Forever sealed from her gaze, the great image of Buddha, completely covered by a mask.

FIFTEEN

I do not think I ever took notice that my family's house had begun to decay. The five-room structure, which included the kitchen and three tatami rooms, as well as the small room on the second level that Father used as his studio, had been built by Grandfather before his marriage to Grandmother. Grandfather's family owned almost all of the land by the mountain, living by its side for nearly five hundred years. They had journeyed on the same dirt roads by which my father and I still traveled. The senior actors rested in the cushioned seats of the carrying chairs, while the younger members walked alongside the horses, saddled with the precious costumes rolled up in carrying cloth.

The masks, however, for the day's performance rested carefully in the lap of the patriarch. They were swaddled in a silk *furoshiki*, the Kanze crest embroidered on the outermost fabric, their comfort and safety considered even more precious than the actors themselves.

They had arrived at the imperial walls of the ancient court, where they performed for the emperor Go-Komatsu, they traveled to Kitayama where they performed for the shogun Ashikaga Yoshimitsu, one of the great Noh patrons. Four hundred eighty-one years ago, in the days when Zeami still lived, Noh was one of the most exalted art forms. And my ancestors were practitioners of the art.

The original house of my ancestors no longer existed. Grandfather's father was the last to live in it before it was consumed by flames. The new Yamamoto structure, the home of my birth, had been built closer to the mountain, as Grandfather, much like the rest of my family, believed that the great Mount Daigo was a shield from evil.

Grandfather chose a thatched roof rather than a tiled one, for he was a man of great tradition and believed that he should honor the way in which his ancestors lived, rather than replace it with a symbol of modernity.

The inner sanctum of the house was dark, constructed from pine trees felled from the adjacent forest. The ceiling beams were left uncovered, exposing the latticework of interlacing planks. Years of the hearth's flames had blackened the wood so now it appeared dark as ebony, the ancient soot thick and gleaming, the wood interred in its own stygian lacquer.

Light penetrated the house only through the rice-paper windows. When the sun served as illuminator, the threads floating in the parchment appeared like silkworms trapped in a flat white sea. I would often place my finger on the paper screen, taut as a drum skin, and trace the curl of each rice fiber. I would see myself in their entrapment and wonder if I would ever have enough courage to free myself from the prison of my destiny, or if I would succumb to my father's wishes and carve as he had, encasing myself in wood.

Father, having removed himself from the perfunctory duties of life, had no spirit for maintaining our home. His instinct caused him to be a tidy man, who began clearing the dishes as soon as he finished eating and who swept up the shavings of cypress wood after he finished carving. But those actions were mere rituals for him, and they could not be separated from the act of eating or the art of carving. I do believe that he would have not eaten at all had the action not enabled him to fuel his body for his carving.

The house, however, had not been born from his hands, and thus he felt no connection to it. When the roof leaked and the rainwater soaked into the tatami, it was I, not my father, who rushed to capture the cascade of water in a ceramic bowl. Father neglected to oil the wooden facade of our home, which thus appeared increasingly weather-beaten with each passing year.

After the last of the ceramic plates we had used for years had broken, Father failed to replace them. We ate from mother's lacquerware dishes as if they were bowls and plates for no special occasion. Once shining and scratch-free, they became dull and streaked with age. A patina formed from years of enduring our careless male mouths.

Father's income dwindled drastically over the years due to the theater's disastrous fiscal state. Given Father's indifference to worldly goods, our expenses were few. We ate produce from the local farmers, and father obtained his carving wood from the forest.

Now, as I look back into my childhood, I realize that we lived quite modestly in a once splendid home that became increasingly older and shabbier. A shell of its former state, no longer proud, it suffered from the weight of our neglect. Weary and needy, the wooden structure sagged like the Noh actors standing on the edge of the stage chanting to an empty theater. Both existed as anachronisms, caught between the traditional world of the past and the increasingly modern days of the present. Like our house, once built on the pride and the popularity of the Noh tradition, the ancient ways had begun to decay. Alas, the reforms of Meiji had come to Mount Daigo and, much to the chagrin of Father and the men of the theater, all that had once been revered began to crumble.

SIXTEEN

Where my father despised the wave of Westernization brought about by the Meiji, I embraced it. I loved the influence of European architecture that was reflected in all of the new structures being built in Japan, the new technology that was beginning to improve our way of life. Railroads were being constructed; stronger bridges were being engineered. Being a teenager at this time was one of the most exciting periods in my life. The government sponsored publishers to send texts to classrooms throughout Japan, to whet the eager appetites of the nation's children, and encouraged the next generation of architects, engineers, and, yes, even artists.

Schooling came easy to me. I devoured texts with hungry eyes and memorized the world map after studying it for countless hours. For the first time in my life, I realized that the country of my birth was an island surrounded by vast dark waters, not an endless strip of land surrounded by unending patches of mountains.

Europe, the land that brought us the locomotive and the daguerreotype, was only a steamship voyage away. At night I would dream of an enormous ship, clouds of smoke billowing from its steel silos, the bell announcing the boarding of all passengers, I among them, dressed in woolen suit and cravat, with ticket in hand.

At sixteen, after acquiring a copy of *Hosun*, an arts magazine that reproduced the works of several European artists, I convinced myself of my future vocation. I was going to be a Western-style painter, for those were the paintings that I loved. The landscapes had depth, the figures had volume, and the palette was rich and varied. I would not be like my father, with his ashen masks, I secretly told myself. I was born on the cusp of a new age.

I can still remember the ricocheting pangs of excitement I felt as I studied those first reproduced images. The first painting remains branded into my memory, its image pressed into the stone palimpsest of my mind: Dürer's *Self-portrait with a Thistle*. The artist's semblance emerges through a skin as translucent as eggshells, his velvet robes a whale blue, piped in carmine ribbon. Carved away from the background of shadows, he turns to me. I meet his small dark eyes. His body is bound, like my own, with an inner dress of white cotton gathered by satin cords pulled across a pleated bodice, and I, a young boy, am dressed in my weekend kimono, with a broad cotton obi wrapped tightly around my waist.

What else did I share with this fair-skinned, yellow-haired painter whose arched nose and full lips rose from the second dimension and pierced the now ragged pages of my magazine? What was it that I recognized, that made me pause for so many hours? Almost four hundred years and an entire continent separated us, but still this image of the young artist reached out toward me.

Perhaps it was Dürer's youth: he was only twenty-two when he painted his self-portrait, and I only sixteen when I first saw it. At such an impressionable age, seeing a painter who is already so masterful with the brush and whose countenance already glows with such intensity, I hoped that someday I would become the same.

I knew that I took easily to the brush; my sessions carving

with Father had proven that. Whereas my carving of the masks was mediocre, my painting of the faces rivaled his.

Of the entire process, it was the painting of the masks that most enthralled me.

I learned much about pigments and the techniques of painting through my apprenticeship with Father. Like a canvas, a Noh mask before it is painted must first be primed in white. We call this gessolike pigment *gofun*, and it is created by blending a mixture of crushed seashells and a pale glue. Once the wooden face is painted white, natural paints—composed of various minerals such as powdered crystal, cinnabar, ultramarine, and rare and precious gilt and mica—are applied. Suddenly the face becomes alive. Through color. And I knew that was what I intended to pursue. But not the painting of masks. The painting of life.

Secretly I wished that my father would take notice of my talent with color and the painting of masks. I suppose I wished he had vocalized his disappointment when he discovered me crouched, secretly sketching his face. But, alas, he kept these thoughts contained.

I too was guilty of silence. I lowered my eyes in reverence when he stared at me. I held my robe close to my thighs when I tiptoed through the house so the cloth would not rustle and I would not make a sound. Silence, it seems, was our curse.

SEVENTEEN

I will remember it always, that fine day in April. The cherry blossoms had begun their season; big, beautiful pink buds fastened themselves to hundreds of heavy ancient boughs that bordered the entrance into Daigo. And the pathway that I walked almost every day was transformed into a magical road; merging branches, dressed in roping strands of pearls and tourmaline, formed a canopy, and sunlight was diffused through the soft skin of petals. I remember that day vividly and mourn its ephemerality: it was the day I bought my first set of paints.

After seeing the painting that Dürer did when he was only twenty-two, I had realized with absolute certainty that I must purchase the proper supplies and begin painting at once. Of course, my father had several brushes and dried pigments that he used when doing the final painting of his masks, but to ask him if I could use them for painting a surface other than a mask was inconceivable.

I could not ask my father for money. I saw my father go to his chest and remove his strands of silver and gold coins with less and less frequency. Although our family rested on the laurels of our name and the long line of actors who belonged to our ancestry, we existed as a family with title only, living in an increasingly decaying house.

Had my father known that I intended to squander money on paints, he would probably have opened our gate and thrown me into an early exile. So I harbored my dream in private. After school I would sketch the portraits of some of my classmates for one ryo and save each coin until I had enough for my first set of paints.

It took me nearly seven months to earn enough funds for the initial purchase. I decided to travel to Yamada's stationery store, down by Shijo-dori, where a friend of mine informed me that the proprietor was importing paints from England. I was soon to learn my first lesson as an artist—that the materials were painfully expensive. I had barely enough money to buy a small set of water-colors and two oxtail brushes. Still, my entire boyhood savings seemed insignificant in comparison with the sheer ecstasy I received from the purchase.

The paints rested in their individual wells, discs of unblem-ished colors neatly arranged within the snug fittings of a wooden box. There were eight different shades—all of the primary colors and their complements—plus the essential black and white. I had never in my life seen such dense, rich color. I remember that, as I began the journey back to Daigo, I held the box at arm's length in front of me; it was my newly bought treasure, and I let it guide me home.

During the years of my lonely adolescence, I discovered that it is not the hands of the artist that are important; it is his eyes. Years later I would reflect back on this discovery and recognize it as the turning point of my career—when I realized that my eyes were connected to my spirit and that they possessed their own vision. But as a young man, I knew them only as tools that enabled me to see, study, and replicate.

Like most Japanese, I taught myself something new by copy-ing something old. In between my academics, I studied the copperplate prints and paintings in the magazine that the Meiji Fine Arts Society had begun circulating throughout Japan. I tried to reproduce some of their images in either a pencil sketch or with my watercolors. In particular, I nurtured an obsession with the human body, spending endless hours trying to obtain an anatomically correct figure. Without a live model, my efforts proved somewhat futile. In the evenings, after I had finished my homework, I would often try to draw parts of my own body—sometimes a leg or part of my hand. But I still found it difficult to construct an entire figure with the proper proportions.

I no longer shared sleeping quarters with my father but chose to sleep in the tatami room that my parents had once shared, where now only the *butsudan* remained. Under the cover of darkness, I would remove my body from the heavy layers of my blanket while the moonbeams penetrated the paper of my window. In these nights of adolescent insomnia, the length of my naked leg served as my study; in the dim light my eyes struggled to discern every sinew, anticipate every tendon, while my hand tried to re-create my own flesh on paper. And sometimes I stripped naked; the cotton weave of my *yukata* grazing my hairless flesh as it fell in folds to the floor.

I offered myself to the moonlight; the whiteness of the stars illuminated my skeleton, while the darkness shadowed my flesh. And in the chiaroscuro of these clandestine evenings, my image found itself on the former blankness of a page. The lines of my sketch struggled fiercely with the laws of anatomy, trying to re-create some semblance of the human form. But I was never able to achieve the appropriate distance or the appropriate angle. I became even more frustrated than when I had begun.

I hid my mountains of sketches inside the drawers of Grandmother's old *tansu* chest. There my work was concealed, carefully shrouded by her neatly folded kimonos, her heavy brocaded obis. "She embraces my work," I would whisper to myself as I wrapped the deep-colored bolts of cloth around the thick pieces of paper. I felt her spirit beside me. I imagined her alive and still living in the old *chashitsu*, her small head nodding, her eyes warm and understanding. "It is our secret, Grandma," I would murmur as I slid the dark wooden drawers shut and silently folded the iron latch. "I will make you proud."

When I was seventeen I entered a watercolor of Mount Daigo in autumn in a school art contest and was awarded first prize. I immediately used it to buy the famous *Kaitai Shinsho, the New Book of Anatomy*. It was one of the first books of its kind to be published in Japan. This medical book, translated from the original German, enabled me to study the body in greater detail and to better understand how the parts of the figure interrelated to the whole. Still, there was a limit to what I could teach myself through books; I knew I needed a more thorough art education if I was to become an accomplished painter.

Had I not thought that I had the potential for greatness, I would never have allowed myself to dream. But somewhere inside me, buried underneath several layers of cloth and skin, a voice called to me. It spoke to me not in Japanese but in a language of its own; it formed its vocabulary through colors and its sentences through images. Every morning as I awakened and every evening as I slept, it reminded me of my destiny. I savored the arrival of these images in my mind. They were in the form of paintings, and they reflected the work of an artist I had seen in a book or magazine. An apple might be snatched from a basket on a Dutch master's table, a figure lifted from a Rubens landscape. And, much like the fragment of a dream one recalls hours later, they remained with me, almost as if they were a premonition of the paintings I had yet to paint.

* * *

In 1894, my last year in high school, aspiring artists had far fewer opportunities to study Western oil painting than their colleagues had ten years earlier. During those first years of the Meiji government, Western art was viewed as a science rather than an aesthetic, a science whose techniques should be appreciated, learned, and mastered. In the 1870s, the Meiji encouraged Western training for its artists so that Japan might compete in all realms of Western society. The government even went as far as to bring Europeans to Japan to instruct students from around the country. These were glorious and exciting times for Japanese artists who wished to study the Western style. Had I been born a few years earlier, I might have attended the Technical Art School in Tokyo and studied with Antonio Fontanesi, the Italian master of nineteenth-century landscape painting who had been sponsored by the Meiji government to teach at the school. But by 1883, long before I was even ready to enter high school, the government abruptly changed its position toward the arts and terminated this progressive institution. While our scientists and engineers continued to receive government support, we artists did not.

Perhaps the Meiji would have continued their support of Japanese artists interested in the Western style had they been more successful in the international competitions of that period. Unfortunately these artists repeatedly lost to those who painted in the traditional styles because Western art critics and judges wanted to see the Japanese continue to create in their native style: the subtle ink washes of the *kano-e*, the colorful and decorative tradition of the *korin*, the technically perfect woodblock prints.

Thus, our artists were encouraged to look back to the nation's rich cultural past, as European and American artists suddenly showed an explosion of interest in all things Japanese. Fueled by a fascination with the exotica of the Orient, European artists found "the East" a well of inspiration. The great salon painters adorned their studios with folding screens painted in black, gold, and cinnabar. They dressed their models in silk kimonos, finely embroidered with colorful flower motifs, untied their sashes, and covered their coquettish smiles with hand-painted fans. The East was in vogue, a source of sexual fantasy and intrigue; Japan had become the land of a fireball sun, the giggling geisha, and the samurai sword.

In no time, collectors and scholars had arrived on our shores hoping to buy, or at least study, our many national treasures. Ernest Fenollosa and his Japanese protégé, Okakura Kakuzo, were two academics who crusaded throughout Japan crying for a return to the old traditions. Fenollosa and Okakura arrived in Japan with the goal of collecting the finest of our national works and taking them back to the Museum of Fine Arts in Boston. Not only were these men successful in their journey, but they also secured positions as advisers to the Meiji bureaucrats and were placed on the Imperial Art Commission.

Blessed with great powers of persuasion, these two men convinced the government to dissolve the Technical School of Fine Arts and combine it with the Tokyo School of Fine Arts. As a result, an aspiring painter in 1894, someone like me, had little choice but to apply to the newly established Tokyo School of Fine Arts. The new school would be the complete opposite of the Technical School of Fine Arts, in which everything was Western. Okakura and Fenollosa, who oversaw the creation of the new school, concluded that it should be completely devoid of Western influence, thus strictly forbidding instruction in Western painting techniques. Its principal goal was to reestablish the traditional Japanese art forms that the nation had turned its back on only a few years before. Even the uniforms of the students, designed by

Okakura Kakuzo himself, were to echo the traditional costume of the Nara period.

Since my record was excellent and my family background was equally impressive, my acceptance and subsequent scholarship to the school came as little surprise. As much as it was an honor to be admitted to the academy, however, I could not feign excitement.

Much to my dismay, the registration papers informed me that there were only three departments in the program: painting, sculpture, and crafts, all in the traditional Japanese techniques. The school offered no courses in *yoga*—what we call the Western style—or in oil painting or pencil drawing.

The prospect of an education in all things traditional made me miserable. I hungered for the West. The school that I had always anticipated attending, a place that I had perceived as my entranceway to a Western art education, had been radically transformed.

In my mind, I had already walked the streets of Paris, lost myself within the magnificent walls of the Louvre, and drunk coffee in a sidewalk café by the Seine. In Tokyo I feared that I would never learn the proper techniques for being a Western oil painter. The classes I was to take would surely not teach me the science of blending pigments, the laws of perspective, or the methods of modeling. I feared that I was not going forward at all; instead, I was leaving one house fiercely grounded in the ancient traditions for another.

I placated myself with the fact that I was at least going to study in Tokyo, where the wave toward modernization was strongest. As much as I loved the quiet and natural beauty of Kyoto, I knew that in the capital I would have bookstores, peers, and most importantly, the mouth to the West—the port in Yokohama.

EIGHTEEN

I postponed telling my father of my application to the Tokyo School of Fine Arts for as long as possible, but as I would be leaving in two weeks, I could delay the announcement no longer. I knew my departure to Tokyo would forever change our relationship and would inarguably demonstrate to him that I would never follow in his footsteps. But much to my surprise, I found myself not dreading informing him of my departure; I actually seemed to long for it.

I suppose somewhere deep in my heart, I wanted to wound my father. To punish him for not loving me more. For cowering from life. Once and for all to make him feel the impact of his blade.

As I had lived my childhood in its mirror.

I plotted how I would finally tell him. I would tell him in his studio. His sacred room, a place reserved only for the wood and those who revered it. Not I! I would slice through that which should have been my destiny. Rebel, and tell him that I would finally be free.

"Kiyoki," he whispers in his quiet voice, "would you please hand me the *tsukinomi*."

I hand it to him, and the blade passes through my hand like a sword. Heavy and gleaming. To be mine no more.

Around me, unpainted masks look down at me from the shelves, their mouths turning up at the corners in silent, slick smiles. The chorus of my judgment.

My own mask rests on a pale swatch of waste silk. Its features are sad and awkward, infused with a spirit it wishes it could exchange.

"Father," I say. And I look at his ancient body crouched over the block of wood. His spine twisting now, as Grandmother's had, his hair slicked behind his ears. "I have something important to tell you."

He does not look up from his carving. He does not turn his head to see my burning eyes. Around me I hear the sound of his saw slicing, the dropping of his chisel.

"What is it, Kiyoki? Do you need me to return the *tsukinomi*?"

"No, Father, it has nothing to do with the wood," I say with premeditation.

He is silent and I can feel the rush of his veins, the perplexity of his mind. He is confused, unprepared for anything else that I might want to discuss.

I loosen my sash and reach to find my letter of acceptance so that I might hold it in my hands, to receive its strength, see the proof of my escape.

"I have been accepted to the Tokyo School of Fine Arts, for the autumn semester, Father."

Silence. Except for the thin rustle of his kimono, the faint stiffening of his vertebrae.

"Father," I say, "they have given me a full scholarship, complete with a living allowance. The government will sponsor me so that one day I might be a great painter."

This is the wounding of Father. More bitter than sweet. Father, sitting there, crumpled like a bag of bones. Cloaked in a kimono. Wood at his knees. Knowing that never will his son be like him.

The mask carver. And he thinks to himself, The only family members who stay are made from timber.

I see him before I leave, as he will be when I am gone. Walking through a house that was never truly his. Where the braziers still glow orange and the altar still reminds him. Alone with ghosts and memories. And when he lays himself down in bed, does his face melt and his feeling surface? Does he wear his pain the way a tree wears its age? In rings of gold. Choked around a crumbling spine.

Does he think of the woman he loved, the son who arrived when he was already broken? Does he wonder why his son does not see him as his wife finally did?

He finds himself in his futon, the coverlet cloaking his chin. And in the night he stares, longing in the darkness to see her. For her shining form to come and forgive. In the whiteness of his sleeplessness, he sees his tragedy clearly. The wood had not been his anchor, but rather his divider. And his son would now leave him, not in death but in defiance. That which he had hoped would save his son had instead shackled him.

But there is nothing he can say. His voice has long since gone.

These are the thoughts that belong to the world of silence. Confessions uttered to a ghost. My father.

Two weeks later I say good-bye to my father with a surprisingly heavy heart. He stands in the *genkan* as I walk down the hallway, his chin lowered to his chest, a lock of his hair falling in front of him, bending like a sweep of calligraphy.

In his clenched fist he holds a shard of plum wood. Black as burned eggplant. Nearly as old as he, softened from the years of his grip. The only thing he carried from the only home that was his.

"Kiyoki," he says and his eyes this time are wet with tears, "take this wood. It is my memory. It is the *ki* from which you were born."

He has not carved for several days and his face falls like melted wax, no longer taut from a mask worn for so long.

He extends his slender arm and beseeches me to take that which he has held on to for half a century. Tight as twine.

I hold the shard in my hands not as my father has over the years, but as his son. And for the first time I see him with compassion. The lonely man that he is. Giving me the wood he has held on to for so many years. Perhaps in the hope that he too can now be free, that one day I shall bury it and all its power will be gone.

"Father," I say, and he motions with his finger that I should be silent. He stretches one arm toward the door and with the nodding of his head urges me through.

I do not utter the words "I am sorry," and do not mention that I can only hope to be as great an artist as he. I am too young, too foolish, to understand the concept of regret. I just bow my head and bend my knees, place his offering of plum wood in my *furoshiki*, and barely graze his shoulder as I walk past.

He stares through the open door, the overgrown garden of wild weeds beyond. A wash of sunlight bathes his gray face and he suddenly appears white. Pure as his pain. An old man who has been old for so very long.

He watches as I leave, wondering what I will do with that shard of wood that he has carried since he was a boy of five.

Part
Two

NINETEEN

The Tokaido railway, its sparkling locomotives only two years old at the time of my departure, shuttled me from Kyoto Station all the way to Tokyo, its brass gleaming, its whistle sounding through the hills. Women with flat bamboo-woven hats turned their heads from rice paddies that soaked their ankles and callused their palms. I thought of them, trapped like gnarled roots forever planted in the soil, and thanked the gods and the ghost of my mother for giving me my freedom.

I would not allow myself to think of Father. The last image of him standing in the threshold. His body bent like a bow, his fingers laced before him like an arrow. I preferred to let my imagination reincarnate him so that, when I left, he now stood tall. The years of sadness woven into the lines of his face eased and then erased, like the cracked earth after a storm.

It was easier for me now to think of him this way. Would he not be genuinely pleased to finally have a space all of his own? I struggled to convince myself. Would he not be relieved now that he no longer had to rise at the break of dawn to prepare my breakfast? Now there would be no one to interrupt his sacred routine of carving, no one to interfere with his beloved craft.

And perhaps most important, no one to remind him of the woman who opened him up for the first time and then closed him shut forever.

I told myself that it was not I who had sacrificed our relationship, it was he. Long ago. When he cowered from life. When he chose to replace the cry of love lost with the silence of wood. I repeated this to myself throughout the train ride, and tried in vain to convince myself of its truth. For there, beside me, the shard of plum wood protruded from my *furoshiki*. I pushed it back into the cloth, its pointed, fraying top piercing the tip of my finger. I thought of Father again. The pain caused by that broken bough was as ancient as it was intense, and I could not help but feel connected to him. I withdrew the sliver of wood and held it close.

I arrived at Tokyo Station and took a rickshaw to the house where I was to board. Shuttered by wooden planks and papered with shoji, it existed like a shadow on a street of large and once lavish Edo-style mansions. The owners of these once splendid residences had since moved into larger homes that reflected the Meiji architectural fashion for stone-carved flourishes, domed roofs, and pillared verandas. All around Tokyo, from the elaborate construction of the Kabukiza Theater in the Ginza to the Ministry of Justice Building in Kasumigaseki, Japanese architecture could no longer be distinguished from the structures of Europe. It seemed as though Greek Revival and Italian Renaissance had replaced wood and shoji. I would soon grow accustomed to seeing my reflection in the pane of leaded glass, no longer my silhouette on rice paper.

The rickshaw left me outside my new residence whose family name, Ariyoshi, was written in calligraphy on the dark wooden gatepost. I opened the latch and proceeded to the entrance, noticing that the outer garden had not been maintained and that a crooked old plum tree grew in the middle of the patch of overgrown grass.

Ariyoshi-san greeted me at the door, a graying man already bent with age. As I lowered my eyes and bowed in greeting, I glimpsed his bluish face. His strange pallor, eerie and translucent, reminded me of Father.

"Welcome, Yamamoto Kiyoki-san," he said politely. His few words would be my first encounter with the staccato pronunciation of the Tokyo dialect. I realized quickly that my articulation of our shared language was slower, softer, and considerably more elegant.

With my usual lack of grace, I handed Ariyoshi an envelope that confirmed my enrollment in the Tokyo School of Fine Arts. He received it with indifference.

"They have already paid me for the first month and have informed me that they will continue to pay me in monthly installments," he told me as he led me from the *genkan* into a long, dimly lit corridor, his shadow stretching before him.

"I have had only one art student live here before you," he continued. "His name was Murakami, but I suppose you wouldn't know him . . . When my wife was alive, she enjoyed having another person in our old house," he said wistfully, his voice trailing like a faint cloud of smoke. "But now that I'm alone, I still continue to do it. It's not for the extra money," he said almost apologetically, turning his head to me as he walked forward. "I suppose I like company."

Ariyoshi's openness and friendly demeanor surprised me. It was wholly unlike Father, who would never have rented a room in our home or spoken so freely to an outsider. I wondered if the old man suddenly found living alone so unbearable that he took on boarders simply to fill the emptiness in his life. Certainly, in the case of my father, the reverse had occurred. Yet when I stared at Ariyoshi, I saw a physical resemblance between the two men: the oyster-blue pallor, the fragile spine bending like a pine in the wind. But Ariyoshi's voice, rising high and trying so mightily to be ebullient, could not have been further from the memory of the man I left so shrunken at the threshold.

For Father was as still as the winter waters. Frozen on the top, yet silently flowing underneath a sheet of ice.

Aside from the faint physical resemblance between my father and my new landlord, everything I encountered from the day I left Kyoto appeared new and different. I cherished the sound of the old man's slippers on the wooden floor, black as satin from years of lantern fumes, because their rhythm seemed vaguely familiar.

Once alone, I slid open the screen door of the closet and removed the futon and the blankets. The room was Spartan, containing only a low wooden table and a charcoal brazier. An iron kettle sat silently on the table with five ceramic cups nestled by its side. This would be my new home, my studio away from school, my first refuge away from my father. Here the tatami were not new, as decades had probably passed since they were last replaced. The grass mats were a white yellow, their former green-ness dried, their strawlike scent evaporated. Here in my one-room flat in Tokyo, my futon was my only companion, white and heavy, the only thing between my flesh and the floor.

I began to unpack my satchels. First I removed Father's shard of plum wood. Immediately I could sense how out of place it felt here. Even though a plum tree grew just outside my window, this piece was from another time. I held it briefly, rolled it back and forth in the cup of my palms. I looked at it again: the twisted stub; the smooth obsidian patina of its outside; the coarse, frayed appearance of its edges. I held it up to the stream of sunlight and tried to discern any distinguishing fingerprints. Had Father's pain pressed itself into its skin? Had his grip been responsible for the waning of its middle?

In the end, I decided not to display it. I was not ready to come to terms with what it symbolized. Instead, I walked to the closet and tucked it deep in one of its interior drawers.

I returned to my carrying cases and *furoshiki* and unpacked my sketchbook. I placed it on the low paulownia table and laid my sticks of graphite and my stubs of charcoal down beside it. I carefully unrolled Mother's painting and placed the five teacups on each corner and one in the center in order to coax the paper to lie flat. I thought her art would serve to inspire me. To remind me of her unfinished talent. That which she had tucked neatly within me before she died.

Last, I withdrew my *yukata* and my sandals. I shook out my silk navy kimono and smoothed out its creases with my palm. Everything smelled of Kyoto. The scent of Mount Daigo and the perfume of cypress wood still clung to my clothes.

That smell was perhaps more emotional than the plum wood. I pushed my face into the cloth of my kimono and inhaled the fragrance of my past. That which I had so eagerly left behind and had tried desperately to force from my mind, I clung to now, perhaps out of longing, perhaps out of nervous anxiety. I did not know. I am only sure of that memory: my face buried in silk, my lungs desperately trying to regain what I had lost.

Within the shoji-lined walls of my rented room in Tokyo, I am reminded that I am now alone. I can no longer gaze out at the mountain whose seasonal changes I had charted since birth. I can no longer walk the soft earthen path to the shrine where my grandmother carried me to be blessed. Here there is no one but my ghosts to watch over me. And here I am no longer known as the mask carver's son.

TWENTY

Picture me then. Close your eyes and forget the gray, wrinkled man who sits before you now. Pretend that you have not seen his brown spots of age, the bits of sticky rice that hide themselves in the white patches of his beard. Ignore the smell of turpentine and the flecks of charcoal underneath his nails. Picture me as I now describe myself to you. A young student. A boy who realized he was born to be an artist long before he discovered that he had become a man.

Tall and as lean as a strip of burdock. Thick black hair. Skin as white as a *maiko*. Eyes the length of a dried almond. Black eyes and pretty red mouth. Some might even say beautiful. *Beautiful*. Like a girl's.

I was discovering myself during those first few weeks in Tokyo. I found myself suddenly exposed and vulnerable. I knew no one when I arrived. And even though I could read, write, and communicate in the same language, my Kyoto dialect revealed that I was not a native of this new and thriving city. I was beginning at a new school as a nervous boy from traditional and ancient Kyoto. I was unused to the crowds of the city, the pace of the nation's capital. My world at Daigo had stood still. I recalled my childhood, how it was speckled with testaments to the past: the pagodas, the temples, the gardens, and the theater of Noh. I remembered the mountain. I remembered Father's masks.

Still, here things were different. Shopkeepers stocked exotic imported goods: tea from Ceylon, ground tumeric from India, shiny copper pots from Nepal. Rolls of British tweed and fine Egyptian cotton were stacked on the shelves of specialty stores. Japanese men wore Western dress freely and proudly, for no special occasion except to celebrate the changing of the times. Never in my wildest dreams had I seen so many new things.

Shortly after my first day at school, however, I discovered that campus life at the Tokyo School of Fine Arts would be far from the progressive atmosphere that this new city afforded. To the contrary, the customs and curriculum of the school seemed archaic and regressive. Its aim was not to prepare its students to paint as Western-style artists in the modern age, but as native painters who worked in the ancient traditions, completely ignoring the influence of the West. I arrived, disgruntled and understandably disillusioned. I had left one citadel deeply pitted against change, only to replace it with another.

Even our uniforms took their inspiration from the traditional dress of Nara period courtiers: a heavily quilted short robe worn over long, flowing *hakama*. Can you imagine how silly I felt walking to school while many of my countrymen were dressed like distinguished Englishmen!

How I yearned to dress like them. I imagined myself in a stiff black jacket, matching vest, and crisp white shirt. I would hold my head high and soak up the sunlight with my proud, beaming face. But instead I found myself walking to my classes through Tokyo with great embarrassment, my head falling forward like a dying lotus, my *hakama* catching underneath my wooden heels.

The School of Fine Arts was cloistered away on its own small campus, adjacent to the community of the Imperial College. But unlike the rest of the college, the buildings of the Tokyo School of Fine Arts were constructed of the traditional materials of Japanese architecture: wood, bamboo, and rice paper.

On the first day of classes, I arrived at a sparsely furnished room where the tatami were woven tight and green, where the walls were covered with parchment and the windows were nothing but small lattice slits beneath a bamboo ceiling.

I watched as eighteen of my classmates filed into this stiff, spiritless room—a room ironically designed to inspire the nation's next generation of artists. We sat on the floor, our legs tucked neatly beneath us, our robes falling to the floor. On the first day I believe every one of us searched the room for an easel or a stool, something that we later heard was strictly forbidden.

"You are the emperor's investment," Morita sensei told us.

"You represent the Meiji's commitment to the arts, to the rebirth of our artistic traditions."

He sat before us, his deep purple robe and black skullcap making him appear priestly. Dark eyes that do not blink. Straight mouth that does not quiver. Morita would be instructing the first-year class in the art of *sumi-e*, Japanese ink painting. His would be the first face that we saw every morning. The one that we saw every time we looked up from our page.

I took three classes: painting, crafts, and sculpture. Each course was overseen by a sensei, but each student was largely responsible for his own work. The school adhered to strictly traditional methods of teaching: all of the students were forced to use their individual powers of observation in order to reproduce an original work of a great Japanese master. We were given a model and expected to copy it.

Noboru was the most gifted student in our class. I noticed this right away, as I am sure did Morita sensei and the majority of my classmates. He never strained his eyes to look at the model. Instead, he opened his mind to it, let it soak into his thirsty spirit and permeate his blue-red veins. With the brush between his long white fingers, the rice paper rolled out before him, he was able to reproduce a painting with the same intensity and perfection as the great Japanese masters. There was absolutely no separation between him, his art, and his brushes.

His talent separated him from the other students, but I worshiped him from afar. He seemed to be not from this earth, as though he had not entered through the sliding door, but rather emerged from the matted floor. Upon first sight of him, I could concentrate on nothing else. The words of Morita sensei evaporated; my peers vanished into midair.

Noboru, a sliver bound in blue cotton, gliding over the tatami. Noboru, with the body of a prepubescent boy and the eyes of a Heian priest. And Noboru, with a face so pure and undisturbed. Like the sacred image of the Kannon: his body lithe and his hands fanned out before him. Golden was his image, and his teeth glistened like pearls.

Never had I seen anyone so exquisite. I had lived a secluded childhood where the most beautiful creature was the one I created in my head: my mother. But this face before me now was different. Porcelain complexion. Eyes shining like beads. My first instinct was to rush toward him, touch him, glide my fingertips over the doll-like perfection of his face. To feel the landscape of his features. To have their impression forever cast into the memory of my palms so they would be forever mine to recall.

But I did not. For, infused into my spirit from the day that I was born a Japanese, was a deep sense of propriety. I bridled my emotions with great tenacity and tried to regain my composure.

I was shocked by my initial reaction to him. I had never experienced such extreme feelings before. Their intensity frightened me at first. I felt as though he was somehow a catalyst for my awakening, and I was surprised that another man could stir me so deeply.

For much of my childhood I had lain dormant, almost afraid to blossom as a full person, fearful it might scare or upset my father. But here I was alone. Father was far away. I was beginning to sense everything anew. Even my own skin felt different to me, as if each of my cells had just risen from a deep sleep.

Near Noboru I felt my senses come alive. I smelled the fragrance of his washing grains, the oil that smoothed his chin-length hair. I anticipated the rhythm of his footsteps, imagined the taste of his salty skin.

I remember watching him during Morita sensei's first lecture, as he was far more interesting to me than was Morita. I lingered over the length of his eyes, the full partition of his lips.

During that first class our teacher outlined, in his slow monotone, the school's objectives for over an hour. With the slow chant of a monk, he somberly informed us that we would be responsible for mastering the techniques of traditional Japanese painting. If we became proficient in these techniques during the four years of our education, only then could we contemplate creating a new style. "You will have to be recommended to the accelerated program, which demands a flawless academic and personal record," he said flatly as I struggled to capture Noboru in my view.

"Here," Morita informed us, "you all will first learn how to hold your brush." He paused before adding: "Hold it the proper way, not the slovenly way in which you all do your calligraphy."

I fidgeted. My robe felt heavy and cumbersome, my face flushed, and my body too warm. I tried to imagine the cool streams of water that I used to drink from near Mount Daigo. I tried to imagine myself submerged.

"After you have accomplished that," Morita continued, "you will learn how to grind your ink . . ." The list continued. Our sensei droned on, referring to the mastering of one technique before the next could be introduced.

I remember that I tried to pretend that my face was a mask, to try to keep my concentration on the teacher's words, but I could not. I sat upright, my legs folded, my shoulders tensed, and my eyes straight ahead. But all I could think about was him.

I pondered the size of Noboru's head compared to that of his body; I relished the curl of his upper lip, the arch of his brow. I sensed the weight of his shoulders, the compactness of his chest. Although he was small and slender, he appeared athletic, tight, and strong. Everything that my willowlike body was not.

In a kimono one can hide nothing, and so it was easy to see the line of his skeleton, the curve of his back, and the sinews of his muscles. He was a perfect specimen of the young boy at the cusp of manhood, someone Michelangelo would have begged to study.

He was beautiful and he became my friend.

I loved his laugh and I loved his way of speaking. I loved the lightness of his walk and the warmth of his eyes.

He was so different from my other classmates, so different from my father. When I looked at him, I was intoxicated by his energy. He exuded a heat, an invisible fire. I saw him like a bodhisattva surrounded by a mandorla of white light.

He was not a ghost, and yet I could feel myself being drawn into him, just as I had imagined the ghost of my mother so many times before; her outstretched arms and her long black hair wrapping me in a tight, protective embrace.

I believed from the minute I first saw him that we were connected. He had looked at me and lowered his eyes. Like a doll that welcomes the heat of its owner.

He was elegant; he had the capacity to break silence.

It was Noboru who initiated our first conversation that first day outside Morita's class. He too had sensed our connection.

"Have you bought your *o-bento* for today?" he had asked.

I was beaming because he had approached me.

"No," I replied, stumbling over my answer.

"Come with me," he said enthusiastically. "I'll show you where to get the best salmon rolls in Tokyo."

Although he was petite, all of Noboru's movements were elegant. For the Japanese, to have too strong a gesticulation would be vulgar, but when Noboru slightly turned his wrist, his hand sketching an invisible circle of air, there was nothing more charming.

Several times during those first days together, I had to control myself from reaching out to touch him. I wanted to capture him, just as a small boy wishes to hold a butterfly in his palms. I wanted to study him, with my face pressed close to his. I wanted to trace the outline of his collarbone with my forefinger; I wanted to inhale the fragrance of his *shiso*-minted breath.

But instead, I laced my fingers behind me, sucked my desires deep within, and wrestled with my emotions in the silence I had endured since birth.

I knew that my feelings toward Noboru were not those that are commonly exchanged between men. I knew of Grandfather and Grandmother's love story and the tragedy of Father and Mother's. But I also knew that I was not typical at all. I had been carved out and brought into this world against my will. Even Grandmother's coddling could not heal my internal wounds. I was the reason that Mother's life had been sacrificed and the reason Father had lost the will to love.

I often wondered, as my feelings toward Noboru intensified, if indeed I was born with my mother's spirit, if I truly carried her deep within. Had Noboru awakened something inside that spirit, a boy whose hands were his genius? Had her spirit noticed them, as it had noticed those of my father? Did her ghost stir inside me these urges? I looked to her for justification, as I had with my painting, so that my guilt would subside and my passion would not be extinguished.

Yet Noboru and I shared more than a mutual attraction; we also shared a love of Western-style painting.

As my first few months at the Tokyo School of Fine Arts passed, Noboru and I became closer. He would assist me after class with some of my ink paintings and encourage me to spend hours after class at the college library looking at reproductions of Western paintings.

I can still see him in my mind's eye, stretching over the long wooden table, his navy kimono clinging to his elongated form. He was so free with his body, like a garden snake that wiggles and coils. He could drape himself over almost anything. Fall languidly and rise gracefully.

Late at night, after we had completed our assignments, he would almost instinctively find the most secluded noodle shop or tea shop, and he would succeed in hypnotizing me with the sweet melody of his voice, the fluttering of his long black eyelashes.

In the privacy of these small, intimate spaces he would confide in me. Speak to me of his desire to paint, to use his hands, to create the incarnation of his voice with pigment rather than words. He would rest his right hand on the shelf of his jaw, his long fingers wrapped around the base of his neck, and that would be the only movement between us for several hours.

I once asked Noboru why he liked me, for I believed I was not his equal in so many ways.

"Your name is beautiful," he told me, and I looked at him, my eyes revealing my confusion.

"Pure wood," he translated the characters, although I of course had known the depth of their meaning since birth. "You are the first person I have ever encountered whose name and face reflect the same."

"Do you mean that I appear to be as cold and as inanimate as the trunk of a fallen tree?" I asked, wounded that someone I held in such high esteem would think me similar to something from which I had spent my entire childhood hoping to escape.

"But why does this cause you so much concern, my friend?" he asked. "Such a beautiful name, such a beautiful face." He paused and moved closer to me, his gaze reflecting his intensity.

"Your face is tranquil and still on the surface. The skin smooth and palpable. Young like a child. But behind your eyes, I see you are wizened," he continued. "You are like an old spirit trapped behind a young boy's mask."

I remember that these words caused me to pull away from him, remove myself from his gaze. It had never occurred to me that I might carry so many traces of my father.

"I am attracted to your purity," he said once more. "The wood makes you more intriguing, but it is the celestial quality to which I am drawn."

I was no longer hearing his words. He had pushed me back into the grasp of those who brought me into this world: my mother's purity, my father's wood. Noboru had seen me as the fossil I truly was, and I shuddered to think he had seen me so clearly.

TWENTY-ONE

There is something to be said for the first person who can look at you and tell you who you truly are. In a way, that person becomes your first mirror, the one who sees your reflection and encourages you not to look away but rather to take a deeper look. Such was the case with Noboru.

After he had confessed why he had pursued a friendship with me, I found myself withdrawing from him and immersing myself in my work.

He came to me one day when I was reproducing a painting inspired by the tradition of Kano Eitoku. I had been working on the rendering of cranes for nearly three hours.

"Hello, friend," he whispered from behind me, and I turned around to see him. "I have not seen you outside of class for several days."

His eyes were gleaming like a mountain lion's, and I turned away from him, unnerved by the intensity of his gaze.

"I have been busy," I answered. "I have had little time for recreation."

"Let's get some tea," he suggested playfully as he extended his sockless foot over the dry section of my painting.

"Not today," I replied, and even I found myself bored by the tone of my voice.

"Aren't we friends, Yamamoto-kun?" he tried once more.

I knew that if I looked at him again, I might crumble. His large wet eyes looked at me languidly, his silky hair dangled in front. But he knew so little of my past. Already he had seen a sliver of my life in Kyoto. He had read it in the markings of my face. But still I struggled there silently. I did not know if I was ready to reveal any more to him.

"I see you are painting cranes," he said wistfully, interrupting my interior monologue.

He looked up at the ceiling, the flood of afternoon light penetrating the thin bamboo slats.

"Have I ever told you, Kiyoki, that I grew up by the sea?"

TWENTY-TWO

Noboru hated nothing more than the smell of salt water, even though he was practically born at the sea's foaming mouth. He told me that his father's house was built on bamboo stilts and that it stood like a long-legged beggar whose feet were submerged in the sand and who pleaded every night with the raging waters not to be carried away.

Most of the men in the village earned their living by making fishing nets. But Noboru's father made paper fans. While his father fashioned the split bamboo into smooth, tiny handles, his mother spent the day painting the rice paper with either the palest landscape or the calligraphic lines of a poem.

Noboru attributed his talent to his mother; she was the holder of the brush and the keeper of color in the family. She would take the half-moon circles of paper and, through her subtle washes of ink, give them life. His father gave them backing and structure. She gave them the pinkness of *sakura*, the orange of *momiji*, the blueness of the waves, and the height of the tsunami.

The ink and paper had been his guardians while his parents worked until dusk, leaving him alone. He learned to control the bleeding of the ink by holding his brush high, and to trace the movements of his brush by propelling each line by the force of his body. He learned that he should never be afraid of black, that he should always be bold.

But Noboru also had the gift of subtlety. He could paint a

sakura hubuki, he could paint the fog, and he could paint the snow.

Every night he slept in darkness, to the sound of the water roaring and his parents' muffled sighs. He tossed between their sleeping bodies, their shadows rising on the walls like the crashing waves beneath the house. In these nights, he would will himself to sleep and delve into the darkness to search for his dreams.

He had heard that there was a place on the other side of the ocean where men had pale skin and burned in the sun. But it was not until he was thirteen that he heard that these men also painted figures that were so real, it seemed they could walk off the page. Because they used thick and luminescent pigments, their pictures had such depth that one could be submerged in the architecture of the images.

He had learned all of this from his uncle, who returned to the village every April. Tall and wiry, his smile accentuated by the black mustache suspended between his nose and lip, he arrived, seeming as foreign as the prints he had rolled up in his suitcase.

He was Noboru's father's younger brother, who had left the village by the sea for the great capital. Now he worked as an importer of Western prints. He wrote and traveled and had been an editor for the art journal *Hosun*. Every time he returned to the house of his childhood, now the house of Noboru's father, he would slide off his loafers, pull up the pleat of his trousers, and complain about the heat. Noboru's mother said she was sorry, the best they could do for him was to give him a cold glass of *mugi-cha*.

She would return from the kitchen with a tray of iced cups of wheat tea and slide open the shoji to where the men were sitting. There she would kneel and beg of him in her soft, melodious voice, beautiful in its distinct southern dialect, to take the cold drink, apologizing that they did not have anything more to give him on this hot evening. And then from the sash of her kimono, she offered him a freshly painted fan.

Pale white stretched over a bamboo spine. The flattened grains of rice floated in the parchment like sleeping worms.

Just as I had, Noboru wondered if he was like them. He wondered if he would ever be free.

The only person the uncle loved more than himself was his nephew. His love for Noboru was the only reason he returned to his village every year. The young Noboru was precocious, energetic, and displayed an incredible artistic sensibility.

The uncle claimed that he had discovered Noboru's gift. But his mother had known of it for years.

Noboru painted everything he could imagine. He sketched the mountains and colored butterflies, and he created intricate battle scenes with sword-clashing, heavy-armored samurai and palanquins containing sleeping princesses.

When he entered high school and learned of the painters of the Kano and Tosa schools, Noboru displayed a prodigious talent for re-creating their landscapes. He experimented with black ink and with the ground pigment he found in his parents' studio. Like that of a wizened calligrapher, his body turned with every movement of his brush; his painting became a dance, and his dancing gave birth to the painting.

Fully aware of his nephew's talent, during one of his visits the uncle brought with him a book entitled *European Artists of the Nineteenth Century.* It was this book that propelled Noboru into his lifelong obsession.

Through the illustrations in this book Noboru tried to teach himself the laws of perspective. He practiced shadowing, drawing the same object during the early morning, late afternoon, and evening, until he understood how the light varied and how it affected the object of his study.

When he came of age, his uncle offered to pay his expenses, should the Tokyo School of Fine Arts accept him into its prestigious program.

When the school's letter of acceptance arrived, his parents embraced their only son. They took what money they had saved over the years and told him to buy the finest set of paints Tokyo offered. The next month he left his tiny village, carrying little more than a small satchel and a homemade *o-bento* containing three salmon rolls made by his mother's tiny and talented hands.

When he bade them his final farewell, they masked their tear-filled eyes by hiding behind their fans.

And so it was that I learned the story of my closest friend at the academy. He had told me of his life before Tokyo, so how could I not tell him mine? We left that night for a tea shop near Asakusa. There amid the light of red lanterns and the warmth of several cups of sake, I told him much of what I have written down here.

This time, after I had conveyed my story—for it was the first time it had been spoken from my lips—I welcomed the silence that came upon the room. For I believed that our friendship was forever sealed, that no matter what came between us, we shared an intrinsic and essential bond, one that I believed could never be broken. In the end, however, I would underestimate certain powers.

Powers such as the sheer force of the sea.

TWENTY-THREE

Noboru's friendship was the only glimmer of light in my otherwise bleak existence. The absence of color in the big city and within the walls of the school pained me. Having been blessed with a childhood that never lacked in autumn hue, snowfalls, or cherry blossom winds, my paper absorbed every color and every season. Here, within the city and within the classroom, I quickly detected a profound difference. Tokyo had long since begun to turn the wheels of change, whereas Kyoto had fought against it. And despite all of the energy and progressive undertakings surging through the city, the walls of the School of Fine Arts struggled to be impervious. Perhaps that was what caused me to be so especially unsettled; I had come from the eternal city of Kyoto to one deeply dedicated to progress. And yet I could not submerge myself in the revolution; I was cast into one of the last remaining strongholds in the city, a wooden fortress firmly rejecting any change.

During the first semester, Morita sensei assigned the class the task of studying the works of the great painter Sesshu Toyo. Struggling to reproduce Sesshu's landscape, we worked silently under the watchful eye of Morita sensei.

Sesshu did not paint with his brush. Instead, he carved. The sixfold screen was not a plane of paper but a piece of stone in which he could unearth an entire terrain of mountains.

He coined the ax-cut brushstroke, slicing away the whiteness of the page to create cliffs. His shrubs looked more like vines, protruding and, in some cases, choking the mountains from which they grew. His mountains were not soft and sloping; they were rocky and jagged. They stood out like rugged towers against a soft, misting sky.

Noboru and I both found such assignments torturous. Although he excelled in them, I struggled to capture the strokes on the page. Both our minds were elsewhere. We both dreamed of someday being *yoga* painters—Japanese painters who used oil and canvas and whose works were executed in the European style. After our long sessions in class, we would walk to a small tea shop and pore over the images of the great painters from the West— Delacroix, Corot, Ingres. We imagined ourselves viewing the creation of *Liberty Leading the People*. We saw the artist blending his pigments on a slab of polished pine. We saw the swish of his brush in the clouds of tinted jars of turpentine; we saw the stretch of naked canvas bejeweled.

We would nearly cry with envy when we saw the first reproductions of the Impressionists—Manet, Monet, Morisot. We memorized their names until they fell from our ears like notes from a well-known symphony.

We closed our eyes and imagined ourselves stepping into Pissarro's *Entering the Village of Voisins*. We saw the steel gray of the sky, the autumn-stripped branches, and the village shadowed by the approaching dusk. Horse-drawn carriage. Cathedral in the distance. If the magazine had provided a door, we would have gladly entered.

With our fingers extended, we traced the lines of their strokes as if it would help us learn the way these Europeans wielded their brushes. We imagined the wooden tray before us was a shining palette and we dipped our fingers into the cups of tea as if they were pots of warm pigment. And I, with the liquid running down my fingers, traced his profile on the glass.

*   *   *

During my first few months in Tokyo, I was conscious that I had begun to change. No longer did I think incessantly of Father and how I had left him behind. I began to enjoy myself and concentrate on my classes. Although I struggled with the curriculum, I was overjoyed to have found Noboru. When I was with him and when we were lost in discussions of Western painting, I was happier than I had ever been.

There were occasional reminders of Father, of course. Ones that I could not ignore. The plum tree outside my window. Its crooked boughs and ripening yellow fruit. The sight of Ariyoshi's aging form.

I had started one or two letters to Father, although I never finished them. I always ended up crumpling the rice paper into tiny white balls and tossing them into the brazier.

I thought he would always be there. Forever in Kyoto. Eternal, like his masks. I had grown up believing love was transient and pain lasted forever.

So you must understand my surprise when around the third month of my studies in Tokyo, a letter was delivered to Ariyoshi's house informing me that Iwasaki-sama, the patriarch of the Kanze theater, was coming to Tokyo. He would attend to some business associated with the Noh community, and in his letter requested to meet with me at a time suitable to my convenience.

I had not seen Iwasaki-sama in years. Not since that day I had traveled as a young boy with Father and his masks to the Kanze theater. I sat down on my tatami and tried to recall his face. I remembered his full cheeks and black hair. I saw him as he had been on that day: when he held Father's masks in his hands and informed him with great embarrassment that the theater could no longer afford his masks.

I took out a sheet of rice paper and in long black strokes wrote that if it was convenient to him, I would meet him in front of the campus gates the following day at six o'clock.

The next day, after I had finished my classes, I walked out of the main building and saw him standing underneath the iron gates.

He stood with the stature of a proud actor, his posture learned since childhood, his feet firmly planted on the ground and his stomach puffing proudly over his sash. Immediately I was struck by his resemblance to Grandfather, who I saw in the face of Iwasaki-sama. He would have worn the scowl of the current patriarch, had he lived to see me take the path I had chosen. He would never have been able to accept that the great family tradition would die with Father. A man not even his son.

Iwasaki's face had aged gravely. And had I not known better, I might have thought that he wore a mask. His skin had grown gray. His hair had been cast over in white. There was hardly a likeness to the man who had ascended to the rank of patriarch so many years before. "Kanze Iwasaki-sama," I said as I greeted him reverently, my forehead straining to reach my sandals. "I am honored that you have called on me. I realize how busy you must be."

He nodded solemnly. "Let us go someplace quiet, Yamamoto-kun. Let us go someplace where we can speak."

As the sun descended into the clouds, the moon slowly became its shining replacement. I walked behind the patriarch, whose shadow enveloped me. And once again I felt swallowed. As if Father had sent a messenger, in the guise of Grandfather.

Only father had not sent him. And as a result, his silence was all the more powerful.

TWENTY-FOUR

I have come to inform you that your father has been ill for the past month," Iwasaki told me in the seclusion of a small restaurant not far from my school.

"Since you left, he has grown frail and thin. The other actors and I have visited him on occasion, only to find that he rarely will come to the door."

The old patriarch rested his full and delicately lined lips on the rim of his teacup. The smoke wafted over his face and made him appear even more ghostly than his already hoary appearance.

"We have been concerned for him. We have been unable to commission any masks, yet we know from the fallen cypresses in the forest that he must still be carving."

I looked down at my plate of grilled fish. My appetite had suddenly vanished, and as I was unable to eat my meal, I concentrated on removing the small grid of bones from the fish's middle.

"Have you been writing to your father since you've come to Tokyo?" he asked, and his tone seemed less kind.

"I have been meaning to for some time," I said, struggling awkwardly.

"It must have been devastating to your father when you left."

I remained silent.

"For all of us in the theater, it is damaging when a child does not follow in our footsteps. In this time particularly, when so many of you are seduced by the ways of the West." He paused and then looked at me with raised eyebrows. I could instantly envision the man who sat before me performing on stage. I need not close my eyes to picture him beating his feet over the polished floorboards in the dance of the demon queller or in the ravaged spirit of Ono-no Komachi.

"It must have been particularly brutal for your father, as you are his only son," he said, interrupting my reverie.

I could feel my face begin to redden. My ears beginning to burn. Had he traveled all the way to Tokyo to remind me of my betrayal? Something I remembered all too well. Had his reason for attending to affairs concerning the theater been a ruse?

"What you tell me of my father is of great concern to me, Patriarch," I confessed politely. "It was wrong for me to have been so self-involved here that I have not inquired about the status of his health. I will write to him immediately and I will try to schedule a trip to Kyoto during the next few months."

"I am glad to hear this, Yamamoto Kiyoki," he said. As he pushed a small piece of sushi into his mouth I noticed the large, swollen quality of his hands. Once again it struck me that I was sitting across from someone who strongly resembled Grandfather.

As we exited the restaurant, the long red curtains falling to the side of the entranceway, he leaned toward me.

"It is a shame, Yamamoto-kun. We all at the theater had always thought you would be a great mask carver like your father."

He turned away from me, and his broad shoulders seemed to slope to the ground. The fading light of the distant lanterns made him appear even older, and he sagged when he bade me good-bye.

TWENTY-FIVE

A-kan! A-kan! A-kan!" the teacher shouted at me from his *zabuton*. Saito sensei was from Osaka, and he always slipped into dialect when he expressed his disapproval.

The silence and sobriety of Morita sensei's painting class was in complete contrast to Saito's sculpture class. Here we worked in constant fear. Here our teacher reigned from his *zabuton*; the slightest incorrect move from one of our chisels was incapable of escaping from his line of vision. Even Noboru, whose work was least likely to be criticized, often felt the sting of Saito's vicious bark.

If it hadn't been for the overbearing presence of Saito sensei, I might have thought I was in my father's studio again. The smell of freshly stripped wood interlaced with the fresh scent of new tatami made me think of home, and this, combined with Iwasaki's visit, caused me to be overcome with a certain bittersweet nostalgia that I was surprised to learn was inside me.

It was not surprising that my classmates and I struggled in sculpture. Most of us were familiar with a brush and ink; we had learned how to write our characters with a brush during our earlier years, and drawing was a skill that came naturally to us. Creating in the third dimension, however, was another matter.

I was probably the only one of my peers who had any knowledge of the art of carving. I watched the others receive their chisels, and their faces betrayed their confusion over the shining blades handed to them.

Had Father been here in this room with me, I know he would have balked at the chisels they were dispersing. The slender pine handles were rough and unvarnished, the silver blades square and blunt to the touch.

I heard the echo of Saito sharpening the edges of his chisels. The sound of the blade against the wet stone brought back more images of Father. Once again I saw him, his back crouched and his knees pressed to the floor, his white wrists jutting from the billowing sleeves of his gray kimono, the blue veins pumping through his skin. He grasped the handles of his chisels like a samurai clasping his sword. Swiftly and powerfully, fingers meshing with wood, Father slid the blades over a shining flat black stone, wet and glimmering in the sunlight. Like the ink stone used by a calligrapher, ground down in the middle.

In accordance with his sharpening ritual, Father always touched the shining blade, sharp as dagger, against his fingertip. The red blood, reminiscent of waxberry juice, ran over his knuckle.

I held the chisels in the palms of my hands. I had traveled so far to avoid the prison of these wooden instruments, yet here I was, picking up the very tools I had rejected years before.

I should have laughed at my situation. The ridiculousness of it could not be met with anger or tears. But in the end, I did grasp the chisels and plow into the wood, just as I had done countless times with Father.

The sensation of wood beneath my blade felt surprisingly refreshing to me. Without the shadow of Father behind me, I worked freely, without the confusion of the man for whom I was carving.

Around me, my classmates struggled. Their hands fell clumsily over their handles. Their blades buckled over the wood. The slab of cedar they were supposed to incise splintered and frayed like a piece of cheap cloth. The irony of my situation amazed me. Here I was, excelling in the only class I had hoped to avoid. The craft from whose chains I thought I had finally sliced myself.

On the second day, Saito called me aside and asked that I remain after class so that he might speak with me.

"Kiyoki," he said that afternoon

"Yes, Saito sensei."

"Is it true that you are the son of Yamamoto Ryusei?"

I was stunned. I had not anticipated that my father's reputation would follow me to Tokyo.

"Yes."

"I am very pleased to have you in my class, I am sure you will do well."

"I am honored to be under *your* guidance, honorable Saito sensei," I replied, stressing the word *your* in order to seem as humble as possible.

"I am sure that you will be far ahead of your classmates, as you have probably been carving since the day you were born." He chuckled to himself as if the fact that I came from a carving family bonded us.

"Carving may come easy to me, but it is the art of Western painting to which I aspire."

"Why do you not make your country and the emperor proud by learning to produce the great craftsmanship of the Kamakura?" he asked, his voice revealing annoyance at my irreverence.

"I am not moved by the wood, sensei."

And then I added, so that the silence between us would be broken, "I am most unlike my father. I am more like my late mother, who was an accomplished painter."

He looked at me with stony eyes. "Such pain you must have caused your family!"

"Pain has always lived within the foundation of my family. That and wood. Forever entwined."

The crooked bend of sensei's nose flashed before me, reminding me of Father's shard of plum wood that still remained deep in one of my closet drawers.

"I had hoped that you might be a student that I could encourage your peers to follow," he said, disappointed. "But, alas, I see that I was mistaken."

The bond that he thought existed was dissolved in seconds. He turned his gaze away from me. I saw the reflection of his face in the glossy weave of the tatami.

"You are dismissed, Kiyoki."

I heard the crick of his neck as he raised his head, and I felt his gaze burning into my back. It was an all-too-familiar feeling. Reminiscent of my childhood. He was like a bough sliced from the trunk of my father. Wooden and restrained. Disappointed and now silent.

I left the classroom to the sound of my sandals clicking on the hall's wooden floorboards. The echo was loud and seemed inappropriate within the walls of the school, this contrived structure built to reaffirm tradition and reject the new age outside its gate. Yet as I clicked down the hallway, I made no attempts to muffle the sound.

In fact, with the arrogance of a foolish young man, I tried to amplify it.

TWENTY-SIX

Nearly a week passed before I gathered the courage to write Father. I was still angry that Iwasaki-san had invaded the new life that I was trying to create for myself in Tokyo.

Dear Father,

I hope these autumn months find you surrounded by many red and golden leaves. Please forgive me for not having written to you sooner, but adjusting to life in Tokyo has been difficult.

I have been struggling with many of my classes. The college is not all that I imagined it to be. Okakura and Fenollosa have certainly established an institution that is staunchly dedicated to preserving the traditional artistic ways of our nation's past. I am sure that you would be pleased to hear this.

I am not getting instruction in Western-style painting, as I had wished. Only after one masters the courses in the traditional classes can one ascend to this highly competitive class. And even this class is not a Western-style class but really one that just encourages the best students to create a "new" Japanese style. All of this is very frustrating to me, but I am happy to be on the path toward painting, which, as you know, I love.

I realize, Father, that I have caused you great suffering with my departure. I write because I want to ensure that you

*are well. Have you been carving? I hope that you will answer
my letter and inform me of your status.*

*I remain your only son,
Yamamoto Kiyoki*

I sealed the letter with rice glue and sent it the following week.

TWENTY-SEVEN

I, Yamamoto Ryusei's son, still silently resented the wood. I endured Saito sensei's class, as humiliating as it was, because I wanted desperately to be accepted to the accelerated painting class. There the students were allowed to experiment with spatial depth and the rendering of light and shadow. Still no oils or canvas, but at least it was something.

Dreams such as those, however, had to be postponed until I completed all of my studio work for the day; otherwise none of my assignments would ever be finished. There were mountains of work to be done. My final project in Morita's class was a replica of a Heian hand scroll, complete with small ink drawings and extremely difficult calligraphy. Additionally, a medium-sized bodhisattva had to be carved for Saito sensei. Then there was still the *bizenyaki* to be done in my crafts class.

Late in the evening, after I had finished my work for the day, I would drag myself home to my small rented room. There I would dream of the paintings I had not yet painted, of exhibiting in spaces I had not yet visited, and of meeting with Japanese painters who had actually studied in Europe. Men like Kuroda Seiki.

All of the newspapers had written about Kuroda's return to Japan in 1893. He had spent nine years in France, abandoning his initial studies there, as a student of law, for painting. Along with Kume Keiichiro and Fuji Masazo, two of Fontanesi's pupils from the old Technical Art School, Kuroda began his study of Western art with the academic painter Raphael Collin and eventually cultivated himself into the role of a well-respected artist.

Noboru and I had often discussed Kuroda and his work, especially after the uproar his painting *Morning Toilette* created during its first exhibition in Japan. With all of the publicity the critics created, denouncing the immodest subject matter and the overt sexuality of the model's pose, Noboru and I decided that we should see the painting for ourselves.

We walked together into the crowded exhibition space not far from the new railway station. It was a far-from-scandalous painting in the eyes of two appreciative art students, especially two art students who wanted so desperately to paint in the Western style. Noboru and I failed to see why the painting shocked the crowds and critics.

It was a rather tall canvas, depicting a young girl standing before a full-length mirror. By introducing the reflection in the glass, Kuroda's composition increased in depth, as the viewer was now able to see both the frontal and rear view of this naked young girl. Unclothed, the woman stared at her own reflection while wrapping a long lock of her hair around her head. Her upswept hair exposes the most delicate, sensual, and most appreciated area of the female for any Japanese male—the nape of the neck.

Noboru and I both loved this painting. Clearly, it was masterful in its technique: its soft palette well blended and the semi-impressionistic brushwork extremely well executed. But the most wonderful thing about the painting to Noboru and me was that it brought out the hypocrisy of the Japanese public.

"Really!" Noboru exclaimed. "Did you hear Okada-san commenting on how vulgar Kuroda was to show not only a nude woman but also one with her neck exposed? It was if he had never looked at one single work of our own Ukiyo-e artists."

"We should be sending the old man a print of Harunobu's *Woman in a Bathhouse*," I suggested.

"Or even better," Noboru said, "we could send a book of Tokugawa *shunga* illustrations."

The thought of seeing the old man confronted with graphic images of sexual practice sent us into peals of hysterical laughter.

We were cocooned in our own amusement that day. We were sated with happiness: by the sun, the exhibition, our impressions of Kuroda's work, and his success in Europe and Japan. We were satisfied like the happy and drunken image of Hotai, his belly full and his face smiling.

That day there was nothing preventing us from believing that we too could achieve the greatness of Kuroda Seiki. We were swollen in our youthful arrogance as we sashayed through the streets, our sandals clicking and our shoulders back. We were truly convinced that someday our own paintings would hang on those walls.

TWENTY-EIGHT

For several weeks I waited for a response from Father, and I began to think of him with increasing frequency. At night he would often appear in my dreams. I no longer felt the beneficent presence of my mother. Now I felt the heavy face of Father gazing down on me, his spirit stretching out to reach into the corners of my mind. I wondered how he responded when he received my letter.

I pictured him as gaunt and frail, as Iwasaki had described him. I envisioned him unshaven and unbathed, the skeleton of a man more dead than living, wrapped in a thinning cloak of gray silk.

When I imagined him reading my letter, I saw him illuminated by the light of a rapeseed lantern, his tired, lined face straining as he read my words. Had he read what I had written? Or had he instead read what he believed I should say? Did he wish that I had said that I was sorry? Or, even more simply, "Father, I know I have done wrong"?

I wondered if he spoke now to my mother. Whether her spirit was the only thing that kept him warm. Or perhaps he cursed her for leaving him. Silently, of course, because words between them were never necessary for communication. Had he closed the *butsudan* so that he could forget Grandfather and Grandmother, the family who had taken him as their own? Had he sworn at their memory because his son had abandoned him?

At night I see him again sitting by the lantern, the taper thirsty for fuel. He lights my letter with its burning wick and sets it aflame so that my words—my inadequate words—evaporate into thin air, trailing behind him in a thin wand of smoke.

Nearly two months passed before I heard from Father. A letter did not arrive, as I had hoped. Something far larger came in the form of a small, neatly bundled package. I opened it as soon as I arrived home from class that day. Yet nothing could have prepared me for the surprise.

I placed the pine box wrapped in cloth down on the tatami and cut the twine with a small knife. There, under several layers of tissue and swatches of silk, I unveiled a mask. Father had enclosed no letter. No simple note. No message except one that could be inferred from the mask.

What did it mean? I wondered as I revealed the pale white face, translucent as a robin's eggshell, and placed it on my lap. It was not the Ishi-O-Jo mask, the mask of the old man trapped in the form of a cherry tree, by which I had always imagined him. Rather, the delicate, youthful features, downswept eyes, gently curving brows, and slightly parted lips led me to believe that it was the Semimaru mask, used in the saddest of Noh plays, *The Story of Semimaru*.

I recalled the character of Semimaru, the fourth child of Emperor Daigo, who is born blind but talented. His melodies on the lute were said to be unrivaled. Yet Emperor Daigo, unable to accept that his son has been born imperfect, orders him exiled and left abandoned on Mount Osaka. Grandfather had once chanted several lines from this play while making his way to the old Kanze theater.

In jeweled pavilions and golden halls
You walked on polished floors and wore bright robes.
In less time than it takes to wave your sleeve,
Today a hovel is your sleeping-place,
Bamboo posts and bamboo fence, crudely fashioned
Eaves and door; straw your window, straw the roof,
And over your bed, the quilts are mats of straw.
Pretend they are your silken sheets of old.

Those words could also have applied to Father, a long time ago, when he was just a boy, when he lived and whittled his masks squatting alone on the forest floor.

Now Father had sent me this mask, and I wondered about its meaning.

I raised the mask closer to eye level. When I held it upright it appeared sad, almost weeping. Its lids weighed heavily, veiling blank eyes. Its mouth quivered, as if withholding a cry. I remembered how, once he is alone, the actor who plays Semimaru takes his lute, his only possession, clutches it to his breast, and falls to the stage weeping. And the mask suddenly came alive to me. Its pain reminiscent of my father. The memory of him all alone except for his masks.

And I recalled how the last scene on the stage is of Semimaru, his blind gaze searching for the vision of his sister who visited and then departed. His tears falling through the mask. And for the first time, I began to understand my father.

I needed no words to realize that he was calling me, asking me to visit him once more. I knew that I had to return to him at once. I decided to return at *Shogatsu*, the Japanese New Year, which would fall in nearly three weeks' time. I told myself that I could check on his health and could confront him about the meaning of this mask. I told myself it would be an opportune time to visit him. That, this year, we could start our relationship anew.

I sat down on the tatami and began a second letter to Father.

Dear Father,

In these months of cold and frost, I write to you. Your mask arrived today, and I wish to thank you in person for sending it. Is it the Semimaru mask, as I suspect? I hope to discuss its meaning with you when I return home. I am planning to visit Daigo at Shogatsu time. We have two weeks' vacation from classes, and I believe I can manage the journey.

I remain your only son,
Yamamoto Kiyoki

I sent the letter the following day and began to look forward to seeing him again. I hoped that we might communicate for the first time our feelings toward each other. But fate, it seems, had other plans.

TWENTY-NINE

Noboru was with me when I received the letter from Iwasaki that informed me my father had passed away. Only minutes earlier, he had discovered the Semimaru mask wrapped in silk and carefully placed in the corner.

"What's this?"

"I believe it is a message from my father."

He picked it up between his palms and studied its face intently.

"Such a beautiful face," he remarked as he continued to stare, transfixed by the intensity of the mask.

"Do you see anything else?" I asked, eager to hear him confirm my suspicion of its meaning.

"Sadness," he said as he looked up at me and then back at the mask. "It is almost as if I can feel its spirit shaking in my hands. It's weeping from underneath its skin."

"Tilt it," I told him anxiously. "Don't you see anything else when you rotate it back and forth?"

He continued to sit on the floor, his feet tucked under him, his palms outstretched, when suddenly there was a violent knock on my door.

"Yamamoto Kiyoki, Yamamoto Kiyoki!" It was Ariyoshi, and he was out of breath from climbing the stairs to my room.

"Yes?" I asked the old man as I slid open my door.

"There is a messenger downstairs who will not leave until he has delivered a letter to you!" Ariyoshi's face was flushed and his words were difficult to make out, each one merging into the other, like a string of beads.

"All right, then," I said, not giving much thought to it. "I'll be back in a moment."

I went downstairs and discovered the messenger breathing clouds of steam into the frosty air. When he saw that I had come to accept the delivery, his shoulders tensed and his posture suddenly stiffened. He could not have been more than fifteen years of age.

"Yes, I am Yamamoto Kiyoki," I told him, and extended my hand to receive the letter.

With his two hands clasping each side of the envelope, the young boy handed me the letter. "It has come from Kyoto."

I handed him two yen and turned to read the letter in private.

The letter was dated December 14, 1895. I closed the shoji to my room and went past Noboru, who had wrapped the mask from my father and returned it to the corner. I sat down on the floor beside him.

Dear Yamamoto Kiyoki,

The year, it seems, has ended badly. The frost has come early to Kyoto, and, sadly, I must be the one to write you the devastating news. Your father passed away last night. Our colleague Isao-san discovered him early this morning after deciding to visit on him on his way to the theater.

We in the theater recognize that you will want to take responsibility for your father's funeral. We thus urge you to return as soon as possible.

With grave sadness,
Kanze Iwasaki Keizo

I received the news of my father's death without any immediate signs of grief. It was almost as if I could not believe that he had left me before I had a chance to return.

I remained on the floor with my knees curled beneath my chin, my kimono smoothed out underneath me. "I must return to Kyoto," I told Noboru after minutes of silence passed between us. "You see, my father has died. I must return at once."

I had missed seeing my father one last time by only three weeks, I thought to myself, as I began to pack for the long journey home. I was stunned by his passing. How could he have left me before I had a chance to say good-bye? I thought to myself. I felt weak and despondent. I had not had a chance to reconcile with him, and I knew that, once the initial shock wore off, this would weigh heavily on my conscience.

Out of respect, I chose to wear my black kimono with the family crest that Grandmother had embroidered. A few years back, I had had the crest removed and sewn to a newer kimono, as I had outgrown the original several years before.

It was difficult to think what I should bring. I rolled up my *yukata* and wrapped an extra pair of sandals in cloth. I bundled the mask my father had last sent me and slid the shard of plum wood into my sash. With each additional movement, I began to feel increasingly nauseated and faint.

"Are you all right?" Noboru asked, concerned.

"Yes, yes," I muttered and tried to show I was fine.

"I should travel with you to ensure that you are all right. The journey will be long and the funeral difficult."

"It is very kind of you, but unnecessary. After all, I will need you to keep abreast of our classes so that you can assist me when I return."

"Are you sure?" he asked, and I knew that he was sincere by the way he lightly touched my shoulder and went to lift my bag.

"Of course," I told him. "Don't be foolish. Both of us can't fall behind in our work."

He smiled faintly. "Let me at least accompany you to the station," he insisted as he went to pick up another of my satchels and my small *furoshiki*.

Once outside Ariyoshi's gate, we piled into a rickshaw and made our way to the station.

"Will you inform the administration that I had a personal affair to attend to?" I asked him as we rode through the bustling streets.

"Of course, my dear friend," he assured me. "I will speak to our professors the first thing tomorrow."

He looked at me with great affection that afternoon. I know he found my father's death difficult to grasp, as he knew that the relationship between my father and me had been strained. Still, he tried to be comforting and had the decency to approach the subject delicately.

"I've never experienced a death in the family, Kiyoki, but I suppose there is little I can say to help you at this time."

I looked at him and tried to smile.

"But the fact that your father sent you that mask," he said, pointing to my *furoshiki*, "must mean something."

"It is too late," I said, looking away from him and into the direction of the approaching station. "I didn't return early enough to reconcile with him. I'm sure he died angry with me."

"You mustn't feel guilty, my friend," he tried to assure me. "You are not to blame."

I looked at him and tried again to smile faintly. He knew my story, yet how could he know the intensity of my pain? For so many years I had struggled to understand my father. He had left me with our relationship remaining a puzzle still waiting to be solved.

So much was my fault, and I would be foolish and self-deluding to deny it. My mother had died because of me, and perhaps my father's grief at my latest decision had caused his early demise. Just as my father had felt responsible for his parents' death, I now felt responsible for my own.

"Let me get your ticket while you go wait on the platform," he begged of me. I did not want to be among the crowds, so I agreed only after insisting that I pay my own passage.

The train rolled into the station, the locomotive expelled its wind tunnel of steam, and Noboru handed me the ticket.

"Take care of yourself, dear friend, and I will see you when you return," he shouted over the noise. He gave me a small push to encourage me to board.

I found a seat next to the glass, so that I could see him as the train pulled out of the station. I arranged my carrying case underneath the seat, placed the *furoshiki* with my father's mask and my *o-bento* close to my side, and tried to maintain a brave front as I waved good-bye to him. It seems, as I look back on it now, that I had taken greater pains to appease my worried friend than I had with my own tragic father.

The journey home went quickly. I slept deeply, and when I awakened, I thought briefly that perhaps my father's death had only been a dream.

The slowing of the train's engines had stirred me. I sat up in my seat and removed the condensation from the interior window with a sweep of my sleeve. Outside, the locomotive was just beginning to pass into the valley. The mountains that surrounded Kyoto were covered in snow, and the pine trees were heavy with frost. I had not realized how much I missed the landscape of my youth.

The train began its descent into the station and the other pas-

sengers and I began to assemble our bags. There would be no one
to greet me on the platform and, once again, I was struck with
an aching sense of loneliness and regret.

I discovered an abundance of rickshaws and drivers waiting
outside the station gates and thus had not the least bit of trouble
finding someone to take me home to Daigo.

Once inside the rickshaw, I was immediately struck by the
crispness of the air. It was a remarkable contrast to the foul smells
of Tokyo. The delectable scent of sweet potato roasting was familiar and comforting. I turned my head from side to side as we
rushed through the streets and small markets and reveled at the
sight of the tiled roofs covered with drifts of snow.

"Where in Daigo are you going, exactly?" the rickshaw driver
called back through panted breaths. Steam seemed to be rising
from his back and billowing from his mouth.

"Before Sanpo-in, the second left after the grave of the poet
Ono-no Komachi."

"Near the mountain?" he asked as he climbed the first of many
steep hills.

"Exactly," I answered, impressed. And at the mere mention
of the mountain, I found myself anxious to get back home.

As we approached Daigo, I could see my house in the distance.
The carved pigeons perched on our roof gables were encased in
ice and the thatched roof sagged from the weight of the snow.
Smoke was noticeably missing from the chimney, a sure sign that
no life stirred within. As we finally pulled up to the door, it struck
me with great force, that he—my father, my last living link with
my family—had truly gone.

I paid the rickshaw driver and made my way to the house.
The gate had been left unlatched, and the garden had become an

overgrown mass of dried tumbleweed covered in ice. Father never had much interest in gardening, I thought to myself, and nearly smiled, remembering how it was I, the only child, who took on the responsibility of the familial chores.

I pushed open the door and entered the *genkan*. The dirt floor had recently been swept clean, and a pair of Father's slippers rested neatly at the door.

I set down my satchels and clutched my arms to keep warm. I knew that I had to start a fire in the braziers and warm the *kotatsu*, for evening would come early.

Around me, things appeared superficially the same as when I left. The lower tatami rooms had been kept just as I remembered; the kitchen still smelled of rice gruel and vinegar. But how cold it was! I went to the barrel by the stove, shoveled some charcoal, and refilled the braziers. Once I lit the braziers, the whole house crackled and warmed in the glow of their bright red light.

Where was Father? I thought to myself as I turned around in a small circle, the bottom of my kimono swelling like a small bell. Where now did he lie?

I discovered my father's body in the tatami room where our family altar remained. But the room had changed. It no longer glowed crimson from the warm halo of the hibachis. It no longer smelled of incense. It had been transformed.

The cold greeted me first. An icy gust blew my sleeves backward as I slid open the first interior doors. Inside, I could see clear into the garden. The thin shoji that led to the *engawa* had been thrust open, and Father lay in the center of the tatami, perfectly preserved. Frost had encased his limbs in a shiny glaze of crystal. Icicles hung from the house's outside beams.

He lay there like a column, his kimono draping his stiffened form. His bluish pallor, his sharp, ax-cut chin. Like a warrior from a glaciered land, he slept oblivious to the cold. I stood there, frightened and weak. The prodigal son whose guilt and pride mingled so deep that he stood paralyzed, unable to bow down to his knees.

I must be honest when I tell you that part of me wanted to rush up and kneel by Father's side and beg for forgiveness. And part of me wanted to scream so loud that the heat of my breath would melt him back from death. But in the end, I did neither. Only when the priest arrived the following morning would I have enough courage to go to him. Then I would finally be able to gaze upon his masklike face and hold him tightly to my side.

That night I slept in my father's old room for the first time since I was five. The room was on the second floor, adjacent to his studio. I entered cautiously, as I felt his presence hovering over me from behind.

Immediately I found myself looking for things that were familiar, hoping they might comfort me in my loneliness, hoping they might give me some inner peace. The mirror and low table where he dressed himself each day still remained, as did his futon, which was still stretched out on the tatami floor. I opened the inner closet and removed my childhood futon and unrolled it next to his. Where was Mother's wedding coverlet? I wondered as I shivered for a blanket.

I walked downstairs to the old *tansu* chest in the hall and discovered it there. The coverlet lay carefully folded, most probably by Grandmother after Mother's death. Beside it were the few mementos of my mother's brief life: a box of her combs, her wedding kimono, and her *tsuno-kakushi*, the ceremonial horn hider she wore at her wedding. How it must have pained Grandmother occasionally to come across these precious articles. They appeared still and lifeless in the old chest, but I imagined how they must have appeared to Grandmother, who had seen Mother wear them.

How Father too must have felt to know they were there. Those tokens of his wife. His beloved. How empty they must have felt in his hands when he brought them close to his face to inhale their faint fragrance when he closed his eyes and envisioned her dressed in splendor on their wedding day.

I shook the wedding coverlet loose and inhaled its stale perfume. The wooden chest had left it smelling like the forest. How heavy the silk was! I thought as I dragged it upstairs. And that evening I slept wrapped in the memory of both my parents. Warm in a way I had never felt, even though I had lived here for years. That night I slept under the blanket of silken cranes. Cocooned in red silk and protected by white birds, I dreamed that I was loved by them both.

The clean-shaven head of the priest appeared at the gate of our empty house the following day. He was silent as I slid open the outer shoji, his gaze firmly rooted to the ground.

Clad in white robes, fastened by a silk-corded girdle and overlaid by a black jacket, a *kesa* hanging over his left shoulder and around his waist, wearing a straw hat and straw sandals, the priest had arrived to offer the Buddhist rites to my father.

He followed me through the narrow halls of our home, the lantern illuminating the rice-paper walls. The heat of our breath formed clouds around our faces. I heard the shuffle of the priest's sandals echoing behind me; I heard his prayer beads rattling between his pious hands.

The lantern glowed like a warm orange ball of fire, and I held it far from my body as we scurried to the ice-cold tatami room where my father's remains lay.

The morning light of the garden had illuminated the room that I had gazed into briefly the night before, but now I could see Father all the more clearly. It had been nearly six months since I left for Tokyo, yet now he seemed wholly unlike the man I left that day at the threshold. He seemed almost regal, stretched out on the wooden platform. As if finally there was no longer any pain.

The priest and I hovered over the silver-haired head of my father, his eyelids smooth in sleep; his skin, now an even deeper shade of blue, betrayed a thin fan of wrinkles, its surface spotted with tiny brown moons. Once again I was reminded of the brittle bark of a century-old cherry tree.

Stroking a bell and withdrawing a long silver razor, the priest commenced the Buddhist Rites of the Dead.

The razor slid over Father's scalp, the wisps of hair falling languidly over his ears and onto the straw-mat floor. White curls, like blond strips of cypress.

I shuddered. Outside, the leaves in the garden tumbled in the night air, their dried surfaces rising like floating paper cranes temporarily suspended by the wind.

The priest continued to recite the scriptures and punctuate his long chants with the stroking of his bell until the moon filled the room with its great white light.

"We must now wash the body," he said as he finally set down his bell. The priest revealed his long, slender arms from the billows of his generous white robe, and reached over the corpse of my father.

"We will clean each of his limbs," he whispered quietly before excusing himself to our kitchen. When he returned, he carried with him a bowl of steaming water and a broad swatch of cloth.

Following the priest's instructions, I assisted in the washing of my father's shrunken body. Lifting each of his limbs reminded me of the weightlessness that one finds among dying trees. His gray, ashen skin fell away from his bones like the papery parchment of silver birch bark.

I can still envision myself taking the cotton cloth and cleaning between each of his once skilled fingers, respectfully paying close attention to his hands. I washed his palms as carefully as I would have an expiring emperor. I smoothed the cloth over the flesh of each palm. There was the initial resistance of death. But in the end, he surrendered himself to my care. And I accepted my duty as his only son. It was a moment that could have existed only with one of us gone. I wished so hard that he would open his eyes and see that I had come home to be beside him. But his eyes remained forever closed and his body stiff as stone. Yet in the end my hands finally rested over his. Mine pink and flushed, his the palest shade of blue.

The hands of the mask carver were entwined, if only briefly, finally, with those of his son.

That night I held my father for the first and last time. I cradled his tiny shaved head in the basket of my arms, and grazed my cheek over his. After the priest maneuvered the cotton shroud over his shrunken form, I released my father into the simple wooden coffin whose only adornment was the faintly carved insignia of our ancient family crest. It was a scene that I knew had occurred within the walls of this room several times before. And I imagined it was a scene that Father had done too many times for his liking. Beginning with the day he buried his master Tamashii in the forest. But this evening was the first to which I bore witness. And I did it alone.

I remained there with Father until the morning. I listened as the priest continued to drone the Scriptures, and I watched over my father as his coffin lay illuminated by the light of several small white candles. The incense floated through the room, and for the first time in my memory, the scent of cypress no longer clung to Father's hands.

I wondered where his soul now mingled and with whom. And I hoped that he was finally returned to the company of his parents, his master, and his beloved wife, my mother, and that their eternity would be spent together in a place without sadness or pain.

But for now I was the one who was left alone in this lonely world of guilt and sorrow. I would need to prepare myself for the approaching burial. The guests would soon arrive, the actors secretly whispering that it was I who had caused my father's— their revered mask carver's—sad and untimely death.

THIRTY

They arrived in their kimonos, having memorized the proper masks of mourning. They followed me as I led the march behind the litter carrying my father to the cemetery. The priest continued to recite the Scriptures as the rest of us walked silently through the streets of Daigo.

Behind me, a stream of actors, wearing the traditional white mourning kimonos of the theater, trailed me like a long train of pale satin. Their faces, revealed to the autumn sunlight, shone like faces for the first time unmasked. Their jowls fell forward freely, like aging Buddhas, their eyelids weighed like the thick hoods of forest toads. The sounds of their sandals echoed my own. Slow and heavy. And the funeral procession moved on.

Iwasaki led the actors in their final walk of respect for my father. From behind, I heard his soft moans. His red ankles were swollen underneath the hem of his robe, his knees barely able to support his aging form.

Upon arrival at the gates of the temple, the body was taken by the novices of the temple and prepared for cremation. One hour later my father was returned to me, and I dutifully returned him to the earth.

When I laid down the ceremonial urn next to Father's inscribed tablet, I knelt beside the grave of both my parents. And there, with the rock dust coarse and painful under my knees, I withdrew the shard of plum wood from my sash and buried it beside Father. Deep in the brown-gray earth. His lifelong pain finally to perish. To be carried by either of us no more.

When I stood up, I turned to my mother's grave and wiped her tablet clean with my handkerchief. My grandparents' tablets stood neatly behind. And it occurred to me that my entire family lay here within my gaze, their Buddhist names articulated in broad strokes of calligraphy, their wooden grave markers shaded by a sweeping branch of a pine.

They had all left me behind. I stood there alone, wondering who would eventually stand beside my grave and bury me in a tall bronze urn. Who would wipe my tablet clean?

I was now the sole bearer of the Yamamoto name. There was no one left to guide me, as Grandmother had done, and no one to feel I had left behind, as I had with Father. In one breath, I could extend my arms and declare, "I am free!" and, in another, I could fall to my knees and see what remained of my family, a stretch of graves shaded by the long green needles of a pine.

The only thing that comforted me at that moment was that Father was finally returned to the side of his beloved. Where he could sleep for an eternity beside her. Where a man who lived his life more spirit than man could finally be released.

And with a heavy heart and a deep sense of loneliness, I left our family grave site, where my entire family would now rest for an eternity. Where they would forever sleep at the base of a bending pine.

The actors and their wives followed me home. It was the custom for me to invite them inside, as they had come to pay their respects to my father by offering money or food in his honor. Many came and knelt with their Buddhist prayer beads, silently praying for Father's safe journey to the next world. Each actor who arrived seemed more ancient than the next. I knelt in the center of the most central tatami room and received their offerings with strained politeness and a few formal replies.

After several hours of sitting, I rose to offer some of the guests a pot of tea. There, within the confines of our modest kitchen, I received their many artfully phrased insults. Their faces could not disguise their obvious disdain for me.

"It is a shame that your father took his craft with him to his grave," one of the actors said to me, his thick voice rising from a cup of steaming tea.

"Ah, so, young man, you are at the Tokyo School of Fine Arts. Do you do mask carving there?" the creaking voice of an actor's wife pressed.

Their words floated through the home like carving blades, but I did not answer them. I refused to make myself vulnerable, to make myself the scapegoat for their disappointment.

I knew I had left many things with my father unresolved, and I regretted it. But these were issues between him and me. I refused to feel guilty for my dreams.

So I remained steadfast in my mind. I would honor the customary fifty days of mourning before returning to Tokyo.

There was much to do before I could return to Tokyo. I had to clear the house and decide either to sell it or board it up until I could return.

I had yet to enter my father's studio. I knew it would be extremely difficult to see the place where he spent the majority of his time, the place where he created and dared to unleash his spirit, day after day.

The steep, narrow flight of stairs that led to his sacred space had always intimidated me. I had never wanted to interfere with his process of creation. I was the disappointing child born from a split and weary womb. There, in contrast, he was surrounded by loyal children of his own creation, their wooden faces resting lovingly in his palms.

When I entered the room, I knew I would discover that I had not been left an orphan. And as I expected, when I finally did enter the sanctuary of Father's small studio, it was true; I had not been left alone. Father had left me over a dozen brothers and sisters, created by his own hand.

The masks rested on the shelves. Some were completely finished and others barely started.

Those uncompleted masks were the most disturbing to me, their faces like tiny embryos whose features were only half formed. They slept there, lonely and somewhat pathetic, born from a god who could no longer complete their missing features. And I, the traitor to their destiny, felt powerless to help them.

I looked around the room for a long time before I held one. I recognized each mask, knew which character each one was intended to become. Despite our separation, my father's world was still deeply rooted within me.

I recognized the slightly downturned mouth and diamond-shaped eyes of Yase-Otoko, the mask worn by the ghost of Lord Fukakusa in *Kayoi Komachi*. I could see the hours of work it had taken my father to smooth the planes of its forehead, carve out the hollowed pockets of flesh over and beneath the eye sockets, and create the sunken cavities beneath its cheeks.

I could see the aggression with which the old man must have attacked the wood when he began carving Aka-Hannya, the mask intended for the Snake Spirit in *Dojoji*. He had nearly completed this mask, having plowed with great power into the soft block of cypress wood and dug out the furrowed brow, the bulging eyes, and the enormous gaping mouth. He had masterfully whittled the demon's large fangs and broad-surfaced teeth. He had smoothed out the sharpness of the chin and carved out the large cavernous ears. He had not begun the horns, however. He always saved that for last.

But the masks that were the most haunting, and which terrified me the most, were those that my father had barely touched.

From the mask that had only a mouth, I heard only screams. From the one that had only a broad, flat nose and the pierced holes meant for nostrils, I heard muffled breathing. But the most disturbing of all was the one that had only eyes.

I believed that these eyes were intended for another Ishi-O-Jo mask. They were the eyes of an old spirit, the wizened, thinly incised eyes looking both downward and within at the same time. But because Father had already given one of these masks to the theater, I was puzzled why he would have begun another version. As the theater would have no need for another, I thought perhaps Father had intended it for me. The eyes burned with intensity as they met my gaze, the rest of the face empty and sad in its incompleteness.

I packed up the collection of Father's masks in its entirety with the exception of that one. That mask, the Ishi-O-Jo mask, I carried down to the room where I was sleeping and laid it next to the Semimaru mask he had sent to me in Tokyo.

The Semimaru mask looked rather grave as it lay on the tatami. I thought of how Father had always told me it was cruel to deny a mask its true destiny on stage. For that was where the spirit, infused by the carver, was finally liberated. As I held the mask up to the light, it occurred to me that, in honor of my father and his lifework, I should give my father's last masterpiece to the theater where it could live and breathe. Where its sadness, its pain, and its resignation could finally be released. To be played out on the stage. To appease the spirit of the troubled dead as only a Noh mask truly can.

I would, however, keep the incomplete mask for myself. To remind me of him. Of our relationship, never reconciled and never completed. But also of my destiny, for now deferred. This mask was the only mask that I could not shake from my conscience. And it would be only this mask that I would take with me back to Tokyo.

THIRTY-ONE

I was sitting in the kitchen during my seventeenth day of mourning, having prepared myself a bowl of miso soup with boiled cabbage and some pickled radishes for my rice. The wind was howling and the wind chimes were rattling in song.

I had forgotten how cold Kyoto could be in the winter. I ate my breakfast with the charcoal brazier underneath the low lacquer table, the futon over my shoulders, and remembered how I had eaten here with my father in the same unnerving silence.

I looked into the basin of my soup bowl and hoped to see my mother emerging like a lotus flower from the dark swamp of liquid. When she failed to appear, I forced myself to remember her visage. I wanted to see her magnificent face, translucent as gossamer, looking at me. I needed to see her omniscient eyes, black as burned ginkgo nuts, comforting me in my struggle and beseeching me to find my way.

The day before, I had visited Iwasaki at the theater. Shrouded in swatches of raw silk, I carried the Semimaru mask that Father had sent me close to my chest.

"I would like to give this to the theater in honor of my father," I told him as I bowed my head to the floor and pushed the covered mask in his direction.

He unwrapped my offering and frowned.

"Why do you give away something that is a reminder of your

father and his craft?" he questioned, his voice betraying his disappointment in me.

"Father always taught me that masks belong to the stage. To the theater," I said softly. "I am sure that Father would have wanted it there."

And then in the painful silence between us, I added, "I believe Father wanted his masks to be his legacy."

"No, Yamamoto Kiyoki-san, I believe he wished *you* to be his legacy." I looked away from him, to the corner where the stretch of stage began.

This was the same room where I had first met Iwasaki and the other actors when I traveled with Father years earlier, when he came to offer his masks to the theater.

"Go," he told me, before I could answer in my defense. "Leave me this mask," he said, and his voice was cold.

"Return to your home and your own reflection," the great patriarch said. He did not lift his eyes in my direction. He did not rise to see me out, nor did he offer me a bow.

I did rise and, out of respect for him, my father's mask, and the stage that supported the feet of my ancestors, I bowed deeply. I bowed to a place I believed I would never return to again.

In my heart, I also knew it was time to leave my childhood home. To finally put to rest my ghosts and my memories.

The following morning I rose invigorated and refreshed. I folded the futons and cleaned the braziers. I wiped the lacquerware with a damp, soft cloth. I swept away the frozen leaves in the garden and emptied the *tansu* chest of its years of stored memories.

Grandmother had carefully placed tiny bundles of chrysanthemum leaves tied in miniature sachets of white gauze. She had hoped to ward off insects and tiny moths from feeding on the heavy silk brocade. As I went to withdraw my beloved mother's wedding dress, one of the sachets came undone. I stood there with the cloth close to my cheek and marveled as a flurry of dried leaves, stored away so long ago by Grandmother, floated through the air and then fell to my feet. The pale green leaves, the color of dried sage, crackled beneath my sandals as I continued to withdraw my mother's heirlooms from the shelves of the deep *tansu* chest. I removed her box of gilded combs, the *tsuno-kakushi*, the ceremonial wig, and the red petticoats.

I remembered that Mother's fan remained in the *butsudan*, placed there by Grandmother so many years before. I had not visited the family altar since I returned home, but I wished to include the fan with a few other treasured articles I would carry with me when I returned to Tokyo.

The main tatami room seemed so empty, this room where Father's corpse had lain only just a few days before, this room where the family *butsudan* was enshrined. On many occasions during my time in Tokyo, I had wondered what would become of the family altar, now that I had abandoned my responsibilities to the household. I had expected my father to ignore the old shrine, as he did most of the domestic chores that did not affect his carving. It was not his nature to remember things outside of the world of Noh. But when I walked and opened the heavy black doors of the shrine, I did not find the altar in a state of disrepair as I had always imagined. To the contrary, Father had painstakingly maintained it.

Mother's wedding fan had been spread out and leaned like a silver wing on a pyramid of Asian pears. Still golden. Perfectly round and only now beginning to show the first signs of blemishing. Father must have picked them the week before he died. Pale candle wax, its drippings permanently dried in the shape of tiny tears, formed at the base of three short, stubby tapers. Yellow chrysanthemum flowers, their many slender petals turning brown on the edges, stood tall in the hollow-bamboo vase. An inch of water remained.

Before me, carefully placed on the shining altar, were all of those tiny fragments of my family's past. I could not stop myself from trembling.

With reverent hands extended, I picked up Mother's fan. I opened the fragile spine and revealed the gilded sides, one silver, the other gold. The sun and the moon in their entirety. How Mother must have looked that day as her face peeked demurely from above the pleated folds. I carefully folded the fan and delicately set it down beside me.

I noticed the familiar sight of the program from Grandfather's last performance. Grandmother had placed that there years before. Now the paper was brittle and had turned a deep shade of ochre.

I read the scrolled calligraphy and inhaled the musty smell of dried parchment. I moved my right hand to turn the page and felt something slide underneath my fingers. Out from the inner fold, another program, bright white in contrast, fell to the floor. I reached down to read it: "November 14, 1895, the twenty-ninth year of our most revered emperor's reign. The Kanze troupe of Noh is most honored to perform Kanze Kojiro Nobumitsu's masterful play, *Dojoji* . . . "

There could be no other reason why the two programs had been placed together. The symmetry was obvious and so beautiful. Father must have known that it would be the last performance he would ever attend at the Noh theater, and when it was over, he had brought the program home and placed it inside the one that had belonged to Grandfather.

I immediately could envision him sitting in one of the front pews. I saw him staring up into the stage and containing his pride upon seeing one of his Hannya masks freed on the stage. And with all my heart I hoped that he felt joy that night. That when he went to sleep he did not think of me. That he did not allow himself to reflect that his connection with the theater would end with him.

It was almost impossible for me to imagine Father kneeling beside the *butsudan*. I closed my eyes and tried to picture him in prayer, a position of reverence. My head battled with the memories contained in my heart, to visualize him in a way I could never see him before, without the company of a mask.

I had stared into his face, white with death, as the priest chanted his rites. I had not seen any signs of sadness. No wrinkles of regret. Underneath the flesh, all that had once been contained, all that had been carefully restrained, had already left.

Life is fleeting. Only Noh and wood are eternal.

And as I knelt in front of our family altar, I truly saw my father for the first time. I finally saw his tragedy. For he had buried his parents, his master, his beloved, and the dreams he held for his son.

"Father," I said aloud, "if only it were true that you loved only the wood."

THIRTY-TWO

As I spent the next few days packing up the contents of the house, it was evident that my family owned few things of substantial value. Since my childhood, I had realized that the bulk of my family's stature was in our name rather than any material wealth. Over a span of many generations and fruitful marital alliances, we had accumulated a modest amount of land, furniture, and lacquerware. But, as Father's masks could no longer be sold for their true worth due to Noh's decline, the gold and currency we once had in plenty had dwindled from our household.

I knew it was wrong to sell to outsiders any of the masks that were carved by my father's hand. Instead, I decided to donate the few that remained to the theater. In the evening, I bundled them in a large, broad *furoshiki* and dropped them at the base of the stage. I left no note and no explanation. In the honor of my father, I knew the masks would speak for themselves.

You must believe me, it was not that I searched our house looking for something to fund my painting aspirations. I came across my father's collection of ancient masks almost by accident. I had returned to his studio to sweep out the last curls of cypress and wipe the shelves clean. The day before, I had packed away what I believed to be all of his carving tools when I discovered that Father had placed my last two letters inside a small pine box with his most precious belongings: his chisels and his jars of dried pigment. They lay there carefully folded and tied in twine. The empty words from a son who returned too late to say good-bye.

But now I was saying farewell to the man whose house I shared and whose craft I could not. It occurred to me, as I finished sweeping the last corners of the room, that I had forgotten the small storage compartment adjacent to the door. I knelt down and crawled into the tiny storage space, needing no candle or lantern to find the large cinnabar chest that lay inside. I could feel the intricately carved cover with my palms and the straight corners with my fingertips. Carefully and with effort, I managed to drag the carved container into the center of the room and remove the lid.

There, deep in the hollow of the chest, Father's coveted collection of ancient masks was revealed to me. They were priceless, having been carved by the great masters who had preceded him centuries ago.

The carved seal on the inside of each mask identified the carver. I had seen him refer to these masks on occasion. Sometimes for a reference to a mask he was carving, sometimes for just a brief glance.

He had a Ko-Beshimi mask by Yukan, a Yase-Otoko mask by Tosui, a Warai-Jo mask by Sankobo, a Sanko-Jo mask by Mitsunaga, a Yoroboshi mask by Jiunin, an Okina mask by Mitsunaga, a Kuro-Hige mask by Zekan, a Shintai mask by Mitsuteru, a Shiwa-Jo by Fukurai, a Ko-Omote mask by Tatsuemon, and a Ko-Jo mask by Mitsuzane.

He had inherited several of these masks from my grandfather, who had inherited them from his father, who had received them from his father. They had been in the family for over three hundred years. The oldest mask in the collection was the Ko-Omote, carved in the early fifteenth century by Tatsuemon.

I picked up Ko-Omote and imagined that this was what my

mother had looked like as a young girl. I caressed the rounded cheeks, traced the half-parted lips, and rubbed the delicate teeth, blackened with the resin of burned eggplant. To blend into the shadows. To be unseen.

I slipped the mask's silk cord over my fingers and gently rocked it back and forth, revealing the mask's magic. When I held her upright, her mouth curled upward into a demure smile. Then within seconds, when I tilted her downward, she succumbed to a deep sadness in which her eyes drooped and her mouth metamorphosed. She looked as though she was about to cry.

Once I overheard my father speaking with an actor who had expressed an interest in studying carving. He had asked my father if Ko-Omote was the simplest mask to carve because it appeared to be so plain.

"No," my father said, his voice revealing his annoyance. "It is probably the most difficult. The planes must be done perfectly. They must be as smooth as a newborn's flesh, and their roundness must be so subtle that the eye cannot discern where they plateau. The beauty of the Ko-Omote mask is that she is so young, so feminine, and so unmarred by the evils of the world. Thus the whiteness of her color and the smoothness of her face are the perfect canvas for shadows to play—to dance on her brow and to mysteriously change her laughter into cries."

My father's explanation silenced the young actor. Humbled by my father's knowledge, he never asked him about carving again.

I looked at Ko-Omote once more before returning her to her silk pouch. I placed her back in the cinnabar box with the others and closed the lid. These were what my father had called retired masks, masks whose spirits had been released over a span of hundreds of years. And although they had grown even more beautiful, aging with a lustrous, inimitable patina, they had become treasures rather than viable pieces for the stage. "Therefore," he had once confided to me, "one should not feel guilty for keeping them safe here in this box."

"Someday these will be yours," he had said in one of those rare moments between us that I could virtually count. Now I looked at this box of treasures and realized that these were the most valuable piece of my inheritance.

I sat there in my father's studio for what seemed like hours. The idea first crept into my mind like a small spider that slowly begins to weave an elaborate web. I could not stop thinking of the freedom these masks could afford me.

Unlike my father's masks, these masks could bring me a large sum of gold. I knew that they were worthy of a collector's eye and I had heard that Westerners were buying our antique treasures at unheard-of prices. It struck me as an exchange. I could learn their artistic traditions and, in return, they could learn from mine.

Indeed I was thinking with the complete selfishness that only the very young can truly have. I was not concerned with bitterness or regret or the complexities of conscience. I could not shake from my mind the idea of all the money these masks could bring! My self-absorption shames me now. My father's ashes had barely been swept from the funeral pyre and I was planning to sell something my family had treasured for generations.

I tried to ease my mind by convincing myself of the sacrifices I had already made by giving the last mask my father carved and the remaining ones I discovered to Iwasaki-san. But these! No one knew of these masks, and with the money from the masks and the selling of the house, I could realize my dream. I could take control of my destiny.

The idea had been brewing inside me since I first discovered that I would not receive the education I hoped for in Tokyo. If I could only travel to France. There I would be able to study with a great master, just as Kuroda Seiki had done. There I would have the artistic freedom that I was denied in Tokyo. I could forget about learning the coloring techniques of the Tosa and Korin schools and, instead, focus on the techniques of the great Renaissance masters and the modern theories of the Impressionists. There I would be able to take advantage of the vast museum collections and the work displayed in the salons.

The excitement of my decision was overwhelming. I needed to open a shoji to let the crisp mountain air into the room.

How I wished that Mother or Grandmother were alive. Surely they would have understood my conflict. Noboru too. How I wished he could be here with me to ease my conscience, assuage my guilt, and share in my excitement. I wanted to pack my bags and rush back to Tokyo to be with him. To confide in him my plans. Would he join me if I went to Paris? Could we together realize our dreams and learn to paint from a true European master? All of this excitement rushed through my veins. But I had to control my urges; I still had almost three weeks left in the mourning period, and I had to find a buyer for both the mask collection and the house.

I promptly decided that the following morning I would contact someone outside the immediate circle of the theater to assist me in making the appropriate contacts. But I was back in Kyoto, and, once again, could not escape the circle into which I was born.

Mitsutani Hiroyuki met me at the tea shop near Yamamoto Dori. I had not spoken with him at the funeral, and we greeted each other with informal nods.

Mitsutani was the son of my mother's cousin who had married an actor within the Kanze family. We were bound by shared blood from our mothers' side and by the bond of Noh. He had lost both of his parents several years before and had carried on the family tradition of acting, even though there had hardly been much of a following since the beginning of the Meiji era. He was far lower in rank than Iwasaki or any of the other elders of the theater, but still I made him swear that he would not utter a word of my plans to a soul.

In between the sips of tea, I informed him of my intentions. He was the closest family member I had, and I wished to see if he was interested in purchasing the masks.

"I know their value, Kiyoki, but I do not have that kind of money now. Unfortunately, few people in the theater do anymore."

I nodded my head, as I understood how the situation had been even when my grandfather was still alive.

"However," he added, "there is a man named Shimakawa who deals with wealthy foreigners from the West. I have heard that they pay well for anything old and valuable from Japan."

He promised to inquire about the value of my collection with Shimakawa and we agreed to meet later that week.

In the meantime, I negotiated with the neighbors next door about purchasing the house and a portion of the land.

The several stacks of pine boxes displayed just how sizable my mother's dowry had truly been. Through their union, my father had gained a house, a household of furniture, lacquer, ceramics, several acres of farmable land, and a secure position in the Noh circle. In return, my mother had gained a husband.

I knew that I would not be able to keep all of these mementos. Aside from Mother's wedding kimono, coverlet, and fan, and father's chisels, I would have to sell the remaining objects along with the house. It pained me to know that these objects would soon belong to another. These were the priceless pieces of their dowries, now dusty with age and neglect. They were needy, as I had been. Longing for a touch, aching for words of appreciation. I wiped away the soot and saw my reflection. I remembered the story of how my mother had first laid eyes on Father, how she avoided his stare by gazing into the top of the lacquer table. How she finally saw him in the mask he had carved.

The few of mother's treasures that did not find their way into pine boxes rested neatly in several bamboo baskets. The smooth blond weave contained all of the objects that for so long had made her tangible to me. But now, with the strength of her spirit infused in my bones, I knew that I no longer had to physically keep these objects to carry her. When I was lost in my drawings, splattered in ink, and damp with paint, she was with me stronger than ever before.

I knew that Mother would gladly have given all of her treasures away had it allowed her spirit to exist freely. To draw more than the belly of the mountain. I felt her protective spirit breathing over my shoulder and whispering to me to go, to travel the seas in order to pursue my dreams. I heard Grandmother's deep sigh and saw the drooping of her lids, the elegant, resigned nodding of her head in the swaying of the pines. I could no longer linger within the constraining walls of the school in Tokyo. I knew that I must travel the waters that separated me from the art I wished to pursue. I must find myself and my talent in France. This was the path that I chose for myself, and I was certain that my mother would have encouraged me to do what was necessary to achieve it.

I convinced myself of this. So when our neighbor Otama came with sixty large silk purses brimming with gold coins in return for the house and all but three acres of our land, and when Shimakawa arrived with his leather-brown face and large-toothed smile, informing me of the foreign buyer's interest in my father's collection, I didn't feel so guilty.

But in the end the guilt still came. Creeping and pervasive.

"I must examine the masks, Yamamoto-san," he said, his yellow teeth glistening in the sun.

I went into Father's studio and brought down the heavy cinnabar trunk. I removed the top and removed the masks from their silk pouches. Shimakawa's face grew serious, and his nose trembled from the dust. In profile, he reminded me of a Sharaku woodblock print. He moved his face along the horizontal path in which the masks quietly lay. He seemed to sniff as he picked each one up in his hands. He grunted. After several minutes he raised his head to me and said, "I probably shouldn't tell you this, Yamamoto-san, but I believe this is the finest collection of masks that I have ever seen."

He paused before continuing.

"The buyer has informed me I can offer you up to seventeen purses of gold, if the collection is of the finest quality. But as you have just suffered a death, perhaps I should urge you to reconsider. This is an outstanding group of masks, and even though I will make money from its sale, I must be honest with you and tell you that it would be a shame for it to leave Japan."

His frankness surprised me.

"The Mitsuzane mask is particularly rare," he continued. "I actually believe it was carved by one of his early apprentices, a carver by the name of Tamashii. Legend has it he carved for only two years under the great master Mitsuzane before vanishing. The seal is different." Shimakawa pointed to the character *mē* in the signature *Demē-Mitsuzane*.

I was unsure whether the mask had belonged originally to Grandfather or whether Father had brought it with him on that day when he arrived at Grandfather's door. But I confirmed Shimakawa's suspicion.

"It is indeed a Tamashii, and I expect its rarity should be

considered when you offer me a price," I said firmly. My boldness and lack of guilt surprised me, but all I could focus on was the money that would allow me to procure my ticket and sustain myself and my studies in France.

I did not want to think about the grave injustice I was doing in selling the masks to someone outside Japan. Even worse, I was betraying my family. My father. What I was about to do was as terrible as thrusting a sword into his belly. As I had done before I left for Tokyo. Had I twisted the dagger and scalded the blade before piercing him, what I was doing now could not have been more painful to him. To his memory.

But what else could I do?

I was alone in this world now. Yet how was my life that different from when he had lived? Then too I was alone. A small boy surrounded by ghosts. My father had never embraced me, I thought to myself, and my bitterness surprised me. He had never placed me above his carving, showered me with the love he lavished over his masks.

"I appreciate your advice, but I still wish to sell them," I told Shimakawa flatly. I cast my eyes down at him. He remained, crouching over the masks, his knees pressed to the floor. "I need twenty purses of gold, however."

"Twenty?" Shimakawa gasped. "I told you I can offer you no more than seventeen!"

"I am sorry, then," I said firmly, knowing that he would acquiesce in the end.

He paused for several moments, and I saw that his eyes rolled upward, as if he was envisioning an abacus and counting in midair.

"All right, then. Twenty purses of gold. I will visit you tomorrow and bring the gold then." He rose to his feet and extended a deep, reverent bow.

"Yes, then. Until tomorrow."

I stood there now alone in our lonely house, having nearly vanquished any remaining feelings of guilt.

I went outside to the *engawa* and dangled my feet over the ledge. The distant peak of Daigo reminded me how far I was from Noboru. I thought how comforting it would have been to have him here with me. I missed the sight of his small robust body, the smell of sweet red bean paste on his breath. I missed seeing his tiny alabaster hands, as white as polished jade, protruding from his sleeves. Perfect when they clutched a piece of charcoal. Elegant as they grasped the slender handle of a brush. Whisking through the air like emancipated doves. Flying and finally falling on the pedestal of my knee.

I closed my eyes and tried to bring his memory to these hills of my childhood. To mingle here with me and my ghosts. To stroke my empty body. To fill me with his laughter. With him.

THIRTY-THREE

It was difficult for me to imagine that, if I indeed traveled to Europe, Noboru might not be able to join me. His companionship in Tokyo had made me feel stronger and more whole. The boy I had been when I left Kyoto had returned a man. Noboru had awakened me. I had become aware of my desires and myself. He had enabled me to believe that I had the talent necessary to pursue a life of painting. He had listened to me as a friend, lover, or father might. With open ears and a kind heart. Giving me the space to dream, to confide, and to love.

If he was not at my side, I could still imagine him. I could call him up from the recesses of my mind, the ventricles of my heart. I carried him as I carried my ghosts. With the same reverence, but with the ecstasy that he lived and breathed. That he was truly my friend. That he lived and touched. That he spoke and laughed. That he looked deep into me, with black pupils trimmed in orange light.

When I spoke to him of my desire to paint, he listened with the intensity of a priest, his eyes looking intently into me. I recalled Noboru nodding and smiling, agreeing in the silence of my Tokyo room.

"You and I share the same dreams, Kiyoki," he replied, his gaze glimmering in the twilight. The sight of our two faces next to each other. White as stars. All of our hopes binding us to each other. His fingers running through my hair, as I had always imagined those of my father. The sensation somewhat unexpected.

Different. Yet welcomed. The embrace I had always yearned for. But now the smells were not of cypress and steely blade, but of turpentine and dark black ink. Swallowing me. Swallowing me whole.

The wind rustling through the naked trees awakened me. I felt the lonely sweep of darkness across the garden and pulled the cloth of my robe tighter across my form. I could not imagine going to France without Noboru, and yet I knew I would have only enough money for my own passage and my own expenses there.

I would not have enough to take him along. But now that I had found him, I knew I did not have the strength to leave him.

He had become my sustenance. I could not pack him away and sell him off as I had done with my memories and my ghosts.

February 3, 1896, marked my fiftieth day of mourning for my father and, as custom dictated, the last day of my official grieving period. Having negotiated the sale of our house and Father's mask collection, I prepared myself for my return to Tokyo.

I walked out of our gate for the last time and swept my hand over the sagging wooden fence. I bowed my head as I turned once more to gaze at the small carved pigeons on our roof's peak, and tilted my chin upward to meet the white crest of the mountain.

I had many more boxes and satchels with me than when I arrived almost two months before. Now, when I boarded the train at Kyoto station, I carried with me Mother's kimono, Father's chisels, and their wedding coverlet. And the mask with only eyes.

THIRTY-FOUR

Noboru met me at the station. I smiled when I saw him standing there. He was wearing his navy blue kimono, his hair black and oiled sleekly away from his face.

The two of us must have looked rather strange in our extremely somber robes. Noboru, so small that he could have been my son, helping me with my bags.

"You look tired, Kiyoki," he said tenderly, his voice floating over me, light and delicious like jasmine.

"It has been a long journey, but it is good to be back." The sound of the locomotive's engine retreated into the background.

"School has been quite dreadful without you," he sighed. "I imagine you will have a lot of catching up to do, but don't worry, I'll help you as best I can."

I smiled and relished the sight of him at my side.

"You must come back to my room for tea," I insisted as we loaded my satchels and *furoshiki* into one of two rickshaws that he had paid to wait for me.

I saw the eyes of Father's unfinished Ishi-O-Jo mask peeking through the cloth wrapping.

"San no ichi Higashi Terauchi cho!" Noboru called to the man who was to carry us. The driver's strong back arched in front of us as he began a quick trot into Tokyo's bustling streets. The wind rushed in our hair, and our kimonos billowed behind us.

* * *

Ariyoshi was out in the garden when we arrived.

"Hello, Yamamoto-sama!" he hollered to me as I withdrew my packages and handed the fare to the driver. "It has been a long time. I hope you had a pleasant journey. A good return to you!" As I walked closer, my mourning robe still cloaking my slender form, he whispered "My deepest regrets regarding your father." I nodded to him, acknowledging his sympathy with the slight bowing of my head.

Noboru held two of my *furoshiki* and nodded to Ariyoshi as we passed through the inner gate and into the inner hall.

"I'll make us some tea," I said to him as he placed the parcels on the dry tatami floor. Noboru always complimented my *o-cha*, saying that he could close his eyes and imagine the cherry blossoms of Tetsugaku no Michi, the splendid road speckled with *sakura*, the only memory he had of Kyoto. A vision not his own, but stolen from a page of one of his mother's books. An image captured by the hand of a woodblock artist. And one that he had tried to re-create time and time again with his own brush and paper.

I was happy that I had brought back some of my favorite tea leaves from Kyoto, since I had already exhausted my initial supply several months before. I prepared the water, making sure that it was hot, but had not quite reached a boil, and then poured it over the small mound of tea leaves piled in my ceramic teapot.

Noboru was sitting neatly on the tatami, his legs folded squarely beneath him. I brought the two cups of tea over to where he was seated.

"Noboru," I said, as I slid the tea over the table and positioned myself across from him.

"Yes." He was so happy to see me. His face was shining like

a winter moon. His lips curled over the rim of the steaming cup, moistening his skin with small crystal beads of condensation.

"I have something to tell you . . . Something quite serious."

His smile vanished.

"With the death of my father, I now have enough money to pursue my studies in France. But I cannot envision myself without you. It is a journey that we should make together." I paused, hoping to hear some sort of sign from him. But he remained silent. "I have decided to wait, Noboru," I said solemnly, "until you have enough money to accompany me." I tried to feign a smile. "Then we will go to France together!"

Noboru, however, did not react as I had anticipated.

He avoided my gaze. His eyes now focused on the steaming tea, the floating leaves, the greenness of the water; his lips curled. His chin remained flat to his chest.

"If you have the funds to make this journey, Kiyoki," he said softly, "I suggest you do it now and not wait for me."

"What?" I asked incredulously. "I would never do such a thing. I'll wait as long as it takes," I insisted.

"I will never have enough money, Kiyoki. I cannot imagine how you ever thought I would be able to gather such a sum of money."

His tone betrayed his embarrassment.

"I did not mean it like that," I said. "I will help you, I will do something to gather more funds." My voice rushed, revealing my desperation.

Noboru, however, continued to gaze at me, his demeanor resigned, his mind already leashed in practicality.

"Kiyoki, you know that my uncle subsidizes my studies here in Tokyo and that he could never afford to send me to Europe. Nor would I ever ask him. I am grateful for what I have here."

"And our dreams? Our aspirations to study abroad, to walk

through the Louvre and paint the Seine?" I was the one sounding betrayed. My words were rushing, and my face was flushed with confusion.

"Kiyoki, it is simple. You must go for both of us. I will stay here and finish my studies. Now that Kuroda Seiki has returned, perhaps I will have the opportunity to join his atelier. Do not worry for me. I will find a way to receive the education I need."

I stared at the beads of condensation forming on his upper lip and forehead. I wanted to offer him my handkerchief, but I knew it would make the moment even more awkward.

"This isn't how I imagined it would be," I whispered. I picked up my tea and discovered it was now cold.

In my mind, I wanted to tell him that I would miss him, to reiterate once more that I couldn't imagine what the journey and the experience would be like without him. But I chose to remain silent for the rest of the evening. I thought that if he could read my silence, he would understand more fully.

Later I would tell him once more that I would not make the journey without him.

"Kiyoki, you are acting ridiculously! This is your chance to receive the education and experience you need to be a great painter." His eyes were glowing in the twilight. "I feel very rude in admitting this to you, but Morita sensei confided to me that if all goes well next year, I will be promoted to the accelerated class. You, Kiyoki, are extremely talented. In my eyes, far more talented than I, but Saito sensei has an acute dislike for you that will hurt your chances of entering the classes that focus on the new style. If, however, you go to France, you will receive the training that you deserve. I see absolutely no question on the matter, especially since you now have the money to make the journey."

As much as his words pained me, I knew he was right. My

chances of being accepted to the accelerated program were slim at best.

Noboru assured me that he would help me make the necessary arrangements. My journey would require several months of preparation, and Noboru encouraged me to start working on my plans at once. First, I would have to begin studying the French language immediately. He promised he would look in the school library for a good text. But before everything, Noboru urged me to write a letter to Takada Ryuiichi, a student whom his uncle had tutored and who was presently studying French language and history in Paris. "Takada will be your guide," Noboru whispered to me that evening. "He has already gone through what you are about to venture." It was evening and I dragged the futon from the closet and onto the floor. We both untied our kimonos and slid underneath the heavy white blanket. I discovered his bare arm gliding over my naked chest. I shivered.

I was drowning in his exquisite perfume. The smell of smoked birch and overripe persimmon was rising off his skin. Intoxicated, I swam into his embrace, as I had imagined myself countless times before in the waters of my mother's womb. I wanted to forget that I would be on a ship, casting off to another place all too soon. It all seemed too far away to conceive at that moment. So I closed my eyes and took comfort in the company of my dearest friend as I desperately tried to push the approaching morning out of sight.

THIRTY-FIVE

It took ten months to settle all of the necessary arrangements. I received a response to my letter to Takada in the spring, and we continued the correspondence through the summer. He was extremely helpful, and assured me that once I arrived in Paris he could introduce me to a friend who was studying at the Ecole des Beaux-Arts. This man, Hashimoto, would perhaps be able to introduce me to an instructor who might be willing to take me on as a student. There were already quite a few Japanese in Paris studying art, he explained, and I should try to meet them in person. They were an unusual crowd, very mixed in temperament. Some, he added, would go out almost every night, spending countless hours discussing art. In one of Takada's letters, he described how he had been sitting in a small café on the Rue du Bac, when he realized he was hearing his own language from a nearby table. The melody of the Japanese, however, was continually broken by a strange word—*impureshunisumu*. Takada could not discern whether it was a French word or just a word that he was unfamiliar with in his own language. He soon realized that the word *impureshunisumu* was in fact the word "Impressionism" converted into a Japanese word. These four Japanese men, who donned only black clothing, had adopted the word into their own vernacular, as it was now something in their everyday life.

Like Noboru, Takada encouraged me to study French as much as my spare time allowed before I departed. And thus, after I had completed my second semester at school and registered at the administrative offices for a temporary leave of absence, I began, with great academic fervor, my study of this foreign language.

My relationship with the French language was one of great frustration and little reward. The few textbooks that were available at the time were sufficient in teaching me the alphabet and the rudimentary grammar, but gave little instruction on pronunciation. But unlike many Japanese who arrived in France after having studied the language at home, and found themselves in a state of shock when no one could understand them, I knew beforehand. I knew that I could not say *madame, demain, Je voudrais aller à Paris*. My tongue was unable to roll the *r*, and I had absolutely no idea how to pronounce the letter *v*. When I spoke, it sounded like "Mahdom, dehman, Je boodlay ahler a Pali."

Noboru could not help me. He had never heard French spoken, and since it was the middle of the summer holidays, we could not ask anyone at the college. I decided to write again to Takada and tell him about my difficulties. He responded with a short note:

August 11, 1896
Paris, France

Dear Yamamoto-san,

The heat continues here, yet I am still able to find beauty in this magical city of carved stone walls and geranium-laced windows. I am so happy to hear that you will be arriving in September; it will be so nice to have another Japanese here in Paris. You mentioned in your last letter that you are having difficulty speaking French. I fear that there is little advice that

I can give you except to keep trying. When you arrive in France, that persistence and dedication to the language will be tremendously beneficial to you.

I assume that you will be taking the boat from Yokohama to Marseilles and then the train to Paris. Please send me the time of your arrival and I will be more than happy to meet you at the station.

Regards,
Takada Ryuiichi

It was a comfort to know that Takada would be there to meet me. It would be a three-week journey by boat until I reached the port of Marseilles; thereafter, the train to Paris would require another full day of traveling.

I had exactly two weeks before my departure. I had accomplished most of my errands and completed all of the necessary arrangements, but had yet to come to terms with leaving Noboru in Tokyo. It remained an abstract reality, one that I knew would be all too real when he said good-bye to me at the boat. Because of my self-delusion, the days in between were spent without any overhanging clouds of melancholia. I truly believed that if Noboru could not leave for France with me on the day of my own departure, he would come eventually.

He would come. I would find him at my doorstep, his eyes would be bloodshot, and his body would seem even smaller from the strain of the long journey. But he would be there with his sketchbook, his paints, and his small leather suitcase. He would be there, in my living room, telling me that they had canceled the accelerated program and he knew that he had to follow his heart and come to France. He would ask if it was an inconvenience if he stayed with me until he found a place of his own. And I, remembering the sensation of his arm on my chest, would insist that he should stay with me forever, that his own place was not at all necessary.

In the mornings, we would walk to our teacher's atelier together. The Parisian sunlight would bathe us in its warm golden light; the wet, balmy air that rose from the watery veins of the Seine would clear our nasal passages and invigorate our lungs. We would carry our leather portfolios, heavy with our bounty of sketches. Our footsteps would echo on the pavement of this great city that almost every great artist had trod upon. Our shadows would hang on the walls of all the fashionable cafés, while our bodies reclined among the intellectuals, the struggling painters, and the poets, our lips touching the rims of champagne glasses. With Noboru at my side, I would not feel obliged to talk; he would entertain the others with his inexhaustible charm and wit. In my silence, I would be lost in my own world of happiness and freedom. Everything would be in harmony.

I was scheduled to sail to France at three in the afternoon on the first Saturday of September in the year 1896.

The boat docked in the port of Yokohama the night before I was to leave. That evening, as I lay awake in my futon, my satchels already packed, I could imagine the sound of the anchor dropping. The heavy iron chain falling into the ocean, the long twisting ropes glistening like golden cords.

I saw myself at the gangway, dressed in my brown woolen suit, waistcoat buttoned, shirt white and unfamiliar billowing under my jacket, like the white clouds of smoke puffing from the great chimneys of the steamer.

The next morning I found myself at the dock, my reflection mirroring the image I imagined. I wore a black bowler that partially covered my ears, and the glare of the midday sun swept over my face like a fierce brushstroke of white.

Noboru had come to meet me. Such contrast. He in his dark blue kimono, wrapped as tightly as a small package, standing by my side.

"You look so elegant in your suit," he mused. He had helped me pick it out the week before at one of the stores in the Ginza that specialized in Western clothes and accessories. It was his way of turning the conversation away from my imminent departure. He looked strained, his sadness waxing across his face like a large black shadow over a once shining moon.

I stared at him from the corner of my eye, hoping to capture one last memory of him before my departure. I wanted to press his image into the files of my mind, the ruby color of his lips, the thickness of his lashes, the cowlick curling ever so slightly among his sea of razor-sharp locks. I wanted to capture the sweetness of his fragrance in a clear glass jar. To seal it away forever, like a child who wishes to preserve the light of fireflies. I wished to hold on to everything of him, for always.

But he stood there stoically. I saw the wind travel into the sleeves of his kimono and undulate in small ripples down the ocean of his cloth. His strong jaw, cocked high, echoed the sharp lines of the ship. His eyes looked above the steaming smokestacks, far away to the distant horizon, the whiteness of his complexion a canvas absorbing all the colors around us: the blue of the ocean, the orange of the sun, the bright yellow of the women's straw hats.

I was clutching one of my three *furoshiki*, and my new suitcase rested by my knee. The sensation of wool against my calf was strange and uncomfortable. The fabric felt coarse and unrefined to the touch. Boiled wool. Scratchy. I was surprised by my longing to slip into a comfortable and familiar cotton kimono for the journey ahead. The humidity of the summer still held fast in the September air. The sun reflected in the shimmering steel of the boat's belly, the portholes casting a glare, making the heat all the more intense. I felt a fire growing underneath my woolen layers, my perspiration leaving a wet shadow on the outline of my spine. I wiped my brow with a square of white cloth that I had tucked into my breast pocket and offered it to Noboru.

He refused the handkerchief with the shaking of his head, the light motioning of his hand.

All around, the sight of foreign passengers, the porters lugging their parcels, steamer trunks, and recent purchases, overwhelmed me. Entourages of thirteen to fifteen persons clustered by the entranceway. Women with large hats, overblown like huge flowers, leaned on folded parasols. The most colorful fabrics I had ever seen cascaded from their tightly sashed waists. Lavender-printed flowers, their insides beaded with seed pearls and accented with lace, danced on duchess satin. Boned bodices heaved in the heat of the sun; handkerchiefs dabbed at perspiring brows. Expensive French perfume intermingled with the scent of raw cabbage and shiitake. Such smells suffocated us in the thickness of the air. The squalid odor of fowl. The fishy smell of mollusks and oysters still sliding alive in their shells. Caged birds, whose resplendent feathers echoed the paintings of Ito Jakuchu, shrieked, and nets of wriggling shrimp and bending snappers were strewn on beds of ice, carted through the third-class-deck entrance to await their imminent fate—to be eaten by the first-class passengers that evening.

The whistle sounding the ship's departure was loud and blaring. Around me, the soft whisperings of Japanese farewells contrasted with the loud cheers and festive bustle of the Westerners boarding. Tobacco smoke mingled with the smell of the ship's coal-burning engines. Silk flowers disengaged from ribboned bonnets, and petticoats were lifted, revealing thin ankles laced in boots, as the crowds rushed toward the entranceway. Heels clicked over the gangplank, steadied by the outstretched arm of a gentleman. With black bowler and white shirt, like me. But different.

Noboru's head turned to me slowly, revealing his face one last time. I saw my reflection in the wet glass of his eyes.

We stood there in silence for what seemed like several minutes. Neither of us knew how to formulate our innermost thoughts into sentences. Our eyes were focused on each other's feet; his slippered in *tabi* and sandals, mine in woolen socks and heavy brown shoes. He bowed deeply, his head nearly grazing his knee. And I reciprocated.

"Good-bye, my friend," he said, while extending his arms to offer a small gift, wrapped tightly in white rice paper. "Do not open it until you have reached Marseilles."

I remained still, my feet like roots anchored to the earthen floor. The package was as light as ash, weighing heavy on me, filling me deeply with its sentiment.

"Thank you," I managed to mutter softly. "I promise to write."

Nodding to me, acknowledging the difficulty of the situation with the bowing of his head, he walked me to the gangplank of the boat, the loud sound of the ship's horn once again serenading the cavernous silence between us. I entered through the dark entrance for second-class passengers and made my way to the lower deck, and as the ship broke away from the dock, I waved good-bye to him once more.

He stood waving in his dark kimono, waving until the fog rolled off the sea and I could no longer see him.

When my ship had finally faded from his sight, he left the port in a hurry. As was the case since his childhood, the smell of the sea again had not been kind.

Part
Three

THIRTY-SIX

I was born under the canopy of loss and created under the union of sacrifice. I was trained as a child to fear the gods and encouraged to channel the spirits of the dead. But as I left Noboru standing on the pier, my heavy European shoes moving me over the gangplank, I realized something that unnerved me. Whereas I had been the one abandoned throughout my childhood, I entered adulthood by leaving those in my life whom death had not yet claimed. First Father, now Noboru. I was the one now causing the pain.

In the background I heard the sounding of the ship's horn and felt the heavy breathing of the passengers behind me. Such confusion stirred inside me! Excitement tinged with regret. Sadness at leaving my beloved friend, nervousness over my future as an artist. I stood in the great Western ship's sparkling salon, a naive Japanese, clothed in woolen garments, perspiration trickling down my temples—unmistakable in my foreignness.

Around me, the brass handrails sparkled, the mahogany walls gleamed a deep red. My eyes squinted, unaccustomed to such brightness. Above, a grand chandelier hovered, glistening with crystal beads and tiny pearls of light.

A French steward, in a crisp white cotton uniform with gold buttons, showed me to my quarters. This was my first direct encounter with a Westerner and, to my surprise, I found him eager to assist me. He knew no Japanese, but he guided me about my cabin, busying himself with fluffing my towels and opening my small chest of drawers. After several minutes, he seemed to wait in anticipation of something. Realizing I had forgotten about the custom of tipping, which I read about in one of my handbooks on European culture, I handed the young steward a few coins. He smiled back and offered me a bow. Such a gesture—from a Frenchman, no less—struck me as charming.

The Western bed took up the largest amount of space in my small cabin. I had heard of several ships that sailed from Yokohama to Europe that offered Japanese accommodations, but I thought it best to begin my initiation into European culture at once. I wanted to blend in with the others as soon as I arrived in France.

The ship's itinerary was outlined on the ticket. We would make several stops along the way to pick up other passengers and food and fuel for the remaining portion of the journey. Our first stop would be the port of Shanghai, then on to Hong Kong, Saigon, and Ceylon. The trip was considered quite a feat of modern technology at the time. With the opening of the Suez, a journey that had previously taken months could now be completed in three weeks' time.

Still, I would find the voyage a long one. My nights were spent longing for the company of Noboru.

The package he had given me lay on a chest in my cabin. The wrapping paper and thin, flat cord concealed its contents, but I marveled at the delicacy of its surface. I imagined him wrapping the small pine box with care.

As I fell into my first sleep at sea, I dreamed he was with me. He emerges, sitting on the carpeted floor in a cabin adjacent to mine, a scroll of rice paper stretched out before him, a long, thin brush in hand. His back is curved. His crossed legs extend like the small silver wings of a Japanese beetle.

I recognize the nape of his neck shining in the moonlight, the thin raised hairs parting over the topmost bone. I sigh at the sight of his white arm extending from his sleeve, slender as a stick of bamboo, grasping a horsehair wand soaked in pigment, dancing with the brush in hand, his entire body swaying over the paper, the thick strokes of black ink exploding over the parchment.

I awakened, my body covered in a cold sweat. Outside my porthole, I could no longer see the shores of Japan. Only a long blanket of water that stretched and wrapped the world in liquid blue. And the breath of my friend slipped farther from me, replaced by the smell of salt and the musk of the distant Mediterranean.

THIRTY-SEVEN

Loneliness can overcome almost any person who journeys across the sea. The water underneath you becomes your cradle. The sun through your porthole, the dial by which you mark your day.

My mind during those weeks at sea, after the Asian ports and before the Suez, became both my best friend and my worst enemy. A constant dialogue between us. My conscience pitted against my passion. My hope mingled precariously with my bouts of despair.

I thought of Father as much as I did of Noboru. Perhaps even more, as he was now elevated, like Mother, to the supreme power of Ghost.

Some nights, I'd uncover Father's unfinished mask from the several layers of cloth in which it slept. I'd bring it to my bed and stare into its nearly featureless face, its round container of two shining eyes.

On our day of arrival, I awoke at sunrise and went out to the ship's bow to get the first glimpse of Marseilles. The ship appeared big and full of energy, smokestacks breathing hot, white air into the sky, the heaving sounds of anchors being dropped and chains being pulled. The steamship's horn announced our arrival with a loud and heavy blast, blowing our greeting into the brown docks that waited only a few hundred meters ahead.

I went to my cabin. My bags were already packed, but I had not yet opened the gift from Noboru. It still looked the same way it did on the day he gave it to me. The white paper remained without the slightest trace of a fingerprint, the corners still neatly wrapped and bound with a thin, flat cord. I sat on my bed and opened it reverently, making sure not to tear the paper. I would save everything—the paper, the cord, and the thin wooden box.

I could not tell what the gift was at first. But when I lifted the box's cover, I saw Noboru's only set of oil paints. Each tube was perfectly white, its bottom rolled and its cap tightly screwed on. My heart sank to think of him without these. They were his most valuable and cherished possessions. His parents had saved for over a year to buy them for him.

As I held one of the small tubes out into the sunlight, my eyes fell upon a small smudge in the lower corner. It was one of Noboru's fingerprints, a pale shade of yellow, pressed ever so faintly into the foil. As I had done with the shard of plum wood my father gave me when I began my journey, I picked up this gift and pressed it close to my heart.

The station for the train to Paris was filled with passengers. Several Western couples waited farther ahead, where the first-class cars would be arriving, the women in their fur collars and their husbands in their round bowler hats. As for me, I still could not believe I was standing on European soil.

The porters bustled through the station, maneuvering their loaded carts through the crowds, whistling melodies my ears had never heard before. They wore uniforms of red and navy with shiny gold buttons.

Here I was, Yamamoto Kiyoki, in France, my black eyes now only beginning to see.

The train arrived. Its massive black wheels rolled over the tracks, and soon an entire symphony of whistles and brakes sounded through the air. I boarded my designated carriage and arranged myself comfortably in a seat next to the window. I spent the remaining ten hours on the way to Paris with my face pressed to the glass. Avignon, Arles, and Orange—the heart of Provence— passed before my eyes. I gloried in seeing my first field of sunflowers, endless rows of yellow, pitted by dark brown, stretching far into the plains.

The houses seemed to be made out of clay, painted either a saffron yellow or a pale lotus pink, their tiled roofs in soft waves of terra-cotta. An occasional farmhouse appeared with a rustic exterior of stone-studded walls. The rooflines varied; some rose as high as church steeples and then leveled off almost in midair. Animals grazed behind low stone walls, the sun-baked remnants of Roman glory. Flowers blossomed within gardens, fenced in by small white planks, displaying colors of the richest purple to the most fiery red.

What contrast to our rice paddies, the wet green swamplands that define our farmland. Instead, I saw shimmering fields of wheat, like soldiers of gold standing tall in the autumn sunshine. There were no women with their backs bent and broad bamboo hats pulled over their eyes. Rather, I saw men with fair hair and red faces pausing from their work to watch the train hurry along the tracks.

I saw all of these beautiful things, although none of them noticed me. The ones who did see me, who studied me, shared the same side of the glass as I. They were the men who wore dark gray suits with crisp white shirts. Men who had thin gold watches with chains dangling from their vest pockets. Men who smoked short-stemmed pipes and adjusted their wire-rimmed eyeglasses every time the sun changed. Women who wore feathers in their hats and silk from their collars to their ankles. Women who nudged their husbands for an answer to the questions they had failed to whisper as quietly as they had intended.

I was trying my best to look inconspicuous and fit in. The man at Takashimaya had assured me that everything in his department was imported directly from Europe. My collar was pressed and of the finest cotton, my cuffs were turned upward and fastened with real cuff links, and my shoes were leather, tied tightly and polished diligently. What possibly could they find so extraordinary?

I knew what they found strange. My eyes were carved like recessed almonds, their irises the color of coal.

I could disguise myself in a fancy, dark Western suit, but my eyes would always betray me.

THIRTY-EIGHT

Stepping onto the platform at Paris, I instantly caught sight of another Japanese, who, unlike me, was dressed in tweed. We exchanged glances, and it was clear by the raising of his brows that he suspected I was the man for whom he was waiting.

As I knew I was competing with the roar of the locomotives, I made my voice unusually loud: "Takada-sama?"

He came over to me immediately, and we extended a mutual bow to one another.

Takada was shorter and rounder than I expected. He had clearly bought his tweed jacket a long time ago, as it no longer seemed to fit him. The lapels spread like strained wings over his upper chest, and the tortoiseshell buttons struggled to contain his bulging belly. His white shirt was crisp and elegantly tailored, but his cravat was awkwardly tied. He seemed sadder and more uncomfortable than I had imagined. Almost like a small boy who had grown too fast, not yet fitting into his skin.

Underneath the Western clothes, Takada was still very much a Japanese. During our initial introduction, we exchanged formal greetings and referred to each other in the most polite language possible. I feigned not being exhausted, just as he pretended that picking me up was not an inconvenience. Under this shared stage of common culture, but against the backdrop of this new and foreign city, we walked toward the station's exit.

As soon as we left the station I was struck by the extraordinary lights of Paris. It had become dark already, the sun having set almost two hours before, so all the boulevards were illuminated by gaslights. The heavy white stone of the station's exterior, the tall, narrow apartment buildings with their small iron balconies filled with potted plants and ivy, dappled with the most magnificent shadows. It was not at all the type of shadow that appears on the side of one our wooden buildings or on the translucent paper of our shoji. Rather, it was warmer, unequivocally more magical. More splendid than I could ever have imagined in my dreams.

"Your hotel is conveniently located near the Beaux-Arts," Takada informed me. He too had stayed there when he first arrived in Paris, but he now chose to sublet an apartment closer to the Sorbonne. "You'll be able to rent a room there for an extended period, if you like it. If not, I'll help you make other arrangements."

"You're far too kind, Takada-sama," I replied, as we walked through the narrow streets draped in hanging geranium leaves and textured by shuttered windows. I craned my neck, my mouth agape, struck by the newness of my surroundings.

"Here we are!" Takada announced as we arrived at the corner of the Rue de Buci and Rue de Seine. The hotel where I would be staying was nestled in a small alcove amid a myriad of small street cafés, art galleries, and tiny food shops.

Takada went directly to the hotel's reception area to speak with the concierge, while I waited close by with my bags in hand. From the corner of my eye, I could see the concierge's bright red vest. In profile, he looked grandfatherly—silver spectacles and powder-white hair. His hands were spotted brown. Brown, as Father's had been when I held them in my palms and washed them with care. As I watched the Frenchman inscribe his register with the information Takada gave him, I was struck with a sudden sense of melancholia. Was Father watching me as I began my journey as a foreigner in a distant land? Or had he abandoned me, as I had done to him when I left the first time, our crafts dividing us into eternity?

"Yamamoto-san," Takada called, interrupting my thoughts. "The owner says he can offer you either a room facing south or one facing east. Which one would you prefer? Perhaps you want the one facing east? It may remind you of Japan." He was smiling at me, and his eyeglasses sparkled in the hotel's lamplight.

"Actually," I murmured, "would it be possible to have the one facing south? The light will be better that way, and if I decide to paint at home, it might be helpful."

"Of course. That would be best, wouldn't it?" he said as he turned his back and resumed his conversation with the concierge.

After several minutes he returned and handed me the key.

"You must be very tired, Yamamoto-san. Why don't you get some sleep and we can meet tomorrow afternoon? There is a good café around the corner if you want to get breakfast in the morning, and I can assist you with the bank if you need it."

"You've been ever so helpful," I said, bowing deeply to him.

"Don't mention it, my friend," he said nonchalantly. "And as far as your studies are concerned, I have a friend in the Beaux-Arts, a man named Hashimoto, who might be able to recommend a teacher for you." He took a pen and small leather notepad from his breast pocket and wrote himself a short note.

"I'll see if I can arrange a meeting between us."

My eyes were beginning to betray my fatigue. I took out a handkerchief and dabbed at my forehead in the hope that it might invigorate me somehow. I did not want to appear rude or ungrateful.

"You have been most kind, Takada-san. I hope that someday I might return your hospitality."

Takada smiled. "It's been my pleasure. Since you are an artist,

Yamamoto-san, perhaps someday you will give me a painting that resembles the way that I see Paris. Perhaps my strange vision of this city can be painted only by another Japanese."

"Should I ever produce a canvas of merit, you will be the first to receive it, Takada-san," I promised. "However, in the meantime, won't you accept this simple gift as a token of my appreciation?" I handed him a small box of dry tea sweets and bowed in reverence as I bid him a good night.

The next morning I awoke at sunrise. The room had two windows overlooking the street, and the daylight penetrated the flimsy green drapes much as it would a shoji. I found my quarters quite spacious and comfortable, but beginning to show signs of age. The paint was chipped and peeling in paper-thin strips around the ceiling's perimeter. The walls, once covered in pale yellow, now had a sort of grayish dinginess that reminded me of my tatami back in Tokyo. Two cigarette burns peeked through the crisp linen like hollow eyes. But still, I was in the city of endless splendors and artistic inspiration, the land of the great masters and the greatest museums. I opened one of the windows and allowed the morning air to enter the room. I stood in my cotton *yukata*, the sunlight warming my face and body.

The light was golden and translucent, like the dappled skin of our autumn pears. How I imagined it would radiate on my canvas, enabling even the simplest objects to glow in its soft, illuminating light.

I would begin painting with Noboru's gift as soon as I got settled.

But first, I sat down and began a letter to my beloved friend.

After I sealed the letter, I set out to find the café that Takada suggested for breakfast.

I discovered it between the Rue Jacob and Boulevard Saint-Germain. There amid wicker chairs piped in gleaming brass and mirrors etched in floral arabesques, I savored my first basket of croissants and a steaming cup of coffee.

With nearly two hours before my meeting with Takada, I decided to walk down the Rue de Seine and then follow the river until I came across the Pont Neuf, where I saw the Louvre for the first time.

There it was: an explosion of grandeur, carved from what seemed like a mountain of marble, an enormous monument housing thousands of the most beautiful works created by the hands of man. I trembled when I saw it. The museum seemed endless; stretching farther than I had ever imagined, it was adorned with countless glass windows, what seemed like a sea of eyes, all gazing down at me.

I walked through the gateway, felt the cloth of my jacket being brushed by so many rushing tourists eager to enter.

I paused in the middle of the Cour Napoleon and felt tiny pearls of perspiration forming over my forehead and around my collar. I was swimming in an artistic ecstasy that benumbed my senses. It was too much for me.

I did not enter on my first day. I would come back and dedicate several days to roaming through the extensive rooms. Instead, I walked toward the second courtyard and then toward the Orangerie. There were so many people out for a midday stroll, and I wanted to be around people now. I wanted to see how the French lived. I hoped that if I studied them in their environment—in their work and leisure, as lovers and as families—I would become more comfortable in this new and strange city.

I met Takada on a corner near the Avenue de l'Opéra, and we set up a bank account for me. It was a sum that I hoped would subsidize my studies and my living expenses for five years. After that, I would have to return home.

"Unfortunately, money goes fast here, my friend," Takada mused after we had left the marble halls of the bank. "If you're hoping to be here for a while, keep a careful watch on your recreational expenses."

"I confess, I have not been known to be particularly social, so I doubt I will have much of a problem being thrifty in that regard. Paints and instruments are usually my greatest expense."

"I see," he said, smiling. "Well, then, we shall limit ourselves to one coffee today."

Outside, the afternoon sun beamed rays of gold onto the sidewalk. I found myself nurturing, if only for a brief second, a ridiculous fantasy that my hair too was as flaxen as theirs. The color of sun-bleached wheat. The sight of my new companion, however, reminded me otherwise. I saw the reality of my reflection in the shiny black mirror of his eyes. I noticed the fastidious manner in which he dressed, for it was the same way I had dressed on my voyage to France. We styled ourselves as Europeans, but in such a flawless manner that, in the end, we tried too hard and failed. I realized much later that we had succeeded only in looking more Japanese, and more out of place, than ever. We slicked our shiny black hair back behind our ears, with not a strand out of place, using a pomade whose smell was as foreign to us as were the ingredients—coconut oil and sandalwood. Still, we continued to buy it for the same reason that we bought our dark brown suits and our matching foulards and handkerchiefs—because we so desperately wanted to fit in.

We failed to realize that we could never escape the reality of our foreignness. Not because we were Japanese, but because we were and would always be self-conscious men.

THIRTY-NINE

For the first time in my life, I was completely free. Takada was a contact, but he knew nothing of my earlier life. He knew nothing of Father. Of my relationship with Noboru. Of the collection of masks I had traded for gold.

Before my studies consumed my mind, I walked through Paris until my feet burned and my toes grew callused. I found joy as I stood among the crowds and watched the street mimes. With their painted white faces and ruby red lips, they juggled bright yellow pins in the air, while men with their children balanced on their shoulders cried loudly and threw a few sous into a large round hat.

The first time I saw the rose window of Notre-Dame, I nearly died from the sight of such splendor.

That glorious window whose radiant cobalt and azure panes glowed in the midday sun. All around me were symbols I did not understand. This house of worship, whose god was not depicted in the form of Buddha but in the tortured image of a bleeding man with a spindly crown of thorns. His mother, with long brown hair and blue robes, knelt at his anguished side, her fingers entwined like vines.

I stood there in the center of mighty Notre-Dame and wished the image of my own mother could have been forever cast in panes of glass, my mother in violet robes, my father swathed in gray.

I imagined Father kneeling at her side, her bleeding womb

cut crimson, my infant form bluish white. Our story played out in colors, a drama that required no masks.

Not far from the Pont Neuf you can pay fifteen sous to ride a boat down the Seine. On Thursday, Takada joined me for an hour as we took a slow ride through the center of Paris.

We admired the Louvre, the Garden of the Tuileries, as we passed them. Takada took a bottle of wine from his satchel and unwrapped two glasses tucked in his *furoshiki*.

"We shall do as the French do and admire beauty with a glass of wine."

He poured the dark red liquid into my glass and clinked his goblet against mine.

"To us Japanese in Paris!" he said boldly. "May we live here amid splendor and return to Japan only on our own accord!" It was the first time I had seen him laugh, and I noticed that his teeth were perfect.

"To Paris!" I said, adding *"Kanpai!"*

We leaned over the rail of the boat, the bottle of wine resting near Takada's feet, and inhaled the fragrant mist that was rising off the Seine. The wind was growing stronger, and Takada was leaning over the rail, his face beet-red from the wine.

"Look, there's Notre-Dame," I said, pointing to its two formidable towers.

"The mighty empress of stone!" he cried as he craned his neck and rested all of his weight on his elbows, the sleeves of his jacket straining to contain his full, round arms.

Then suddenly there was a tremendous gust of wind. It rose from the waves, as if directed by a force other than its own and, before I could warn Takada, his black hat had been swept off his head and sent clear into the water.

"Oh, no!" I cried with despair. "What will we do now?" The small black hat was bobbing up and down on a ribbon of waves.

"We just watch it and enjoy it," Takada said, and he was still laughing. I looked at him, and I will always remember his face. It was the only day on which I can recall that he was forever smiling.

Takada and I said our farewells and agreed to meet in a few days. By that time he hoped to have scheduled a meeting between his friend Hashimoto and me. In the meantime, I decided to acquaint myself with the area adjacent to the École des Beaux-Arts, so I would seem more knowledgeable of my surroundings.

I awakened early and at once began wandering through the long and winding back streets that reminded me slightly of the *unagi no michi* of Kyoto, the streets that we say are as narrow and curvy as eels.

I passed the patisseries, with their jelly tarts and their buttered rolls. The luxurious and rich smells of the sweet shops permeated the damp air, and I recalled my first smells of Tokyo: the rank stench of the fermenting *nato*, the heavy grease frying the tempura, and the fish skins roasting on the fire. In Paris, women's perfume intermingled with the smell of preserves, a cloud of sweetness masking anything foul.

The cobblestones under my feet, however, felt hard and awkward. I missed the feeling of earth beneath my sandals. I felt as though I had lost a sixth sensation: with the heavy leather shoes encasing my feet, I no longer could be sensitive to the floor beneath me.

I wondered how my father might have felt here in this city. The cold feeling of constantly being surrounded by stone rather than wood. I wondered how he might react to the throngs of people, the abundance of color and light. I saw him in my mind. His blue face shining like lapis. His hand covering his eyes from the blinding sun. I saw him in the shadows. His fingers withdrawn into the folds of his kimono. Wearing his ache. Sniffing for his wood.

And I saw my mother too. Imagined how she would have rejoiced in this city's splendor. Marveled at the freedom of the spirit that dripped like garlands from the lantern posts. What the creative mind unleashed could accomplish! she would have thought. I vowed to make her proud.

I bit my lip, tasted a feral droplet of blood, and was brought out of my daydream of glory and ghosts. Daigo was far from here, curled within my heart and forced into a long sleep. Here there were no mountains with which I could mark the seasons. Here there was no Noboru in whom I could truly confide.

But here there was freedom.

I wandered through the streets and let the presence of my parents' spirits fall away. Hours later I found an art supplies store neatly tucked behind a modest facade on the Rue de Rennes. I walked inside, mesmerized by the quantity of material stacked throughout the store. They had five different types of easels and an entire section of drawing utensils: colored and graphite pencils, block and vine charcoal, pastels and colored chalk.

At the back of the store, the proprietor had stacks of paper and rolls of canvas and, at the base of the middle display case, he had watercolor sets, gouaches and individual tubes of oil pigment. Brushes were arranged like flowers in large silver canisters. Sticks of charcoal were wrapped in tissue and tied with twine.

There was so much I had never seen before. I did not recognize the jars of gesso and linseed oil, nor did I have any idea how to use so many other materials. I had never stretched a canvas; I had only painted on paper or wooden boards. I was humbled by what I had to learn.

I bought some paper so I could attempt a few watercolor sketches during the late afternoon. I needed to increase the relatively small portfolio I had brought from Japan, which included only a few of my paintings and some pencil and charcoal sketches. I was most pleased with my anatomical studies and my watercolor of Daigo. The paintings I had done in Tokyo were overworked and lacked the freshness of my earlier work. Against my own will, I had also brought some of the ink paintings I had done in Morita's class. Noboru had thought it best.

I knew he would have loved the art store. He would have walked through the narrow aisles like a priest through a temple. He would have touched the bristles of each brush, examining the softness of the hairs, the firmness of the point. He would not have been shy or intimidated, like me. He would have held the amber varnishes to the light and marveled at the hue. He would have brushed his fingers across the rolls of canvas and intuitively known which was best.

But now he was so far from here, this place of stone and golden light. The rush of rickshaws was replaced by the trotting of horse and carriage, and the trembling spire of the church was substituted for the pagoda from the local shrine.

How long would it take for him to receive my letter? Would he write as soon as he received it or take his time in his response? So much was changing in my life and it had only been four days since I had arrived. I wondered how I would keep track of all that was transpiring. I would be meeting with Hashimoto, Takada's art student friend, on Tuesday and perhaps he would be able to assist me in finding a teacher. I shivered with excitement. Tossing a scarf over my shoulder, I returned to the hotel in the hope that I could capture on paper some of the new and fresh images I had just seen.

FORTY

It is the following afternoon; my easel is in front of me. I work quickly so that I might capture the view from my window before it turns dark.

Dressed in my *yukata*, I am daubed with smudges of pigment; I am intoxicated by the fumes of turpentine and shiny-palmed from the leaking of the linseed oil.

I paint the peeling yellow walls of my room and the large windows opening to the city. I paint the faded fringe of the green linen curtains and the steely arabesque of the wrought-iron balcony. I paint the red of the potted geraniums and the black of the church's cross.

I paint with an energy and a bliss that is common among those who have had no formal training. I re-create the images I see before me with no guide other than my eyes. The colors lack proper mixing, the perspective is askew, and the shapes are distorted, but I have created a painting that is sincerely felt and one that retains its artist's original eyes.

My painting is not memorized. Here the colors, the shapes, the cockeyed perspective are all intuitive. It is far from the reproductions of ancient paintings that I did in Morita sensei's class, where every line I created was a regurgitation, where every brushstroke was the same one copied by each entering class.

*   *   *

Years later, even after I had begun my formal training, I would always return to that first painting. I have kept it in my studio and have never disposed of it, despite its many technical flaws. It is my first self-portrait, even though my face is nowhere on the canvas. Yet it is I: an excited Japanese looking past the open glass and onto a city that I know now I can never call my own.

FORTY-ONE

Hashimoto Ryazaburo appeared at the entrance of the café wearing a black suit, a white shirt, and a white cravat. He was a strange-looking Japanese, his skin as pale as the powdered face of a *maiko*, his hair cropped so short around the crown of his head that it resembled a skullcap made of black satin. His eyes were framed by tiny silver pince-nez, and his ears were shiny and large.

Takada and I were sitting at a table, our chairs facing the glass so we could view the Parisians on their afternoon strolls. Our eyes followed the women's silken bustles, the lines of their parasols, the coattails of their escorts, while our ears were lost in the clicking of their heels on the cobblestones, the idleness of their chatter, the lightness of their being.

Hashimoto recognized us immediately. Arriving without hesitation, he came to our small table and introduced himself to me. I stood up to offer him a bow, but he extended his hand. "Let us not forget that we are in *France*, gentlemen," he said in French.

"Do not worry, Yamamoto-san," he said in his impeccable Tokyo accent "I have not forgotten my Japanese!" He forced himself to laugh loudly like a European, and his white teeth were broad and sparkling.

The waiter poured three cups of coffee. I placed one hand around the cup and the other at the bottom, drinking the liquid as we drink our tea in Japan. Takada coughed, and I looked over to see that he was concentrating his gaze on the handle of my porcelain cup. I changed the position of my hands.

Hashimoto at once began to speak of his own experiences in France. He had arrived five years earlier thanks to generous funding from his father, a doctor in Tokyo, to acquire the artistic training that was then unavailable in Japan. His father had been a close acquaintance of the Kuroda family and, upon his arrival in Paris, Hashimoto met with Kuroda Seiki, who made the introductions necessary for him to be accepted into the Beaux-Arts.

"There aren't many Japanese in Paris," he said between sips of his coffee. "Kuroda Seiki and Kume Keiichiro left two years ago, and I have not seen or heard from Fuji Masazo in a long time. I am one of the few left! Of course, now there will always be Takada." He looked over at Takada, now looking ashen and deflated in his brown suit. "And a new brother—Yamamoto!

"Yes, the Japanese art community is small here, but we are in the best city in the world for art. Where else does one find such museums, such color, and such stimulation for the eyes and the soul? Nowhere on this earth, I tell you. Nowhere!"

I was nervous in the presence of this excitable Japanese. He seemed so unlike Takada and me. So unlike Noboru and Father. In fact, I had never before encountered anyone so brazen.

I was nervous to ask him questions. But I also realized that he was my main resource. So finally, after ingesting several cups of coffee, I managed to ask him where I might find instruction.

"Hashimoto-san," I said delicately, "perhaps, you could tell me how you came to attend the École des Beaux-Arts?"

Hashimoto sat back in the rather small café chair and reclined against the pane of glass. After two sighs, he responded.

"My father would not support me unless I attended the same school as the great French masters. Before I even submitted my application, I received private instruction in French language.

My father had me tutored for five hours every day by a student of French at the Imperial College. I traveled to Paris for my interview and started my lessons at the école that September."

"I doubt that I could attend such a rigorous program," I said with a tone of despair. "My French is not particularly good, and even if it were, it seems I have completely missed the interviewing period."

"Do not worry, Yamamoto," he said with a wave of his hand. "I suggest that you get in touch with Raphael Collin."

I looked at him blankly, not having recognized the name.

"Collin instructed both Kume Keiichiro and Kuroda Seiki," he continued. "Unlike some of the other teachers, Collin is a well-respected master who was trained as an Academic painter, but does not object to introducing some of the newer, fresher techniques of the Impressionists. At the Beaux-Arts, we are limited to the Academic style, so our creative freedom is shackled. In the five years that I have been in Paris, I have changed tremendously, but you could hardly glean that from my paintings."

As he spoke, his experiences reminded me of my time at the Tokyo School of Fine Arts. Disillusioned by his description of the Beaux-Arts, I turned my head to the window. I needed to remind myself that, no matter what happened, I had at least been bold enough to make the journey.

Hashimoto lit a cigarette. He placed it between his thin lips and sucked deeply, inhaling the smoke into his lungs. I was terribly impressed with his sophistication, his savvy, his ability to adopt Western mannerisms.

As he spoke of his time in Paris, his voice became softer, his tone firmer, and his words carefully chosen.

"I will tell you, Yamamoto-san, my first few months here, before I began my studies at the Beaux-Arts, I made only sketches in charcoal of everything that I thought was beautiful. I went almost every day to the Louvre and tried to perfect my renderings of the human form. It was as if I lived there, among the marble statues of the garden—I, a Japanese, crouched at the feet of so many Greek and Roman gods. There in that stone chamber, with my hands blackened by the crumbling bits of charcoal, I learned, after countless hours of practice, the formula for perfect human proportions. What I did not learn, however, was how to actually make my figures seem human. They appeared exactly like what I was drawing—perfect figures without flesh or blood. I had succeeded only in copying.

"Once I entered the Beaux-Arts, we worked from live models, and still, my figures were as stiff and lifeless as stone. I was so consumed with rendering them perfect that I couldn't bear to create anything human, because human figures are not as perfect as Roman statues. No, they move, they have slightly crooked limbs, asymmetrical faces, and skin that falls in all sorts of directions. Now I understand that. It is part of my growth as an artist.

"And it is with that same growth that I feel constrained by the stiff, old-fashioned style of the Academics. I see the work of the Impressionists, the way they diffuse light by diffusing their brush-strokes, the freedom of their palette as well as their subject, and I am envious. I cannot do that type of work in the classroom. My hours are dedicated to learning the techniques of the old masters—a worthwhile education, indeed—but I am bound to it until I graduate. Then, in my future, once I return to Japan with my degree, I will begin to experiment, using all of the knowledge I have acquired here. I only hope I will be able to do that. To achieve something in my art that will make me memorable."

"You are too hard on yourself, Hashimoto," comforted Takada.

Hashimoto pressed his pince-nez to the bridge of his nose and inhaled again from his cigarette. "I guess you could say that I have always had a special weakness for the image of San Sebastian. My original inspiration for wanting to paint in the Western style came after I saw the painting *The Martyrdom of Saint Sebastian* by Piero della Francesca."

As he spoke, his eyes glistened as if he were seeing the painting for the first time. "I was absolutely awestruck by the realism of the painting. The egg-white color of the tortured man's skin, his body pierced so many times by the unforgiving arrows, and his eyes facing the heavens, brimming with tears. Was it the anguish or pain, or was it the thrill of spiritual ecstasy that marked his face? It always left me perplexed."

Hashimoto stared at me with his now naked eyes. The pince-nez dangled from his forefinger and carried the reflection of his face in the spectra of the far lens. I could tell by his demeanor that he was challenging me.

"I believe all martyrs feel a spiritual ecstasy through their pain, just as artists find inspiration from their suffering," I replied. "This does not mean that we do not suffer, or that Saint Sebastian does not feel pain, but rather that we welcome the pain in order to experience the ecstasy and the artistry."

Hashimoto smiled this time with his mouth closed. "Very well said, Yamamoto-san."

"Artists are not the only ones who suffer," Takada mumbled into his coffee, now cold.

"What's that, Takada old man? You have it *too* good. What's that rumpled envelope in your breast pocket? Another check from your father?"

Takada placed his palm over the gray letter. "It's nothing," he said and he stuffed it deeper into the satin lining of the pocket.

"Well, I must be going, friends," Hashimoto said, as he motioned the waiter for the check. "I will send Collin's address to your hotel and relay a message to him that you might be interested in attending his atelier—if he will have you, of course."

"Thank you for your kind assistance," I said to him while rummaging through my pockets for some coins.

"Do not worry about it," Takada said to us both. "I'll take care of the bill." Hashimoto was already out the door, waving his hand in the air, and reaching for his hair pomade with the other.

I sat in the café, waiting for Takada. He was staring at the mirrored columns. The man I had spent the afternoon with only a few days ago seemed to have disappeared. He had hardly uttered a word.

"What's wrong, old man?" I asked, trying to imitate the gregarious Hashimoto. "Are you all right?"

"Ah, yes, so sorry," he said, as if I had awakened him from a dream. "It is only that I received a letter from home today and I am a bit distracted." He pushed the envelope deeper into his pocket and stood up, stumbling gently over the legs of his chair.

"Let me pay for the check," I insisted. "After all, this meeting was arranged to assist me, right?"

"No, no," he pressed. "You must save your francs for your art supplies, remember. I will have few expenses in the future, I assure you."

I felt uncomfortable with his generosity, but he would hear of nothing else.

"I promise to make you that painting!" I vowed as we exited the café and entered the sea of pedestrians. I was exhausted. But somehow, in the silvery autumn light of this afternoon in Paris, with the sound of horse-drawn carriages and an occasional umbrella tapping on the cobblestones, I managed to walk the distance home.

FORTY-TWO

I arrived at Raphael Collin's studio the following Thursday. He stood in the entranceway, sliced from the shadows, his voluminous beard flowing like a waterfall of white. He was a tall man with a thin build and generous, thick gray curls parted in the middle. His eyebrows were platinum and full, the thick tufts of hair offsetting his dark eyes.

"I have been waiting for you," he said, and his voice seemed refreshingly kind. His tall, slender body leaned on a long ebony walking stick; its carved ivory handle, in the shape of a small mongoose, fit snugly in his palm.

I bowed reverently to him, so deep that my black hair nearly grazed the floor.

"You must be Yamamoto Kiyoki," he said, and he bowed his head in return, not extending his hand for the customary shake.

I followed him through two large doors as tall as elm trees, the veins of the wood running through them like rivers. I thought of Father. Touched the wood as I walked past and remembered the sensation of cypress. Recalled its high green smell and, for a brief moment, forgot where I was.

"Monsieur Yamamoto," Collin called, and I raised my head to discover a large room encircled by easels. I noticed the drop cloths speckled with paint, the tall windows with the heavy curtains drawn aside.

"I thought I would show you this room first," he said, with

his lean arm extended. "But let us walk to the second-floor parlor so we may talk in comfort."

With my sketchbooks tucked underneath my arm and my portfolio clutched between my fingers, I walked behind him. I followed him up a small iron staircase, carefully switching my satchel so I could balance with a free hand, and arrived to a second-floor sitting room that was tastefully arranged.

"Take a seat, Monsieur Yamamoto," he urged politely, and I awkwardly smoothed the back of my jacket before sitting in a bright red armchair. Around me, long windows were dressed in chintz, and paintings by lesser-known Academics covered the walls. My eyes darted around nervously, hoping to anchor themselves on something comforting and familiar. I noticed a small piece of Imari porcelain discreetly displayed on an end table and found comfort in its red and blue glaze.

"Might I offer you some coffee?" he asked politely.

"If it is no trouble to you."

Collin rapped his walking stick against the wooden floor. The sound echoed throughout the room, startling me with the strength of its strike.

"Flora . . . Flora!" he called out. From behind a silk pleated screen, a woman appeared.

I was served coffee from a large silver tray. Cream and sugar were generously spooned into the porcelain cup. The steaming pot rattled nervously against the milk jug, Flora's tiny hands gripping tenaciously at the coiled handles.

"She is my model, not the servant," Collin said almost apologetically. He turned to her and smiled as he reached for his cup.

"I want to paint another version of *Floréal* this afternoon," he whispered into her ear, and I caught the thin flash of her smile in the mirror behind him. She exited demurely, and I buried my face in the cup of steaming coffee.

"Have you brought any of your paintings, so that I might see your experience?" he finally asked.

I placed my cup on the table and reached for my portfolio. "Yes, sir, I have," I answered, my voice betraying my anxious nerves.

"Well, let me take a look." I handed him the leather folder and let him withdraw the sketches and small selection of my awkward ink paintings.

His brow now curled intensely, his small eyes focusing on my every line.

"You were studying in Tokyo, at the School of Fine Arts, *non?*"

"Yes, for nearly two years."

"Your sketches are not bad. I especially like this one of the mountain." He turned the paper to face me, revealing my sketch of Mount Daigo.

I felt a breeze coming through the curtains and wondered if it was the ghost of Mother.

"Have you painted in oils yet?" Collin asked.

"I have tried, but it is difficult, not knowing the proper techniques."

"As you must already know, I instructed two of your countrymen, Kuroda Seiki and Kume Keiichiro. And I hear that Monsieur Kuroda has become quite famous back in Japan."

He pronounced the names of my compatriots with ease, and I found myself greatly impressed.

After a few moments of contemplation, he spoke. "If you are serious about painting, Monsieur Yamamoto, I will offer you my instruction."

I could not believe that gaining acceptance into his atelier could have been so easy.

"I am so honored, Master Collin." I blushed.

"Don't be. I learned a lot from my former Japanese students.

They influenced my work greatly. The paintings that Kume and Kuroda did before returning to Japan revealed enormous proficiency. I really was quite pleased with their work." He paused, looked at my eyes—wide with shock that I would be receiving instruction from this great master—and decided to change the direction of our conversation.

"Would you like a tour of the studio?"

I stood up, glad to have a chance to see once more where I would be working. I followed him carefully and respectfully, much as I imagined a small child would follow his father.

Collin descended the stairs gracefully, the vents of his black coat billowing behind him. When we reached the large drawing room that had been converted to the atelier for his students, he walked past the circular rows of easels and stepped onto the podium where the model typically reclined.

"This is where the students spend the majority of their day. If I do not ask them to go to the Louvre to sketch, they paint here," he said, encircling the room with the tip of his walking stick.

The high-ceilinged, white-walled sanctuary was filled with easels and littered with short wooden stools. There were bottles of turpentine and flasks of linseed oil on the shelves. A pail of gesso stood next to the sink.

"I encourage a five-year course of study, and I insist that you learn the foundations of drawing before you begin to paint. A complete comprehension of anatomy is essential. You will never be able to paint the human form without having studied it extensively. The beginning students practice sketching from sculpture before they are allowed to join my advanced students in the classes in which I have a model. And I caution you, Monsieur Yamamoto, that itself can take up to two years."

I nodded, trying to disguise my disappointment that I would be unable to begin painting at once. I was inspired, however, by the paintings around the studio. They revealed that Collin encouraged his students to develop their own style of painting, as long as they could support their vision with a mastery of technique.

"As for my own style," Collin began, "I have great respect and enthusiasm for the work of the Impressionists, but I myself will always be a bit of an Academic painter. It's my training, and I believe it mirrors my nature.

"That isn't to say," he continued, "that I don't encourage my students to seek the influences surrounding us in this day and age. The work sometimes scorned by the Salon is in fact fresher and more impressive than that of a lot of the Academic painters, perhaps myself included."

I looked at the old man standing on the podium, his white beard now fluffed with the energy produced by his exuberant mouth.

"But, Monsieur Yamamoto, I must warn you. You will probably encounter the same difficulties as Kuroda and Kume did while studying with me."

"I am not sure I understand," I admitted.

"During Kuroda's and Kume's last years with me, after they had achieved great proficiency in the techniques of the old masters and the comprehension of anatomy and perspective, I encouraged them to forsake the concept of copying and to begin cultivating their own style. This, however, proved the most challenging task for them in all their years of training."

"In Japan, copying the masters is the only method to learn," I said. "It is also the way we pay respect. Only when one possesses the skills necessary to replicate the techniques of our great masters has one achieved a level of excellence."

"We train similarly, Monsieur Yamamoto, but we are expected to create something new in the process. In Europe we encourage our students not only to master the fundamentals but also to reveal their unique *vision* of a particular subject."

His words were revolutionary to me. Originality was indeed a foreign concept to us Japanese. In the past, when I had seen reproductions of Western paintings, I only dreamed I would be given the chance to create similar paintings. Never before had I considered bringing something to the canvas that was uniquely my own.

I wondered silently if I had anything inside me to bring.

"Perhaps it might be easier if I show you what I mean," the old man said as he descended the small model's podium and placed a blank canvas on an easel at one side of the room.

"Have a seat on one of the stools, Monsieur Yamamoto, and make yourself comfortable."

Collin now stood only a few strides in front of me, stationed at his easel, tall and straight. He removed a brush from one of the tins and squeezed it dry between his thumb and index finger. I watched as he effortlessly prepared his palette.

Titanium white, red ocher, cobalt blue, cadmium yellow, and vermilion were neatly arranged on his palette. He dabbed the brush's bristles into the undiffused lines of pigment and began creating subtler shades around the perimeter. He hesitated for a moment, looked at me, and then at the canvas. Then at me once more.

With a newfound intensity, his eyes returned to his palette. He cleaned his brush in a clear glass of turpentine and then gently dried it with a small white rag that had been tucked under one of the easel's legs. Returning to his palette once more, he dipped his brush into a light brown wash, and then suspended it briefly over the stretched canvas.

He pressed the side of his brush onto the board, dragging the first stroke of color across the page. That first gesture of color. Blue-green. Like a vine of seaweed floating across a sea of white.

"Your face is quite extraordinary, Monsieur Yamamoto, even when you are standing perfectly still. It seems to change before my very eyes."

His voice awakened me from my trance. Seeing the great master apply stroke after stroke had transfixed me. Each thin layer of pigment was built up with another. Strong color was contrasted with weak color, and the juxtaposition of complementary shades created depth. I realized I had not been concentrating on *what* Master Collin was painting, but rather *how* he was painting. What emerged from his abstract strokes and swatches of color was a portrait of me.

A strange feeling of nausea began rolling inside my stomach, as Collin stepped back to study his most recent creation.

He had painted me in my dark brown suit, each stroke feverishly rendered. My fingers were long and white, palms facing downward, stretching almost painfully over the slopes of my covered knees.

But it was my face that haunted me.

My face, painted blue-white, transparent glaze after transparent glaze, was ghostlike. My cheeks were sunken, my eyelids thin and sweeping, my gaze directed downward. Somehow Collin had inadvertently portrayed me as the very image of the Shunkan mask, the mask that we use to personify a man in exile. I was aghast.

"Is something the matter? You look ill," Collin said, his concern revealing a deep, paternal nature.

"Oh, no, it is nothing," I lied. "I am only nervous that I will be an inadequate student for someone who is so gifted as you."

"Do not worry," he said kindly. "You, Monsieur Yamamoto, will do just fine. It is the concept of originality that frightens you

Japanese. In contrast, our European students suffer over precision and accuracy. The very areas in which you'll undoubtedly excel."

I stood up from my stool and looked past the lines of easels into the tall windows overlooking the street. The sun was beginning to set over the city. The street lanterns were just being lit. And after I bade my farewell to Collin, instead of making my way back home, I walked for hours, lost in the city's dark haze.

FORTY-THREE

We are all haunted. I learned that early on in my sojourn in Paris. Everyone has his ghosts. Mine belonged to the other world. I would see my mother in a cloud of lavender, her robe long and lilac. I would see my father's gaze in the swirling grain of a block of wood.

But for men like Takada, it was different.

Whereas my ghosts swirled around me, their features often blurred, their voices forever muted, Takada's still lived. Separated by only an ocean, their outstretched hands grasping to reach his shores.

"Yamamoto-san," he told me one day, "I envy you."

I looked at him, sunk in a wicker chair at the café, and wondered how my friend could possibly envy a lonely, mediocre exile like me.

"You have nothing calling you back. No family. No obligations."

"I did leave someone behind," I confessed.

"Love evades me, my friend." And he looked into his coffee, stirring with the spoon as if it were a bowl of tea leaves capable of foretelling his future.

"Why do you wrap yourself in such sadness?" I asked him, somewhat confused. Emotion articulated always made me uncomfortable. Because, deep down inside, that was what I craved.

"I have received a letter. My father has requested that I return to Japan."

"Can you not ask for an extension of your studies?"

"He has already begun investigating future brides for me. An arranged marriage awaits me. A career in politics is already secured."

He tapped his chest, and I could see the faint outline of an envelope behind the fabric of his jacket.

"When I return, my life will be unbearable. Married to a woman I do not love. Shackled to a career in which I have no interest. Such is my fate! I cannot bear it!"

Takada's glasses slipped from the bridge of his nose. His pink cheeks inflated with angst, his speech filled with a mixture of ire and despair.

"I envy you, Yamamoto-san, because you are free. There is no such struggle in your life."

Only I knew how very wrong he was. As he spoke, I saw myself once again at the *genkan*, my father standing there like dead timber. Watched as he pressed the shard of dried plum wood into my palm. And wondered if such a thing was even possible. That one day I could be *free*. Free of my memory.

"My struggle is with ghosts, as real to me as your own parents," I said over my steaming cup. "They too hold me tight. So do not envy me."

FORTY-FOUR

It was inevitable that Takada—a short, quiet man with heavy cheeks and swollen fingers, who packed all emotion inside his tiny, turgid frame—would one day reach his threshold, his anguish splitting him at the seams. No large bang would be heard. Just the empty, hollow sack of a man who one day just appeared to burst.

Takada was born the son of a politician. That was easily detectable, for his posture was proud and his belly prominent. Indeed, he had never gone hungry for a day or even an hour. But if one probed deeper inside him, it became apparent how truly empty he was. Filled with air. Inflated with pain. Steeped in despair.

His father had carefully planned his birth, just as his grandparents had meticulously orchestrated the marriage of his parents. An arranged marriage, where love was forsaken for duty, and happiness was forsworn for familial prosperity. His parents' union was as empty and as politically driven as their child's conception.

Takada's father was the second youngest man ever elected to the national parliament. Handsome and cunning, he carved out his niche at an early age. Thinking himself something of a *Genji*—the elegant prince of courtly tales—he had no plans to remain faithful to his small, delicate bride. With careful planning and a keen understanding of the dynamics of architecture, he saw to it that his large Edo-style mansion was refitted with secret passageways and private quarters solely for the purpose of accommodating his evening dalliances.

It was not that his wife was unattractive, for she was indeed beautiful. Had she not been, he would never have married her. Instead, he believed himself to be all-powerful and to be wholly and unquestionably entitled.

The first time he saw his wife, he noted that her forehead was aristocratically high, her mouth delicate as an orchid, and her hair as glossy as freshly ground ink. But what impressed him the most was her lineage and her good name. It would bode well for his career to have an heir born from such blood.

Takada's mother was of noble birth. Her father and his father before him had both served the emperor in his court. But as the fifth daughter born to a mother who bore only girls, she had a wretched position. Her elder sisters informed her years later, as they combed each other's hair, how her parents had failed to name her until two months after her birth. "What's the use?" her mother had asked. "I have no more names left for yet another girl."

Ultimately her parents called her Shizuka, and hoped that she would grow up and mirror her name: silent one. And they loved her the least because she was clearly a burden. Tiny and weak, a constant reminder that she had not been born a son.

"She is the last of my daughters to be married off," her father had told the handsome young politician, "so you need not worry about her mother's or my interference."

Takada's father looked at his hands, now full with a large envelope containing her dowry, and felt extremely pleased.

"Should we have a son, we would surely hope that you'd visit."

"Indeed," said the old man coldly. His indifference chilled the air of the already cold room. "We will return after the birth of her firstborn."

They were married in a small Shinto ceremony. The young girl dressed in traditional garb, her gaze weighted to the floor. That night, after the bridegroom had lain with his new wife, he stood up and left her to sleep alone. So she lay there by herself. Behind walls of rice thread. Behind the mask of tear-streaked powder and long black hair. Like the Akashi Lady of the classic tale, the woman who is one of many. The woman who grows old waiting. The woman who is longing to be loved.

Takada was born in the early days of winter. When frost formed an icy haze over the shutters. Where the breath froze from the lips of all who sighed in relief that the child produced was male.

His story, like mine but different. In his story there is silence and there is sadness.

But his ghosts are living.

His mother, unlike mine, did not die the night of his birth. Instead, she died more slowly, living her death as slowly as she dragged her robe.

"Males are always born to women of tears," her mother told her as the child was taken away from her and swaddled in silk, all in accordance with the politician's instructions. The old woman's face, powdered in rice flour, hung over that of her daughter, her envy greening the talc.

Tears spread like puddles over Takada's mother's face as her tiny son was carried away. Her breast heaving for his suck, her heart aching to be the one to comfort his cries. She looked into the darkness in search of her husband, her birthing bed illuminated only by thin burning tapers, but he had vanished from the room. She could hear in the distance his booming voice, his raucous and drunken laugh. The giggling of the women she foolishly believed were servants filling her ears.

"For sixteen weeks you may nurse him," her husband informed her, as he watched his infant son sleep in his mother's arms.

He watched every time she nursed the boy. Watched with narrow eyes and furrowed brow. He saw how the child, with smooth pink skin and patches of soft black hair, joyfully nestled into her breast. He saw how she held him dear.

But after sixteen weeks of having the child suckling at her side, so close that she could feel the tiny thump of his heart echoing inside her, the child was brought into her chambers no more.

"You will see him when he is strong," her husband told her while reaching to undo her hair. "Be patient and I will reward you," he uttered through heated and furtive breaths.

She arched her neck to give herself over to him entirely. The dutiful wife. So hollow that she felt concave. "No son of mine will grow weak from being coddled by the arms of his mother," he said as his body sweated and shuddered over hers.

And inside she felt herself dying. Floating up from underneath the weight of her husband's body and his wicked words. Evaporating like a trail of extinguished steam. Years later she would return to the memory of that evening. Mark it into her memory. The first day that began her death.

She felt him finish. Saw him as he paused and reached to snuff out the flame in the lantern beside her bed.

"It's that way, with the rearing of boys," he added mindlessly. "You wouldn't know that, wife," he said as he closed his eyes.

"After all, it's your poor destiny to have been born a woman."

* * *

As the weeks passed, Takada's mother grew increasingly despondent. "Please," she begged of her husband when he came to her on certain nights. "When might I be able to see my son?"

"*My* son," he said severely, with eyes that darted into her own.

She looked up at him, noticing how his cruelty hung over him like a rank, damp robe.

He crept up to her, and he smelled of imported tobacco and wine.

"You must be patient, wife," he told her again as she turned her head away and looked at the shadows behind the translucent wall, where her son slept just meters beyond. She saw the outline of his nursemaids. Heard his stifled cry. And as her arms stretched through those of her husband, she knotted her fists so that her nails might pierce her skin. Leeching herself of her own cries. Releasing the pain that had been choking her from within.

More time passed and Takada's father still forbade his mother to see her son. Her chambers were structured so that she faced west. The only bit of scenery she saw in her carefully controlled view was a formal garden, designed by her husband, with small sculpted trees and a log of hollow bamboo that dripped water onto a perfectly round rock. But on her north wall, from where she heard her son's weaning cries, her son's room abutted hers. There, at night, she would watch his shadow and wonder if he was old enough yet to recognize her.

In the second year of her son's life, her husband informed her that she would periodically be permitted to see her child. But the visits would be limited to one hour a week. "Social obligations," he called it. During such times, when he saw to it that everything was structured under his careful eye and suffocating control, he would order the child dressed in small silk outfits and request that his wife's hair be plaited and arranged in the traditional style of a married woman of the day. He too would prepare for the pomp and artificiality of the engagement, dressed not in a kimono but in a suit, tie, and bowler. He would call for a carriage to bring his picture-perfect family to a staged public outing. He would request one of his favorite servant girls to hold a parasol over his wife and child, so that they seemed like a family stolen from an imported painting. Neatly arranged on the manicured lawn of a garden like the beautiful trees that were sculpted by razor, the scars from where they have been pruned hidden beneath the flashing of a flower.

On these rare and strained occasions, Takada's mother would always hold the child close to her, recall the time when she was able to hold him next to her heart, and tighten her face so that the tears could not fall. She would bury her small nose in the child's sprouting locks of hair, smell the sweet scent left by his bathing powder, and try to rub some of it onto the collar of her robe, hoping she might smell it hours later, after he had been taken from her again. Afterward, she lay alone in her room, only to watch him as a shadow.

She knew he would grow up fast. Like a sprout of sweet pea, tall and lean. She could not help but weep, knowing she would not be present to share his first teetering steps, to hear the first words he managed from his lips. But the memory of their first months together kept the candle of her faith aglow.

"There is a bond between us," she would whisper into her north wall, as if the porous paper would absorb her words and relay them into her infant son's ears. She would lay her head next to the slats of bamboo and try to listen for his breaths. Hoping to be his *silent* protector. Hoping to be his mother, even if rarely seen or heard.

In her heart she nurtured the idea that they had formed a bond between them, their fluids in each others veins. "My husband cannot break that," she prayed over lit candles. "Let it be beyond his control."

As her son grew to be a toddler, their time together still limited and arranged, Shizuka could not help but see how the child was drawn toward her space. As if it was impossible for him to forget her. As if he too longed to be at her side.

On the days in between their structured meetings, mother and child were never allowed a moment alone. The house, with its many narrow passageways, was constructed so that they could never use the same channels. A house woven with countless paper screens and hidden doors. A labyrinth created to prevent love.

Denied daily contact with his mother, Takada was brought up by nursemaids who attended to his needs in the day and early afternoon, and to his father's needs in the evening. They sweetened his milk with sugar cubes, hoping he would grow fat and would no longer cry. They fed him *o-seki-han*, the festive azuki rice, nearly every day rather than just on holidays, and scented his tea with chrysanthemum petals. But, as large as he grew, he remained forever empty.

When he found himself alone at night, he would be accompanied by his mother's muffled cries. Separated from her by a screen, his first unchaperoned contact with her was by spreading his fingers like a spider over the webbing of her shadow, cast in black over the shoji. Rice paper stretched in a sea of white.

He learned to memorize the rhythm of her footsteps. Recognize the rustle of her heavy robe.

But still he longed to spend even just a single moment with her alone.

Month after month passed. With every night, he yearned to touch and feel something more than the cool black outline of her form.

Slowly, the square of rice parchment, which Takada had grown accustomed to touching, began to grow thin from wear. And one night, when his nursemaids had tucked the futon underneath his chin and gone to busy themselves with their other more fulfilling duties, he found his fingers piercing the near-transparent skin. There, suddenly, in the middle of the shoji, was a hole.

If he listened closely, he could hear his mother's breathing. Partitioned from her only by a thin screen, her head rested where for so many years she had learned to sleep and wait.

"*Okāsan, Okāsan . . .*" he whispered. *Mother. Mother.*

Suddenly there was the soft illumination of her lantern. And for the first time, he heard her speak freely.

"Yes . . ." It was the sound of her voice, murmured ever so faintly.

And as she made out his first few words, she saw from her side—her side of the screen that had separated them for so many years—the small protrusion of a tiny pink finger needling through a hole as minute as a marble.

She drew herself close to the shoji and knelt, her cotton robe dragging underneath her knees, her long, black hair trailing behind her. And for the first time she reached out and touched her son alone.

The child behind the screen, the young Takada, grasped the finger of his mother. He held on to her so tightly that she thought she might just have to scream. But she bit her lip instead, preferring to taste the tiny droplets of blood rather than forgo this moment—the moment she had awaited for so long.

The two of them could conjure up no words. The sensation

of each other's warmth silenced them for what seemed like hours. When the first hint of daylight approached, Takada heard the faint murmur of his mother.

"Child," she whispered, "should your father discover us, he will banish me. This is too great a risk. Should I be unable to watch over you, even if it is only your shadow, I will surely die. So you must allow me to cover this hole."

"Yes, Mama," he whimpered, embarrassed that, should his mother hear his cries, she might not think him a man.

As the sun began to rise, he listened as his mother furiously cut the paper from her now extinguished lantern. He heard her break its bamboo spine and carefully discard its remaining pieces in the stuffing of her pillow. He caught the sound of her fumbling through her lacquer boxes, searching for her needle and thread.

In the moonlight he caught the glimmer of her face, beautiful like a doll's, as she began to sew over the pierced square of torn parchment with a patch of the lantern skin, her eyes shining much like his own. But she looked away from him, his glance too painful to bear, the separation already weakening her soul.

But he kept on watching her. Wanting to remember her as she looked without the weight of his father's glaring eyes. As if to engrave her into his memory. Forever. Because even that didn't seem long enough.

So he watched her as she sewed over their little square window. Watched as her eyebrows furrowed and she fought back the tears. Watched as she replaced the square of parchment that had allowed her forbidden contact with her son. And he studied her two fingers, slender as reeds, as they grasped the spinning silver needle. Mending the parchment stitch by stitch till the envelope was sealed. Till slowly he could see her no more.

*   *   *

He grew from a sad small boy to a melancholy young man under the careful and cold guidance of tutors handpicked by his father. Still limited in seeing his mother, he saw her rarely and became accustomed to communicating with her shadow.

Takada studied vigorously: Japanese classical literature, history, and abacus calculation, as well as intensive study of French and German. He loved the study of the French language most of all. His teacher, a young man from Osaka, had recently returned from studying abroad.

"I'll send you too!" his father promised in between clouds of smoke. "Before you're married, before you begin your political career." He looked at his father, slick in his Meiji-style suit, the pipe clasped between his yellowing teeth, and shuddered.

"I would like to leave for France in my twentieth year."

And to his shock, his father agreed. Knowing that it would bode well for his son to have some foreign experience, he consented to have the boy go off to Europe for a few years. But only on the condition that he would return by his twenty-fourth year.

The day Takada prepared for his departure, his father, to his surprise, called one of the maids to fetch his mother.

"Let the old woman say good-bye to her son," he said with the laugh of a wolf.

And as Takada waited on the first floor, his neck arched to the banister, he saw her once more before he was to leave. Not as she had been the night they grasped fingers. Mother to son. Not as she had been as he watched her veiled by the sweep of her black hair as she sewed the tired parchment. But still beautiful to him.

She stood at the top of the staircase, her hair neatly coiled on top of her head, streaked with gray. Her skin still smooth and white.

She wore a heavy kimono that cloaked her thin arms, but she withdrew her hand to wish him farewell.

She did not speak. But he sensed her thoughts: *Yes, go far away from here, my son.* He knew that she wished she could join him. Flee this prison that had kept her for so many years. As he watched the tears flooding her eyes, his too began to brim. He raised a handkerchief to his brow, covering his face with the cloth. By the time he returned it to his breast pocket, she was gone.

Takada's twenty-fourth year approached. He had spent the past years joyfully reading French literature at the Sorbonne, rarely thinking that time would catch up to him so fast.

But now the letter had arrived, calling him back.

Dear son,

Tokyo is filled with autumn leaves and the emperor has commissioned two more government buildings to be built in the Greco-Roman style. I am sure that you will not recognize our city when you return.

I have enclosed the last installment of your living allowance. You should use this for your passage back to Yokohama. I have been busy securing a job in the lower part of the parliament for you. I have also sent your photograph to a matchmaker who will arrange several o-miai meetings for you when you return. A good bride who will bring you a son someday, as well as maybe some more connections for your burgeoning political career.

I look forward to your return.

Your father.

Many nights Takada lay awake, splayed over his sheets, his arms extended across his bed, his legs tucked tightly together. Like a cross. Like a man preparing for his execution.

He thought of the world he had lived in for the past four years. Free of rules, regulations, and responsibility. Free of the oppressive weight of his father's presence. Where he could read to his heart's content and roam freely through the streets. For the first time he had friends of his own. Mostly Japanese, but Frenchmen as well. Here no one expected anything from him. No one demanded anything.

But there, oh, how different things would be! He so dreaded his return.

FORTY-FIVE

My life in Paris began to take shape over the weeks that followed the start of my studies under Collin. Every morning I started out just as the sun was rising over the Seine. With my black hat pulled down over my ears and my paint box clutched in my hand, I would walk twenty minutes to Collin's atelier.

There the older students would already be preparing their easels, arranging the paint on their palettes, the model still wrapped in silk chiffon.

The beginning students, myself included, worked in a smaller room off to the side. Our hands were yet to feel the splendor of a sable brush between our index finger and thumb. Instead, charcoal now blackened our palms and dusted our lungs. We sketched for hours, our necks stiff with pain, our wrists tired and sore.

Collin would appear every hour, from behind the half-closed French doors that separated us. He would walk behind each of us, his careful breathing blowing on our necks as he examined our work. Occasionally he would walk to the center of the room and turn the marble statue that served as our model. "Now draw her from this side," he would say before vanishing, and all of us would try our best to muffle our exasperated sighs.

Yet we all knew that, not until we were successful in reproducing these anatomically perfect creatures of stone, would we be able to work with a live model. Deeply frustrated, I recalled how I endured the same sort of struggle back in Tokyo.

For that first year with my mentor, my hands only clasped a stick of graphite or a lump of charcoal. We sketched in monochrome, and we were instructed in black and white. Only after class could we find color again.

We'd find it in a café. In a glass of claret. This red wine refilling our tired veins. William, the only other student who was not French, would tell us of his life in London. Where the English equivalent of the café was the pub. Where the maids were flushed and friendly. Where friends and brothers drank till dawn. I, of course, remained quiet and shy, my stories stored in my interior, the warmth of the drink never bringing them to the surface. I smiled when appropriate and learned to laugh with an open mouth and a hearty guffaw. But I never learned to reveal myself.

My brushes, in the meantime, remained in their jars at home, liberated from their glass cisterns only after I returned each evening. Then I would paint on my own, still somewhat clumsily. The color of paint was one of the few things that could alleviate my loneliness and keep my ghosts at bay.

My spirit nearly collapsed during my first year as a student with Collin. There was so much I struggled with; my confidence sagged, my belief in my talent nearly shattered, and my bouts of loneliness often debilitated me. I rarely saw anyone outside my class. I spent hours inside the atelier or at a museum working on figure drawings. Finally, the first year came to an end, and Collin announced that he would allow us to begin working with oils. I rejoiced at the opportunity to start experimenting with such silky, rich emulsions under the guidance of my teacher. There was so much to learn about handling the pigments properly. Soon I was learning how to mix certain proportions, layer the paint, scumble it so that all brushwork seemed to vanish, and even apply it in a thick impasto. Suddenly my canvases seemed to take on a new dimension. They finally began to reflect light and the figures appeared voluminous and fleshlike. I felt as though I had entered the canvas through the hairs of my brush. I felt as though I had finally begun to understand what Collin had spoken of, and for the first time all the sacrifices I had made to come to France appeared to have been worthwhile.

My surroundings began to inspire me. I looked at the sky and realized that it was full of colors other than blue. I gazed at the fields of grass and wondered how an artist could articulate each blade. Everything around me caused me to wonder how to portray it with paint.

Inevitably, I saw less and less of Takada and Hashimoto. Takada, however, appeared one rainy afternoon after I had finished class, standing outside the atelier.

"Why do you stand here without an umbrella?" I asked him, shocked to see him soaked through.

"I didn't notice it," he said absently. The black of his hair fell over his face like threads of seaweed, and his face was shiny like melted wax after it has cooled.

I was carrying a canvas wrapped in cheesecloth and I bent over it, trying to protect it from the rain.

"I thought we might get a cup of tea," he muttered.

I stared up at him. First, at his white shirt, now transparent, his brown skin revealed through cloth. I noticed his lips were turning a purplish shade of blue.

"Sorry," I uttered as apologetically as I could. "I have to finish this canvas by tomorrow. Even if I stay up to all hours of the night, I'll be hard pressed to complete it."

"I see," he said, unable to mask his dejection.

"Perhaps, I could manage just a quick cup of tea," I muttered. "But let us find a place not too far from here. My canvas is heavy and I have mountains of work to do before morning."

* * *

In a café on the Rue de Sèvres, not far from the Jardin du Luxembourg, we ordered two cups of steaming tea and settled into two roped iron chairs. Several large Frenchmen had gathered in a nearby booth, their table noticeably littered with empty carafes of wine, their voices and peals of laughter annoyingly loud.

The rain had left Takada dripping. Like a snuffed candle, a thin veil of breath rose from his skin, and tiny droplets rolled down his cheeks. Had I not believed him to be such a formal Japanese, I could have mistaken them for tears.

"Father has insisted I return next week," he said, as he pulled at his drenched shirt and ran a small handkerchief over his damp hair.

"You could stay, you know. You could try to get a job, or you could move into a smaller place to minimize your expenses."

"It's far more complicated than that, my friend."

"Yes, of course it is, but you must try."

Behind me, the noise of the crowd was growing increasingly distracting, and I tried with great effort to tune out their voices and the swirl of their tobacco smoke wafting through the air.

"Someday you will be in the same position as I," he said, and I knew I would remember those words forever. As I do now, even as an old man.

"We belong to neither world now. We live here and revel in a freedom that before was unknown to us. You find your spirit in color and line. I, in a stanza of Molière or a verse of Rimbaud. But we are fools to think that they accept us." He paused. "Look over there." He pointed to the crowd. "They mimic us behind our backs. Tell jokes at our expense and consider us unutterably beneath them."

I turned my head, as he urged me to do. To see what I so

desperately did not want to see. There they sat in clusters. Wineglasses raised to their lips. Their cravats loosened around their necks, their white shirts billowing out from their wristbands.

"Voyez les Chinoises!" one said as he pointed his crooked finger in our direction. *"Ils sont vraiment dégueulasses!"* another cried mockingly as he used his two forefingers to push up his eyes into tiny, thin slants.

"They think we are Chinese," Takada said as his lips touched the rim of his nearly empty cup. "To them we are all the same."

I sat there, my heart now sinking, my spirit nearly crushed.

"You are a bit naive, my friend," he said with a half smile. "The walls around your house in Kyoto must have been incredibly high."

I smiled, as I could feign no other reaction. I had hoped that those walls would crumble with this journey. But I knew that I still carried with me my own pain. My own guilt and my own hauntings. For Father would never leave me. I carried with me the unfinished Ishi-O-Jo mask as penitence. To wander forever with it as a reminder. A symbol of my betrayal, perhaps never to be reconciled.

"You have a canvas to complete," he said. "I shouldn't have kept you this long."

"No, no," I insisted. "It is fine."

"Tonight has helped me with my decision," and once again he took out his handkerchief and patted at his brow.

"Such a shame about the surroundings, though," I said apologetically.

"It's not your fault, Yamamoto-san," he said, his voice once again sounding sad. "Things like this are beyond our control."

I walked him outside, where we bowed to each other as we said farewell.

"Maybe we can get together again tomorrow," I hollered out to him.

But he did not answer me. He had already turned to leave. And I watched as his rain-soaked form walked into the distance, his back strangely slumped forward and his shoulders sloping toward the ground.

The sound of his shoes tapped over the cobblestone, until all I could make out was the lower half of his shadow, his echo surrendering to the wind.

FORTY-SIX

Takada hanged himself on the fourth day of November 1897, when I was in my thirteenth month of studies with Collin. Hashimoto, in the same black clothes he was wearing the day I first met him, met me outside of Collin's studio and informed me of the bad news.

I felt myself sinking as I stared back at him, felt as though my feet had suddenly succeeded in melting the stone. There was the initial ache I had experienced before. The sense of loss. The disbelief. But also a creeping feeling of anger.

Hashimoto began to retreat, sliding his feet backward over the cobbled street, bowing his head in departure. I listened, stunned, as he made an excuse for his departure—a figure-drawing class at the Beaux-Arts.

I found myself standing completely alone, rubbing my face furiously with the sweaty palm of my hand. I continued to do this absurd motion for what seemed like several minutes. I began at my forehead, running roughly over every one of my features until I reached my chin.

I wanted to convince myself that I wasn't wearing the same look of vacancy that I had just seen on the face of Hashimoto. I wanted my face to look red, swollen, miserable, shocked. Angry.

Takada was dead.

The sunny yellow painting I had begun for him during my first few days in Paris was now complete. It had been lying for several weeks now in my room, and I was only waiting for a free moment to drop it off at Takada's apartment. I stood outside, leaning against the cold stone of Collin's building, and felt a swelling nausea flow from the pit of my stomach into every one of my veins. I banged my fist into the rock-hard surface of the outside walls, and wished for once that this city were built of paper and wood so that I might tear the whole thing down or set it ablaze with one strike of a match.

Takada had come to me for help and I had selfishly put my art before him. I had responded as I imagined Father would have, and I hated myself for it.

The day I discovered that Takada was dead, I cried. I cried from tear ducts that should have dried up long ago, in a way I could not cry for my father's death. There no longer seemed to be any sense to my world. I did not care if anyone stared. I did not care if it was an act of weakness or cowardice.

So I wept. Wept like a child who never cried for the loss of his mother, the death of his father, who lived with him twenty-some years before he was buried at the base of a pine. As all Yamamotos are, the needled branches covering their tablets with broken yellow thatch.

That evening I went to Takada's apartment and found that Hashimoto was already there, boxing his things. I began helping him pile the volumes of French literature and criticism into card-board crates and address them to be sent home to his family. The room reflected the image of the dead man, restrained and mono-chromatic, with white walls and dark brown furniture.

"The police report said he hanged himself from the ceiling. He used a pair of brown leather suspenders," Hashimoto reported dryly. As he spoke, he was rolling a poster from the ballet *Le Rêve* that was printed in the style of a Japanese woodblock print. I had seen that poster plastered all over the streets—the image of the

Western woman in a tutu with a kimono thrown over her shoulders and a chopstick in her hair. Hashimoto placed it in a box and sealed it tightly with tape.

"Supposedly they confiscated a small rapier."

"Takada attempted *seppuku* as well?" I found all of this too much to comprehend.

"I don't think so. He probably contemplated it and then decided that the suspenders would suffice."

I thought of Takada's brown trousers, the ones he always wore with his tweed. I pictured him stringing himself up to the ceiling. The suspender loops knotted, his yellow-brown head strung through the self-made noose. His jacket slipping from his shoulders. Falling to the floor. His feet finally dangling free.

And now the brown wooden boxes were all taped, stacked, and labeled in a room suffocating in its own silence. In that room in Paris, where two Japanese, in brown shadows and the setting sun, packed with few words between them what remained of their fallen friend.

FORTY-SEVEN

He had been my closest friend in Paris, and although he was no substitute for Noboru, I had seen myself in him. The fact that he had chosen death as the only means of escaping his demons terrified me. It was not that suicide had never occurred to me, but my dream to achieve artistic excellence was always stronger. I needed to be pure to myself. To my father and in the memory of my mother. I could not rest until I had tried. After that, I did not know what would happen.

With Takada gone, my loneliness increased. The letter I received from Noboru intensified this.

January 4, 1898

Yamamoto-kun,

The days in Tokyo are cold. I have had to sleep with two hiba-chis next to my futon.

It is wonderful news to hear that you are now studying with Raphael Collin. I trust that you will be in good hands.

The Meiji Fine Arts Society has a few reproductions of Collin's work, and I was greatly impressed. I especially like the 1886 painting Floréal. *His rendering of the Western female figure seems to be executed with precision and an acute appre-*

ciation for detail. His choice of palette is soft, subdued, and elegant. It appears that he is experimenting with the Impressionists' style of diffused light. Is this correct?

Things have begun to change for the better here at school. It was announced that Kuroda Seiki will head the school's new Western Painting Section this year. We students had pressed hard for the creation of this department, and we are quite pleased with the results. There will be approximately twenty of us studying under him at the beginning of the fall semester, and some of his former students from his private atelier will be joining us.

I am confident that you are receiving a far better education in the techniques of Western painting than I am, however. You deserve such privilege. I am struggling to become an accomplished painter. It is difficult, as you know.

I will not be able to join you in Paris and this saddens me. I must wait here for your return.

Noboru

He feigned modesty in the letter. He also never mentioned missing me, as I so desperately missed him. It was all so difficult. I could not gauge the intimacy of his feelings through his letters. They were always somewhat formal, written in the traditional Japanese manner in which the weather is most sensitively described and the information that follows is relayed in a skeletal framework in which one must fill in the flesh to sense the true meaning of the words.

What I did learn was that he would not be coming. He had begun his life anew. The new program under Kuroda's guidance would ensure his success in Japan and his absence from me.

His mind would be elsewhere now. Lost in the pigments, consumed by the canvas. Never struggling to search the sea, to find me.

If anyone knew of the obsessive relationship between an artist and his work, it was I. I had lived it for the first twenty years of my life.

There is little room in an artist's life for anything but his work. Father had shown me that. I had been born the son of such a man, and my behavior toward Takada showed me that I was becoming such a man. Each day I fell deeper and deeper into my paintings. As if the brushstrokes I made could reach out and grasp me.

But still the memory of Noboru came to me. Most often at night, as I imagined Mother had come to Father.

I would see him in the fluttering of the curtains. The wind twisting them to create his form, the shadow of the lamplight playing tricks to create his face. And I would feel my heart swell with longing, because I knew that there was still a chance to love him. To hold him again. For Noboru was not yet a ghost.

My bed was cold and my body twisted in the damp white sheets. Where Noboru was, now it was already day. The sun was shining and surely he was already dressed in his kimono, his brushes gleaming in his polished hands. Did he think of me? Dream of me? Or had his passion for his painting replaced me, as Father had done with me. For love had abandoned Noboru when I left him at the gangplank. When I chose painting over him, when I opted to journey across the sea.

How I longed for him some nights. This night in particular. I had to believe he would remain true to me, as I would to him. My letters had become increasingly emotive. Perhaps the vivacity of France was rubbing off on me.

Dear friend,

I received your letter today. It seems the post is very slow and I wait impatiently for a letter each day.

Life here continues to be a struggle. Painting has become my life, my sustenance, and I miss you and our time together in Tokyo. How I still wish you could be here! To see all the beauty, the art, to meet Master Collin and become his pupil. I know he would be impressed with your talent. You would put me to shame!

There is no one here like you. Takada's death has made me lonelier than ever. And I fear I am becoming like my father. All of my life siphoned into my craft.

It seems you have been working as obsessively as I have. Congratulations on being accepted into Kuroda's program. You will be his favorite student, no doubt.

As much as I love the beauty of Paris, I look forward to the day when I can return to Tokyo. I can't wait for you to look at my canvases. Your opinion means so much to me, as does your friendship.

Faithfully,
Yamamoto Kiyoki

I had not revealed the true extent of my loneliness and longing in my letter. It would have been inappropriate for me to be any more emotional.

Several times I picked up Noboru's last letter and reread it. Each time it seemed more distant. Perhaps he was only distracted by the exciting news about Kuroda's class. I desperately wanted to be happy for him, for he would finally receive the education he deserved. But my heart still mourned his absence—and even more so because of Takada's suicide. Now I truly had no one in Paris, except Hashimoto, who was far too elusive to form a friendship.

Although Hashimoto had originally expressed excitement for a new Japanese arrival in Paris, his enthusiasm toward me had waned as my second year in Paris approached. I soon realized why Hashimoto had so little time for me. His interests lay in other areas besides the cloistered and serious walls of the Beaux-Arts.

FORTY-EIGHT

Eva didn't just walk; she rotated and swiveled. The balls and sockets of her hip bones seemed barely connected, as they managed to send her well-padded sides far into each corner of the sidewalk, propel her prominent pelvis into the foreground, and her two globular buttocks into the rising and swooshing of her rear. She was a more curvy version of the bodhisattva, a woman whose posture was permanently positioned in a seductive *S* curve. Her breasts were like two overripe mangoes, firm and exotic. Their color was unusual by Parisian standards because they were forever blushing a fervid pink, a burning shade of coral, which no amount of powder could hide.

In the middle of her heaving décolletage, framed by a plunging collar bordered in ribbon and lace, rested a small ivory amulet, strung on a black silk cord and squeezed between Eva's breasts. It was a strange amulet for a Frenchwoman of that time to be wearing: a miniature carving of the Buddha with a rotund face and protruding belly. This small, fleshy talisman, whose image seemed to be repeated within every fold, every curve, of this gargantuan female entity, was indeed an unusual piece of jewelry to substitute for a cameo. But Eva was far from conventional, especially considering the man she chose to dangle from her arm.

Eva had left her small village just outside Le Havre for Paris a few weeks after her eighteenth birthday. The birth of a seventh sibling had sent this young maiden to look for work in the big city.

She found it quickly. The manager at La Bucherie hired her as a barmaid only seconds after her request for work floated off her perfectly puckered lips. Her lack of experience was a trifle compared to her other assets. She had no ivory amulet between her breasts during those first few weeks. Later on, when she would recall her early days in Paris as a young single woman, miserable in her long hours of work and her *pauvre vie*, she would always insist it was because she had not yet been blessed with her ivory Buddha.

Hashimoto met Eva at La Bucherie during her second week as a barmaid. According to both of them, it was love at first sight.

He had stopped in for a quick whiskey. The bitter cold of a winter in Paris could not be endured without the medicinal charms of strong alcohol. He had grown up on warm sake to combat the freezing temperatures of winter in Tokyo, and simply looked upon his daily shot of whiskey as nothing more than an aspirin.

Eva's painted mouth and non-Parisian smile greeted Hashimoto's Arctic-glazed eyes with immediate results: he soon began to thaw. He dissolved like a teaspoon of honey in a cauldron of boiling water even before the whiskey touched his lips. He immediately wanted to paint her. He saw her white and milky body sprawled over a divan in his studio. He saw her fiery red hair unpinned and flowing over her pale shoulders, falling over her rose-inflamed breasts. He saw that she was a woman who had all the possibilities of a flower: she would open up to him, his very own fleur-de-lis.

She was not cold and frigid, like the other women of Paris he had encountered. They never shed a glance of warmth from the icicles that served as their eyes. They looked at his tiny yellow body, the black crescents of his eyes, the lacquered ebony of his hair, and immediately chastised themselves for gazing too long, for letting their stares find a victory over their expressionless faces, all because he was a foreigner.

But Hashimoto realized, from the moment he entered the café, moving toward the shiny mahogany bar and the voluptuous caryatid who rose from behind its wood and brass barrier, that the woman who stood there was fantastically different.

Eva was indeed different. Anyone who had the opportunity to dine with the amorous couple could tell that she was far from ordinary. When she reclined against Hashimoto's shoulder, her perfumed body smelling of vanilla and lime, she'd eagerly recall her first encounter with her Big Buddha, the man who had saved her from being a barmaid for the rest of her life, the man who had given her her talisman.

Eva insisted she sensed Hashimoto's arrival even before he entered the café. According to this northern farm girl, the café that had been so poorly heated for several days suddenly became as hot as an island in Polynesia. When she noticed that her permanently flushed bosom was beginning to perspire, Eva knew that something wonderful was about to happen. Her mother had always told her that a woman never sheds an ounce of moisture from her breast unless she is either pregnant or in view of the eyes of her betrothed, and Eva knew she was not pregnant. By the time she had mopped up the spots of water that puddled the surface of the bar, her countenance beaming in the golden reflection of the brass, she noticed that a strange calm came over the café. There was a pause when Hashimoto entered, that profound silence which conversationalists have spent lifetimes trying to interpret.

Their love affair began the moment Eva's eyes met Hashimoto's, and soon Hashimoto's yearning for Eva was so intense

that he found himself incapable of attending his classes at the
Beaux-Arts.

Eva, however, did not distract him from his painting. On the
contrary, she drove him to unimaginable heights of artistic inspiration. Mornings, afternoons, evenings, at all hours except during
interruptions for passionate lovemaking, Hashimoto sought to
reproduce Eva's image in his paintings. He painted her as her
unadorned self, settling in to the comfort of a silken divan; he
painted her as Venus rising from the waters and haloed by seashells; and he painted her as the Madonna, with a strangely Eur-
asian Christ Child.

There was no denying that Eva had replaced Hashimoto's daily
need for whiskey. It was she who warmed him now, fueled his
painting, nourished his heart, and sent fireworks exploding
through his soul. Together the two of them lived and feasted on
each other, a curtain of finished canvases bordering their boudoir
in a tiny studio on the Rue de Daviel in Paris.

Seeing Eva and Hashimoto together made me feel more alone
than ever. I was uninterested in having an affair with a Frenchwoman. What I really desired was to retrieve that sense of fulfillment, that wonderful unconditional companionship that I'd had
with Noboru in Tokyo. He understood me. He inspired me. In
his own way, he loved me. I had grown up in a family where my
father was silent, my siblings wooden masks, and my mother a
ghost. Noboru had, without ever putting his mouth to mine,
breathed life into the deflated chamber of my body. With him, I
felt the closest I had ever felt to being in love.

Sometimes, in the evenings, when we stayed late at the studio
and then found ourselves in the quiet sanctuary of my apartment,
the evening sky studded with stars and exploding with the giant

white cannonball of the moon, our gazes would linger in the recesses of each other's eyes. Now I know that it was exactly the same quiet that Eva spoke about. I would try to remember that feeling when I was alone in my rented room in Paris. Try to recall his body after having soaked in the steaming waters of my *o-furo*. His skin, red and smooth, revealed from within the cotton packaging of his *yukata*. He had such tiny hands with such long, threadlike fingers. He loved to sit neatly against my wall, his head resting on the pedestal of his bent knees. And I, so unremarkable in comparison, a long mass of skin and bones, with large hands and sinewy fingers, yearning to be so daring as to penetrate the thin box of space that encased his body. I yearned to enter the sphere where he inhaled his air, exuded his natural perfume, positioned his legs. Just to smell the scent of his neck, the faint traces of sweet red bean paste on his breath, the chrysanthemum oil he used on his hair. To have the cilia of my eyelids sweep over the entirety of his body, and to have the ability to cling to him, as I do now to that memory.

FORTY-NINE

It was a cold, blustery day in February when I ran into Eva and Hashimoto. Their black carriage pulled alongside me, and Hashimoto pushed his head outside the black satin top.

"Hello there!" he called out, and the very sound of his voice sent me recoiling. The horseman pulled over to the side of the street and pulled his bowler hat over his eyes while he waited for us to finish our conversation.

"We haven't seen you in a bit," said Hashimoto. His glasses were beginning to frost from the shocking cold outside his warm carriage.

Eva cocked her head to one side. Her flaming hair was tucked inside a frilly bonnet, and her large bosom was hidden under a heavy velvet cape.

"Yes, hello, dear Yamamoto. Why have you been keeping yourself so scarce?" Her voice was flirtatiously high.

"Work, work, and more work," I mumbled. "Doesn't the Beaux-Arts keep *you* busy, my friend?"

"Busy?" he asked in a mocking tone. "No, not at the moment, although I must admit I've been missing many a class lately." He turned to Eva and placed a hand on her voluptuous thigh.

"We actually have an Art Students' Ball this Saturday. I daresay we could get you an invitation if you wanted."

Eva squealed with delight. "Yes, yes! He can take Isabelle as his guest."

She leaned forward again so that I could see her, and miraculously her cape fell off her shoulders, exposing her radiant cleavage. "It's a masquerade ball, Yamamoto," she crooned. "You'll have to wear a mask and costume. It will be great fun!"

"I'm afraid I'll have to decline," I mumbled. "Anyway, that horseman of yours is getting cold."

"We will hear nothing of the sort," Hashimoto insisted. "You are absolutely coming to this party. All the most talented art students of Paris will be there."

"And Isabelle is quite a beauty!" Eva added, smiling. "You'll thank me by the time the evening is over."

I highly doubted that would ever happen. If I could have attended with Noboru, that would have been an entirely different matter. But why would I want to go to a ball where I knew no one and, worse than that, as the escort of a woman I had never met?

"No, no," I insisted. "I absolutely cannot do it. I have several canvases to complete and I'm not much fun at social events. I assure you, I would be quite a bore."

"Don't be such a little boy," Eva cried. "Won't you try to persuade him, Buddha?" And with that, she nuzzled her round cheeks into his shoulder.

"There is no discussion, old friend," Hashimoto insisted. "We will pick you up on Saturday." The horseman cracked his whip and the carriage pulled out into the street. "Don't forget, it's a masquerade," Hashimoto added, sticking his head momentarily outside the tarp and then, within seconds, retreating back into the carriage.

I was left standing beside a lantern post, the cold, damp wind stiffening my hair with frost.

The following Saturday morning, I awakened with absolutely no plans to attend the ball. I had several paintings I wanted to complete, and I had felt sluggish for weeks. My canvases were not turning out as I expected. The colors were muddy, and the nude I was trying to render seemed awkward and uninspired.

I silently blamed Noboru for my malaise. He had not yet responded to my latest letter, and his last correspondence still weighed heavily on my mind. I had become convinced that there was a distance to his words that surpassed the typical Japanese formality. Had I been a fool to nurse my affection for him as long as I did? Had he forgotten the intensity of our relationship in the two and a half years since I had left?

I was finally beginning to accept that he would never come. But I was unwilling to believe that he would forget me.

I would have come, had our situations been reversed. I would have swum the waters, floated through the Mediterranean, my kimono sleeves billowing like sails. I would have written every day, as I nearly had, answered each letter immediately, and finally sold my soul, if it meant I could have come.

But, perhaps in my old age I can see things more clearly. Now I realize that, like my father, I put my craft above love. And in the end, I was the one who left.

I wrapped myself in my kimono and sat down on my only chair. Outside, the sun was set against the church spires, and the bells of Notre-Dame were ringing in the hour.

I was surrounded by my work. I had somehow managed to sneak a part of myself into the composition of nearly every still life, every nude. Collin had thought the idea innovative, "As you are an artist, why should you not paint a faint reflection of your-self in the window, or over here?" he said, pointing to the toe of my brown shoe on the edge of my canvas. "Why should I tell you to take that out?" He smiled. "For the first time, Yamamoto, you are beginning to be original. Congratulations!"

I had not meant to be original. I was only painting what I saw. If I caught sight of my scalp in the windowpane, or the toe of my oxford on the tile beyond my easel, I thought it only right to paint myself into the canvas. As an artist, I recorded everything that I saw in front of me. I had always been an observer; participation was not my strength. I watched life. I relayed my vision in color and line. That was what separated me from others.

I wished Hashimoto had understood that, but obviously he did not. At half past eight, there was a furious knocking at my door.

"Let us in, Yamamoto dear!" cried Eva. "We will be late."

"Yes, yes," Hashimoto echoed. "The carriage is waiting for us downstairs."

I opened up the door and saw that Eva and Hashimoto had arrived as Marie Antoinette and Louis XVI. She was wearing a towering golden wig dripping in faux pearls and an elaborate brocade costume that made the best of her ample décolletage. He was wearing a matching brocade vest, tailcoat, and pantaloons in robin's-egg blue and silver, an inexpertly powdered wig, white knee-high stockings, and high-heeled shoes. Their masks were studded with rhinestones; his made of felt, hers of ostrich plumes.

And behind them stood the most exquisite creature I had seen since Noboru. From where I stood, I could not tell if she was a man or a woman. She had come in costume as a faun. Her robes were made of fur, each hair as if touched by a brush drenched in a pot of raw sienna and burnt umber. Her long arms extended from her robes like delicate columns, her neck slender and her collarbone shining.

Her long red hair had been piled high. And tiny ears had been inserted on her headband of golden leaves.

"Let me present the lovely Isabelle, or the Fairy Faun for the evening," Hashimoto said with a bow. She tipped her brown mask to reveal a beautiful face. High cheekbones. Skin as pale as alabaster. Green eyes and an orchid-bloom mouth. The three of them walked inside.

"I am afraid, if you have decided to go as a Japanese in his bathrobe, Yamamoto, you might just catch cold," said Hashimoto with sarcasm. "Why don't you change into a kimono and go as a Japanese? You'll be the most authentic one there, I assure you."

"Yes!" Eva chirped. "And we brought you a mask, just in case you had forgotten to buy one. One must always come prepared for these things."

From behind her mask, I could see Isabelle trying to disguise her smile.

"If you will excuse me," I said calmly, "I will change into a kimono, as my friend Hashimoto has suggested." I gathered my navy robe from the closet and informed them I would only need a moment.

Inside the bathroom, I splashed cold water on myself and changed from my linen *yukata* into my silk robe. My reflection in the mirror revealed that the past few months had weathered me. My face was beginning to be lined, my once jet-black hair now showed the first sprouts of gray. I was almost gaunt; my cheekbones looked like large triangles swathed in a transparent stretch of skin. My lips were cracked, my eyes watery and unclear. What a sight I must have appeared to them! Had Noboru seen me, he would hardly have recognized the man before him, reduced to skin and bones. I had become quite the stereotype of the starving artist.

Suddenly I was Interrupted by Hashimoto's impatient cries.

"Come on, old man, we really must be going."

I opened the bathroom door and hurried to put on my sandals.

"Put on your mask," Eva insisted. She handed me the small

red covering with the eyes cut out and the ribbons to tie in the back. This is what they call a mask? I thought to myself. The flimsy piece of felt that I held in my hand was nothing like the masks of my childhood, nothing like the one that slept underneath my mattress here, its eyes inscribed by one man's knife. This mask had no weight, no intensity, and no spirit. Its only purpose was to disguise.

"Let me help you with the ribbons," Eva offered. She came over to me, her perfume rising off her flushed chest, and tied the mask strings in a bow. It was the first time I had ever worn such a thing, and there was so little thought behind it. It was not like Grandfather, who meditated over his mask for hours before raising it to his face.

"Are we finally ready?" Hashimoto's voice was completely exasperated.

"Yes, yes, so sorry to have kept you waiting." I motioned them to exit, and I fumbled to lock the door behind me.

As I watched Eva and Hashimoto descend the staircase, clouds of smoke rising from his wig, I was caught off guard by Isabelle's slender arm sliding into mine.

Although I felt awkward, I allowed it. Because she was different and because she was so beautiful. This gazelle-like creature who—for the evening, at least—was mine.

The entrance to the Art Students' Ball was marked by torchlight. Garlands of freesia and ivy were strung over the frieze. Bouquets of fruit, tiny champagne grapes and pale green quinces, filled Grecian urns. The sound of strings beckoned us. Violins and cellos. The smooth melody from the clarinet, and the flute's fluid breath. Isabelle squeezed my arm as her deep red fur brushed over my silken robe.

"This is terribly exciting, isn't it?" she said softly. Her French was smooth and melodious, blending like an instrument with the violins.

"Yes, yes," I said, although I was feeling dizzy, overwhelmed by the sumptuous surroundings. Men and women swarmed around us, each costume more elaborate than the next. A Turkish Moor swathed in a turban sipped champagne next to women in long velvet robes, golden bracelets, and violet shoes. A sun-bronzed pharaoh stole a kiss from a raven-haired and turquoise-bejeweled Cleopatra, and a short, balding gentleman dressed as Napoleon drank champagne from a helmet whose exterior he had adorned with yellow feathers.

I spotted Hashimoto and Eva speaking to a man dressed as Caravaggio's Bacchus. A garland of grapes encircled his head, his brown chest protruded from the white toga he had draped over his side, and a goblet of claret nestled in one of his chubby pink hands.

"Have you known Eva long?" I finally mustered the courage to ask my night's companion.

"I met her when she first came to Paris. She bought a hat from me." She was smiling from beneath her chestnut-colored mask. Behind the slits, her green eyes were dazzling.

"I've been making hats since I was a little girl." But soon she had turned from me, her russet robes sweeping like a fox's tail over my shins. The music filling my ears.

"Do you see the orchestra playing over there?" she mused. "How I wish you'd ask me to dance."

I knew that Frenchwomen were far more forward than their Japanese counterparts. But still, her words froze me with fear. I had never danced with any woman before, Japanese or European. I knew not even the proper dance steps to attempt such a feat!

"Come, come," she chided gently, "or we will miss this round!" She thrust her arm around mine and dragged me onto the dance floor.

She pulled herself close to me, her acorn-colored hair and gilded wreath aflame, the torchlight illuminating my perspiring brow. She smelled like the forest, deep and musky. I inhaled the sweet fragrance of the leaves she had fastened to her hair.

"Don't be afraid, I will guide you," she said from behind her mask. And it was true, she led me as the music swayed on. As celestial as a fairy, she moved over the notes of music, her body close to mine, so that I could continue to inhale her woodland perfume. Was it the high green of cypress, to match her cinnamon-red hair? My head bowed toward hers as she led me over the floor, the music filling my ears, my navy robe billowing with air. Indeed, I was lost in the winding curves, the dips, and the curtsies. For that brief moment, as the orchestra played on, I was hers.

The moon beamed ivory. Round, as if it were the sun cloaked in ermine, it shone on a sea of artists and their friends. It was only then that I felt slightly guilty that Noboru was not there with me.

Where was he now? I wondered as Isabelle and I removed ourselves from the dance floor. Was he asleep? Was he alone or with another, as I was? I had not betrayed him, I said to myself, even though this was the first time I had felt so intoxicated by another person besides my devoted Noboru.

When the night began to transform itself into dawn and Isabelle and I found ourselves separated from Eva and Hashimoto, the other guests departing, and the orchestra beginning to pack away the instruments, I did not protest when she suggested that we return together to my room.

She stood in my small chamber, the fading moonlight radiating off her doeskin form, the fur robe falling from her shoulders, and I could have wept from the sight of her golden limbs.

Was it the champagne that made me dizzy, or was it fear? I stood in the corner, watching as she remained steadfast in front of me, her mask still cloaking her face, her hair still bound with pearls.

She removed her robes first. The mask remained, the hair still piled high. And I gasped as she let the russet silk fall to the floor, like an autumn tree shedding its leaves, her nakedness revealed to me.

Her body glowed like amber. Translucent and deep yellow. Her thighs soft and round.

"If not for you, then for whom shall I undo my hair?" I said, remembering how Grandfather had used the ancient Heian poem to describe Grandmother.

And she raised her long, lean arms to unpin her titian curls. They fell like Bordeaux waters over her perfect, round breasts.

"Come to me," she said, and stretched out her arms for me. I hesitated before I went to her, and when I did, she untied the ribbons of her mask.

"Yamamoto," she whispered, and her fingers reached down under the folds of my robe. She could feel my body trembling next to hers, a body wrestling with fear, desire, and guilt.

My kimono fell to the floor. The navy silk formed a dark puddle around my feet, like spilled ink bleeding into the floor.

She kissed my forehead and ran her ivory fingers over my bony chest. Around me I inhaled the deep woodland smell of the forest and stroked the downiness of her loins. The night had left her wet, her skin damp and fragrant.

I was not so naive that I did not know what she desired from me. In Japan we have woodblock prints that could make a Western man blush. But in the end, my own loins failed me.

My heart was elsewhere, true to the person I always believed I would love.

I removed myself from the embrace of her sensuous form. Her breath was racing and her body flushed strawberry. My own sex hung slack and small.

I stood over her, both of us naked, she more beautiful and luminous than the most exotic flower. I marveled over the curve of her back, the plumpness of her derriere, the fullness of her breasts. The nipples the color of crushed poppies, the shadow cast underneath her arms the color of wet lilacs.

"What is the matter?" she finally asked. Her soft voice was nearly lost in the wind outside my window.

"It is just that you are so beautiful, I prefer . . . I prefer . . ." I stuttered nervously, looking past the curtains of my dank room into the quiet of the night.

"I prefer to paint you."

And so, as the night gave over to dawn, I painted her. My Isabelle. Mine for the evening, in any event. Where I could record her on my canvas. Never before had I been so inspired. That night I blended my pigments like a great master. Her flesh rendered in a palette of primrose and burnt carmine. Her scarlet curls adorned by golden leaves and tiny faun ears. Like a character from Greek mythology, she hovered between flesh and foliage, a goddess of the woods.

Lulled by the rhythm of my brushstrokes, Isabelle slept in pose, only to awaken to find her mirror image forever cast on canvas.

"May I have your robe?" she asked me when she awakened from her sleep and found herself lying on my floor like an odalisque. The bright morning light had caused her to blush with embarrassment.

"Certainly," I said as I rushed to hand her my *yukata*.

She tied the sash tightly and walked over to my easel.

"Is that *me?*" she asked modestly.

"Yes," I said, scared that she would declare my rendering of her atrocious. She walked two paces back and squinted at the canvas.

"*Monsieur,*" she said with a smile. "I think it's *wonderful!*"

FIFTY

This is your best painting to date, Yamamoto!" Collin cried when I showed him the painting of Isabelle, *The Fairy Faun*. "If you can work a little on the brushwork, you might just be able to enter it in the Salon next year."

Collin placed the canvas on the center easel and took a few steps back. "Such an exquisite model! Where ever did you find her?" He looked back at me, his eyes shining.

"Such a splendid idea to have her mask half between her fingers and half dangling to the forest's floor. And such a lovely body! You've finally gotten the proportions just right!" He moved closer and squinted at the detail of the nude. "It's quite magnificent . . . the contrast of her creamy white body set against those rich red-brown robes."

"I'm so glad you like it, Master Collin," I managed to say. "It still needs improvement, I know."

"Your brushstrokes need to be stronger, Yamamoto," he said as he pulled at his voluminous white beard. "Start working on some other canvases and then come back to it. Your mind will be refreshed, and you'll thank me for the advice afterward, I assure you."

My painting of *The Fairy Faun* remained on the center easel all day, the easel that Collin reserved for his students' most commanding paintings.

I began my day's work, stretching out another canvas and priming it with gesso.

That night, I carried the canvas of Isabelle through the streets as I made my way back to my room. I held the painted side toward me, so that her nakedness wouldn't be revealed to the crowds, and so I could protect her unvarnished surface from the blustering wind.

I worked on perfecting her at home. I mixed the colors of my palette on my wooden board and blended the pigments until they were as rich as jewels.

The reds glowed like rubies, the greens like jade and ultramarine. I tried to give her face a truly three-dimensional quality. I painted in the delicate flare of her tiny nostrils, the faint trace of auburn hair that cascaded over her brow.

For the forest, I used my memory of Daigo as my guide. I imagined the tall, lean cypresses; the curling leaves of the cryptomeria; the flat blades of the sumac. I remembered the shadow of my own form as I lay down in sleep on the damp earthen floor.

There in the wooded kingdom she sleeps. The fairy faun. Her umber robes, her bedding, the sunlight bathing her flaxen form. And I keep her in my studio, to work on her until I have perfected her, as Collin inspired me to do.

FIFTY-ONE

Looking back, I can see a thin thread that connects my experiences in life with those of my art. All of my relationships, like all of my paintings, were struggles. During my days with Collin, I often found myself staring into my sketch pad or my canvas, hoping perhaps that it would speak to me. Guide me. Show me where I was headed in this often frustrating journey to create art.

But in Collin's atelier, I was not Yamamoto Ryusei's son. No one knew me as the only child of the mask carver and his lost love. I was simply Yamamoto Kiyoki, the Japanese who had come to Paris to pursue painting.

As the end of my third year of studies with Collin approached, I started to feel that my work was coming together. The painting of Isabelle, *The Fairy Faun*, had marked my turning point as an artist. Collin was perhaps the first to vocalize it, but I was beginning to feel it within myself as well.

For over three years, I had struggled within the walls of Collin's atelier to reproduce the images that I saw before me.

I grieved painfully over my inability to reproduce what my eyes beheld, what my heart understood. In the slender figure of the young girl before me, I saw the slight curve that ran from her armpit to the valley underneath her breast; I saw the shadow that marooned itself like a puddle of Madeira at the back of her bent knee; and I saw the perfect shape of her shoulder blades, her spine falling like a single ribbon down her back and then curving outward like tied laces around her behind. I saw everything, sensed every contour, memorized every shape. But many times my eyes fell upon the image on my page, and I didn't recognize it at all from the subject that stood before me.

But now I believed my luck was changing. Collin had gazed upon my rendering of Isabelle as the fairy faun and had seen what I had: her magnificent beauty cast in autumn hues. I had captured her radiance, her perfectly proportioned figure, her mystical allure, and seized it! I had forever preserved her within the threads of my canvas.

"You still have to concentrate on your brushwork, Yamamoto," Collin said gruffly while looking over my shoulder as I painted with the others one afternoon.

"I will not have you returning to Japan until you have developed a style of your own, young man."

"Yes, sir," I said meekly.

"Don't paint for the sake of the judges at the salon. Paint for your own sake. If you continue to paint exactly what has been painted for the last hundred years, how will art ever evolve?"

The others in the class were looking on. William peeked out from behind his canvas and winked with familiar fun.

"True, you all know I am a bit of a stodgy Academic in my own right, but even I have learned something from those Impressionists!"

The others managed a chuckle.

"As artists we must bring our own experience into our vision. Vision is as important as light and shadow!"

"Yamamoto," he said, as he crept close behind my hunched shoulders. "Did you not tell me once that your father was a mask carver?"

And I stared at him as he brought the ghost of Father into this room where the emulsions we used would have rotted wood.

"And have you any carving experience?"

"Yes," I replied, almost ashamed.

He then took a palette knife and a rag from the pocket of his white smock. He carefully stroked the shining blade with the pressure of his fingers and the cloth. Like my first set of chisels, the blade was silver in the light of the sun.

"Who says a canvas cannot also be carved?"

And then he walked away. The palette knife lay beside my scattered tubes of paint. I stared at the steel instrument and then at the soft bladders of pigment. The blade and the paint coexisting. That which I had always considered separate now mingled together.

Collin allowed me my own discovery. He vanished somewhere into the atelier as I applied those first few strokes of paint with my knife.

Perhaps the palette knife is not only for blending pigment, I thought to myself. And I held the blade in my hand. So much lighter than the chisel, its blade flexible to the touch, it extended before me and I swept it across the page.

I watched as it cut over the canvas, rippling the paint up over its edge. Then I applied some paint to another section and used the knife like a pencil. The image of Isabelle reclining on the forest floor seemed to be coming off the canvas, her flesh almost within my grasp. With the tip of the knife, I carved her out of the pigment.

Collin came over to me hours later, after I had transformed my canvas. She was as beautiful as she had been that night when I first painted her as a faun. But now she came forth. Entered space. Took possession of one's eyes.

My master stood behind me, his eyes pressed into a squint, his long fingers laced before him like strings. "Very good, Monsieur Yamamoto."

And I turned to him, my black smock smeared with paint, my hair wild from work, and I smiled. I can still recall how strange my teeth felt against my upturned lips. The sensation of a smile was as foreign to me as a loud, long laugh. He placed his pale hand on my shoulder and squeezed.

"Your eyes have finally met your hands," he said.

And I extended my hands before me. Stared at their paint-spotted skin, flashes of orange and gold pigment flecked over the joints. I turned them over and marveled at the palms, these appendages of mine that gripped palette knife and brush in order to create.

"You have accomplished something here, my son."

I stared up at him with glassy eyes. I wanted to remember this man before me for always. This teacher who called me his son. And I wondered if my own father looked down on me that shining afternoon and saw me carve. Because I realize I was not doing it for Collin, or for myself, but as a tribute to Father.

FIFTY-TWO

I am so proud of you," Collin said, when my painting was selected for the Salon. He extended his hand and clasped mine. "When a pupil's work is admitted to the yearly Salon, his teacher cannot help but bask a little in his glory!" he said, and his eyes were beaming.

I smiled. "It is all because of your patience and guidance, Master Collin. Without you I would still be doing awkward sketches, no doubt."

"You are too hard on yourself, dear Yamamoto. In these four years you have made tremendous strides in your work. Your canvases reveal that."

The same day I ran into Hashimoto and Eva on the street. They were not in the comfort of a carriage, and she was shivering underneath her cloak and muff.

"Congratulations, Yamamoto," Hashimoto wheezed over a cough. "I heard that one of your paintings was accepted this year by the Salon!"

"Yes," I said and blushed. "I was quite surprised."

"I've been trying for eight years!" he lamented. "It must be some painting!"

"It's really nothing," I said adhering to a strict sense of Japanese modesty.

"Well, we definitely will come to see it when the Salon opens next week," said Eva. "The Salon is always such a social event in Paris. One simply must attend!"

I looked down at her rosy cheeks and plaited hair and nodded in agreement.

"Perhaps we'll bring Isabelle. She speaks of you often. It was quite rude of you, Yamamoto, not to have called on her after the ball," she said playfully.

"Oh," I said, trying to muster a defense, "I've been so busy recently, truly lost in my work. I hardly ever see a soul." But the thought of Isabelle attending the Salon and seeing herself displayed to the public petrified me. It would be almost too embarrassing to bear!

"I really doubt Isabelle would find the Salon very interesting."

"Nonsense!" cried Hashimoto. "Who doesn't find the Salon interesting? The lines to enter snake across the street. The cafés nearby make enough money to last the year! It is the art event of the season!"

I was mortified at the thought of embarrassing Isabelle. Even though I had not seen her since that night, I was still sensitive to her feelings. Had our positions been reversed, I would have been mortified to see a nude portrait of myself hanging in a public place. Worse yet, what would Eva and Hashimoto say upon seeing their friend displayed, her naked limbs and raspberry hair flowing across a massive canvas?

Yet there was nothing I could do. By Sunday afternoon, I would find out.

On Sunday I found myself standing next to the huge wall where my painting was exhibited among at least fifteen other canvases.

The Fairy Faun hung exactly in the center. No one who entered the South Salon could miss it.

I listened as the crowds filed through the ribboned channels around the room.

"Such a lovely face she has," one woman whispered to her husband, her tightly tied bonnet veiling her face.

"Celestial!" one man exclaimed to his friend, who might have been a journalist, for he carried with him a small leather-bound notepad and a pen.

Others criticized the fierce brushwork. "The brushstrokes are far too ferocious for such a delicate creature," a wizened old painter of the Academic tradition mused hoarsely.

"Yes," his gray-haired companion agreed. "And have you ever seen such trees in the Bois de Boulogne? Never!"

Around three o'clock, after I shook hands with some of my fellow students from Collin's atelier, I spotted Eva and Hashimoto entering through the west entrance of the room.

Eva was dressed from head to toe in viridian green, her russet hair aflame against the bright color of the cloth.

"Yamamoto," she cried over the crowd, "we were so excited to come!"

Behind her, I caught sight of Isabelle, a striking figure cut in deep crimson.

Hashimoto reached back to usher her forward. He was beaming as he made his way through the throngs, a dashing figure dressed in black, escorting two radiant females.

"Which one is yours, old man?" he chirped.

Before I had a chance to answer I saw the once florid complexion of Eva suddenly turn pale.

She had already turned to Isabelle, who was not blushing as I had imagined. Her smile was radiant, her expression proud and determined. In her carmine robes, she looked beguiling.

"Why, of course it is me," she said to her friend. "Do you not remember that night I wore a costume of a faun."

"I daresay," Hashimoto said as he nodded at my canvas. "It certainly is a bold work of art."

"Thank you," I said, embarrassed at the commotion between the two girls.

"I am honored to have inspired such a masterpiece," Isabelle said as she came forward and offered me her hand to kiss.

"Indeed you did," I said. I was now a far deeper shade of scarlet than her overskirt.

"You will be the talk of the town, Isabelle!" Eva cried, and I wondered if there was a tinge of envy in her voice.

"There is nothing wrong with that," Isabelle said playfully as she undid her bonnet and shook out her deep red curls. She withdrew a tiny ivory fan from her purse and fanned herself.

With a few succinct movements, she seemed once again transformed. "My only regret is that you never called on me to pose again, Monsieur Yamamoto."

"Had you left me an address, I surely would have, mademoiselle."

She smiled and her teeth flashed like her fan. "Well then, you should make it up to me, my dear Monsieur Yamamoto! How about a night on the town? Perhaps tonight? As a small gesture of gratitude for the good fortune I have bestowed on you, for I suppose I had a little something to do with your magnificent painting, *The Fairy Faun*."

"Indeed, that sounds like a marvelous idea," Eva mused. As usual, she had answered the question before I even had a chance to open my mouth.

"But we have a previous engagement, dear one," whispered Hashimoto, his arm draped protectively around his beloved's waist.

"Such a shame," Eva said with a pout. "It would have been such fun."

"But *you and I* can still go," Isabelle said coyly.

I stood there silent, my eyes bewitched by her beauty, my heart beating so loudly, I could hear its rhythm in my ears. She had the capacity to make me feel dizzy in a way I hadn't felt since Noboru. Even all these years later I have never encountered another woman, another being, quite as beautiful, or as beguiling, as Isabelle.

That night we dined near the Bois de Boulogne. We ate raw oysters and drank three bottles of champagne. One week's worth of my allowance, swallowed in a matter of hours, but how glorious it was!

Isabelle was wrapped in yards of bloodred taffeta, her complexion as creamy as meringue. Her piles of copper hair, released by the plucking of a single hairpin, fell languidly over her shoulders. Her porcelain-white hands were open and majestic, as if inviting a monarch butterfly to sleep in the valley of her palms.

Even now I can close my eyes and see her there, her back pressed against the velvet cushion, her eyes drawing me into an imagined embrace. Gone, for the moment, is my devotion to Noboru, my passion for painting. Evaporated is my ambition. My only desire is to be near this beautiful creature, to nestle and sleep deeply by her side.

And these feelings are confusing to me because they are so different from the ones I hold so deeply for Noboru. The ones that are interlaced with a shared love of painting and with my yearning to be loved by the one who escaped me.

Yet tonight she, Isabelle, lay in my bed, her crimson robes strewn on the carpet, her petticoats unabashedly removed. And I hold her without entering her. Because I still am devoted to Noboru, and because I am unsure that I can love her that way. Yet I allow her to wrap her slender arms around me as she falls into a deep sleep, her auburn hair spreading like marmalade over my stark white sheets. Bringing with her the smell of the forest. Clinging to her is the heavy fragrance of cedar. Damp, like mulching maple. High and green, as familiar as the scent of cypress.

Behind the screen lay my canvases, some finished, some just begun. But I hardly think of them. For the smell of Isabelle's perfume, her heat, and her thin curve of smile are ever so satisfying. For this woman, who could be mistaken for a faun, lay here in my bed with me, her limbs soft and slender, her neck arched like a swan's.

And I imagine Father, as he lay entangled in the arms of Mother. His beloved. The only rival to his craft, for even I, his son, lacked the power to bring him back to the world of love.

His struggle revealed to me his division over two of the purest truths: the truth of love and the truth of wood. Each vying for his spirit. And when love came and left, it was the recurring words of his master that saved him: "Love only the wood."

And I realize that I am a product of such words. I knew that Isabelle would rise and leave. That after this night I too would return to my old self. That, once again, I would be consumed by my craft.

But I was just as certain that the mask carver's legacy would end with me. For should I have a son, I would fear the cycle would be repeated, with yet another artist forced to choose between his craft and his love.

The next morning, Isabelle awakened, stretched her lovely bare limbs, placed her bare feet on the floor, and walked unabashedly through my room retrieving her undergarments.

"You're a strange gentleman, dear Yamamoto," she said as she smiled and placed each leg into the center of her petticoat. "You must find women a distraction to your work, *non*? Not that I mind, since you have already immortalized me on your canvas."

"It was you who immortalized my canvas," I said.

She beamed and I blushed.

"Well, my young painter," she said with a tinge of exhaustion. "I know you will not call on me. Your work is your mistress, but I must tell you I've enjoyed myself."

"As have I," I said quietly.

"Tell me something, Monsieur Yamamoto. I have the feeling you left someone at home to whom you are still very devoted. Am I right?"

I stood there quietly, my face flushed and my mind racing. Finally I managed to answer her. "Yes, you are quite right."

"She is a lucky woman, if I may be so bold as to say so. Not many women have a man who stays faithful for nearly five years."

I smiled and remained silent as she reached for her evening bag and pushed her curls up into her bonnet.

"Well, I hope we meet again," she said sweetly, as she leaned over and kissed me on the cheek.

I bade her an uncomfortable farewell, with a slight bow and a grazing of my hand on her left arm. The sound of her heels echoed in the stairwell, resonating for only a few moments before fading into a hushed silence.

Unable to rid my head of her memory, I took out a sheet of paper and began a letter to Noboru. He had not written to me in so long. Noboru who, I prayed, had not yet forgotten me. And in my heart I knew I had to begin making preparations for my return.

FIFTY-THREE

During my four and a half years of studying under Collin, I had exhausted almost all of my funds. The few francs that remained in the bank would barely cover my passage home. So, in the spring of 1901, I seriously began my preparations to return to Japan.

The years in Paris had often been difficult for me. In the end, I succeeded in mastering the techniques I had traveled so far to learn. But, more important, I had discovered a style of painting that was uniquely my own. I had completed nearly forty canvases. Still lifes, portraits, landscapes, and nudes. I tried my hand at all of them. Whereas I had thought myself a landscape painter when I arrived, upon my departure I knew that it was portraiture, particularly my series of self-portraits, that best revealed my strength as an artist.

My favorite was *Self-Portrait in Violet*, one of the last canvases I completed before my return to Japan. My head, painted in a deep palette of violets and dark, Prussian blues, sits on top of a body cloaked uncomfortably in a suit. The long, lavender fingers clutch a closed fan, its wooden spine strangely resembling a shard of knotted wood.

My eyes stared out to the corner, my mouth caught between a stiff smile and a cry. It is me, carved out of thick impasto. The markings of my knife embedded in the paint.

I recall Dürer's *Self-portrait with a Thistle*, the painting that had moved me to tears as a child. That image of the young artist, with the silk cords pulled tightly across his chest, the pale flower clutched between his hands. I knew that I had finally expressed something that cried from deep within me. That I too had captured the angst and the peace that mingled in my soul. I was taking the first steps toward making amends.

The week before my departure, I realized that I had neglected to inform Master Collin of my return to Japan. I remained behind after our Monday class. As the other students slowly packed up their satchels, withdrew their arms from their white smocks, and rearranged themselves in their black waistcoats and silken ties, I lingered over each and every one of their movements. It had been my routine for four years, but it would all too soon become another memory. I tried to savor the sight of the dirty water jars being cleaned and replaced, the sound of the turpentine top being screwed tight.

For those are often the things we later forget.

"I will be leaving Paris shortly, Master Collin," I informed him. "It seems that I have only enough money left to carry me home."

He looked down at me, his tall frame and dark eyes hanging over me like a shadow.

"So soon a departure? I was hoping for another year with you at least!" He let out a small laugh that helped to diffuse the seriousness.

"Monsieur Yamamoto, you have proven yourself well over the last few years. You are no longer just a painter. You are now an artist."

"Thank you, Master," I said. "I am all that I am because of you."

"Nonsense!" he bellowed. "Go back to your people and breathe life into their veins. Pierce their eyes and hearts, and fill them with color!" He was shaking my hand with vigor.

"Good luck, Yamamoto," he said. Then he added, "You should be proud."

That word, strange and unfamiliar to me, made me feel odd. Perhaps even sad. Once again I thought of Father, and lamented that he had never uttered it to me. Had I never merited such a compliment from him?

"Good-bye, Master, and thank you," I whispered. "You have been like a father to me."

"It's an honor to have known you, and should you return to Paris, please call on me."

We stood face-to-face for the last time, our shadows stretched over white plaster walls. And then I bowed to him. Ensuring that my neck was straight and my back flat, I bowed deeply out of respect for my beloved master.

And to my surprise he bowed to me in return, his fluff of white grazing the floor. "Go on, then," he said, as he smiled. "Go gather your things." And with those last words, he pressed his hand on my shoulder and turned his black-suited back to me. The sound of his walking stick echoed on the marble. *Tap, tap . . . Tap, tap . . .* fading into the sound of Flora's calls.

Now I was alone. The four walls surrounding me were to house me no longer, so I removed all traces of myself from his studio. I cleared my sketchbook from the student racks and retrieved all of my remaining work. I rolled up my canvases and wiped down my tubes of paint. I wrapped my brushes in newsprint and tightly closed my flasks of turpentine and linseed oil.

As I walked out into the Paris evening, the iron lanterns already lit, I inhaled one last deep breath. And, strangely, the memory of that afternoon with my father, when he took me to find my first cypress tree, returned to me. That day I had also wanted to savor the smells of the musky forest floor. So that afternoon I had concentrated so hard that I knew I'd never forget. And now, as I placed each foot on the cobblestones, I found myself once again remembering the sensation of earth beneath my sandals. The sight of the red temple gate above my head. And I knew that I was ready to return.

FIFTY-FOUR

Noboru sent a telegram informing me that, because of a school-related function, he would be unable to meet me upon my ship's arrival. It was the first communication I had received from him since I could remember and, as it was a telegram, the message was painfully brief.

Although I was saddened and disappointed by Noboru's message, I was not particularly concerned. I knew that I would be able to find my way, for I was returning home, not arriving in a foreign land. What I had not expected, however, was how much different the Japan that I had carried in my memory for nearly five years was from the Japan to which I returned.

It would be wrong to deny that I too had changed. As I traveled on the steamship home, I spent what seemed like hours studying myself in the mirror. Only twenty-six years of age, yet I seemed far older. Gray hairs were emerging from my scalp. My skin was sallow. Fine lines were appearing underneath my eyes, at their corners, and around my mouth.

Would Noboru recognize me? I did not doubt my internal transformation; I realized that my experiences had forever changed me. But by my outside—by my mask—I had been betrayed. Now I had a body and a face that mirrored its age. Old before my time. As Grandmother had said, "Who would have known a man could grow ancient in a day?" The same words that she once used to describe Father could now also describe me.

I fanned my fingers over my eyes, my pupils peeking through the space between my knuckles like slats of a bamboo fan. It was strange that I would do something so vain. It seemed like something a woman would do when she approached her twenty-fifth year. When she was no longer a *hana zakari*—a flower at the peak of its bloom.

I imagined Noboru as he had been when I left him. Memories that one carries never seem to change to accommodate time. I saw him wrapped in the same navy blue kimono, I knew in the back of my mind that it would now be worn and faded to a pale gray, but I still imagined him dressed in it. The color sharp and intense. His small round face shining like the inside of an oyster shell.

Hold me, I thought to him. Of him. Because returning was frightening. And my canvases, my experiences, and my memory were now all I had. But what I was to learn was that one should never keep memories of the living. For the living can change.

Tokyo, 1901. I hardly recognized you. Whereas I grew old, you grew young and new. The wood of my youth had been replaced by stone and tile. You approached your transformation into the modern age with solid structures and an affirmative air. The Meiji architecture, begun before my arrival in Tokyo as a young art student, now dominated the city. The Ministry of Justice in Kasumigaseki was complete, echoing the architecture of the French court. French and Venetian motifs decorated the facades of Tokyo mansions. Brick and mortar. Stone and stucco. Shoji and shadows disappearing from view.

My luggage would follow me in two weeks' time. So, with only a small satchel containing my bare essentials, I wandered through the streets that were once familiar to me, and eventually found my former boardinghouse where an older woman was tending a small garden of wild eggplant outside the *genkan*.

"Excuse me for my rude intrusion," I said. "I used to rent a room here from a man named Ariyoshi."

"Ariyoshi Togo died three years ago. I am his sister."

"I am sorry for your loss. I remember him as a dear and honest man." She nodded in agreement, her head bent like that of an aging peacock.

"If you do not have a vacancy, can you suggest another place for me? I have just arrived after a long and difficult journey from abroad."

"We are full here," she said sweetly. "However, the house on the corner has a vacancy. Ask for Suga-san and tell him that Ume sent you."

I bowed deeply and thanked her for her graciousness, again offering her my sympathy.

Upon my arrival at Suga's boardinghouse, I was shown a small but clean room. The spring light was shining through the shoji, and outside the street was lined with sakura trees whose buds were just showing the first signs of pink.

"Is the bathhouse on the next street over?" I asked.

"You are familiar with this area?" Suga-san seemed surprised.

"Yes. Nearly six years ago, I lived in the Ariyoshi house."

"So much has died in these parts in such a short time. It is hard for an old Oji-san like me to keep up with the times."

"It is hard for everyone," I said comfortingly. "I have never known change to be slow."

He bowed graciously and left me to my new surroundings. I walked over the tatami and slid open the closet and removed the futon. I was tired and needed to rest.

There was something eternal about the room. Although my first glimpses of Tokyo years ago seemed foreign, here, in a room never before visited, I felt at home. The crisp smell of the tatami was refreshing to my senses. The diffused light of the shoji was soft and easy on my eyes.

The next morning, after I had returned from my bath and eaten my breakfast, I paid a young boy to deliver a message to Noboru.

"I have returned," I wrote, "and I look forward to our meeting. Please visit me soon. It has been a long time."

I wrote my address at the bottom of the piece of rice paper, folded it neatly into a triangle, and pressed two silver coins into the boy's hand.

"Go quickly and with care," I called after him.

I slid open the latch to the gate and walked up the narrow stairs to my quarters. I wrote a letter to Sakamoto, the gallery owner who had mounted Kuroda's first exhibition in Tokyo, inquiring if he was interested in seeing my work.

That evening, as I was resting in my *yukata*, Suga called for me.

"Yamamoto-san," he hollered, "you have two visitors who await your company."

Who could they be? I thought to myself. It would be a tremendous coincidence if Sakamoto and Noboru had arrived together.

I stood up, smoothed out the creases in my robe, and walked downstairs to greet my guests.

Noboru and a young gentleman in his early twenties were standing in the *genkan*, dressed in formal suits. Both had their hair parted and oiled, both had mustaches, and both had foulards billowing over their stiff white collars.

I knew the other gentleman was not Sakamoto, the gallery owner. He seemed far too young. He had the cool, unblemished, unspoiled beauty that only the very young can have. For the first time in recent memory, I found myself envious. The same sort of jealousy I had as a young boy, watching my father surrounded by his beautiful, pristine masks.

Noboru extended his hands into the air. I stood on the steps looking down.

"My friend Yamamoto Kiyoki, it has been such a long time!"

I remained speechless. He noticed that my gaze was directed not at him but rather at his young friend.

"Forgive me for my rudeness. This is my friend Matsushima Noriyuki. We are both students of Kuroda Seiki."

He had chosen not to greet me alone, an action far more powerful than any words could be.

I gathered my emotions. "Would the two of you care for some tea in my room?" I motioned to the dimly lit hallway above my head.

Noboru turned to his friend, and they both nodded in agreement.

"That sounds very good, if it is no trouble to you. You must still be very tired from your journey."

"I am fine," I assured him. "Please, it is just up here." They followed me up the stairs and into my room.

As they settled into the room, I reached for the boiling kettle on the brazier and began preparing the tea. It had been a long time since I had prepared *o-cha*, and I tried to disguise my unease.

"We drink coffee too!" Matsushima chimed proudly.

"Yes," Noboru agreed. "It has become somewhat popular here."

"I regret that I have no coffee to offer you. Suga has only provided me with tea."

"That is fine, my old friend," Noboru said with a laugh. "I have come because I want to see you and be the first to hear of your travels, not for your drinks."

He was not wearing his navy kimono, as I had imagined him.

Age had not yet arrived on his face. His skin was still smooth, his complexion still pale. I raised my head as I poured the steaming tea. Viewing him through the clouds of vapor reminded me of the days we spent envisioning our lives abroad over a pot of shared tea. Those days now seemed to be from another lifetime. And I felt my heart ticking inside my chest, as if viewing the demise of our friendship from the outside, the distance between us now seeming far greater than the span of water I had traveled on my return.

Noboru broke the silence. "Do you have any samples of your work here, or are they arriving with your luggage?" he asked.

"I have brought some of my canvases and one sketchbook. The canvases are rolled up, but I will show them to you. I am hoping to meet Sakamoto soon to see if he is interested in exhibiting my work."

"Sakamoto, eh?" Noboru raised his brows. "He has a respectable gallery. Isn't that where Kuroda had his first show?"

"I believe it is," I said.

"I'm sure he'll be interested. He is always looking for the next Kuroda." Then he added, "Now let us see those canvases!" His tone seeming almost wolfish.

I did not want to appear secretive, so I excused myself and retrieved my work. Grateful for the opportunity to compose myself, I spent several minutes hunched behind a folding screen rummaging through some satchels.

I returned to the main tatami room with two still lifes and three self-portraits. Whereas my earlier work had been influenced by the Impressionists, for the most part, my later work was far darker in its palette, angrier in its tone, and fiercer in its brushwork. They were somber but passionate paintings, born from my pain and isolation, the images resurrected from my experience.

Noboru leaned over each canvas as I rolled them out on the tatami floor. He squinted and pushed his face close to each work in order to examine the brushwork more closely.

"Is the still life of the fruit your earlier work?" he asked.

"Yes. Is it that apparent?"

"Well," Noboru said slowly, "the Japanese usually prefer a lighter palette. The public seems to have a penchant for subtle color and subdued brushstroke. Your work seems fierce. Angrier than your normal temperament. I must say, I'm a bit surprised." I could tell from the way that he carefully chose his words that he was trying to disguise his distaste for my work.

Raising his head, he added, "But what do I know, Yamamoto? I am confident that Sakamoto will pick what he thinks is best.

"Is this the painting, *The Fairy Faun*, from this past year's Salon?" he asked as he picked up the canvas that lay in the far corner of the room.

"Yes, it is," I said quietly.

"The model is most beguiling. Her face seems almost a combination of the sexes. She has the defiant eyes of a man and the delicate features of a woman." He paused. "Such a splendid creature!"

I nodded in agreement while looking at his friend, Matsushima, whose face was beautiful but as blank as a water-washed stone.

I knew that I looked at Matsushima coldly, as though looking at myself ten years ago, and I was filled with disgust.

"What have you been doing lately?" I asked Noboru in a tone I would have used to address someone only slightly more familiar than a stranger.

"Well, after I complete my final works for Kuroda next week, I plan to start an atelier of my own. The students who are not accepted at the Tokyo School of Fine Arts will need a place to learn Western technique. The demand for instructors is actually quite high. You might consider it."

I knew that the income from such instruction was quite good, but I still had dreams of supporting myself purely from my own craft. Much as Father had from his. I would prove to everyone that I was capable and talented enough to achieve such a feat!

"I will have to see what opportunities unfold for me, now that I have returned," I said as I rolled up my canvases and returned them to the closet.

"Well, I hope all works out well with you and Sakamoto," Noboru said as he stood up abruptly, the young Matsushima mimicking him like a puppet. "Please forgive us for our rudeness, but we must be going. I am sure you are quite tired as well."

"Yes, yes," I said, somewhat eagerly. "But it was good of you to come."

I saw the two of them to the gate, and I felt as if I had all of a sudden switched places with my father in my memory. I was now the one standing outside the *genkan*. Standing there alone. The one betrayed.

Sakamoto sent a letter requesting I visit him at his gallery three days later. I gathered my portfolio and set out to meet with him.

His gallery was near the Ginza, on the first floor on an exclusive street.

"You must be Yamamoto Kiyoki," he said, greeting me at his door. "Please come in." He was wearing a black suit, a white shirt, and a black bow tie. A black bowler hat was resting on a bamboo table in the *genkan*.

I slid off my shoes and bowed deeply.

"Please, Yamamoto-san, please come in!"

The building's traditional dark wooden outside was in sharp contrast with the brightly illuminated interior. Asai Chu's *Fields in Spring*, among other paintings, hung on the wall.

"Would you like some tea?" he offered.

"I am fine, thank you."

"I received your letter and am quite interested to see your work. Did you bring samples from your portfolio?" He began clearing his desk.

"Yes," I said, unrolling them onto the desk's wooden surface.

He spent several minutes on each one. He nodded his head up and down. He looked closely and then stepped away in order to gaze from a distance.

"I have never seen anything quite like these," he said, pointing to my three self-portraits. Indeed, they were dark and serious portrayals of me. I had sought inspiration from the works of Rembrandt, but chose to reinterpret his style. I preserved the same black monochrome background, scumbled the pigment, and infused an ample amount of varnish. But when I painted myself, I used a thick, coarse brush and avoided the smooth, delicate lines of the old master style, and I opted for more frenzied, almost kinetic ones. I painted myself in a kimono. I also painted myself in a suit and tie. I wanted to convey that my experience had transformed me into a chameleon. But my favorite painting remained *Self-Portrait in Violet*.

Sakamoto looked over my work with narrowed eyes. Eyes permanently squinting from countless years of scrutiny, his skin crinkling over his bones like burned paper.

I watched as he extended his forefinger and traced the movements of my brush, the traces of fibers fossilized in the bright spread of pigment.

"I have never seen anything like your work, Yamamoto, but it bodes well for you that one of your paintings was exhibited in last year's Salon," he said as his eyes skimmed each canvas. "Only time will tell if Japan is ready." He sighed.

He was brave enough to take a chance on me. "I have shown

Kuroda Seiki, Asai Chu, Fujita Tsuguharu, Fujishima Takeji, and I will show you, Yamamoto Kiyoki, too." He looked at me with his cautious gaze. "But I will show you only once. The rest is for the public to decide."

We scheduled my debut exhibition for July, nearly two months for me to prepare my work. It would be a grand affair, Sakamoto promised. All the art critics would attend, as well as all the accomplished and accepted painters of the day. The pressure was great and I worked day and night in order to complete new canvases to complement the portfolio I had brought with me from France.

Sakamoto arranged studio space for me outside the gates of the Tokyo School of Fine Arts, in an old apartment where the rent was cheap and the tatami worn from age.

Noboru visited me occasionally, sometimes bringing a box of sweets or a canister of tea. It would always break my heart when he arrived. The reality of our friendship, its superficiality and the distance between us, was often too much to bear. My memory of the past was still grasped tight between my palms, like the sable brush that had once belonged to him that I held dear.

He would walk behind me and look at my canvas, illuminated in the afternoon sun. He would not speak, and neither would I. But I knew that what he saw before him was something he did not understand. Perhaps it was my anger that scared him. Perhaps it was something as shallow as the palette I chose. All I know is that, on the night of my exhibition, he did not acknowledge me. He stood in a corner meeting everyone's eyes but mine.

The exhibition was a disaster from the outset. I awakened the morning of my debut to dark clouds and rain. Who would even come? I wondered as I prepared a bowl of tea. Outside, the torrents transformed the streets into muddy rivers and the rice-paper windows became thick and opaque.

I arrived at Sakamoto's gallery early, in order to make sure my paintings were installed to my liking and that the program had been printed with the correct information.

"The canvases are far too close to each other!" I protested.

"That's the way we do it here in Japan," Sakamoto replied curtly.

"But they are on top of each other, each bleeding into the next!"

It was not at all how I imagined them displayed.

"Let me do my job, as I have allowed you to do yours," he said as he turned his back on me and returned to his low, paulownia wood desk. "I will see you at eight o'clock."

I chose to wear my black kimono, embroidered with Grandmother's crest, for I believed it was the finest thing that I owned. Believing the critics and collectors would also come in kimonos, I never thought twice about my selection. I stepped into the hooded rickshaw, shielding myself from the rain with a parasol, and made my way once again to the gallery.

I arrived only to discover a group of critics had already gathered around several of my paintings. They had chosen to wear Western dress. Black coats and crisp white shirts punctuated the room like a long line of dominoes. And I, the Japanese artist who had just returned from Paris, slumped shyly in the corner, my silk kimono hanging from my shoulders like a shroud.

Their distaste for my work was apparent. They scrunched up their noses and shook their heads with confusion. They took off their glasses and wiped them clean.

I should be fair when I tell you that Sakamoto did try to introduce me, and promote me, as he had promised. He came over and tried to impress upon the guests that I was an ambassador of the new French style. "See the passion of his paintings," he said to one critic who pressed his face close to the canvas and then simply responded with a shrug. "And his use of color and texture. It is the influence of the Impressionists, you see." But no one seemed to care.

The weeks that followed were the cruelest. Every newspaper, magazine, and art journal in Japan seemed to have something unfavorable to say about my work. They said my paintings were "renditions of the grotesque" or "the work of a madman." They speculated that I had suffered some sort of dementia while I was abroad, and prided themselves on having the sense not to be fooled into believing that my work was art. Even *The Fairy Faun* did not catch their fancy. The critics condemned it as odd and disarming—a mythological creature that they could not understand.

The moment my work was unveiled to their eyes, my career as an artist in Japan was ruined before it even began.

No art academy would have me as a professor. No private student would seek me as an instructor. Yet what destroyed me the most was not the reaction of the critics, collectors, and journalists who were responsible for my fate; it was Noboru's response.

He had paced through the gallery with his eyes averted. Hovering in a corner when I was with Sakamoto. Lost in the crowds when I was alone. But always with his eyes cast down and his back slightly turned.

Noboru visited me shortly after my disastrous exhibition. I had read in the paper that day that he had just been awarded the first prize at Japan's yearly salon, the National Bunten, that year. He did not, however, mention it when he arrived.

He came into my room, the faint traces of diluted turpentine permeating his coat. I greeted him in my cotton *yukata*. I had not changed out of it since the exhibition. Two weeks had since passed and I had yet to shave or comb my hair.

"Good afternoon, Yamamoto," he chimed, and I think he fell into surprise, seeing me in such a wretched state.

I grumbled my greeting to him and let him find his way past the pillows and unmade futon, to a square of exposed tatami.

"You may sit down," I muttered from where I stood. My back was now turned to him, my head faced the blurred rice-paper window.

"I am sorry this is the first chance I have had to visit you alone," he said apologetically. There was kindness in his voice. But there was anger in mine.

"You greet me now when we are alone, but avoid me at galleries."

"I thought it best under the circumstances."

"Circumstances! What circumstances?" I cried as I whirled back from the window. "Does one not greet the artist whose exhibition it is? Let alone, one who is your friend?"

I glared at him. My eyes, wet from too little sleep and too much sake, fell upon him like sharpened claws.

"I am in a difficult position here. Can you not see? I am trying to make a name for myself and earn a living. We all can't be pure as you, Kiyoki!"

And the irony of my name once again besieged me.

"I have always been envious of you, Yamamoto Kiyoki." This time his voice was even softer, as if he needed to whisper these sentiments that he had kept hidden within himself for so many years.

"When you left for Paris, I knew that you would experience things I never would have had the opportunity to gather. That you would see things and meet people to whom I would never be exposed." His eyes fell to the floor. "Can you not pity me? My work is far emptier than yours. Merely a patchwork of soft colors and imagined light."

I looked at my friend. The one that I remembered from long ago had finally returned.

"You paint for yourself, and I paint for them," he said. "I may have money and security, but you have purity of the soul. As painful as that may be now, as the years go by, you will be the one who is remembered."

"I doubt that very much," I said. "I am already forgotten."

"You are ahead of the times, my friend."

"I will wait, then," I said. "I will do as you say and wait for my country to catch up to me." I began to laugh, because the conversation seemed so preposterous.

"You are a great painter, Kiyoki, and I believe in you. Now you must concentrate on the future."

"I am planning to return to Kyoto. I still have some land in Daigo that I intend to sell. I will need the money."

"You won't teach?"

"Who would want to learn to paint from a madman?"

"You are being too hard on yourself."

In actuality, I did not feel I was being hard enough. How could I be, considering how much I had sacrificed and how many people I had hurt, just so I could afford to paint.

"I have no plans except to return," I told him. "I need to see my mountain."

"I would like you to see my work before you return. It is important to me that you come."

I promised to visit him the following week.

FIFTY-FIVE

No matter how much he had warned me, Noboru's work surprised me greatly. The artist I remembered from our years at the Tokyo School of Fine Arts was far different from the one now standing in his spacious studio, showing me his work.

He had been spoiled. His years under Kuroda had developed his talent as a fine painter but destroyed the purity of his soul. Just as he admitted, he had learned to paint what the Japanese wanted to see, but not what he saw with his own eyes and soul. His fire had been extinguished, his vision dulled.

His paintings were nothing like what I had imagined. They were pleasing and innocuous. But they were completely unevocative. Paintings that were *inspired* by the work of Renoir. Paintings that *echoed* the quiet landscapes of Cézanne. They revealed a mastery of technique but, in the silence of their perfection, crumbled under their lack of substance.

I could not comprehend the work of art students like Noboru, who had never left Japan but painted with their eyes peeled westward. They had learned to paint from images reproduced in books and art magazines, and had never seen the sights they copied.

None of them had ever set foot in the Louvre. I recalled the moment when I had first entered the Sully gallery. I never felt more humbled as an artist, or more foreign as a man away from his home. Everything that was so exhaustingly beautiful was created by European hands. And the faces that stared at me, from either the linen of canvas or the rock of marble, were eyes that accentuated the imperfection of my own. Each gallery was an orgy of flesh; larger-than-life women towered above me, their breasts dangling like goblets, their ribs tapering into the slender stem of their waists. Wings fluttered from the backs of angels, the puckered mouths of putti kissed the Virgin, and I walked the corridors without the history of a shared religion, a common face, a mutual past. For the first time in my life, I yearned to see a familiar *kano-e* painting. After three hours, I had become numb to so many great works. The paintings of Bellini, Tintoretto, and Filippo Lippi ceased to move me.

These men who have never left Japan cannot conceive of the notion of being overwhelmed by the greatness and the excess of art in Europe. They are ignorant of what it is like to be so far away from their home, to lose their confidence in who they are. Foolishly, they think that they can simulate the attitude of a Western artist without ever having journeyed, suffered, celebrated, *lived* with the intensity that we all do when we are far from home. They do not know. And they never will.

It saddened me. Within me, a tremendous amount of pathos stirred. My friend, who would have fame and fortune, would have it all at the expense of his artistry. I had not the heart to tell him what I truly thought of his work.

I could feel the weight of his eyes on my shoulder. And I envisioned myself turning to him with my face disguised by one of my father's masks. Could he read my eyes? I wondered as I looked quickly past him and then at the floor.

"How wonderful that you have been working under Kuroda!" I managed to muster, because lying seemed equally cruel.

He looked at me with eyes no longer bright. The flame extinguished. Begging me to go.

"Forgive me," I whispered as I turned to leave. I am not sure if he heard me. But I said it anyway, because I felt I needed to say it to him. To Father, to Grandfather. To their memory. For my leaving. Because had I not left, I knew my life would have been different. And although I doubt I would have been happier, I know that I would not have been the one asking to be forgiven.

FIFTY-SIX

It was September 1901. I packed all of my belongings in my brown leather suitcase, rolled up my canvases in a long, hollowed-out piece of dried bamboo, and dressed myself in my old navy blue kimono. I wore sandals and *tabi* as well. Externally, I brazenly displayed the incongruity that I felt internally. The brown leather suitcase containing my neatly folded brown woolen suit, which cushioned the unfinished Ishi-O-Jo mask of my father, rubbed at my side with every step.

I arrived at Tokyo station, bought a one-way ticket to Kyoto, and boarded the train.

I remember nothing of that journey. I pulled down the blinds of my compartment and shut my eyes. My eyes were so tired. They could not absorb one more color, one more image. I pressed my head to the glass and slept for almost the entire passage.

Outside the station, many chair men were waiting to carry people to their final destinations. I was too weary for the long walk to Daigo, so I motioned to a young carrier that I would require his services.

"Where do you need to go?" he asked me. His accent was rough and revealed his lower-class background.

"I need to get to Daigo."

He grunted. "Get in. That will be ten yen!"

"I'll pay you when we arrive," I told him firmly.

I squatted and inched myself into the rough carriage. The

chair man called his partner, who grabbed the other side of the pole, and we began the trip up to Daigo. This part of the journey was far from luxurious. The men walked with their characteristic stiff-legged gait, and the chair jolted with every step. I braced myself by using the leather strap attached to the pole that ran through the top of the inner chamber. Still, my body jerked and ached.

An hour and a half later I arrived at the base of Mount Daigo to discover the entire peak ablaze in its autumn glory.

It smelled like autumn. Crisp and smoky. I felt that I was awakening from a black-and-white dream and entering a world of unending color. Had I really been away for so long? The mountain seemed as eternal as ever, formidable in her foliage. Like an empress, bejeweled in amber gold and ruby red. I had missed her.

I walked toward Sanpo-In, traveling up the rocky path that I had traveled so often as a child. The earth underneath my feet felt wonderfully familiar; the air filling my lungs felt clear. I passed through the orange torii, craned my neck to see the gate's delicately flared sides, and hesitated for a moment as I entered the old temple.

I could hear a priest from within the temple's inner chamber ringing the monks to prayer. Their shadows filtered through the shoji, their round shaven heads bowed to their chests. I could smell the burning incense mingling with the drying leaves, and I could see the unripe persimmons hanging from the trees. It was as though the fondest memories of my childhood had been preserved.

I continued my walk through the temple's grounds. I trod softly on the dirt pathway and tiptoed on the neatly placed stepping-stones leading to the carefully manicured gardens and a glistening shallow pool of water. The low, twisting pines were perfectly pruned. The plush patches of green velvet moss were glistening with moisture. The pond was shimmering in the setting sun. For the first time I thought that the silence surrounding me was exquisite. There was no sound except for an occasional toad belching or a cricket chirping, and I thought of the story of my father as a young boy. Was Sanpo-In similar to the sanctuary where he had first learned to carve?

I leaned over the man-made basin of water, my reflection confirming once more that I was no longer a boy. The landscape here had stayed at a standstill, but I had not. Age had besieged me. It had anchored my eyes, pulling the flesh sightly downward, and toughened my once translucent skin. I was now nearly twenty-seven. Nearly the same age my father was when Mother died.

That night I slept at an inn not far from where my father and I had once lived. As I took a hot bath, I thought of Noboru. Experience had changed us. Separated us. It was not the distance; it was something far stronger than the sea.

I soaked in the steaming water for almost an hour. Too long for one's health. When I stood up to reach for my towel, I felt my legs grow weak, and my vision began to escape me. With great difficulty, I managed to find a small wooden stool and I sat down. Naked and cold from the outside air, I cradled my face in my cupped hands.

The next morning I decided to visit the old Kanze theater. As I traveled there, I thought I saw the faces of my father, grandmother, and grandfather in the bark of the gnarled trees. I remembered how I had walked the path so many times beside them. Yet now, as I walked the path that led to the theater, I walked alone.

The soil underneath my sandals was the same dirt that had cushioned the feet of my ancestors. The trees above me were the same branches that had shaded them from the sun. Still, the path initially surprised me. Unlike the pristine walkway that was engraved in my memory, the path had become overgrown. Once impeccably groomed, the thick green shrubbery that lined the trail had grown wild and unruly. Long twigs twisted across the earth, black and brittle; they splintered as I crushed them under my feet.

The Noh stage stood in the middle of a field, just as it had for hundreds of years. Its ornate roof, with rolling curves and fancy woodwork, had darkened with age; the imperial-style structure, thundering its independence, stood alone.

I moved closer to see it. The heavy and ornate roof loomed like a protective hood for the sacred stage. The floorboards were immaculate, impeccably preserved and free of scuffs. As tradition dictates, each plank was free from knots and glistened like finely polished lacquer.

The pine tree painted on the rear wall had faded greatly. "The pine is symbolic to Noh," Grandmother had told me after I saw my first performance. "It echoes the spirit of the theater. Like our traditions, its greenness persists regardless of the season. The pine is a strong tree, and it is unyielding."

He was right. The tree, although worn, retained its malachite luster. In contrast, the pillars that flanked the stage remained unpainted, and their *hinoki* bark was weather-beaten with age. They had been painted when I was a child, I was sure of it. But somehow parts of the stage had fallen into a state of disrepair, while other parts, primarily the floorboards, seemed to survive, unscathed by time.

Suddenly, as I stood there alone among the crumbling splendor, I heard a sound. It came from the *hashigakari*, the floating bridge that served as a passageway for the actors as they made their powerful entrances onto the stage.

"Who's there?" an elderly man's voice cried out.

"Who's there?" he said a second time and more persistently.

"My name is Yamamoto," I said. "I mean you no harm."

"Why are you here?" he responded angrily. "We do not give public performances here anymore. You have to go to the stage at the Nishi Hoganji Temple for that!"

"I apologize for the intrusion. I have memories of this stage, and I only came to refresh them," I said gently. "If only you would be so kind to allow me that pleasure."

The old man revealed himself and stood at the center of the bridge. He held a long wooden broom with bristles made of tightly wound thatch. Age had twisted him; he appeared crooked and uncomfortable but still altogether proud, like Grandmother with her bent back. The similarity between him and the pine tree was uncanny.

"What sort of memories could a young man like you possibly have?" His voice was bitter and sharp.

"My grandfather was a great actor who performed here."

"What is your name again?" he asked. I had obviously piqued his curiosity.

"My family name is Yamamoto. My first name is Kiyoki."

"Yamamoto . . . Yes, of course!" One could see that he felt triumphant that his memory had not failed him. "Your father was the great mask carver, Yamamoto Ryusei!"

I was surprised that he chose to mention my father over my grandfather.

"Yes, that is right. I am his son."

"We heard that you went to Europe after his death."

"That is true. But I have returned."

"What for? Do you carve like your father?"

"No, I do not. I paint."

"Well, I don't see why you've returned to Kyoto. What do you intend to do with yourself here?"

"I thought I might set up an art school instructing students in the Western tradition."

"Your time would be better served helping an old man like me polish the floorboards. It's a disgrace to Noh to let them be blanketed in even a single speck of dust. I sweep them every day and polish them every other week."

"You are very admirable," I said.

"Well, I'm unable to perform anymore."

"What is your name?" I asked him.

"My name is Hattori Keizo."

His name seemed familiar to me. And although his face was creased with age, I recognized the unsightly mole underneath his eyebrow. He had been present that day, years earlier, when I traveled to the theater with Father.

"I studied under your grandfather. He was a great man and the best actor this stage ever had." He paused. "I believe we met once a long time ago, when you were just a boy."

"I remember, Hattori-sama," I said with great reverence.

"Things have fallen apart around here over the past few years. We haven't had a performance in three autumns. There is no interest among the younger generation." He looked at me, his face crumpled in scrutiny. Suddenly, almost like a madman, he blurted, "You know, you are to blame!"

I looked back at him, my eyes betraying my sadness. "Why do you say such a thing? I cannot be responsible for the fate of the theater in its entirety."

"You were born into a family of Noh and you betrayed that family! Why go and travel the seas to learn art when art lives and breathes in your own backyard?" The old man's voice was sharp and his pitch squeaked with cruelty.

"I am a painter now, Hattori-san. Yes, I have been trained in the Western school, but I can still paint outside it. Let me repaint the stage. The great pine tree should be retouched, and it would be my privilege to do so, if you would allow it."

"Why should I allow you to paint the Yogo Pine?"

"Will you not allow me to make amends?"

He looked down at me from the stage. The broom he leaned on twisted from the pressure of his body's weight, the bristles bending over the floor.

"Come Friday and I will rummage around the back to see if I can find you some paint."

"Do not bother," I replied. "I have plenty to spare."

"You cannot use *any* paint, Yamamoto-san. We have special pigment that is used only for the sacred painting of the pine!"

"I see. Very well. I will see you, then, on Friday," I said, careful to bow deeply to him before I made my way back.

FIFTY-SEVEN

That Friday I retraced my footsteps to the theater and met Hattori Keizo-san once again at the steps of the stage. He withdrew three canisters of dried mineral powder from his sash and instructed me on how to mix them with the rest of the emulsions.

"I will leave you for the remainder of the day," he informed me. "I understand that an artist must have his privacy."

He rose elegantly. His knees cracked beneath him as he smoothed out his kimono over his legs. And for a second I saw him as an actor once more, his *tabi*-clad feet sliding silently over the floorboards, his hands waving good-bye like small, sacred wings.

The world of Noh had slipped by me, nearly vanishing overnight. I had heard that many troupes still enjoyed the patronage of the wealthy and that foreigners paid handsomely to see the exotic theater. But Grandfather's troupe had slid into the shadows of the past, though it was the purest of them all. Perhaps it had been too pure to survive.

Had you told me five years ago that I would return to Kyoto only to paint the Noh stage, I would never have believed you. But here I was, blending my pigments and staring at the great Yogo Pine. I recalled how it was this very pine that I once questioned Grandmother about. "Who was responsible for painting it?" I had insisted, and she shrugged her shoulders and tried to shift the conversation to the rhetoric of Noh, emphasizing the symbolism of the pine rather than the painter who placed it there.

Now before me, the stage existed as a faded memory. Her once green pine needles were but faded traces on a badly weathered wooden board, no longer viridian but a pale shade of ochre. Had I swept my hand over its once splendid branches, the pigment would have crumbled into my palms like pistachio dust. Yellow green.

I knelt on the floor of the stage and began to lay out my brushes. I arranged them in order of size and took out a small piece of cloth from my sash and polished the handles until they gleamed bright.

The twisting branches of the Yogo Pine were directly at eye level. Tubular trunks parched and cracked like kindling, mighty branches whose once rich umber hue had disintegrated into gray.

But I would now restore it. To the memory I had held since I was a child. The Yogo Pine, at the base of the Kasuga shrine where, under its blooming boughs, an ancient man once danced. Where the gods in heaven first channeled the art of Noh.

I, Yamamoto Kiyoki, was now painting the great Yogo Pine, not as an original canvas but as tradition dictated. I would not betray this memory, this tradition, as I had betrayed Father and the others so many years before. I would probably betray them again, as a selfish man always seems to repeat his betrayals. But not today. Today was for them.

I blended the malachite green with my knife and expelled every last one of my breaths before I had enough courage to place my first stroke on the wood.

I layered green upon green. Gold upon gold. Until the green flourishes of the shrubbery swirled like verdant clouds and its brown trunk twisted and bowed, its gold knots tied in loops and its branches pierced and peaked. My body swayed and glided across the floorboards like a dancer. Like a Noh actor gripping a brush instead of a fan.

Yamamoto Kiyoki, Pure Wood, had finally come home.

Grandfather, I thought, can you see me here on your stage? Grandmother, it is I who paints the pine!

And, Mother, do not worry, I will still paint my own paintings. But it was to Father, I yelled up to the heavens: *"I have returned!"*

FIFTY-EIGHT

I hoped to create an atelier of my own. I would rent the first floor of an old house and make it into a large studio where I could paint and instruct a few students. I envisioned myself as a Japanese Raphael Collin. I would grow a beard and wear a long blue smock over trousers. I would teach by day and do my own painting during the night.

I needed money, of course. Five years before, I had sold all but one of my father's masks. I had sold our ancestral home, its contents, and all its land, except three acres. Looking back now, I am surprised that, as hasty as I was as a young man, I had not sold everything that I had inherited. Wisely, I had kept three acres of the land that my grandfather's family had maintained for centuries. It was almost adjacent to Mount Daigo and Sanpo-In, and it had originally been the site of my grandfather's childhood home.

There was nothing left of the old wooden house. According to Grandfather, it burned down during the first year of his marriage to my grandmother. The only thing that remained of the ancient structure was the *kura*, a storehouse that stood almost a hundred yards from the original house.

The *kura* stood tall and lonely. Its exterior plaster walls were peeling, exposing its extremely crude insulation made from layers of dried mud and bits of rope. The roof was peaked and decorated with heavy black tiles. There was a bolted window on the second story that had been further sealed by the hammering of several wooden planks over it.

I never believed that there was anything in the old storehouse. I believed that any valuables that had once been there had long since been recovered by either my grandfather or my father. I had kept the land only because I thought that one day I might need it. I was right.

One night I dreamed that I lived inside its thick plaster walls and painted beneath its high vaulted ceilings. In my dream I could smell its damp wooden beams and feel its heavily rusted locks. I felt safe inside, impervious to the outside and its elements, nestled like a child in the womb.

I awakened the next morning, bought a hammer and some candles from a local shop, and headed for the land that I could still call my own. I chopped at the outside door, breaking the locks with one heavy swing, and eagerly pried open the old dilapidated door.

I was immediately hit by a piece of falling wood. I fumbled for a candle and a match and went deeper inside the crumbling structure. The room, now transformed from a dark cave into a glowing sanctuary, brimming with bales of brittle hay, seemed in need of repair, but was still filled with endless possibilities.

Once I was inside, the structure seemed to be better preserved than I had initially thought. The roof had withstood the test of time, as the inside of the storehouse was surprisingly dry. Still, the air was cool and a bit stale. I walked a little farther and discovered a wooden staircase that led to the second story.

The beams creaked under the weight of my body. I concentrated to keep my balance and not lose one of my sandals. To my amazement, six or seven cedar chests were neatly pushed against the far wall of the second floor. Each one was bound shut with yards of rope, but none of them had been secured by iron locks.

*   *   *

It took me nearly fourteen hours, almost two days' work, to go through the contents of the chests in their entirety. But in the end, what I discovered was well worth it.

The chests contained twenty-four costumes of the Noh theater. Some, I would later learn, were nearly three hundred years old. I can still recall the magnificent robes as I pulled each one from its cedar lair. Each had been carefully folded and meticulously placed on top of the other. They had remained unscathed, protected from the elements, for at least the duration of my lifetime.

As I removed one robe after the other, each one seemed more splendid than the one that preceded it. There was a *maiginu,* a dancing robe, with an iridescent pattern of bamboo leaves that ran throughout the entire garment. There was the fragile and ethereal *mizu-goromo.* I held the transparent and gauzelike fabric between my fingers. I could see through the loosely woven threads and discern my hands beneath the robe's cloth. The *mizu-goromo,* or water robe, was the costume typically worn by the old men of a play. It was soft and humble. It was ghostlike and, although there were so many robes in the chests that were far more dazzling, it was my favorite.

Later on, when I finally took the collection to a dealer for an appraisal, I would see for the first time each robe laid out beside the others. I would learn that these were probably not the robes of my grandfather, but those of his father and his father before him.

The robes were truly extraordinary. The collection contained at least three silk *choken,* the long silk kimonos worn by either male or female characters. One was decorated with a strong *ishi-datani* pattern, another with a sumptuous festoon of snow-covered camellias. Many were woven with threads of gold. Some had been dyed using the Edo-period *katazone* paste-relief technique.

They were the costumes worn by my forefathers. They were the robes that draped their backs and heightened their performance. Perhaps some were gifts from generous shoguns, who stripped them from their own backs and flung them onto the stage to show their appreciation. Perhaps others were commissioned by them. I will never know their history. I will only know for how much I sold them. It was enough gold for me to live on for a very, very long time.

FIFTY-NINE

Had I not needed the money, I would have never have sold the robes. The dealer sold them for a price that few Japanese could have afforded at that time. The theaters did not have the money to purchase costumes of that quality. It was only the wealthy Western collectors who had developed an interest in esoterica and in the mystery of the artifacts.

When my distant cousin Mitsutani Hiroyuki heard of the sale, he paid me a visit at the old *kura*. I was busy clearing out the second floor and was covered in dirt and sweat. I hardly recognized him, having not seen him since that day after the funeral when he helped me sell Father's ancient masks.

"Kiyoki!" he shouted up at me. "How could you sell those robes? They should never have left the country. They belonged to our blood! They belonged to the theater!" He was puffing, and his face was crimson and swollen.

"You already sold your Father's masks. We actors are reduced to wearing threadbare robes and everyday sashes! Do you not care?"

"I needed to eat, cousin!" I shouted back.

"So do I and so does my family. Do you think a Noh actor makes a decent living these days? I perform only once every two months at the Nishi Honganji. Do you think the other actors and I rip up the floor beams of the stage and sell them for firewood so that we can eat and stay warm in the winter?"

He was shouting at me at the top of his lungs. His face was far redder now, and I feared he would die in front of me, just as Grandfather had.

"I am sorry, Hiroyuki. I will do anything so that I can paint."

"You are not a painter," he bellowed back. "You are nothing but a whore."

He turned his back on me, as I had thought about doing to the old man at the theater weeks before. But his words were bitter and hurtful all the same. And I didn't have to look very deep into myself to recognize that there was a certain amount of truth to them.

Three months passed before I completely refurbished the storehouse as I had intended. The first floor would contain my studio and the area where I would instruct the students; the second floor would be the area where I would sleep. I built a crude kitchen and dug a well and installed a pump not too far from the structure. It was far from luxurious, but it was my own.

I left word at the paper store and art stores near the university that I was offering classes to promising students who had an interest in Western-style painting. News of my atelier circulated slowly, as I had no fame or award to distinguish me from any other struggling painter of the time.

As I waited for the students to come, I concentrated on my own painting. On bright days I would erect my easel outside of my studio and paint the mountain or the pagoda at Sanpo-In. Some days I would travel to the park outside Kiyomizudera and try to paint the prickly pines and the wide-leafed oaks.

The sky in Japan began to depress me, however. If I adhered to the natural palette of the scenery, the colors on my canvas would inevitably become gray and muddy. If I chose the bright colors that I loved, my work seemed false and unrealistic. The natural shapes and foliage of Japan were inconsistent with the palette that I loved and had used so freely in France.

The architecture here was somber. It was far from the confectionlike quality of the Parisian buildings, with their rolling curves and arabesque ironwork. I began to miss France terribly.

The students came, but eventually they left. I became frustrated that they did not have the ability to spend hours in the Louvre and see the work of the old masters in person. I became angry that the sunlight here never seemed as golden as it did there. Unlike Collin, I was incapable of inspiring the few students who came through my door, and in the end, I drove them away.

I could not paint here as I could when I was in France. I could not teach. I had no fame, and I had no distinction. As I walked down the streets, once so familiar to me in my childhood, I felt chills deep within my spine. People were staring at me, my own countrymen. Staring at me, as though I were a foreigner intruding in their sacred space.

The old *obasans* with their hunched backs and crooked smiles glared at me through their cataracts. The village youngsters snickered as I walked past their school. Whether it was small children or elders who probably knew me as a young boy, all could sense that I was not like them. In the end, I believe that was what drove me back to France. For in France there were no expectations as to how I should be. I was undeniably different and would never be French. But I could do as I pleased and act as I wanted to without anyone ever condemning me for my oddness. Only my foreignness disturbed them. As an expatriate, I was free to do as I pleased.

This time, however, I did not return to Paris. In 1903 I went south. I elected to paint in the small village just outside of Nice called Antibes. I bought a small apartment near the Mediterranean shore. Every morning, when I opened the windows, I was greeted by the blue of the sea and the light of the sun. I painted for solace and sold my work in both Cannes and Nice. I would have never left that beautiful village had the First World War not forced me to return to Japan.

In the end, I would grow old here in Japan. Not in Kyoto, as I refused to return there, but in Tokyo. I would be too old to fight in either of the world wars. But they inevitably found their way onto my canvas. When paint became rationed, I found a way to make my own pigments. I used the yellow from ground chrysanthemums, the blue from berries, and the red and yellow from smashed plums.

It was as if I were a child again.

When the sirens sounded during the air raids, I often thought of my apartment in the south of France. I would imagine its terrace, and I would hold my hand to my face and try to recall the smell of the lavender bushes outside my door.

The walls that now enclose me are less forgiving. I live in a dusty grotto that refuses me any light. I have windows, but the sky here is not the sky of Europe, that blue-white color, the same frail color as a quail's egg. The grass does not find its colony in meadows but in the prison between slabs of concrete, the artifice of parks. I don't recall when it was that my body began to deteriorate, that my legs shriveled like dried strips of burdock, that my muscles atrophied and my skin was singed like burned rice paper.

Sometimes, late at night, I see myself again as that young boy, holding my first set of watercolors before me, walking for hours like a diligent monk, delivering his treasure to the formidable mountain of Daigo. In my dream, the mountain forgives me for having abandoned her for those of another land. She blankets me in a thunderclap of falling cherry blossoms and washes away my sorrow with a soft, misting rain.

And my dream always closes with the same image. Father, frozen on his deathbed, my fingers clasped tightly over his. Our hands forever entwined. But no longer can I make out that my palms are a fervid pink and his a pale, ghostly blue.

In my dream they are now one and the same.

And if I am feeling brave, when I rise, I allow myself to wonder. Wonder if my life has been in vain. That I might have made the wrong choices. For the Yamamoto line stops here. With me. The mask carver's son.

And still, all this time, I have carried with me my father's mask. The one that has only eyes.

I know my father carved this one especially for me. And so it is the only one that hangs on my wall. It stares at me with the same dark, bottomless eyes that only my father had. It stares at me without mercy. Those eyes, which see me for all I ever was and all that I am now. Those eyes, still pleading with me to uncover my chisels, those eyes that beseech me to complete its face.

Asahi Shimbun
November 16, 1967

Yamamoto Kiyoki of Daigo, Kyoto, was found dead last week by city authorities in his apartment not far from Shinjuku station. The cause of death was apparently old age. Yamamoto Kiyoki, born 1875, was the son of Yamamoto Ryusei and Yamamoto Etsuko of Daigo, Kyoto, and the only offspring of the couple. His father, Yamamoto Ryusei, was the acclaimed mask carver of the Kanze Noh theater, and his maternal grandfather, Yamamoto Yuji, was the patriarch of the Daigo Kanze Theater from 1848 to 1881. The Daigo Kanze theater is no longer in existence.

To the surprise of the authorities, discovered with the body of Yamamoto Kiyoki were nearly three hundred finished works of art attributed to the deceased, including approximately thirty unfinished canvases, as well as one Noh mask. According to the Department of Western Painting at the Tokyo Imperial Museum in Ueno, the works that Yamamoto Kiyoki left behind are of great interest to the museum and are being considered for the museum's permanent collection. Also of interest to the museum are several volumes of diaries that Yamamoto Kiyoki inscribed documenting his travels to France, where he studied under the acclaimed French painter Raphael Collin (1850–1916), and detailed his experiences as an artist in Meiji Japan. The museum plans to examine all such material before releasing any further details to the public.

Cremation services will be handled by the government and the ashes returned to the family grave in Daigo, as no existing family or friends could be located.

As reported by Homori Naoki,
reporter for the Asahi Shimbun

Readers Guide

The Mask Carver's Son

DISCUSSION QUESTIONS

1. The first part of the book, narrated by Kiyoki, describes events that happened before he was born. Why is this background information important for Kiyoki's own story? How do you think Kiyoki learned so many details about his family's history? Does history repeat itself through the generations?

2. Shattered by the deaths of his parents, his mentor, and his wife, Ryusei becomes silent, believing he should shut out emotion in favor of the wood. Kiyoki says, "I firmly believe that my father began carving only because he knew that whatever he created with the chisel could never die." Does carving prevent Ryusei from feeling the pain of loss, or does it only cause more heartache by dividing him from the rest of the world?

3. Does Ryusei blame Kiyoki for his wife's death? Does he resent Kiyoki? Do you think he truly loves his son? What passages in the book indicate his feelings?

4. Kiyoki discovers his late mother shared the same passion for art. How would Kiyoki's life have been different if his mother had lived?

5. Is the concept of wearing—and creating—masks symbolic to Kiyoki's struggle to identify his own self? Is he ever able to rid himself of the identity of "the mask carver's son"?

6. Do you sympathize with Kiyoki's struggle to carve his own path in life, separate from the duty and obligation he feels to his family? Or

do you think he betrayed his father? Was selling his father's masks a selfish act, or a necessary one?

7. Compare and contrast Kiyoki and Ryusei. Does Kiyoki think he is similar to his father?

8. When Kiyoki meets Norobu, he is surprised to feel romantic feelings for the first time in his life. Describe Kiyoki's interpretation of his own sexuality.

9. What role does each of Kiyoki's acquaintances in Paris—Takada, Hashimoto, Isabelle, Collin—play in his development as an artist and as a person? Does he allow himself to get close to anyone there? Why or why not?

10. What are the main differences in the art world in Japan and France as described by Kiyoki's narrative? What are the differences in the culture of both places? How does the Westernization of Japan during this time period affect the story? Does Kiyoki "fit" into one better than the other?

11. After returning from France, Kiyoki's first Japanese art exhibition is widely criticized. Do you think Kiyoki considers himself a failure?

12. Kiyoki returns to his hometown of Kyoto and offers to repaint the Yogo Pine at the ancient Noh theater. Why does he do this, and what is the significance of this act? How does it make him feel?

13. As Kiyoki grows older, do you think he regrets the choices he made as a younger man, or feel guilt over his actions?

14. Just like his father, Kiyoki dies alone. However, his obituary says that the artwork he left behind will be acquired and possibly exhibited by a museum in Tokyo. Does the acclaim for their art justify both Kiyoki and his father's solitude and sacrifice in dedication to their craft? Do they both ultimately achieve the life they wanted?

If you enjoyed *The Mask Carver's Son,* don't miss

The Lost Wife

Alyson Richman's rapturous novel
of first love in a time of war.
Read on for a special preview.

New York City
2000

He dressed deliberately for the occasion, his suit pressed and his shoes shined. While shaving, he turned each cheek carefully to the mirror to ensure he hadn't missed a single whisker. Earlier that afternoon, he had even bought a lemon-scented pomade to smooth his few remaining curls.

He had only one grandson, one grandchild for that matter, and had been looking forward to this wedding for months now. And although he had met the bride only a few times, he liked her from the first. She was bright and charming, quick to laugh, and possessed a certain old-world elegance. He hadn't realized what a rare quality that was until he sat there now staring at her, his grandson clasping her hand.

Even now, as he walked into the restaurant for the rehearsal dinner, he felt as though, seeing the young girl, he had been swept back into another time. He watched as some of the other guests unconsciously touched their throats because the girl's neck, stretching out from her velvet dress, was so beautiful and long that she looked like she had been cut out from a Klimt painting. Her hair was swept up into a loose chignon, and two little jeweled butterflies with sparkling antennae rested right above her left ear, giving the appearance that these winged creatures had just landed on her red hair.

His grandson had inherited his dark, unruly curls. A study in contrast to his bride-to-be, he fidgeted nervously, while she seemed to glide into the room. He looked like he would be more comfortable with a book between his hands than holding a flute of champagne. But there was an ease that flowed between them, a balance that made them appear perfectly suited for each other. Both of them were smart, highly educated second-generation Americans. Their voices lacked even the faintest traces of the accents that had laced their grandparents' English. The *New York Times* wedding announcement that Sunday morning would read:

> Eleanor Tanz married Jason Baum last night at the Rainbow Room in Manhattan. The rabbi Stephen Schwartz officiated. The bride, 26, graduated from Amherst College and is currently employed in the decorative arts department of Christie's, the auction house. The bride's father, Dr. Jeremy Tanz, is an oncologist at Memorial Sloan-Kettering hospital in Manhattan. Her mother, Elisa Tanz, works as an occupational therapist with the New York City public schools. The groom, 28, a graduate of Brown University and Yale Law School, is currently an associate at Cahill Gordon & Reindel LLP. His father, Benjamin Baum, was until recently an attorney at Cravath, Swaine & Moore LLP in New York City. The groom's mother, Rebekkah Baum, is a retired schoolteacher. The couple was introduced by mutual friends.

At the head table, the lone living grandparent from each side was introduced to each other for the first time. Again, the groom's grandfather felt himself being swept away by the image of the woman before him. She was decades older then her granddaughter, but there was something familiar about her. He felt it immediately, from the moment he first saw her eyes.

"I know you from somewhere," he finally managed to say, although he felt as though he were now speaking to a ghost, not a woman he had just met. His body was responding in some visceral manner that he didn't quite understand. He regretted drinking that second glass of wine. His stomach was turning over on itself. He could hardly breathe.

"You must be mistaken," she said politely. She did not want to appear rude, but she, too, had been looking forward to her granddaughter's wedding for months and didn't want to be distracted from the evening's festivities. As she saw the girl navigating the crowd, the many cheeks turning to her to be kissed and the envelopes being pressed into her and Jason's hands, she had to pinch herself to make sure that she really was still alive to witness it all.

But this old man next to her would not give up.

"I definitely think I know you from somewhere," he repeated.

She turned and now showed her face even more clearly to him. The feathered skin. Her silver hair. Her ice-blue eyes.

But it was the shadow of something dark blue beneath the transparent material of her sleeve that caused shivers to run through his old veins.

"Your sleeve . . . " His finger was shaking as it reached to touch the silk.

Her face twitched as he touched her wrist, her discomfort registering over her face.

"Your sleeve, may I?" He knew he was being rude.

She looked straight at him.

"May I see your arm?" he said again. "Please." This time his voice sounded almost desperate.

She was now staring at him, her eyes now locked to his. As if in a trance, she pushed up her sleeve. There on her forearm, next to a small brown birthmark, were six tattooed numbers.

"Do you remember me now?" he asked, trembling.

She looked at him again, as if giving weight and bone to a ghost.

"Lenka, it's me," he said. "Josef. Your husband."